...s, author of the True Blood series

'Thrilling, sexy, and funny! These books are addictive.
One of my very favourite vampire series'
Richelle Mead, author of the Vampire Academy series

'We'd suggest dumping Stephenie Meyer's vapid Twilight books
and replacing them with these'
SFX Magazine

'Ms Caine uses her dazzling storytelling skills to
share the darkest chapter yet . . . An engrossing read that
once begun is impossible to set down'
Darque Reviews

'A fast-paced, page-turning read packed with wonderful
characters and surprising plot twists. Rachel Caine is an
engaging writer; readers will be completely absorbed in this
chilling story, unable to put it down until the last page'
Flamingnet

'If you love to read about characters with whom you can get
deeply involved, Rachel Caine is so far a one hundred per cent
sure bet to satisfy that need'
The Eternal Night

'A rousing horror thriller that adds a new dimension
to the vampire mythos . . . An electrifying, enthralling
coming-of-age supernatural tale'
Midwest Book Review

'A solid paranormal mystery and action plot line
that will entertain adults as well as teenagers. The story line
has several twists and turns that will keep readers
of any age turning the pages'
LoveVampires

a&b

PAPER AND FIRE

VOLUME TWO OF THE GREAT LIBRARY

RACHEL CAINE

Allison & Busby Limited
12 Fitzroy Mews
London W1T 6DW
allisonandbusby.com

First published in Great Britain by Allison & Busby in 2016.

A CIP catalogue record for this book is available from
the British Library.

First Edition

ISBN 978-0-7490-1732-3

Typeset in 10/15 pt Sabon by
Allison & Busby Ltd.

The paper used for this Allison & Busby publication
has been produced from trees that have been legally sourced
from well-managed and credibly certified forests.

Printed and bound by
CPI Group (UK) Ltd, Croydon, CR0 4YY

RACHEL CAINE is the author of more than forty novels, including the bestselling Morganville Vampires series. She was born at White Sands Missile Range, which people who know her say explains a lot. She has been an accountant, an insurance investigator and a professional musician, and has played with such musical legends as Henry Mancini, Peter Nero and John Williams. She and her husband, fantasy artist R. Cat Conrad, live in Texas.

rachelcaine.com

To the scholars. To the students. To the librarians.
To those who fight for all of those, every day.
Shine the light.

EPHEMERA

Excerpt from a Report Delivered via Secure Message to the Archivist Magister, from the Hand of the Artifex.

I thought that you were being soft when you ordered us to keep the boy alive, but he's been incredibly useful already. As you said, a brilliant mind. When we allow him access to books and papers, which we do as a reward, his observations on engineering are quite groundbreaking. After breaking him using the usual means, we provided him with chalk, and on the walls of his cell, he began to write some unusual calculations and diagrams. These I have enclosed for your review.

He also had observations, which he confided to a guard I had ordered to be friendly to him, about the maintenance of the automata within the prison. Clever boy. And dangerous. He might have succeeded in turning one of them to his own uses if we hadn't kept a constant watch.

I know you want to keep him alive, but even after this long, he continues to be outwardly cooperative and inwardly quite stubborn. I haven't seen the like since . . . well, since his mentor, Scholar Christopher Wolfe.

As bright as he is, I don't how we can ever control him completely. It would be far kinder to kill him now.

Reply from the Archivist Magister, via Secure Message.

Under no circumstances are you to kill the boy.
I have great plans for him.

CHAPTER ONE

Every day, Jess Brightwell passed the Spartan warrior statue on his way to and from his quarters. It was a beautifully made automaton, fluid and deadly, with a skin of burnished copper. It stood in a dynamic pose on its pedestal with a spear ready to thrust, and was both a decoration and a protection against intruders.

It wasn't supposed to be a threat to those who belonged here.

Now as he passed it, the shadowed eyes under the helmet flickered and flared red, and the Spartan's head turned to track his passage. Jess felt the burn of those eyes, but he didn't return the stare. It would take only an instant for that form to move and that spear to drive right through him. He could feel the very spot the point would enter, like a red, tingling target on his back.

Not now! Jess sweated, terribly aware of the leather smuggling harness strapped to his chest, and the slender original book hidden inside. *Calm. Be calm.* It was incredibly difficult, not only because of the threat of the automaton, but the anger that burnt away inside of him. As he walked away, the tingle in his back rose to a hot burn, and he waited for the rush of movement and the horrible invasion of the spear stabbing through his body . . . But then he was a step past, two steps, and the attack didn't come.

When he looked back, the statue had gone back to resting mode, staring blindly straight ahead. It seemed safe. It wasn't. Jess Brightwell lived on sufferance and luck at the Great Library of Alexandria. If he'd been half as clever as his friend Thomas Schreiber, he ought to have figured out how to disable these things by now . . .

Don't think about Thomas. Thomas is dead. You have to keep that thought firm in your head, or you'll never make it through this.

Jess paused in the dark, cool tunnel that led from the Spartan's entrance into the wider precincts of the complex where he was quartered. There was no one here to watch him, no fellow travellers at either end of the tunnel. The automaton couldn't see him. Here, for this one sheltered moment, he could allow himself to feel.

Anger sparked red and violent inside, heated his skin and tensed his muscles, and the tears that stung his eyes were driven by rage as much as grief. *You lied, Artifex,* he thought. *You lying, cruel, evil bastard.* The book in the harness on his chest was proof of everything he'd hoped for the past six months. But hope was a cruel, jagged thing, all spikes and razors that turned and cut deep in his guts. Hope was a great deal like fear.

Jess bounced his head against the stones behind him, again, again, *again*, until he could get control of the anger. He forced it back into a black box, buried deep, and secured it with chains of will, then wiped his face clear. It was morning, still so early that dawn blushed the horizon, and he was tired out of his skin. He'd been chasing the book he smuggled now for weeks, giving up meals, giving up rest, and finally he'd found it. It had cost him an entire night's sleep. He'd not eaten, except for one quick gyro from a Greek street vendor nearly eight hours ago. He'd spent the rest of the time hiding in an abandoned building and reading the book three times, cover to cover, until he had every single detail etched hot into his memory.

Jess felt gritty with exhaustion and trembled with hunger, but he knew what he had to do.

He had to tell Glain the truth.

He didn't look forward to that at all, and the idea made him bounce his skull off the stones one more time, more gently. He pushed off, checked his pulse to be sure it was steady again, and then walked out of the tunnel to the inner courtyard – no automata stationed here, though sphinxes roamed the grounds on a regular basis. He was grateful not to see one this time, and headed to his left, towards his barracks.

After a quick stop to wolf down bread and drink an entire jug of water, he moved on, and avoided any of the early risers in the halls who might want to be social. He craved a shower and mindless sleep more than any conversation.

He got neither. As he unlocked his door and stepped inside, he found Glain Wathen – friend, fellow survivor, classmate, superior officer – sitting bold as brass in the chair by his small desk. Tall girl, made sleek with muscle. He'd never call her pretty, but she had a comfortable, easy assurance – hard won these past months – that made her almost beautiful in certain lights. Force of personality, if nothing else.

The Welsh girl was calmly reading, though she closed the blank and returned it to his shelf when he shut the door behind him.

'People will talk, Glain,' he said. He had no temper for this right now. He needed, *burnt*, to tell her what he'd learnt, but at the same time, he was on the precarious edge of emotion, and he didn't want her, of all people, to see him lose control. He wanted to rest and face her fresh. That way, he wouldn't break into rage, or just . . . break.

'One thing you learn early growing up a girl, people always talk, whatever you do,' Glain said. 'What bliss it must be to be male.' Her tone was sour, and it matched her expression. 'Where have you been? I was half a mind to call a search party.'

'You damn well know better than to do that,' he said, and if she was going to stay, fine. He had no qualms about stripping off his uniform jacket and unbuttoning his shirt. They'd seen each other in all states as postulants struggling to survive Wolfe's class, and the High Garda wasn't a place that invited modesty, either.

He really must have been too tired to think, because his fingers were halfway down the buttons on his shirt when he realised she'd see the smuggling harness, which was a secret he didn't feel prepared to share just yet. 'A little privacy?' he said, and she raised her dark eyebrows but got up and turned her back. He didn't take his eyes off her as he stripped off the shirt and reached for the buckles of the leather harness that held the book against his chest. 'I need sleep, not conversation.'

'Too bad. You won't get any of the former,' she told him. 'We're due for an exercise in half an hour. Which is why I was looking for you. The orders came after you'd gone sneaking into the night. Where exactly *did* you go, Jess?'

Jess. So they weren't on military footing now, not that he'd really thought they were. He sighed, left the harness on, and replaced the old shirt with a fresh one. 'You can turn,' he said, as he finished the buttons. She did, hands clasped behind her back, and stared at him with far too much perception.

'If that bit of false-modesty theatre was meant to distract me from the fact you're wearing some kind of smuggling equipment under that shirt, it failed,' she said. 'Have you gone back into the family business?'

The Brightwells held a stranglehold on the London book

trade, and had fingers in every black market across the world, one way or another; he had never told her that, but somehow, he also wasn't surprised she'd know. Glain liked to learn everything she could about those close to her. It was a smart strategy. He'd done the same with her, the only daughter of a moderately successful merchant who'd nearly bankrupted himself to earn her a place at the Library. She'd been raised with six brothers. None of them, despite sharing her strong build and height, had been inclined at all to military life. Glain was exactly what she seemed: a strong, capably violent young woman who cared about her abilities, not her looks.

'If you're a Brightwell, you're never really out of the family business,' he said, and sat down on his bed. The mattress yielded, and he wanted to stretch out and let it cradle him, but if he did, he knew he'd be asleep in seconds. 'You didn't just barge in here to make sure I was still alive, did you?'

'No.' She sounded amused, and completely at ease again. 'I needed to ask you a question.'

'Well? As you said, we've got only half an hour—'

'Somewhat less now,' she said. 'Since we're having this conversation. What do you know about the Black Archives?'

That stopped him cold. He'd expected her to ask something else, something more . . . military. But instead, it took his tired brain a moment to scramble to the new topic. He finally said, 'That they're a myth.'

'Really.' Scorn dripped from that word, and she leant back against the wall behind her. 'What if I told you that I heard from someone I trust that they're not?'

'You must have slept through your childhood lessons.' He switched to a childish singsong. 'The Great Library has an Archive, where all the books they save—'

'Not fire or sword, not flood or war will be the Archive's grave,' Glain finished. 'I memorised the same childhood rhymes you did. But I'm talking about the other Archives. The forbidden ones.'

'The *Black* Archives are a story to frighten children, that's all. Full of dangerous books, as if books could be dangerous.'

'Some might be,' she said. 'And Dario doesn't think it's a myth.'

'*Dario?*' Jess said. 'Since when do you believe anything Dario Santiago says? And why is he talking to you at all?'

She gave him a long, unreadable smile. 'Maybe he just wants to keep track of what you get up to,' she said. 'But back to the subject. If it's where they keep dangerous information, then I say that's a place that we need to look for any hints about what happened to send Thomas to his death. And who to go after for it. Don't you?'

Thomas. Hearing his best friend's name said aloud conjured up his image behind Jess's eyes: a cheerfully optimistic genius in the body of a German farm boy. He missed Thomas, who'd had all the warmth and understanding of others that Jess lacked. *I can't think about him.* For a wild instant, he thought he'd either shout at her, or cry, but somehow he managed to keep his voice even as he said, 'If such a place as the Black Archives even exists, how would we go about getting into it? I hope Dario has an idea. I don't.'

'You know Dario – he's always got an idea,' Glain said. 'Something to think on, anyway. Something we can do. I know you want to find out how and why Thomas died as much as I do.'

'The Archivist told us why,' he said. 'Thomas was convicted of heresy against the Library.' *Tell her what you know, for God's sake.* The thought beat hard against his brain, like a prisoner battering at a door, but he just wasn't ready. He couldn't tell what saying the words out loud, making them *real*, might do to him.

'I don't believe that for a moment,' Glain said softly. Her dark eyes had gone distant and the look in them sad. 'Thomas would never have done anything, said anything to deserve that. He was the best of us.'

Just tell her. She deserves to know!

He finally scraped together just enough courage and drew in a deep, slow breath as he looked up to meet her eyes. 'Glain, about Thomas—'

He was cut off by a sudden, hard rapping on the door. It sounded urgent, and Jess bolted up off the bed and crossed to answer. He felt half relieved for the interruption . . . until he swung it open, and his squad mate Tariq Oduya shouldered past Jess and into the room. He held two steaming mugs, and thrust one at him as he said, 'And here I thought you'd be still lagging in bed . . .' His voice trailed off as he caught sight of Glain standing against the wall. She had her arms crossed, and looked as casual as could be, but Tariq still grinned and raised his eyebrows. 'Or maybe you just got up!'

'Stuff it,' Glain said, and there was no sign of humour in her expression or voice. She moved forward to take the second cup from Tariq and sipped it, never mind that it was probably his own. 'Thanks. Now be about your business, soldier.'

'Happy to oblige, Squad Leader,' he said, and mock-saluted. Technically, they were off duty, but he was walking a tightrope, and Jess watched Glain's face to see if she intended to slice through it and send him falling into the abyss for the lack of respect.

She just sipped the hot drink and watched Tariq without blinking, until he moved to the door.

'Recruit Oduya,' she said as he stepped over the threshold.

'You do understand that if I hear a whisper of you implying anything about this situation, I'll knock you senseless, and then I'll see you off the squad and out of the High Garda.'

He turned and gave her a proper salute. His handsome face was set into a calm mask. 'Yes, Squad Leader. Understood.'

He closed the door behind him. Jess took a gulp of the coffee and closed his eyes in relief as the caffeine began its work. 'He's a good sort. He won't spread rumours.'

Glain gave him a look of utter incredulity. 'You really don't know him at all, do you?'

In truth, Jess didn't. The squad had bonded tightly, but he'd held himself apart from that quite deliberately; he'd formed deep friendships in his postulant class and seen some of those friends dismissed, injured, and dead. He wasn't about to open himself up to the same pain again.

Still, he considered Tariq the closest he had to a friend, except for Glain. Glain he trusted.

His uniform jacket was still clean, and he put it on as he finished the coffee. Glain watched in silence for a moment before she said, 'You were about to tell me something.'

'Later,' he said. 'After the exercise. It's going to be a longer conversation.'

'All right.' As he stopped to check his uniform in front of the mirror, she rolled her eyes. 'You're pretty enough for both of us, Brightwell.'

'Charmed you think so, Squad Leader. You're quite handsome yourself today.' *Handsome* was a good description. Glain had chopped her dark hair closer for convenience; it suited her, he decided, and fit well with the solid curves of a body made for endurance and strength. There was no attraction between them, but there was respect – more now than before, he thought. Some, like Oduya, might mistake it for something else. She might be right to be concerned. Jess met her eyes in the mirror. 'That compliment stops at the doorway, of course.'

She nodded. It seemed brisk, but there was a look in her eyes that he thought might be some form of gratitude. 'Stop preening and let's go.'

They left his room together, but, thankfully, no one was in the hall to see it. The squad had gathered towards the end, talking casually, but all that stopped as Glain approached. Jess silently took position with the rest of the squad, and Glain led them out at a fast walk for the parade ground. Despite his sweaty weariness, he looked forward to this; it was a chance to let a little of his anger out of that locked, chained box. There wouldn't be any real surprises. It was just an exercise, after all.

He was dead wrong about that, and it cost him.

They were in the tenth long hour on the exercise ground when Jess saw a flash of movement from the corner of his eye and tried to turn towards it, but he was hampered by thick layers of cloth and the flexible armour, and just simply too slow, too tired, and too late.

A shot hit him squarely in the back.

Then he was on the ground, looking up at a merciless Alexandrian sky scratched white by the heat, and he couldn't breathe. The pain crushed all the air out of his chest, and for a split second he wondered if something had gone badly wrong, if all the safety measures had failed, if he was going to die . . . And then his frozen solar plexus muscles unlocked, and he gulped in a raw, whooping mouthful of air.

A shadow blocked out the burning sun, and he knew her by the short-cropped halo of hair that bristled up. After blinking a few times, he saw that Glain was holding out a hand to him.

He bit down on his pride and took it, and she hauled him to unsteady feet.

'What the hell did you do wrong, Brightwell?' she asked him. There was no sympathy in her voice. He shook his head, still intent on getting breath back in his lungs. 'I told you *all* to watch your backs. You didn't listen. If these weapons had been loaded with real ammunition, you'd be a mess to clean up right now.'

He felt halfway dead, anyway. The training weapons that the High Garda of the Great Library used were not toys; they delivered real jolts and *very* real bruises. 'Sorry,' he muttered, and then, a second too late, 'sir.'

Now that she wasn't just a silhouette against the sun, he could see the warning flash in her eyes. *We're not equals here.* Forgetting that was a stupid, personal issue he needed to overcome, and quickly; she couldn't afford to let it slip for long without seeming to encourage a lack of discipline in the ranks of their squad.

Hard habit to break, friendship.

The rest of the squad gathered together now from around the corners of the mock buildings that served as their training ground. It was mercilessly hot, as it always was, and each of his fellow Garda soldiers now looked as exhausted and sweat streaked as he did. Glain wiped her face with an impatient swipe of her sleeve and barked, loud enough for the rest of the squad to hear, 'Report what you did wrong, soldier!'

'Squad Leader, sir, I failed to watch my back,' Jess said. His voice sounded strained, and he knew from the still-burning ache in his back that he was going to have a spectacular sunset of a bruise. 'But—'

Her face set like concrete. 'Are you about to excuse your failure, Brightwell?'

'No, sir!' He cut a look at Tariq, who was openly grinning. 'It was friendly fire, sir!'

'Oh, be fair. I'm not *that* friendly,' Tariq said. 'And I did it on orders.'

'Orders?' Jess looked at Glain, whose face was as unreadable as the wall behind her. 'You ordered him to *shoot me in the back?*'

Glain's expression never flickered. 'In the real world, you'd better watch your friends as much as your enemies. Allies can turn on you when you least expect it. I hope the bruises remind you.'

He hardly needed the tip, and she knew it. He wasn't a fool; he'd grown up never trusting people. Trust, for him, was a recently acquired skill that had developed in the company of his friends and fellow postulants. Like Glain. Who was trying to remind him not to rely on it.

Jess swallowed a bitter mouthful of anger and said, 'No excuses, sir. Tariq always struck me as shifty, anyway.'

'Then why'd you let your guard down, you bright spark?' Tariq said. 'I admit, I like playing the heinous villain, sir.'

'Playing?' someone else in the squad muttered, and Tariq mimed a finger shot in her direction as he swigged from his canteen. Jess would have laughed if it didn't hurt so much, but Glain's lesson had been pointed . . . and on point. *I can't afford to relax*, he thought. *I knew as much from the beginning. Glain's just trying to remind me*. With, unfortunately, Glain's typical subtlety.

'Settle,' Glain said flatly, and the squad did. Instantly. Nobody questioned her – not for long. Jess certainly didn't. 'We're nearly at the end of training,' she told them, and paced back and forth in front of them with a lithe, restless energy that never seemed to go away, no matter how long the day. 'We *will* finish in the lead. Screw that up, *any* of you, and I'll slap you out of service hard enough to brand my palm print on your grandmother's face. Clear?'

'Clear, sir!' they all responded, instantly and in perfect chorus. They'd learnt how to move and speak in concert long, painful months ago. That was Glain's doing. She'd end up High Garda commander one day . . . or dead. But she'd never settle for less than perfection.

'I'm tempted to make you run it again,' Glain was saying, and there was a barely perceptible moan that ran through the group which she didn't acknowledge, 'but you've bled enough for one day. You weren't terrible, and next time had *better* be an improvement. Shower, drink, eat, rest. Dismissed.'

That, Jess thought, *is why she's good at this*. She'd pushed them all very hard, to the point of breaking, but she knew when to give just a touch of encouragement. And, most of all, she knew when to *stop*. None of them, not even him, were being carried to the Medica tents, which couldn't be said for a lot of other squads who weren't as highly ranked as Glain's.

Around them, this section of the High Garda training ground was almost deserted; it was reserved for trainee testing. Everyone else had called it a day long ago, since the mess bells had pealed half an hour back, and now that Jess had the chance to think about it, his stomach growled fiercely. He'd burnt off the light breakfast hours ago.

He fell into step with Shi Zheng and Tariq, but stopped when Glain said, 'Brightwell. A word.'

Others gave him sympathetic looks but didn't pause; they walked around him as he halted and turned back. Glain was still pacing, and doing it in full sun; she never minded the scorching Alexandrian heat. The sun loved her just as much, and her skin had darkened to a warm, woody brown over the months of exposure. Jess, who'd been in the climate precisely the same amount of time, had managed to achieve only a light coating of translucent tan over layers of memorable burns. 'Sir?'

She fixed a stare somewhere over his shoulder, towards the horizon. 'Message came in earlier to me from Captain Santi. He says to tell you . . . no.' She suddenly shifted to fix her gaze right on his. 'No to what, Jess?'

'Glain—'

'That's Squad Leader Wathen to you, and *no to what*?'

'I asked to talk to Wolfe. Sir.'

'Why?'

It was the coward's way out, but he gave her the second reason he wanted a meeting with their old Scholar Christopher Wolfe, who'd pushed them through a memorable period of hell as postulants. 'I wanted to know if he knew anything of the Black Archives.'

She blinked, and her look shifted – still suspicious and dark, but a good deal more concerned. 'You told me you thought they were a myth just this morning. You must have asked days ago.'

'I did. For the same reasons you gave. Seemed to me that if the Black Archives existed – and I never said I thought they did – then it might be a place to look into Thomas's death.' He looked down. 'I got a letter from his father, thanking me for being his friend. He asked if I knew exactly how his son died.'

Glain said nothing to that, but after a moment, she nodded. 'You didn't want me looking into the subject because you already were.'

'And they watch us, Glain,' he said. 'All of us.' It was burning his tongue to tell her the truth, but he knew, *knew* how she'd take it. And he was too tired. He wanted to tell her in better circumstances, when the clock wasn't ticking down. If there was an exercise, she needed her focus more than he did . . . or, at least, that was what he told himself.

'Which brings us to the point: stay away from Wolfe. You know it's not safe, for him *or* you.'

'I won't ask again.'

'Dismissed, then, Brightwell. We'll talk later.'

He nodded and jogged away to put space between them. Curious that Captain Niccolo Santi had passed the message, and Wolfe hadn't sent it himself. But, then, their teacher had been a barbed puzzle since the start.

Wolfe was not a kind man or a natural teacher, but he'd tried his best to save his students. That didn't make him a friend, exactly, but Wolfe would want to know the truth about Thomas, too. Once he did . . . *No wonder Captain Santi wants to keep me away from him*, Jess thought. *Wolfe wouldn't let it go.* No more than Jess could. Or Glain, once he told her. Good that he had a little more time to think. He needed a plan before he set that particular cat among the pigeons, didn't he?

His back ached, and his head pounded from the heat and exertion. Dinner was as fast as breakfast, fuel he ate without really noting it, and afterwards Jess fell into bed for a few short hours – far less than he needed – before dragging himself up. He still had things to do that couldn't be done in the open.

He showered, changed to civilian clothing, shovelled down food in the common dining hall, and slipped away from the High Garda compound into the embrace of a rich, sea-cooled Alexandrian evening, beneath a blue-black sky scattered with hard stars.

This was work better done in the dark.

EPHEMERA

Excerpt from Report from Obscurist Gregory Valdosta to Obscurist Magnus Keria Morning.

. . . regarding our new problem child, Morgan Hault, I have seen little improvement and much to worry me. I'd have thought six months of intensive training and supervision here in the Iron Tower would have wrought some changes in her, but she remains stubborn, sly, and dreadfully smart. Only this morning I found that when I put her to work writing out standard representational formulae for changes to the Codex, she instead came up with a system to disguise entries – in effect, to hide them. I gave her a simple task of alchemical preparation of a calix of gold, and instead she seized the opportunity to try combining mercury, vitriol, common salt, and sal ammoniac to create a virulent mixture to melt the thinnest part of her collar. She was unsuccessful, of course, and is being treated for a burn, but the concern is that she came very close to discovering a compound that might work.

I've set her to work, supervised, on the boring task of

transcribing official messages into the books, but I don't dare put anyone with her for long. The little criminal can be quite disarming. I realise that giving her access to some of the messages might be dangerous; she still retains her allegiance, as far as I can determine, to Scholar Wolfe and all her fellow students. But, believe me, she'll do far less damage with pen and paper than with alchemical preparations.

And for the love of Horus, keep her well away from anything to do with translation. I shudder to think how we could hold on to the girl if she was able to translate herself away from here.

She continues her resistance to the rules of the Tower, but I have determined, through the proper charts and analysis, that her ideal time for propagation will come soon. I have not warned her of this. Gods know what she would do to avoid doing her duty.

I know you are sensitive on this subject, Obscurist, so forgive me for my frankness, but I still feel you give the girls too much freedom in this matter, allowing them three refusals before they undergo the compulsory procedure.

She has, of course, already used up all three of these refusals.

Your faithful servant, Gregory

CHAPTER TWO

The Alexandrian black market had two obvious faces. The more public one, known as the shadow market, sold illegal but harmless copies of common Library volumes – punishable, at worst, with fines and short prison stays. It catered to those who wanted a book purely for the criminal thrill of it, even if the book was shoddily transcribed and incomplete, as they often were.

A smuggler called Red Ibrahim presided over the darker, more private end of the trade, and he was legendary well beyond the city; his reputation was spoken of even in Jess's house back in London. He was a *cousin*, someone in the trade you could rely on in a pinch and for a price. Jess had actual *blood* cousins in the trade, but the main tests to becoming a trade cousin were long-term success and a certain ruthless loyalty to fellow smugglers. They were bound – pun intended, he supposed – by the business of books, of history set in leather and paper.

Forbidden fruits.

For months, Jess had steadily dealt with a succession of Red Ibrahim's subordinates – he had a network of at least thirty – and found them all cold-eyed and capable. His Brightwell bona fides had been checked again and again at every stage; he was, after all, a High Garda soldier, wearing the copper band of service to the Library, even if he *was* a smuggler by birth. Reconciling that and earning trust, even with the Brightwell name, had been a tricky job.

Tonight, as he walked, his initial directions wrote themselves out into his Codex in the Brightwell family code, and he immediately erased them. He visited a market stall, where he was told verbally to go to another shop, and then to a third, darkened bar, where sailors cursed each other over dice games and a proprietor slipped him a paper note. The route took him halfway across the city, and his legs were truly aching by the time five words scribed themselves in his Codex: *knock on the blue door.*

He stopped, put the book away, and looked at the houses on the street where he stood. They were neat rectangles painted in pale shades with Egyptian decorations at the roofs, and fluted columns in miniature on the porticos. Respectable homes for modestly well-off families, something a silver-band Scholar might own, perhaps.

There was a house with a dark blue door on the right, and he stepped through the square gate and passed through a garden of herbs shaded by a spreading acacia tree. An ornamental pond cradled lazy fish and large lotus plants. It was a traditional household, with Egyptian household god statues in a niche by the door, and he made the required respect to them before he knocked.

The man who opened the door was nondescript – not young, not old, not tall or short or thin or fat. A native Egyptian, almost certainly, with sharp, dark eyes and skin with a rich coppery sheen. The local fashion was to shave all body hair, even eyebrows, and this man clearly abided by it.

'Jess Brightwell,' he said, and smiled. 'I'm honoured. Be welcome to my home.' He stepped back to allow Jess entry, and closed the door behind him. It had a significant lock, and Red Ibrahim engaged it immediately. 'We've heard much about each other, I'm sure.'

'I expected you to be ginger,' Jess said. The man raised what would have been his eyebrows. 'Sorry. English term. Red-haired, I mean.'

'I am not called Red for that.'

'Then for what?'

Ibrahim smiled, just enough to send a chill down Jess's back. 'A story for another time, I think. Please.' The man – Jess placed him at about forty, but he could have been younger, or even older – gestured to a small, delicate divan, and Jess sat. A young girl with straight black hair worn in a shoulder-length cut walked in with a tray of delicate coffee cups and a silver urn. She was maybe fourteen years old, petite and pretty, and smiled at Jess as she poured for them both.

She took a seat on the divan at the other end from Jess, to his surprise.

'This is my daughter, Anit. The gods have smiled upon my house, and she is an intelligent girl who wishes to study the trade. Do you mind if she listens?'

'No objection,' Jess said. He remembered his father doing the same for him and his twin brother, Brendan, though he didn't recall either of them having much of a choice. 'It took quite a while to arrange to see you.'

'Yes, of course, and I mean no offence by my caution. Does your father, the excellent Callum, receive every stranger claiming to be in the trade?' Red Ibrahim handed him a cup so small, it felt like a child's toy in Jess's fingers, but the coffee inside was sweet and potent enough to make his heart race after only a sip. 'Or does he ensure his business's – and his family's – safety by being wary?'

'He's a careful man,' Jess agreed, though he remembered his father ruthlessly risking him, and his brothers, without much thought for the consequences. His older brother, Liam, had swung from a gallows for the *careful* way his father did business. 'He wants to obtain some information, and you're the best positioned to have it at your fingertips. It's a delicate matter, of course.'

'Of course,' Ibrahim agreed. 'Naturally.' He waited with polite attention.

'Automata,' Jess said.

'There are no truly rare versions of Heron's work, as you no doubt know—'

'Not interested in rare volumes,' Jess said. 'We're looking for books that describe the inner workings of the creatures. And how to disable them.'

Red Ibrahim was in the act of drinking his coffee, and though he hesitated an instant, he finished so smoothly Jess almost missed the reaction. Almost. Then he laughed, and it sounded completely natural. 'Do you know how often this request is made, young Brightwell? The automata are the enemies of both smugglers and Burners in every city on earth! Do you not think that if such information was available, we would have obtained it and made an incredible fortune with it by now?'

'A unique treasure like that is more useful when used strategically, for your own purposes.' Jess put an edge on his voice. 'This is the most dangerous place in the world to smuggle a book, and yet you've made a career of it – an empire, of sorts. You'd make it a mission to have that information at your disposal.'

'No one can disable these creatures. It's impossible.'

'Nothing's impossible,' Jess said. 'They're mechanical creatures.

They're made. Someone knows their secrets, and secrets are always for sale to those who look hard enough. And if I know anything about you, sir, it's that you would look *very* hard.'

'At everyone,' Red Ibrahim agreed. He put down his coffee cup with precise control. 'What does your father offer in exchange for this gift of all gifts? Presuming such a thing exists at all.'

Jess tried to keep his face as calm as Ibrahim's, his pulse as slow. He didn't blink. 'I have a copy of the *Book of Urisen*, by William Blake.'

Ibrahim's expression was just as still. 'There are eight copies of such a book in the world,' he said. 'I would need something a great deal rarer. It is, as you say, precious treasure indeed, this information.'

'There *were* eight copies,' Jess said. 'Six of them were purchased by ink-lickers, who ate them in some sort of sick ritual four months back. As I'm sure you already know. That leaves two: the one in my father's vaults . . . and the one I have stashed here in Alexandria. Which can be yours, if you have what I want.'

'Ah,' Ibrahim said softly. 'Now we come to it, I believe. What *you* want. It is not your father who asks. He'd never let you trade away such an important, valuable volume. He's got along well enough without such information, despite the best efforts of the London Garda. No, I think it is *you* who needs it so badly.'

Jess didn't answer that. He felt sweat break out in a hot mist on the back of his neck, but he hoped his face remained unreadable. After a moment, he said, 'One of two copies left in the world. I'm offering it in fair exchange. It's a prince's ransom.'

Ibrahim exchanged a look with his daughter. Anit said, 'It is a good price, is it not?'

'It is,' Ibrahim agreed. 'But that isn't the point. The point is that young Brightwell here is trading against his family's interests, for personal reasons. Tell me, does it have to do with the book you spent so much time and *geneih* tracking down, and bought only yesterday, perhaps? The one about the prisoners of the Archivist?'

This was dangerous. Very dangerous. Jess said nothing. Ibrahim sat back against the cushions and rested his chin on one hand. He wore a ruby ring on one finger, and it looked like a drop of fresh blood. 'I want no involvement in Library affairs,' he continued. 'Nor in the private crusade of a brash young man. This is not our trade.'

'I'm asking for information, and that *is* your trade,' Jess shot back. 'Do we have a deal or not?'

Ibrahim continued to stare at him with those unsettling dark eyes for so long Jess felt words bubbling up and trying to escape – angry words. He swallowed them down and waited. Finally, the man stirred, rose to his feet, and looked at his daughter, who still sat quietly watching. 'Anit. I leave it to you.'

'What?' Jess shot to his feet, but Red Ibrahim was already going, heading for the doorway that led to the interior of the house. For a hot moment, Jess thought about chasing after him, but he also knew a man like that didn't survive by being careless. If he'd turned his back, there were plenty of knives ready to protect him.

'Sit,' Anit said, and there was an unexpected layer of steel to her voice. 'Sit down, Jess.' Young and tender she might be, but she was something else, too. Hard in a way that he had never seen before – not unless he saw it in the mirror. She put her hand to a chain around her neck, one that held a ring dangling from it – a large carved ring, with an Egyptian hieroglyph of a bird.

He stared after her father as the man closed the door, but he sank onto the cushions again. 'What's he training you in tonight? How to refuse to help and still keep the Brightwells as allies?'

'He meant what he said. It is my decision. He has left it to me.' Jess moved his gaze to her, and found her nearly as unreadable as her father, but there was a little lift at the corners of her mouth. Amusement. 'I imagine you're thinking what a cruel fate it is, being left to the whims of a mere girl.'

'Something like that.'

She played idly with the ring on the chain. 'We are survivors, Jess,' she said. 'You and I. We come from the same dark places. If you think I don't understand you . . . Tell me, why didn't you go to your brother for this instead? Surely it would have been simpler and cheaper?'

'Brendan?' Jess felt his brows lower in a frown. 'He's not in Alexandria. He's gone. Back to London.'

'No,' Anit said. 'You should perhaps keep better track of your twin. I don't wish to offend you, but he can be a nasty piece of work.'

'Sounds like my brother, all right. Why is he still here?'

She lifted both palms. 'Ask him. I'll tell you where he stays.'

'And you'd like to be rid of him, is that it?'

'One Brightwell in Alexandria is more than sufficient. We would rather that be you.' She lowered her hands to her lap and cocked her head, with a real smile dancing on her lips now. 'I had two brothers myself. I know how difficult they can be.'

Jess cleared his throat. 'So, what's your decision? Your father left it up to you.'

'He did.' She studied him for a long moment, then said, 'Will you swear you will never betray where you got this information?'

'I swear on – what would you like me to swear on?'

'The soul of your firstborn.' She outright grinned this time. 'It's traditional.'

'The rate I'm going, it may be an empty promise. All right. I swear on the soul of my firstborn that I won't tell anyone where I got this information. Not my friends or my family. I'll never betray the house of Red Ibrahim.'

'I believe you,' she said. 'And if you break that oath, Egyptian curses are cruel, Jess. And quick. Remember that.' She rose to her feet and headed for the door.

'Wait! Where are you going?'

'To get the book you asked for,' she said.

'I didn't bring—'

'I trust you,' Anit said. 'If I didn't, you'd be dead already.'

It wasn't a long wait, which surprised him; they must have kept this incredibly dangerous information here, in their *home*. His father would have been scandalised. The Brightwell business was always kept completely separate from the Brightwell residence, though Jess had sneaked in plenty of illegal books in his time – to read, not trade.

She was back in only moments, casually carrying a little leather-bound volume. It looked worn and plain, obviously someone's personal notebook. As he took the volume from her, his fingers felt a rougher patch on the leather, and when he looked closer, there were dark stains soaked into it. Blood.

He opened it to look at the contents, stared, and then raised his gaze to hers. 'It's in code.'

'Of course,' she said. 'And I will give you the cipher to read it when you bring me the payment you promised. I said I trusted you. I'm not a complete fool.' She hesitated for a moment. 'Jess, I said I had two brothers.'

He was busy flipping pages, trying to see a pattern in the cipher – a useless effort, of course, but better than giving in to frustration. 'Are you threatening to set them on me if I don't deliver? I will.'

'I *had* two brothers,' Anit said, and put her hand to the chain around her neck and the engraved ring that hung there. 'They're dead. The reason they are dead is the book you are holding in your hands.' The ring, Jess realised, was sized for larger fingers. A young man's fingers.

It stopped him cold, along with the realisation that the dark stains on the cover could have been her brother's blood. He looked up and into her eyes. They were as unreadable as her father's.

'If you try to use this information,' she said, 'you'll be killed. I would hate to see that happen. It's a fool's bargain, Jess. My father paid a great deal to get this book, and it's cost us more than it could ever be worth. I'm only giving you fair warning.'

His throat felt suddenly tight, and he forced a smile as he said, 'I'll be back with the Blake in an hour.'

She nodded. 'I will be waiting.' Somewhere in the back of the house, a bird began to sing loud and musically, and Anit turned her head towards it with a smile. 'It's our pet skylark,' she said. 'My younger brother built a house for it. The song is so beautiful, isn't it?'

Jess held the bloodstained book in one hand and said, 'It is.'

If this ended badly, at least he could enjoy the bright, familiar song of a bird he'd grown up hearing back home.

EPHEMERA

Text of a message between the Artifex Magnus, head of the Artifex school of the Great Library, and an unnamed recipient.

Greetings and fair wishes, brave soldier. You have already been made aware of your mission, and I know you have doubts of the morality of such an action. You need have no fear. In firing this shot, you will remove from the ranks of the Library one of our most difficult and dangerous traitors, one for whom there is no cure but death.

I do not give this order lightly, and I know you do not take it so. The Burners cry that a life is worth more than a book, but we know the truth: knowledge lives on. No single life can claim so much.

And so a man who threatens knowledge must be dealt with – by persuasion, by force, and, if all else fails, by death.

Blessings upon you from your god or gods, and from the hands of the Archivist Magister himself, who has approved this action.

HIS SEAL.

CHAPTER THREE

By the time he'd retrieved the Blake from his personal stash of rare books and delivered it to Anit in exchange for the cipher, it had been well into the dark hours of early morning. Then Jess spent hours poring over the contents of the book, writing out a translation page by careful page.

The results were startling, and he'd ached to keep going, but by the time his clock showed three in the morning, his eyes were too grainy to focus, his brain too numb to think. Jess finally admitted defeat and fell into bed, where he slept the sleep of the dead . . . Until a pounding on his door resurrected him.

'Mup,' he mumbled, and rolled sideways off his bunk. He desperately wanted to flop down again and die; his body felt nine kinds of sore from the trauma of the exercise the day before and the night's adventures. He hadn't had nearly enough sleep. *The book*, he thought, and grabbed for it and the sheaf of translated pages. He stuffed it into the smuggling harness, which was getting a good deal too crowded for safety, then threw on a robe to answer the summons.

Glain stood there, crisply uniformed, and she said, 'Unplanned exercise. Get ready. It's our last one. Thirty minutes.'

'Glain—' But she was already moving on to knock at another door. He'd hoped to find a moment to talk. But this wasn't the right one again. Maybe that was better saved for after, when all this was done, and he could guide her more gently through the levels of shock, grief, and anger that he'd already experienced.

Dressed and fortified with a cup of sweet Egyptian coffee, he jogged with his squad to the training grounds and their assigned place to form up on the field. Other squads were coming, too, but none, Jess saw, had beaten them there.

Glain hadn't made the run with them.

She isn't here.

He realised that only as they formed their rank and stood at attention. It wasn't just unusual for Glain to be missing, it had *never happened*, and he exchanged a sidelong glance with the young man to his right – Tariq, who'd shot him the day before – without moving another muscle. Tariq seemed calm, but he was already sweating. The loud morning tone sounded from the top of the High Garda watchtower, and . . . Glain still didn't appear. Other squads were inspected and dismissed. Jess's group stood silent in the hot sun, at attention. If the others worried as much as he did, they were too well trained to speak.

Finally, Jess saw one of the Garda's armoured carriers speeding across the ground; his eyes tracked it as it approached them. Glain Wathen jumped out almost before the hissing steam-powered vehicle came to a halt. She was followed by someone Jess recognised only slightly: High Garda Captain Feng, who was smiling this morning, though his eyes were like chips of cold black ice. Feng had never appeared on the parade ground before. Never interacted with their squad at all. He had quite a reputation as a hard man to please.

From the rank behind him, Jess heard someone take in a startled breath, but he concentrated on staying as still as he could. Feng's gaze – cold and impersonal – swept over each of them as he walked the rank. He gave Jess exactly the same assessment as the others, no longer or shorter, and said nothing until he reached the end of his inspection and returned, with Glain, to stand before them. He and the young squad leader were silhouetted by the merciless glow of the rising sun. It effectively hid their expressions.

'Scores,' Feng said to Glain. She briskly unhooked the small waterproof box on her belt and snapped it open. Inside lay a blank, a book connected to the Great Library's vast archives, though this was one whose cover shimmered with the Library's gold seal and the feather of Ma'at – her recording journal, which copied itself daily into a mirroring blank on the shelves somewhere in the distant bowels of the High Commander's offices. Military issue.

Glain presented it to Feng with both hands, and he took it the same way – a sign of respect for the book itself, not for her. He paged through, reading her reports and notes, and then handed it back with the same care. 'Well done, Sergeant Wathen,' he said. 'Well done, squad. Take ease.'

That was a relief, and Jess heard a quiet sigh as they all spread their feet and relaxed their spines a bit. That was a mistake, as Feng continued, 'You lead the roster in points, and, as such, we have decided to issue you a special test today, one that will challenge you to the level we wish you to achieve. Are you ready to excel, recruits?'

'*Yes, sir!*' they all responded at once and as one. Nobody had to feed them *that* response. Every member of Glain Wathen's squad was driven to excel, and their gods preserve them if they weren't. Glain added her own voice. She stood even taller, even straighter. She was in her element here.

Jess envied that. Right now, he desperately missed the quiet comfort of his books. *This*, he thought, *is going to be hard.* Feng hadn't set up a special challenge for them for the fun of it, and Jess had no doubt at all that it was going to be a brutal affair.

'Squad!' Glain called, and they all gave back a deep-chested *sir* in response. Even Jess. 'We lead by two points in the rankings. *This is not enough.* We *will* bring in this exercise with a comfortable five-point lead, and we *will* finish with the top score! Is that understood?'

'Yes, *sir*!' Jess barked, in unison with the rest. He wanted to finish this bloody training in first position as much as Glain did, but having attracted the attention of Captain Feng was a mixed blessing at best.

Feng walked slowly up and down the row, but he looked into the blank middle distance as he said, 'Your assignment today is a confiscation. Your job will be to enter and search a home for contraband books, and, if found, tag and recover them for the Library. You may meet resistance. Be ready.'

That sounded deceptively easy. Glain and Jess had been on *real* book-confiscation missions as postulants competing for their current positions; every person in the squad had qualified on situations much harder than this. In fact, it sounded *so* remedial that it was utterly out of place, given where they were in their training.

Jess shot a look to his right, where a Scandinavian girl named Helva stood at rigid attention. Helva's glancing look told him his unease was shared. *Not right at all.* If Glain thought the same, she gave no indication of it, but, then, she'd always had the best face for secrets that Jess had ever seen.

Glain swivelled to face her squad. 'In the carrier,' she said. 'Move!'

They scrambled in. It was a tight fit, but designed for a full squad and gear. Jess found his seat as the steam engine hissed and gears engaged to rattle the carrier forward. It picked up speed on the flat ground. No windows, so Jess couldn't tell where they were going except far and fast. The parade ground itself was enormous, and held close to twenty different environments and set pieces around the edges. He'd been in most of them during training, including one that doubled as a set for an Alexandrian street. He assumed that was where they were being driven.

He was wrong.

When the carrier jolted to a stop again and the squad jumped out, Jess found they were at the farthest western edge of the High Garda compound: a restricted area near the edge of the field where trainees were not allowed to venture. Jess's misgivings twinged again as the squad lined up again behind Glain's rod-straight form. *Not right*, he thought. The entire area was surrounded by a high stone wall, with just one visible gate.

Behind them, the carrier's bubbling hiss rose to a gusting sigh as gears engaged again and it raced away. The tracks spat a long plume of sand over the squad. As Jess blinked grit away, a solid man in High Garda uniform with two Horus eyes on his collars – a full centurion in rank – looked them over with bleak, unforgiving eyes. 'All right,' he said. 'Gear to your right. Get it on. You have sixty seconds.'

Jess joined the rush to the equipment piles off to the side. High Garda flexible armoured coats emblazoned on the back with the Library symbol, and a heavy black weapon. No reloads for it. Jess was all too familiar with the gun; he'd carried one in

Oxford, when he was still a postulant. Even after all the practice he'd had with it over the past few months, it felt like a hot alien creature in his hands, unfamiliar and hostile.

It brought back such bad memories.

'Live rounds?' someone behind him asked as Jess checked his weapon.

'You have live stunning rounds and half-strength regular rounds,' the centurion said. His accent had the lilt of southern Africa, Jess thought, and it matched with the burnished darkness of his skin. 'They're still dangerous, so pick your targets and try not to kill each other.'

Jess shook his head; they weren't beginners. They were a tight, trained squad now, and they'd all got to know how the others moved. He could pick up cues from body language and peripheral vision. They hadn't had a targeting mistake since the first week together. Well, except for that incident with Tariq, but that had been *orders*, not accident.

Half-strength rounds were *not* normal. These would leave real, lasting damage, and if they hit in the right places outside of armour, could even break bones, damage organs. *Why use them today?* Another piece that didn't fit in place. The assigned job was too easy, the location too remote, the ammunition too odd. There was something not right about this, and though Glain had an excellent, impassive mask of a face, he could see the tension in the sharp way she moved. She knew something she wasn't sharing. He was tempted to confront her, but he knew better; here, in front of the rest of the squad, she'd just slap him down.

He silently checked his weapon and nodded readiness, and once the others signalled, the squad moved to the door. The centurion creaked it open, and a puff of sand blew out in a smothering wave. *It's not real*, he told himself. *Just a mock-up of a street, some actors thrown in for colour and sound. It's safe enough.* But he'd never been in this particular standing exercise set before. He didn't know what it would be like, and it made him itch all over to have it as a final challenge.

'You have thirty minutes to complete the assignment,' the centurion said. 'This is your only exit, so remember where it is. Heads on a swivel, and good luck.'

He seems a good enough sort, Jess thought. More than that, he seemed competent. He had another, more silent and nondescript comrade standing in the shadows. *A skeleton crew*, Jess thought, and wondered what resources they had in case something went wrong. *Not much*, he thought.

Another wrong piece to an unreadable puzzle.

He didn't have time to try to put it together, because his squad was moving into danger.

'All right, it's simple enough,' Glain told them as the door creaked shut behind them. 'I want *perfection*. Watch yourselves. Assume nothing is safe. Understood?'

Jess always assumed the world was dangerous, however it appeared, because . . . well, it was. He knew that very well, had from the time he was old enough to be sent running across London with a contraband book strapped to his chest. Why would she bother to remind any of them? They weren't careless. Where the instructors had taken away points, it had been for small things – form, speed – never lack of awareness. She must be as nervous as he was.

If I was any more paranoid, I'd never function, he thought. The amusement tasted bitter and strange on his tongue, like metal, and he swallowed hard and followed Glain into the barren, twisting streets.

The exercise set wasn't at all what he'd expected. These were *not* Alexandrian streets – which were wide, clean, and beautifully planned – but architecture that spoke more, to Jess, of England. Weathered, cramped buildings. Shadows and rubble. Shop windows filmed with grime, and what he glimpsed behind them seemed chaotic and cheap. A rail-thin dog with ribs showing under fur stood like an automaton in the shade of a narrow alley, and Jess felt a pang of pity for the poor creature. Was it supposed to be here? If this hadn't been a serious test, he'd have stopped to toss it a bit of food, but even as he thought of it, the dog flinched and silently turned to run into darkness.

He didn't see any actors playing parts here. He didn't see anyone at all.

Glain, on point, was methodically checking the stops and doorways, while Jess and the young woman on his right, Helva, watched the dark windows that overlooked the street. There was no need to assign the jobs; each of their squad understood their roles in this action. They proceeded smoothly and quietly down the street, and at the end of it, Jess saw a lone figure standing at the corner. The man wore a sand-coloured Library Scholar's robe that floated on the harsh wind, and beneath, practical clothing showed black. Shoulder-length hair blew in a tangled mix of black and grey, and even before they got close enough to make out features, Jess knew who was waiting for them.

Scholar Christopher Wolfe.

Jess read the sudden tension in Glain's body as she processed this new information; no one, he sensed, had warned her that they'd have a Scholar to escort, and certainly not that it would be *Wolfe*. The man was supposed to be lying low somewhere. After all, the Library's highest levels wanted Scholar Wolfe gone or dead, and for Wolfe to put himself out in public like this, in a *training exercise* . . . Yet another thing that felt madly wrong.

The reason three of their class of thirty had died, Jess remembered, had been because the Library so earnestly wanted Christopher Wolfe silenced. It wasn't a comfortable memory. Well, perhaps even Wolfe hadn't had a choice in this. There had been no sign of his partner, Captain Santi, today on the parade grounds. Where was he? A threat to Santi's safety would make Wolfe do a great many things. It had before.

If Wolfe was here under duress, it didn't show. He presented nothing but bitter strength to the world, just as he always did, as demonstrated by the dismissive look he swept over them. Even Jess and Glain.

'You move like you're strolling down the boulevard,' Wolfe said to Glain, who nodded to him as if that was a normal greeting. 'I thought you were meant to be High Garda soldiers. Are they training you to walk elderly ladies across busy streets?'

'Better safe than dead, sir,' she said. 'As you well know.'

'Do I?' His face, Jess thought, looked more set and grim than ever, and there were dark shadows beneath his eyes that hadn't been there before. He looked thin and haunted. 'Well, then. Do try to keep me alive, and let's finish your mission, Corpse Squad.'

Jess shot a look right and saw Helva flinch at the words. She wasn't used to Wolfe's humour, which verged on cruel; new recruits were commonly called Corpse Squads by the veterans, but it was never said to their faces. Trust Wolfe to flick it at them like a lash, to keep them on their toes.

'You're in no danger, Scholar. Stay behind me, and between Brightwell and Svensdotter.' Glain, if disturbed by his jibe, didn't show it a bit. *She's learnt much since her early days*, Jess thought. There was even a glint of humour in her eyes, but it died in a second as she turned to scan the street. Wolfe pushed in between Jess and Helva. Jess cast a quick look at him and verified that not only was the Scholar unarmed, but he was also without armour beneath that silk robe. If he took even a half-round straight on, he'd go down hard and risk serious injury, even death. Why hadn't they kitted him out with the same gear the squad was wearing?

This isn't right, he thought again, but he couldn't fire questions at Wolfe, not the ones he wanted to ask, like *Who ordered you to do this?* and *Did you have a choice?* Because as a soldier, it wasn't his place to demand that information. He had a job. He simply had to do it perfectly. There was no margin for error.

Glain led them down the street at a steady, calm pace, checking doorways and shops. Jess and Helva watched the upper storeys and rooftops, and, thus far, except for the skinny, starving dog, the place seemed deserted. Nothing moved except cloth whipped by the wind and sand over cobbles. The place smelt dead and deserted.

It startled Jess when Wolfe said, 'The house is on the right, the third on the block. That's where we'll find your prizes. The faster we finish this, the better, I think.' Jess had an almost irresistible urge to turn and look where Wolfe indicated, but instead he kept his gaze locked high and let the others do the gawking. 'There's likely to be some resistance to your confiscation.' His tone was so dry it nearly evaporated on the air. Of *course* there would be resistance. Original books were highly illegal. Coveted, traded, sold, and smuggled, nevertheless. People rarely let them go with a shrug.

This was one of Jess's least favourite High Garda duties:

taking books out of the hands of those who loved them – unless, of course, they were perverted ink-lickers, who delighted in consuming rare and original works in some orgy of possession. In that case, he was happy to slap them in restraints and haul them off to the Library's prison cells. Confiscation was the aspect of the Library that Jess felt the most uneasy about in general, the lengths to which the Library went to ensure *all* knowledge, *all* learning flowed through its doorways. It was not a sign of confidence to him. Nor of a pure heart.

Wolfe went quietly, and Jess wondered if he'd been told more than they had. As little as the Library trusted him these days, perhaps he'd been given the exact same information they had. He was used to thinking of Wolfe as the holder of secrets, but for all his confidence and ability to *seem* all-knowing, Wolfe operated at just as much of a disadvantage as Jess, and likely always had. Seeing Wolfe as merely human was an unpleasant reminder of just how fragile all their safety could be.

They proceeded down the street, and though she might not have realised it, Glain quickened the pace; she'd not been told that they'd have Wolfe to protect – he could see that in the increased tension in her shoulders. She didn't like the silence of these streets any more than Jess did.

When the attack came, it came very fast and from above. Jess almost missed it; the attacking force had positioned itself very cannily to take advantage of the morning glare, and he only registered a tell-tale flicker of movement that *might* have been a bird but in his gut he knew was not, before he shouted, '*On our left!*' at the same moment that he heard Helva ring out, '*On our right!*' just as the first shots rained down at them. Both of them began firing up at the shadows on top of the rooftops, the clattering noise of bullets drowning out any other shouts.

Someone grabbed Jess by the back of his uniform coat and yanked him hard enough to make him stumble three steps; his aim went wild, but the action saved his life. From the new angle, he saw a glass bottle tumbling towards them, catching the light in a flash of green liquid inside.

The bottle shattered on the street as they scattered, with Glain herself covering Wolfe and shoving him towards a doorway as she fired upward. Jess felt the sudden, strange feeling of an indrawn breath on the back of his sweating neck, and then the thick, clinging substance known as Greek Fire that had been contained within the bottle ignited with a hissing roar. The heat flashed over him, and for a moment he feared he was caught in the flames, but when he turned to look he saw a huge, burning column rising to the sky.

This is not a test. That was not half-strength. A million questions raced through Jess's mind, but all useless now. Surely Santi couldn't have known and hadn't agreed to this. Wolfe wouldn't have, if he'd been able to refuse.

Didn't matter. The force on the roof had weapons of their own, besides the shock tactic of Greek Fire. That attack seemed to have missed all of them, and now Jess's squad had taken the meagre shelter available in doorways, and bullets – not half-strength, either – chattered holes in the bricks near them. Glain broke the dirty glass on a wide shop window and ordered Helva through to check it while she covered Wolfe, who crouched to present a smaller target. He looked, as always, focused. Tense. Ready.

Unarmed and completely vulnerable.

Jess tried to control his shaking. Though he knew he ought to be frightened, his trembles were more from adrenaline, eagerness to take the fight to the enemy. He was *angry*, he realised. *Angry* that he'd been dumped, once again, into a situation beyond his control, and with utter disregard for his survival. Angry that Glain, Wolfe, and these comrades he'd tried so hard not to care about might pay the price *again*.

He saw a target on the rooftop, aimed, and fired, and saw the impact. Someone went down, just a dim shape against the glare. *Good.* He aimed again, fired, and missed, but got a hit on the next shadow that appeared.

He cast a quick glance towards Glain and Wolfe, just to be certain they were still secure; Glain was in perfect form, face calm, eyes bright as she aimed and fired, and every shot counted. The sheen of the greenish Greek Fire against her skin made her look almost like an automaton herself . . . except for the slight, contented smile on her face.

Glain had found her perfect moment, it seemed.

Jess ignored Tariq's movement from his post nearby at first, thinking his comrade was looking for a better firing angle up. But he watched him, anyway, out of instinct and the sense memory of getting shot in the back. Tariq wasn't looking up at their attackers, he realised after a second. His squad mate was staring straight at Glain and Wolfe, and the steps he took from cover were angled to put him clear of Glain and give him an open shot on Wolfe's unprotected body.

Jess didn't believe it, not instantly. He *comprehended*, but belief came a second later, as Tariq raised his weapon. Wolfe, without armour, without protection, wouldn't be as lucky as Jess had been in the same situation – and this was no shock-weapons exercise. Half-strength rounds could maim and kill . . . If Tariq was armed with half-strength at all. Somehow, Jess knew in a flash that he wasn't.

Tariq had been ordered to kill Wolfe.

Jess felt it in his gut, a conviction so strong he didn't question where it came from. Tariq, who'd been given orders to fire on his own squad before, might not even know what he was doing was wrong. He might be completely innocent.

He would still be the instrument of a Scholar's death.

Jess realised he didn't have enough time to reach Tariq and warn him or spoil his shot. There were no good options.

He raised his weapon, aimed, and fired before Tariq pulled his own trigger.

His squad mate, his *friend*, collapsed against the wall with his mouth a dark O of surprise, and the weapon slid out of his hands to crash on the cobbles.

Then Tariq sagged down to a sitting position, hunched and breathless from the shot Jess had placed right in the centre of his chest, and his face turned a terrible creamy shade just as his eyes fluttered shut. *Not dead. Please, God, don't let him be dead.* If the Greek Fire was real, maybe all the ammunition was real as well. But he'd put it into armour, not flesh. Jess didn't see blood, which was one small mercy. *I didn't have a choice.* It was either Tariq or Wolfe.

Jess scrambled from his position to Tariq's side and pressed his fingers to the young man's neck. He found a pulse, and pulled the young man to the shelter of a doorway before he took a zigzag pattern towards Glain and Wolfe.

Glain had seen the whole thing, and she swung the barrel of her gun towards him as he neared. 'Stop!'

'I saved Wolfe's life, you idiot!' he shouted back, and ignored her to hug the wall beside the Scholar. Jess faced out, blocking Wolfe from any more possible friendly fire from that angle. 'This isn't just an exercise!'

'Really?' Glain snapped. She sounded slightly annoyed, as if someone had taken the last croissant from the tray at breakfast before she could reach it. 'I saw what happened. Tariq was aiming straight for Wolfe. Did you kill him?'

'No.'

'Good. Then he can answer questions and get a taste of my boot.' She sounded extraordinarily good-natured about it, which was a little chilling. She cast a lightning-quick look over her shoulder into the darkened interior of the shop and called, 'Helva! Is it clear in there?' No answer. She glanced at Jess, then said, 'Take him in. Carefully.'

'You're sure?'

'Whatever's in there, it's safer than here. They're moving to new positions. They'll have us soon.'

Two of their comrades – not counting Tariq, who might not be part of their squad at all – were down, not moving, and as he scanned the rooftop opposite, Jess realised she was right: the firing from up there had stopped, though they'd thrown another container of Greek Fire that was belching gouts of flames and toxic smoke towards the cloudless sky. Distraction, while the attackers gained new firing positions. Inside the shop was safer.

Jess grabbed Wolfe's shoulder, but the older man shook himself free with an acidic look Jess remembered all too well from classes. 'I'm fine, Brightwell,' he said.

Jess drew his small sidearm and handed it over. Wolfe looked at the weapon with what Jess was *almost* sure was longing, then shook his head. 'If I'm not armed, my death's much harder to explain,' he said. He turned and scrambled lithely through the broken window, avoiding the sharp edges, and dropped inside. Jess cursed under his breath and shoved the hand weapon back in place before following. *He* didn't manage to avoid all the shards, and felt the hot kiss of a cut along one cheek as he plunged after.

He found Wolfe only a step inside, standing very still, and Wolfe's arm went up to block his path when he would have pushed forward. 'No,' he said quietly. 'Wait.'

'Why?' Jess was acutely aware that his back, *Wolfe's* back, was to the open street, and took a step slightly towards the man, to try to block a shot if one was coming. 'Get to cover!'

'*Listen.*'

Jess heard it then, the soft moan of someone in pain. It had been Helva who'd come in here, he remembered; he hadn't heard her signal clear. 'Get down!' Jess barked, and shoved Wolfe behind the fragile shelter of an overturned table. 'Stay there! Glain, Helva's down!'

Glain's voice from outside sounded clipped and calm. 'Secure the Scholar first.'

'Secured,' he said, and fixed Wolfe with a look. 'Stay that way. Sir.'

Jess took out a small sealed bottle, twisted the cap, and shook it. A soft yellow glow formed inside as chemicals mixed, a milder version of Greek Fire – a reaction that created light but not to produce explosion. He held it up and off to the side, in case someone should be aiming at the glow, but though a few bullets still flew outside, nothing came his way.

He saw Helva down near the back of the small, cluttered room. Her eyes were open and she was still breathing; he could see the rise and fall of her chest. 'Helva!' She didn't move, not even to turn her head towards him, though he thought her gaze shifted his way. Whatever was wrong with her, it was serious. Jess pointed at Wolfe. 'Stay here.'

Wolfe nodded. Jess moved carefully through the clutter in the way – broken, dusty furniture; bolts of rotten cloth; unidentifiable bits of shattered lives that had been dumped here

for show and to make their job harder. He didn't see any enemies
lurking; there wasn't room for them. One door at the back, still
closed, though he supposed someone might have shot Helva
through it, then shut it again. He rattled it, to be thorough. It
was securely locked.

He knelt down next to her, put the light down, and checked
her for signs of trauma. No blood. No, wait; a small trickle of
it running down her hand . . .

Something moved in the crook of Helva's arm, and for a
bizarre, insane moment Jess thought she'd grown a third arm,
until some screaming, instinctive wisdom in the back of his
mind recognised the sinuous way the thing moved as it glided
over her chest.

Cobra.

Jess involuntarily flinched and the cobra reacted, rearing up
to eye level and flaring its hood wide around its sleek head.
Black eyes glittered in golden light, and for an eerie moment the
thing looked like the ghost of an ancient pharaoh risen again. It
swayed slightly, watching him.

From somewhere behind him, Wolfe whispered, 'Don't move,'
and Jess didn't. He stayed as still as he could, exchanging stares
with the reptile that swayed slowly in front of him. He didn't
know much about snakes – there weren't many in England, and
none like this deadly creature – but he knew sudden moves were
a *terrible* idea, even if all he wanted to do was throw himself
backward. Cobras, he remembered his friend Khalila telling
him, could strike the length of their body, and this one looked
as long as Jess was tall. At least Egyptian cobras didn't spit.
He was remembering a surprising amount of information from
new-minted Scholar Khalila Seif's lecture, to which he'd only
half listened. Most critically, he remembered that the venom

could easily be fatal without immediate treatment.

'Move back very slowly,' Jess heard Wolfe say. The Scholar hadn't moved, thankfully. 'Very deliberate movements. Native Egyptian cobras are not overly territorial; it wants escape, not confrontation. Give it a chance to go.'

'It had a chance,' Jess said. 'It didn't go.'

'It was attracted by her body heat. And *stop talking* and do as I say!'

Helva's eyes were fixed on him, too. Her face was a dirty grey, covered in sweat, and he didn't like the laboured way she was breathing. The cobra continued to focus on Jess, which he supposed was the best outcome; if it turned on Helva again, she'd have no chance at all. *I could try to shoot it*, he thought. If he fired accurately, he might kill it. If he didn't, it could bite him or Helva, and shooting Helva even with half-strength rounds might kill her, anyway.

'Back away,' Wolfe said again. '*Do it, Brightwell!*'

It was the snap of command in Wolfe's voice that made Jess finally comply. He'd grown so used to following the Scholar's orders as a student that before his forebrain could argue with the order, his hindbrain had already begun to move him backward, one slow scrape of his knees at a time. The snake shivered, as if considering a strike, but it held back and watched him shuffle in retreat.

The hood slowly deflated, and the snake – sleek and fast now – slid off Helva and made for a darker corner of the room. Jess watched it without moving until he was certain it was set on escape, and then breathed a burning sigh of relief and lunged forward to Helva. She struggled to sit up, but he held her down. 'How long?' he asked her. She gave him a weak, pale-lipped smile.

'A few minutes,' she said. 'I was afraid he'd bite me again, so I didn't dare call out. Thanks.'

'For what? I didn't even kill the thing.' *I should have*, he thought, looking down at his comrade's sweating, pallid face. He should have killed it. What if it came back?

The cobra had been shocking enough that he'd all but forgotten the shooting until he became aware it had stopped, and then alarm spread a net over his body, pricking every nerve to alert. He looked back to see Glain stepping through the broken window into the store. She kept attention fixed on the street outside, but for the moment, at least, it was quiet.

'How is she?' she asked Jess without turning.

'Cobra bite,' he said, which he knew would tell her everything. They *should* have had a Medica officer with them, if this had been a real mission, but for training all they had were basic first-aid kits, and nothing that would help against that venom. 'We need to get her out of here.'

'No,' Glain said. She sounded calm but grim. 'Jess, I need you to bring help. Get *Santi*. Bring back Medica for Helva and anybody else who needs it.'

'You think we're under real attack.'

Glain nodded sharply, but he saw the set of her jaw, the line of her shoulders. She was angry. 'Get to the gates,' she said. 'Get Santi here and *not* Feng. Watch your back. Go, Jess.'

He didn't like leaving her here, all but alone to protect Wolfe, but, then again, there was no one he'd trust more with that job. And, he thought with a bitter spike of awareness, no one *she* would trust more to risk this. He'd grown up running books for his father through the maze-like, dangerous streets of London. She knew that.

'Here.' Jess pitched her his weapon. 'I won't need it, and it'll just slow me down.'

Glain caught it one-handed and promptly handed it to Wolfe. When he tried to protest, she fixed him with a straight glare and said, 'Take it. We're beyond all that now, I think.' In Wolfe's hands, it looked entirely out of place, but Jess well knew the Scholar was no stranger to fighting or killing, if it came to it.

He cast one look down at Helva, who managed a smile. She was holding her own weapon now – a smaller sidearm – and said, 'Run fast.'

'Always,' he said, and – mindful of the cobra lurking in the dark corner – moved to the closed back door. He opened it and checked. It seemed clear. The alleyway was bright after the dimness of the shop, and he took a breath to let his eyes adjust, then stepped out and turned to scan the roofs. No one in view, which meant he *might* have a chance.

Running for his life was a feeling that settled on him like old, familiar clothes. He wasn't frightened by it: he'd played keep-away with the local London Garda all his childhood, and running in that vast labyrinth of a city was much harder than these straight lines and clean angles. It meant, though, that there was less cover, less chance to lose pursuers in blind corners and narrow passages. He'd have to make up for that with sheer speed.

Jess took in three deep, stomach-straining breaths, oriented himself by the sun and memories of how far they'd come from the entrance, and *ran*. At the next alley, he cut around to the main road – it was, as the centurion at the gate had warned, the only way out. No point in wasting time.

The first block was easy; he'd caught their attackers by surprise, and when he exited the back of the alley at a flat run, he was moving like a blur. He heard the shouts rise like smoke, and a scramble up on the roofs, but they were nowhere near the right position. Someone shot at him, but it went wild. Five steps farther down, there were more shots flung his way, but with the same lack of accuracy.

Someone up there made good time or was in a lucky spot, and he saw a bottle of Greek Fire arc towards the ground two body lengths away from him. No good choices: if he swerved, he'd lose momentum, and there was no telling which way the fire would splash. Going through it wasn't an option. The thick goo would cling to skin and fabric and couldn't be wiped or washed away. He'd burn.

As the bottle hit the ground and the fire rushed to life, Jess ran straight at the side of the nearest wall. He put more energy into his stride and ran two gravity-defying steps sideways on the wall, then pushed off hard and launched himself like an arrow past the roiling green blaze in the middle of the path. He landed hard on the cobbles on his shoulder, and close enough that the toxic smoke crawled hot into his lungs, but he coughed it out and rolled to his feet and *kept running*. Shots scattered behind him, but they all missed, and now the inferno behind him was also – usefully – cover.

Only another block to the exit gates, and Jess made the turn and poured on even more speed. His heart convulsively pumping now, his lungs rebelling from the effort and smoke, but the goal was within sight.

That was when a shot hit him squarely in the back with enough force against the flexible armour beneath his Library coat to knock him off stride and stun his lungs into paralysis. Deprived of breath, blazing with pain, Jess tumbled to the ground, rolled helpless as a beached fish, and convulsed as he tried to pull in air. *Right in the same spot Tariq hit me.* He saw black and red spots, and the pain came in waves as hot as Greek Fire. *I'm going to die*, he thought, and it seemed incomprehensible to him, because the gates were *right there*. Rescue for Wolfe, Glain, Helva – all of them. It depended on him.

He wasn't going to make it.

You will, he told himself over the screaming, mindless fear he felt. *You have to! Get up. Get up! Do it!*

His lungs released suddenly, and he sucked in a breath so fast it burnt, then coughed it out and tasted bloody copper. The pain didn't matter; he had air, and the pain couldn't stop him. *Wouldn't* stop him.

Jess crawled to his knees, then his feet. He was bitterly aware of seconds slipping by and pursuers catching up as he lunged forward. Half a block to go – hardly anything; just a few steps. *Go. Just go.*

Another half-strength bullet (he thought they must have been half-strength, or he wouldn't have been able to get up the first time) raced past him, so close he felt the heat of it score his cheek. The hot desert sand hissed up into his face as if the street itself tried to hold him back, but he plunged on, only half coordinated now, step after pounding, uncertain step. He was leaving a trail behind him of bloody drops, and for a panicked second he was back in the streets of London, worried about leaving a trail for the Library lions to follow . . .

Focus.

He put his head down, forced his muscles to ignore the pain and managed one last, desperate burst of speed.

He made it to the closed gate at the end of the street where they'd entered and collided with the wood. His fist pounded weakly on it, but his lungs still felt too traumatised to shout.

Exposed. Pinned like a bug to a board. This was his greatest moment of vulnerability; he was a perfect target for anyone who cared to aim a well-placed shot.

Jess pulled in a painful breath and shouted, 'On the gate! Open! Open *now*!'

To his sweet and unexpected relief, it swung wide in the next few seconds. He nearly toppled out, but the centurion who'd let them in caught him. The man barked, 'What in Ra's name is going on in there? Did you idiots start a war?'

'Santi,' Jess gasped out. 'Captain Santi. Get him. Now.'

'Look, recruit, you don't request the presence of an elite captain of the High Garda just because—'

Jess grabbed the centurion's collar and yanked him close enough to smell his morning breakfast. '*Get him!* We have wounded, and our Scholar *will be killed* if you don't shift your arse *right now*!'

'Scholar? What Scholar? You don't give orders, you little—' The soldier stopped talking. Jess had pulled his utility knife and now it pressed gently on the man's abdomen, right where it could do its worst.

'Someone betrayed us,' Jess said. 'Tell me it wasn't you.'

The centurion's face was hard to read, but he seemed more angry than guilty. 'You'd better use that toy if you think I'd put baby soldiers at risk. Betrayed you how?'

'Greek Fire. Real bullets. You heard it. That was no exercise.'

The centurion's expression didn't change, but something did around the edges of Jess's awareness; a slight shift of his feet, tightness around his eyes. 'Drop the knife, boy. Before my comrade gets upset.'

Comrade. Jess felt the movement at his back and knew the other soldier was there, ready to shoot.

'Tell me you're not with them,' Jess said quietly.

'I'm not.' The centurion looked past him and nodded. 'Stand down.' His gaze locked back on Jess. 'You too.'

There wasn't any other play to make. Jess stepped back and put his knife away. He said, more quietly, 'I need cobra antivenin for one of our squad. Get that, too.'

For a terrible second, the centurion didn't move, and then he looked at the soldier behind Jess. 'Send a message. We need Captain Feng.'

'Not Feng,' Jess said. 'Santi.'

'Santi's not in charge of this—'

'*Get Santi!*'

The centurion might not have believed him, but he was willing to play along for now. Jess thought there would be plenty of reprimands in his immediate future, but he no longer cared. And that, most of all, must have got through to the centurion, who abruptly nodded. 'Antivenin is in my pack. Let me get it.'

'Don't move,' Jess said. 'I don't trust you.'

'Boy, I could have got that knife from you like taking a toy from an infant,' the man said. 'I'm getting the pack.'

With the pounding surge of adrenaline starting to recede, Jess figured the soldier probably could have taken him down easily, and he nodded. The soldier reached down, grabbed a field pack, and snugged it on. Then he took up his heavy black weapon – more powerful than Jess's, and not loaded half-strength, for certain.

'Well?' he said, when Jess stared back. 'Go on, then. You're taking me inside. I need to assess the situation.'

'I'll need a weapon.'

'Where's yours?'

'I gave it to the Scholar.'

The soldier gave him a sharp look, then took out his sidearm and handed it over. 'Shoot me and I'll end you,' he said. 'I'm Centurion Thabani Botha, in case I die.'

'Brightwell, sir.'

'Good. Now we're mates. Move.'

Jess was still winded and hurting, but he didn't protest; he just turned and led Botha back through the gates and watched the rooftops. It was eerily quiet now, no more shots coming their way, though the Greek Fire still blazed away in a snapping fury. Looking at it now, Jess was shocked he'd managed to get around it, since it occupied all but a small strip of safety against the farthest wall. He and Botha squeezed past as quickly as possible. Once they were out, Botha said, with quiet grimness, 'I wasn't told there'd be a Burner simulation along with your confiscation assignment.'

'What if it wasn't a simulation? Could Burners get in here?'

Botha didn't answer. Maybe he didn't know, or maybe he just didn't want to say. But Jess doubted that the enemy who'd attacked them was really part of the Burner movement. *This came from inside the High Garda itself*, he thought. Tariq had turned on them, after all. There would be questions to be asked in the wake of this, hard ones.

Botha put up a fist and Jess came to an instant halt. They were just at the corner, and Botha looked around, then back at Jess. His eyes had gone narrow and cold. 'How many out there?'

'I don't know. Just saw shadows on rooftops. Maybe ten?'

'Armed with Greek Fire?'

'And guns,' Jess added, though he knew Botha hadn't forgotten. He just felt a little defensive. He swallowed and said, 'If you see any of my squad, watch them, too. I think some of them may be—' He trailed off, because he didn't want to come right out and say *traitors*, but the implication hung heavy in the air between them.

Botha shrugged. 'I always keep an eye on recruits. They might shoot me in a panic.'

Jess decided then that he liked the man. 'Better follow me, then. I trust *your* aim, at least.' He stepped out into the street. For a second, he felt dizzy, waiting for the inevitable bullet to hit, but nothing did. Silence, except for the hiss of sand stirring in the wind, and the roar of the fire behind. The blaze that had kicked off the whole mess was dying down in the middle of the street ahead, and Jess used that as a guide to look for Tariq. There he was, still lying where he'd fallen. Jess wanted to stop, but Glain, Wolfe, and Helva had to be his first priority. He'd find out the rest later.

Glain stepped out of the shadows of the broken window and pointed her weapon past Jess, at Botha. 'Halt,' she snapped, and Jess felt Botha coming to alert. 'Drop it!'

'He's here to help,' Jess said. 'He's got antivenin for Helva, and Santi's on the way.'

'You bring it in, Jess,' Glain said. 'I don't know that one.'

Botha laughed. It sounded genuinely amused. 'Smart,' he said. His pack thumped the ground by Jess's feet. 'Take it in, recruit.'

Glain's posture stiffened just a little more. 'Check the pack,' she told Jess. He crouched down, opened the flaps, and looked in. Standard field equipment, with a full Medica kit inside. He looked back over his shoulder at the centurion.

'You're Medica?'

'Cross trained,' Botha said. 'I do field medicine. You don't need me for this, though. Just give her the injection.'

'Do it,' Glain said. 'Hurry.'

Jess found the antivenin and eased by Glain, who kept a sharp watch on the centurion. He found Scholar Wolfe beside Helva, taking her pulse. Wolfe held up his hand without even looking up, and Jess handed the shot over and watched as Wolfe slid the needle in. The injector hissed a little as the gas capsule triggered, and the clear liquid contents pushed into Helva's vein. She was still and quiet, and Jess would have thought his fellow soldier dead if not for the flutter of her pale eyelids. Her colour was bad – as bad as it could get, Jess thought, without Anubis appearing to personally drag her to the underworld. 'Is it too late?' Jess asked. He didn't want to care. He'd tried hard not to care about any of them.

'I don't think so,' Wolfe said. He put his hand on the young woman's forehead and held it there for a moment – *Not medically useful; just comfort*, Jess thought. The action of a kind man, though Wolfe wouldn't like being thought of in that way. He went out of his way to be seen as a hard, uncaring bastard. 'I've seen this stuff revive those worse off.'

How often? Jess wanted to ask, but didn't. He didn't want to know. Instead he turned back to Glain, who was still aiming her weapon squarely at Botha. Botha was watching her with a smile, but had dead-serious eyes above the upturned lips. 'I'm going to check the others,' Jess said, and stepped through the broken window with a crush of glass under his boot. 'Centurion, come with me. She probably won't shoot you in the back.'

'Probably,' Glain agreed, deadpan. She didn't relax her vigilance until he'd led the centurion away to Tariq.

Botha rolled the younger man over and checked his pulse. He sat back and shook his head. 'He's gone,' he said. It staggered Jess, but he steadied himself quickly. *Tariq was aiming at the Scholar. I had to do it. I had to.*

'They said we had half-strength rounds,' Jess said, and that got a look from the other man. A pitying one.

'This wasn't you, recruit.' Botha rolled Tariq's limp body over to the side, and Jess saw the red-rimmed hole in his ribs. 'The shot punched straight through and came out the other side – armour-piercing. From the angle, this came from above while he was already slumped down. Definitely wasn't you.' Botha, while he talked, kept his gaze up on the area above them. Jess looked up, too. Nothing but sky and blazing morning sun. 'Decent shot from that angle. Your squad mate would have been gone in an instant, never knew what hit him. Come on. Let's find your other lost lambs.'

Jess hoped they weren't, like Tariq, lambs to the slaughter.

They found one inside another storefront, well concealed and unhurt; the others were grouped together in a defensive position down the street. Unlike Tariq, the worst wounds were bruises and cracked ribs from half-strength rounds. Tariq had been deliberately executed, Jess thought, for failing in his mission to kill Wolfe.

'What in Allah's name happened?' That was from Zelalem, one of their squad who was taller than Botha, and cadaverously thin. 'What kind of test was *that*?'

'Pass or fail,' Botha said. 'Fall in, all of you.' The three of them groaned as they stood up from their meagre cover of a fallen block, and Zelalem swayed like a reed in the wind before Jess braced him. 'I said fall *in*, not fall over. Move it. I want all my ducklings together.'

Lambs; now ducklings. Botha must have been a farmer in a previous life. Jess thought about mentioning it, but he didn't think the man was in a particularly jovial mood. As they moved back towards the storefront, there was a storm of movement at the far end of the street, and all of them instinctively drew to the cover of doorways with their weapons out.

It wasn't necessary, because the movement turned out to be Captain Niccolo Santi, leading a half century of his troops down the street, all at high alert.

The centurion stepped out to flag Santi. 'All clear here, sir,' Botha shouted. 'Coming out!'

He gestured to the rest of them, and Jess fell in as they jogged their way to the main force. Glain stepped out of the wrecked window with an arm around Helva to prop her up, while Wolfe took the other side.

Niccolo Santi held up a closed fist to halt the advance of the troops, and the look he gave Wolfe was long and unreadable. 'Scholar,' he said. 'Any damage?'

'Not to me,' Wolfe said. 'This one needs Medica. Cobra bite. We've given her antivenin.'

Santi gestured, and two of his command stepped out of formation and rushed to take Helva. Some of the pressure in Jess's chest lifted. *She'll be all right.*

Jess expected a barrage of questions from Santi, at the very least, or an outpouring of concern for Wolfe's safety.

So it came as something of a shock when Niccolo Santi, long-time partner and lover of Scholar Christopher Wolfe, turned to Botha and said, 'Put Scholar Wolfe in restraints. He's under arrest.'

The strangest thing of all was that Wolfe didn't seem at all surprised.

EPHEMERA

From the personal journal of Scholar Christopher Wolfe (interdicted to Black Archives).

There are mornings where I wake and I am back in the cell, and I see nothing but the dark. Feel nothing but the pain. On those mornings, I am convinced I never escaped that place, and the life I have had since never existed at all, except as a fantastic illusion.

I should leave you, Nic. I know that, because I'm not really here at all. I should vanish and never come back, because one day either I will break and fail you or I will make you break your own vows to the Library to save me from myself.

But I can't. Leaving you would destroy everything in me that remains true and good. Leaving you means giving up on a better world.

I'm sorry, Nic. I love you more than you can ever understand. I wish I could be strong enough to protect you from my own stupidity.

CHAPTER FOUR

Jess got no answers all the way back to the barracks, where he was put in a waiting room with the rest of the squad. They were all exhausted and confused, drenched with rank sweat, and though they were allowed to strip away their armour and were given food and water, the bare room offered no other comforts but wooden chairs. They had a watchful guard who, when Jess posed a question to Glain, snapped, 'Quiet. No talking.'

He leant back against the bare, cool wall and closed his eyes. At least they couldn't keep him from resting.

His Codex gave a small, strange tingle, like a tiny shock; it was a sign someone had written him a personal message, and it pulled him out of a slow slide towards dreams. He straightened and fumbled for the book in its case at his side. Every time he opened it, he remembered his parents gifting it to him before he'd left to train at the Library – a rich gift, leather-bound, with his name inscribed in gold Egyptian hieroglyphs on the front. It had suffered some from hard use, and the scratched, roughened, battered surface looked nothing like the crisp new thing he'd brought just a year ago to Alexandria.

Felt like his, though. A part of him, now.

The first part of the Codex held the standard Library listing of volumes available for reading and research – constantly updated by means of a science that was the secretive work of Obscurists, but that wouldn't have triggered the shock – and, behind that, the contents of the latest reading he'd requested, which happened to be a history of the ancient Romans in the time of Julius Caesar. For all his faults, the man had put aside his quarrels with Cleopatra and Antony to save the Library. In many ways, the modern world owed its whole existence to him.

Behind his reading, on a separate tabbed page, were messages that came in handwritten directly to him. Normally they were from his family – innocuous questions about his progress and health, deep coded with requests from his father for information about books. Nothing new from family, though. Today, on a new, blank page, a message had come from a nameless source, and he recognised the neat, precise writing immediately as an invisible pen moved over the paper on the other end of the connection.

Is Wolfe all right?

He stared at those words hard for a moment as they faded from view. The message was from Morgan Hault, locked up in the Iron Tower of the Obscurists; the girl could not leave and had no chance of escape, and yet every time he saw her handwriting, he remembered the silken feel of her skin and the heat of her body against his. The scent of her hair washed over him in a warm wave. He'd told himself to forget her; she was trapped, and she must still blame him for that. He'd been the one to hand her over. He hadn't fought to keep her free.

She didn't ask how he was. Only about Scholar Wolfe. That said volumes. And stung more than a little.

He wrote back, *He's fine. Are you all right?*

The words faded, and there was no immediate reply. He hated that she didn't tell him what was happening to her inside the tower. Still, she had to be safe enough: Obscurists were rare. Valuable. Necessary to the continued operation of the Great Library and the entire system of the Codex, and Serapeum. They'd have no reason to hurt her. And surely she wasn't yet old enough for them to be demanding a child from her, to continue the Obscurist line. That would be in her future, but not yet. Surely not yet.

At long last, as he watched, a pen moved over paper somewhere in a room far away. *Does that matter?*

As simple as that was, it ripped a piece of his soul away. She hadn't forgiven him.

Of course it matters. Are you?

Is anyone? she replied. *As long as the Library rules us?*

She was right, of course, but he wished, futile as it was, that the Library could be what he'd always believed it to be as a child: the light of knowledge, the protector of science, arts, history. A force for great and eternal good.

The terrible truth was that the Library still *was* all those things. It *was* a force for good; it *did* protect what would otherwise have been lost in wars and chaos and disasters. It *did* encourage scholarship and knowledge across the world, across religious and national lines. It *did* set knowledge and learning in a place of honour above all other considerations.

It was just how it went about it that turned his stomach and made it all wrong.

The Library will change, Morgan wrote, and he could hear the whisper of her voice saying it, too. *It has to change. We must make it change. Is that still our bargain?*

As if they had the power to do that. Jess's optimism had

guttered out months ago, and whatever embers remained were fast losing their heat. He took up his pen and hesitated. He knew what he needed to write to her; it was the same information he needed to give to Glain, and to Wolfe, about Thomas. But, as with Glain, he couldn't think of the words.

Morgan's pen moved one last time, to write, *I will have more information soon. Look after Wolfe.*

He wrote, *Don't take unnecessary chances.*

She didn't reply to that last, only marked down a final X to let him know she was finished, and then the words vanished from the page as the Codex scrubbed any trace that she'd ever written to him at all.

He didn't understand how she could do this – cover her traces so thoroughly from other Obscurists who should have been watching them both. Morgan was clever and resourceful; she'd concealed her abilities as an Obscurist for most of her life without being detected. Still . . . he knew it was a risk every time she sent him a message, and yet he still craved any contact from her like a drug. One day, she'd let something slip, some sign she was letting go of her anger and bitterness.

One day in the distant future, she might even forgive him.

He returned his Codex to the case on his belt and saw Glain looking at him from across the way. She might have suspected Morgan was still in contact with him, though he'd not been completely forthright about it. Glain knew too many of his secrets as it was.

Jess was just about to shut his eyes again when Santi strode into the room, swept all of them with a look, and pointed to Glain, then to Jess. 'You two,' he said. 'With me.'

He executed a crisp turn and left, leaving Jess and Glain to scramble up and after with as much decorum as their battle-sore bodies could manage, while the rest of their squad stared holes in their backs. Santi didn't pause as the door shut behind them. He continued a quick march down the long, plain corridor, then up a flight of stairs decorated with Anubis statues in alcoves, and to an office door guarded by yet another armed guard. Santi accepted the soldier's salute with one of his own.

'Dismissed,' he told the guard, and watched the man leave. Then he opened the door and led the way inside.

Christopher Wolfe sat on one side of a large solid table. He was shackled at the wrists.

'Sit down,' Santi said to Glain and Jess as he shut the door, and gestured to a wooden bench at the side of the room. He was still wearing that cool military expression, and it gave Jess a creeping sense of unease. Wolfe in chains, Santi acting utterly unlike himself . . . And the four of them in a locked room.

Glain slowly eased herself down on the bench and glared at Jess until he sat next to her. Santi dragged a wooden chair, a noisy slide over the stone floor, and thumped it in place across from Wolfe at the table.

Wolfe finally looked up. He seemed drawn and exhausted and – so wrong to Jess – vulnerable. He lifted his bound wrists silently, and, when Santi shook his head, dropped them back with a heavy clank of metal to the table.

Though he'd brought the chair over, Santi didn't sit. 'You're still under arrest, Scholar Wolfe,' he said in a quiet, calm voice that raised the hackles on the back of Jess's neck. 'You're going to stay that way. You know why.'

'Nic—'

'No.' Santi cut Wolfe off clean. 'I don't want to hear it. Don't you understand the consequences? One of my recruits is dead. Another may never regain the use of her arm. That's *you*. That was *your* choice to put yourself at risk when you damn well knew better, and I told you to stay away!' There was a flare of emotion at the end of that small speech, and Santi paused, as if he hadn't meant to let it out. When he started again, his voice was once again pressed flat. 'Tell me why I should ever let you roam around unmonitored again.'

Wolfe hadn't looked away from Santi's face the entire time. Hadn't blinked. Hadn't displayed the slightest flicker of guilt or anger. There was a strange light in his eyes that Jess couldn't reckon. 'Because hiding me away isn't *working*.'

'It's keeping you alive. That's what I care about.'

'Then you care too much,' Wolfe said. There was a tremor in his voice now, and in his hands, too. Something broken behind his stare. 'You've *locked me up*. I don't take well to that. As you know.'

Santi sat down slowly, as if he didn't even realise he was ceding ground. 'It was necessary. You haven't been yourself.'

'You tried to get a message to me,' Wolfe said, looking past Santi at Jess and Glain. 'What did you have to tell me?'

Santi quickly leant forward and grabbed the chain of his manacles tightly to pull Wolfe forward. 'No,' he said flatly. 'Stop. For the love of the gods, don't you understand that someone just tried to kill you out there? The Archivist wants you dead. I trust today finally hammered the point home, since it was written in the blood of others this time instead of your own!'

'Captain,' Jess said, and Santi actually flinched, as if he'd forgotten them in his intensity. 'Why did you bring us here if you won't let me answer?'

'Because I want you to understand too,' he said, and turned to stare at them. 'Leave Wolfe alone. Don't contact him. Don't try. You see what happens – you're the reason he came out of seclusion, to talk to *you*. He could have been killed. The Archivist is burning for an excuse to see him dead.'

Wolfe's smile this time was strangely warm. It nearly looked normal. 'The Archivist needs no scrap of an excuse to do that. No, Nic, be honest: you brought them here because you thought they'd take one look at me and leave me alone out of sheer pity.'

'Chris . . .'

Wolfe didn't appear to regard his lover at all. He kept looking right at Jess and Glain. 'I'm not insane,' he said. 'I'm not on the verge of it. I may be stretched to my limits – my limits being admittedly lower than they should – but you have something to tell me, and that thing is important enough that despite all the well-meaning captivity Nic has put around me, I will continue to risk my life until you *tell me*. He can't stop that, and he knows he can't.'

Santi gave a wordless shout of frustration and fury, knocked his chair over backward, and stalked around the room. His face was tense and pallid, and there was something else there – real fear, Jess thought.

'All right,' Wolfe said. 'Ask.'

'It isn't so much a question as something I need to tell you. All of you, I suppose, though I hadn't thought it would go quite this way.' He swallowed, because he'd drawn Santi's attention now, too. The weight of their stares felt heavy as an elephant on his chest. And speaking of his chest, the harness beneath his shirt seemed to pull even tighter on his bruised skin.

He silently unbuttoned his uniform jacket and shirt beneath. Both were sodden with sweat, and the kiss of cooler air on damp skin made him shiver. No one said a word as he pulled aside the fabric to reveal the smuggling harness, and then unsnapped the pocket to pull out one of the two books inside.

'Your life is on a thin edge right now,' Santi told him softly. 'I'm still an oath-sworn member of the Library High Garda. That contraband had better be worth your risk, Brightwell.'

Jess's hand felt cold and sweaty as he gripped the battered, flexible leather of the cover, and for a long moment he said nothing. Couldn't think how to begin to tell them. Then he said, 'This is the last confession of one of the Archivist's personal guards. The man killed himself a couple of months ago. In it, the man gives detailed records about who he arrested, who was tortured, who was released. Who was executed and how.' He swallowed. 'Your name is in in here, Scholar Wolfe.'

No one moved. Jess raised his gaze from the book to meet each of theirs in turn.

'There's another name in here. Thomas Schreiber's.'

Glain took in a breath, then slowly let it out, and bowed her head. 'Does it say how he died?' she asked. 'What they did to him?'

'It has a record of Thomas's arrest,' Jess said. 'And they did . . . they did hurt him.' He didn't want to think about that. He'd read the entries, forced himself to do it, and he'd hurt for days after, like his mind and body had been cut and torn by it. 'But Thomas wasn't executed.'

None of them seemed to quite grasp what he'd said at first. Not even Wolfe, who was usually so quick off the mark. The silence stretched, and Glain finally said, in a hushed and muffled voice, 'Then how did Thomas die?'

'He hasn't died at all,' Jess said. 'He's still alive. *Our friend is still alive*. And that means . . . That means we still have a chance to save him.'

He should have predicted that Glain would be angry, but,

for some reason, he underestimated the speed of it, and when her fist hit him square on the left side of his jaw, he didn't have time to duck. It was a solid punch, with considerable muscle behind it, and when the red haze faded, he was lying on the floor on his back, and Santi was holding Glain from behind by the elbows. From the absolute fury on her face, she was ready to haul Jess off the floor and give it another go.

'Thomas is *dead*!' Glain shouted, and it sounded raw and full of anguish. Tears glittered hard in her eyes. 'They took him from our house, they tortured him, and they *killed him*! They told you *to your face*!' She launched into a blistering stream of Welsh that he was sure called everything from his manhood to his parentage into question, and didn't stop until Santi whipped her around and shook her.

'Calm down, Squad Leader! That's an order!' Maybe it was his stern presence or her awareness that she couldn't hit a superior officer, but Glain stopped cursing and went still. She breathed fast and hard, but after a moment of silence, she nodded sharply. Santi let her go. Glain sank back down on the bench and balled her hands into hard fists that Jess watched warily as he got up.

Santi turned on him, and there was violence in him, too. Just better controlled. 'Jess. How do you know this book isn't a fake?'

'Because absolutely no one wanted me to have it,' he said. 'I stumbled over the existence of it only because I was working my way through –' he caught himself in time; regardless of how much he trusted these three, his family's business matters weren't to be shared '– through an errand for my father. I overheard a reference to this book, and when I tried to follow up, I was blocked at every turn. It took me months just to verify the news of the guard's suicide, and even longer to make contact with his family to finally pay for the book. They've got no love for the Archivist, believe me.'

'Or that could all be the signs of a very well-baited trap,' Santi said. He crossed his arms and leant against the wall. No help from him, Jess saw. He concentrated on Wolfe.

'Sir, it's authentic. I've investigated.' He swallowed and held Wolfe's stare, somehow. 'I have sources you can check.'

'And I will.' Wolfe's voice was as soft and dry as the desert sands. 'I'll expect a full account of them before I believe a word of this.' But he glanced at Captain Santi, and there was something in it that made Jess play a guess.

'You already knew this, didn't you?' That got both Wolfe and Santi's attention, and though Wolfe was hard to read, Santi, in that moment, wasn't. 'God. You *did* know Thomas was alive.'

'No,' Santi said. 'We didn't. Not for certain.'

Wolfe removed all doubts when he said, 'I believed that he was. And no, before you scream at me, I had no real proof, not like this book of yours. The pattern follows what they did to me: arrest, torture, prison, erasing me as if I never existed. The Archivist doesn't like to waste talent. Thomas Schreiber is gifted, and he knows that. He'll want to . . . use him, if he can. The greater good of the Library and all that.'

There was a bleak sound to that, and Jess felt chilled as he remembered the entries in the journal, the shock he'd felt on seeing the name *Scholar Christopher Wolfe* written there, early on in the book. The guard had seen Wolfe arrested and taken for questioning, but had never seen him executed.

Wolfe had simply disappeared from the records.

Just like Thomas had disappeared, taken from the safety of their student housing. Gone in a whisper.

Dead, they'd been told.

'Is Thomas being kept here in Alexandria?' Glain's voice had gone hard and cold. She leant forward to put her weight on elbows braced on knees. 'Where did they hold you, Scholar? What happened to you when they—?'

'Stop,' Santi said. It was just one word, but the force behind it – not a shout; just pure *menace* – made her look at him in surprise. 'He doesn't need to relive any of this.'

'He does if it's the same place Thomas might be held.' Jess stood up, and Wolfe's gaze followed him. It seemed black and remote, but there was something behind it Jess couldn't understand. 'Where *are* they keeping him? Here?'

'No. They wouldn't keep him in Alexandria, knowing he has friends such as us.' Wolfe leant forward, and his shackles dragged across the wood. 'Let me see it.'

'No,' Santi said.

Wolfe's voice stayed warm. Almost kind. 'I know you are trying to protect me, but, Nic, I see all this every night in dreams. You can't protect me from memories.'

Santi finally gave up. The anger and frustration radiated off him like waves of heat. He wanted to *act*, and Jess understood that; he'd felt the same for the past months, knowing about this tantalising book, hearing of its list of prisoners and executions. He'd intended to only punish himself by finding out exactly how Thomas had died, but instead . . . Instead, he'd found hope. And hope hurt.

Jess held out the book, and Wolfe took it. They were all silent a moment while he flipped the pages. Jess found himself watching the man's face, waiting to see him react, but he might have been perusing some dusty academic work instead of reading about his own darkest hours. When he was done, he closed the book and sat back with a sigh.

'I suppose I should begin with what Glain doesn't know,' Wolfe said. 'Three years ago, I invented and built a device – something that threatened the entire foundations of the Library, though I didn't see it at the time. My device was destroyed, and I was charged with heresy. My work was erased. I was made to disappear, too.' He glanced at Santi, who was still staring hard at the floor. 'Nic was a fool and risked himself trying to find me. He nearly died himself in the attempt. At any rate, I was finally released, under the conditions that I never again publish or pursue any lines of research that the Library deems dangerous. I live on sufferance.'

Jess knew all this; he'd learnt it from Santi and Wolfe when Thomas had disappeared. He'd never breathed a word of it to the others, and it jolted him that Wolfe was speaking of it now.

'But you got out!' Glain said. 'That means there's hope for Thomas.'

Wolfe was already shaking his head. 'My mother is the Obscurist Magnus, and her influence and power meant that the Archivist couldn't execute me out of hand, no matter how badly he wanted to. Even so, I didn't just *get out*, though I was a man of high standing, of many accomplishments, with honours and friends. Thomas was just a student. A postulant.' Wolfe paused a moment, and Jess thought he was censoring himself about what to tell them. 'If Thomas *is* still alive, it's because the Archivist recognises his worth to the Library. That means they'll keep him until his will and spirit is thoroughly broken, and then they'll put him to work in some secret corner. Eventually. It won't be a life, but he will still be breathing.'

That was a horrible thought, but it was one Jess had already experienced. Thomas wouldn't simply be *held*. It would be far worse than that. He didn't want to imagine how much worse, but he could see from the lightless look in Wolfe's eyes that the Scholar remembered. There was something not quite right in that stare, and Jess shivered. Maybe Santi had been right: maybe involving Wolfe in this was a mistake.

But we need him, Jess thought. For the first time since he'd held that book and read the account of Thomas's arrest and questioning, he felt less alone. Less helpless. He knew Glain wouldn't let it go; despite Santi's reluctance, the captain wouldn't, either.

And with Wolfe's guidance, Thomas's fate seemed more and more like something they could change. Together. He'd never once, since realising Thomas still lived, thought about leaving him where he was, to whatever mercy the Library might have.

Thomas was his friend. And he would find him. It was as simple, and dangerous, as that.

Glain, in the silence, turned to Santi. 'Captain. Do you *really* think Thomas is dead? Or are you more afraid that Jess is right and it sends us all down a dangerous path?'

That was a pointed and perfect question, and Jess had to give Glain credit: she was much more clear-headed about this than he could be. For him, it was a raw, personal wound; he'd loved Thomas like a brother, and he still felt responsible, in no small part, for what had happened to him.

Santi chose his words carefully – too carefully, maybe. 'I don't want Christopher dragged back under this threshing machine. The book could be faked. They might be waiting to draw us in. There's every reason to believe Thomas is dead, and almost none to believe he's alive.'

'*Almost* none,' Glain repeated, still in that calm, quiet voice. 'Which means there is, in fact, some. Do you really think we wouldn't want to know that? That we wouldn't want to find out?'

'It may get us all killed,' Santi said. 'Think what you're doing.'

Jess exchanged a look with Glain. A long one. And in it, he could see they were perfectly in agreement. 'We have thought about it. We need to rescue Thomas,' he said.

'No matter what it costs,' Glain said. 'We don't abandon our own.'

Santi and Wolfe exchanged another look. Wolfe inclined his head a little to the side, with a strange, crooked smile. 'You see? They're as bad we are.'

'Worse,' Santi sighed. He rose and unlocked Wolfe's restraints, and packed the flexible cuffs back in the holder on his belt. 'They haven't even got a proper sense of fear. But that will come.'

Hadn't got a proper sense of fear? They'd survived the bloodbath of Wolfe's choosing of his postulants to the Library; they'd survived Oxford. They'd just this morning survived ambush, attack, and the death of one of their own, even if he'd been a traitor to them. They definitely knew fear. Jess just didn't intend to let it stop them. 'So, where did they hold you when they were questioning you?' he asked Wolfe.

Wolfe sighed. 'That, you see, is the problem. I don't remember. Can't. Believe me, I've tried. I can see pieces, but not . . . not anything significant. And I will admit, it's not a memory I'm eager to relive in detail.'

'Even for Thomas?'

Wolfe looked away. 'I'll do what I can,' he said. 'But you'd best try to find another way to get the information you need.'

'Do it carefully,' Santi said. 'Unless you want it to be buried along with you.'

Jess spent the rest of the evening locked in his room with Anit's little coded book about the automata. It wasn't much, he realised: hastily written notes, likely a simple memory aid for someone in the Artifex division of the Library who'd worked on the design or repair of the machines. Some of it was utterly incomprehensible to him, even when he'd translated it from the code. Much of it would take an engineer of Thomas's calibre to understand.

There was a notation of some kind of *script* that had to be changed when orders were altered, but it was a passing mention that noted the change could only be done with the help of an Obscurist. Interesting. Not helpful.

The one golden fact that he picked from the volume was that there was a way to turn an automaton *off*. In hindsight, it was obvious; anyone who had to work on these devices would need to shut them off for safety. But somehow, Jess had always thought of automata as having a sinister, independent, immortal life of their own. In the end, they were mechanical marvels . . . but still mechanical.

Maddeningly, the book didn't give specifics; it wasn't so much of a manual as an *aide memoire*, and it assumed the reader already knew most of the inner workings. All it said was that there would be a manual override located on the exterior of the automaton. Not terribly helpful. Jess could suddenly understand how Anit's brothers had come to a bad end if they'd experimented with this particular, tantalising clue: a Library sphinx wouldn't simply stand there while you ran your hands over it, looking for the hidden switch. It would claw you to death for taking liberties.

Not to mention the fact that there were *many* kinds of automata: sphinxes, lions, the Spartan that watched Jess balefully in the courtyard. Surely different models had different locations for such an override. *Morgan might be of some help*, he thought, but he had to wait until she contacted *him*; there was no way he could write directly to *her*. Frustrating.

What would Thomas do? Jess closed his eyes and imagined the automaton that was most common to Alexandria: the sphinx. From pharaoh's head to lion's tail, it was a fearsomely intimidating creature the size of an actual lion, and armed with the claws and power of one, too. He'd never seen one with an open mouth; did they have lion's fangs, too? Or human teeth? Somehow, imagining them with an open mouth and human teeth to bite with made them more frightening. *Where would Thomas put an off switch?*

Thomas had never built automata like the Library's versions – his had been toys, dolls, chess sets – but one thing he'd said seemed significant now. *You never put the activation button on top*, Thomas had said when he was constructing a miniature horse. *You see? Anywhere it could be accidentally pressed would be bad design. It must go underneath.*

Underneath. But what engineer in his right mind would want to slither underneath a sphinx to turn it off? *Has to be somewhere the average-sized person can reach*, Jess thought. He was imagining the sphinx so vividly now, he could imagine its blank eyes staring straight into his own. A pharaoh's stiff headdress. A human face with a nose and mouth. A chin. A neck flowing down into the broad, muscular body of a lion.

Does that mouth open? Would Thomas have put a switch inside? Not if there was a risk the jaws might close, Jess thought. The idea was efficiency and safety.

He just didn't know, and he thought, with a tired shudder, that Anit's brothers had likely done this same mental exercise and got it wrong. When it had come to their final test, they'd lost their lives. No wonder Red Ibrahim didn't use this information. He'd sacrificed enough to it. *And Anit gave it to me to let me try, at a considerable profit.* Clever girl. No risk to her family, and if Jess managed where her own brothers had failed, she'd probably buy that information back from him.

Jess tucked the book and translation back into his smuggling harness, curled up, and fell asleep for a blissfully quiet night. His dreams, though, were not so restful, full of blood, fire, death and Thomas's screams as Jess ran down an endless tunnel towards him, never quite arriving.

He woke up with the bitter taste of ashes coating his tongue, and realised it was well before dawn. *Good,* he thought. He'd told Glain, Wolfe, and Santi what he knew about Thomas. There were others who needed to know, too.

And he needed the feeling of motion, even if it was only an illusion of progress.

Breakfast came from a sleepy street vendor with a tray full of warm almond pastries, and he ate one on the long walk down gently sloping streets to the harbour. Alexandria was a breathtakingly beautiful city, and no matter how long he'd been here, it never failed to grab his attention. This morning, ships floated in shadow, while the tallest point of the pyramid of the Serapeum flared with the brilliant glow of sunrise. It was promising to be a clear morning, and the sea looked as calm as milk.

A long, straight road ran to the far end across the bay to the island of Pharos, and there, covering a huge part of that island, stretched the massive Lighthouse of Alexandria. It was shaped like three graduated stacks of square buildings, each atop the other, tapering to a graceful tower in the upper third of its height.

It sparkled golden at the tallest point, where a statue of Hathor lifted her hands to the sun, and the dawn's colour shaded down the tower from soft orange into twilight blue at the base. Even at this early hour, figures moved in the large, open courtyard in flowing robes: no doubt they were Scholars and attendants, heading to their work. There were four main entrances, one on each side of the square – open, but with automaton sphinxes standing guard.

He had no particular reason to think the sphinxes would attack, but he also didn't want a record of his visit here, in case someone was watching his movements. No one doubted he was High Garda, after all; he wore the bracelet of service, prominently visible on one wrist, and a crisp, official uniform. He wasn't *actually* sneaking in or evading security. Merely . . . blending.

All it really took was a stack of five pastry boxes high enough to conceal his face, and to wait for a group of High Garda uniformed soldiers to arrive for duty. He fell in with them and kept his walk and posture as relaxed as he could.

The sphinxes turned their heads to track him, but with his face buried by the boxes, they quickly lost interest to scan the rest of the incoming rush of Scholars, guards, and assistants. The automata were trained to detect Greek Fire and the delicate scent of original books, but the pastries would have more than covered any hint that escaped the smuggling harness's pouch.

The pastries smelt delicious enough to make his stomach rumble again.

Jess paused inside the courtyard to get his bearings. It was still night-shaded inside the thirty-foot walls that served as defence both from sea and enemies, though some glowing lamps hung in alcoves. The outer edges were furnished with long marble benches and expertly maintained little contemplation gardens, each overseen by a god statue with some connection to scholarship. There, in the far corner, Athena lifted her spear with her familiar owl on her shoulder. Saraswati had her own quiet garden, where her statue sat with lute in hand by a little fountain. Nabu of Babylon and Thoth of Egypt presided over their own groves, each a patron of the written arts. The Lighthouse courtyard had the feel of something incredibly ancient, and, at the same time, something vital and alive, walked and enjoyed by thousands every day. Antique and modern together.

The Lighthouse rose in a stacked spire towards the heavens. It had looked large at a distance, but it was truly massive – and, more than most things he'd seen in Alexandria, it had the look of ancient wear. It had been rubbed by so many hands and shoulders that the corners at the base to the height of his head were almost rounded away. The stone steps leading inside dipped in the centre, the mark of hundreds of thousands – if not millions – of feet.

Jess began the long trip up the winding stairs. There was a steam-powered lifting device in the centre, but it seemed slow and crowded, and he didn't altogether trust mechanical things today. By the time he reached the twenty-second floor, he was only a little out of breath. Brutal as it might be, the High Garda's conditioning certainly worked.

He rapped on the closed door, balancing the boxes in one hand, and heard a muffled voice invite him to enter. He stepped in, closed the door, and put the stack of pastry boxes on the desk, careful to avoid any of the loose pages littering the top.

Then he looked up into the wide, startled eyes of Scholar Khalila Seif.

She was just as he remembered, as if the months had never passed: pretty, composed, modestly dressed in a loose floral-patterned dress beneath her sweeping Scholar's robe. Her pale pink hijab lay neat and perfect and framed her face to accentuate her large brown eyes.

After that shocked, frozen stare, Khalila let out a girlish squeal and launched herself around the desk and into his arms, hugging him with a ferocity that was surprising for a girl her size. 'Jess! It's so good to see you! What are you doing here?'

'Bringing breakfast,' he said, and gestured to the tower of pastry. 'I thought you might be hungry.'

'Did you think they starve me? Or are you expecting a famine?' She swatted at him with a small, elegant hand and pushed him towards a pair of chairs near the windows. Her view was of the city of Alexandria, and it was spectacular. Seabirds glided at eye level, while the streets and buildings climbed up the hill around the harbour. The giant structure of the Alexandrian Serapeum dominated the sky, along with the black, rounded gloom of the Iron Tower. She ignored the sights. Her smile was full of delight, and she leant forward towards him with her hands clasped together in her lap. 'Whatever are you doing? Really?'

'I wanted to see you,' he said. It was true and it was untrue at the same time. Khalila was a friend. A brilliant mind. A rising star of the Library. When they'd been all together in Wolfe's class, she'd been as much part of the team as any of them, and more than some, but now . . . now she was fast-tracked to the highest levels of scholarship. One day, she'd rise to greatness. Power. Maybe even fill the chair of the Archivist.

If he didn't get her killed. *I shouldn't do this*, he thought. *I'll ruin everything for her. Everything.*

But he knew Khalila well enough to know that she'd find out, and when she did, she wouldn't thank him for that protection.

Jess slowly reached over and took one of her hands in his,

and said, in a very low voice, 'Is it safe to talk here?'

'Yes,' she said at the same quiet level. 'They don't monitor my conversations. Still, we should be careful. And fond of you as I am, you should not stay here long.'

'I know,' Jess said. 'I'll be brief.' There was, he realised, no easy way to tell her; the shock wouldn't be kind. Better to do it in one go. 'I have proof that Thomas wasn't executed, as the Archivist told us he was. There's every reason to believe Thomas is still alive, in prison.'

Khalila's smile faltered, then died, and her dark eyes fixed on his for so long and so silently that he wondered if she'd really heard him. Then she stood up; walked to the door with brisk, firm steps; and turned the lock. 'That will put on a privacy signal. My assistant could arrive at any moment,' she told him. 'I shouldn't wish for her to hear this.' Her voice sounded completely normal, as if he'd told her that there might be rain in the afternoon, or the price of saffron could go up in the markets. 'I would ask how *you* are taking this, but I think I can guess.'

'You seem very calm,' Jess said.

Khalila turned to face him. Tears glittered in her eyes, on the verge of falling. 'Do I? Who told you he might be alive?'

'No one,' Jess said, and told her a shortened story about the illegal book and his confession to Wolfe, Santi, and Glain. 'Santi's worried we'll all do something stupid now. To be fair, he's probably right about that.'

She crossed back to her chair and sat, then absently dabbed at the corners of her eyes with the sleeve of her robe. A few blinks, and the tears vanished, leaving a hard, luminous shine. 'And you believe this? You're sure?'

She was asking him to be logical, not emotional. Jess took a moment to order his thoughts. 'Devil's advocate? It's exactly the kind of ruse the Archivist would love to try,' he admitted. 'And maybe he'd be careful enough to make me work for months to lay hands on this information. So I'm not completely sure, not yet. We might never be completely sure. Maybe we'll have to take a chance.'

'You *must* be sure,' she told him. 'If it's a trap . . .'

She wasn't saying how much she'd lose for it, but he was acutely aware. 'We need to find records of where the Library likes to keep its most dangerous prisoners,' he said. 'I'm just not sure how to get to them – and that's where you come in, I think. You're the best researcher I know, Khalila.'

'Without a doubt.' She had the sweetest smile, one that dimpled just at the corner to let him know she was silently mocking him. 'And you want me to proceed?'

'Carefully. Khalila, I mean it: *carefully.*'

'Of course. I understand the risks.' She paused for a moment, then came to sit next to him again, hands folded in her lap. 'Jess – having been here in the Lighthouse for the past few months, I have heard . . . disturbing things about Scholar Wolfe. That he may be not himself, or—'

'A few books short of a full library?' Jess finished, and was rewarded with a nod. 'It's true: he went through terrible things before we met him, and it left scars. But I don't think he's broken beyond repair, and I think we can count on him. All this makes sense. Thomas had – has – too good a mind for the Library to just discard. They'll want to *use* him. Isn't that logical?'

'Perhaps,' she said. 'Or it's just difficult for us to believe the arrogance that would destroy such a beautiful mind. Such a . . . such a beautiful person as Thomas.' That thought killed another of her lovely smiles, and Jess hurt to see it.

'We have two choices,' he said. 'We can choose to believe he's dead or choose to believe he's alive. Believing he's dead is safer, but—'

'But so cruel,' she whispered. 'What if he's alive? Suffering? Thinking we will come for him, and we never do?'

Jess nodded. It never left his mind for long, the idea that somewhere, Thomas Schreiber was counting on him for rescue. 'That's why I can't let this go, Khalila, trap or no trap. I just can't. I won't ask you to do anything more than a little research—'

'Don't be stupid,' she interrupted, and that smile returned, more certain – and more devilish – than before. 'Of *course* I will do everything I can; it's the only honourable thing to do. It might take time. I say that not because I am afraid to jeopardise myself, but because wrong moves will only get me locked away from key information. It will have to be done slowly, for all our sakes. But when it's time to get him out, Jess, I will go with you, of course. You don't even have to ask.'

There had been a tightly tied knot of stress in his chest, and he felt it give way under a wave of relief. And then another tension set in. Worry. 'I mean it: *be careful*. Thomas – I don't want to explain why they took him; that would only put you at more risk. But they'll do anything to keep what he discovered from being known. I don't want you joining him somewhere in the dark, being—'

'Convinced?' she finished for him, with a sharp arch to her brows. 'Yes, I would like to avoid that, too. I don't think I'd be very brave.'

He doubted that. Khalila had a soul like a diamond – fiery, brilliant, and difficult to scratch. Even diamonds could shatter, though, and he didn't want to be the cause of such an awful thing. 'I mean it,' Jess said. 'Don't trust *anyone*. Someone tried to kill Wolfe yesterday, and they didn't care how many others died with him. Just like when we were postulants.'

'*Someone?*' she asked, and gave him a slight tilt of her head. 'Jess. Don't treat me like a fool. We both know who would be behind a thing like that.'

'The Archivist,' he said. 'Not that we'd ever manage to prove it. There'll be a whole chain of disposable puppets, and he'll already have cut any strings that lead back to him.'

She was silent for a moment, staring out the window at the view – at the towering pyramid of the Serapeum, he realised, whose gold top caught the morning light and blazed like a second sun. 'Such a tragedy. The Library was meant to be a light lifted against the darkness,' she said. 'But we've lost our way. We're wandering in the shadows. That has to change.'

It has to change. Morgan had said the same thing many times, and he heard the echo of her frustration in Khalila's voice. 'Well, if that's going to change,' he said, 'then we're the ones who will have to see it done.'

'Because revolution rarely comes from those in charge.' She turned her head back to him, and the smile was firmly back in place. 'Yes. I read history. But we shouldn't be talking in abstracts and philosophy, Jess. How have *you* been? It's an injustice, you being wasted in the High Garda. You deserve so much more!'

He grinned. 'I've done all right,' he said. 'You know me. I survive.'

'You shouldn't have to simply survive!'

'They tell me suffering builds character,' he said. 'Glain's turned out to be a right good leader, by the way. She'll climb the ranks fast, I've no doubt.'

'And you?'

He laughed outright. 'No, thanks.'

'I wish I knew a way to get you back here. I think you miss this.' She gestured at her office. It was a plain affair, with a desk, shelves, Blanks. A few precious originals carefully shelved behind a panel of glass. His gaze fixed on them, and instantly he felt that sensation: longing. He wanted to take those books in his hands and experience the texture of the cover, the smell of the pages. Books spoke mind to mind, soul to soul across the abyss of time and distance.

He did miss all this. Desperately. 'I'm fine, I tell you. How's Dario? Are you two still . . . friendly?'

She shrugged. 'Dario is an arrogant ass.'

'So you're still seeing him, then.'

That made her laugh outright, and he liked seeing happiness on her face. 'We understand each other.' She blinked, and the amusement faded fast. 'Speaking of understandings . . . Have you heard from Morgan?'

He didn't want to lie to her again, but he did. Effortlessly, to protect Morgan, if nothing else. 'Morgan isn't likely to ever leave the Iron Tower again. You know that.' *And I did that to her. She could have run. Maybe she would have made it.*

'I'm so sorry. I know—' She seemed to search for just the right words. 'I know how much she meant to you, though you try not to show it.'

He said nothing to that. The compassion in her voice made the half-truth hurt as if it was true. And it *could* be true, despite what he wanted to believe. Morgan might forever be nothing more than words on a page to him, like those originals safe from his touch behind glass.

'Jess.' Khalila drew his gaze back to her. 'What is it Scholar Wolfe used to tell us? "Anything is possible. The impossible just takes longer".'

'Stupid saying.'

'Surprisingly true, though. How should I contact you? Not by Codex, I assume.'

'Paper messages,' he said. 'Put nothing down that you wouldn't want the Archivist reading. And give your notes only to those you trust completely. Nobody else.'

'I've missed you. We can be friends again, finally. I've missed you so *much*, Jess.' She hugged him once more, and he hugged her back. In some ways, the bonds he'd formed with her, Dario, Glain, Morgan, Thomas . . . those had been more important to him than the ties he had by birth to his twin. *I let Morgan down*, he thought. *But not them. Not this time*. 'Do you want me to tell Dario about Thomas?'

'No, I'll do it. Is he here? In the Lighthouse?'

'Yes, he's three floors down, in Scholar Prakesh's offices. He's working as her assistant. You're going to see him?'

'Does that surprise you?'

'A little. I admit, I never thought you two would pay each other visits like reasonable adults. Tell him. He'll want to help as much as I do.' She patted his cheek in an almost motherly way. 'The two of you are so alike.'

'Oh, so now I'm an arrogant ass, too?'

'Of course,' she said, and her smile grew deep enough to reveal that dimple again. 'A fiercely smart, ridiculously brave one. My favourite kind. Now, take some of these pastries away before I eat all of them and make myself sick!'

He took most of the boxes with him and went down three flights. He'd never heard the name, but Scholar Prakesh's offices took up an impressive expanse, and when Jess pressed the bell to the side, he was surprised to find the door opened not by Dario, but by an elderly woman in a vibrant pink sari with gold trim at the edges under her black Scholar's robe. 'Scholar Prakesh?' he asked, and bowed to her. She smiled and gave him a slight nod. 'Please forgive me for disturbing you. Do you like almond pastries?'

She watched his face intently as he spoke, and to his surprise, began to move her hands in fluid, rapid motions. He recognised it, though he didn't speak it: sign language. He tried to look uncomprehending without seeming stupid, and must have failed, because she sighed and clapped her hands.

As if she'd summoned him out of thin air, Dario Santiago appeared from a side room. He raised his eyebrows when he saw Jess and the pastry boxes. Scholar Prakesh repeated her gestures, and Dario watched her hands, then said, 'Scholar Prakesh says, "Young man, your charm is wasted on me, but your pastries are not. You are . . . ?"'

He knew enough to address his words to the Scholar and not her translator, and bowed to her. 'Jess Brightwell, Scholar, a soldier in the High Garda. I am very honoured to meet you.'

Dario watched the exchange that followed and spoke for her again. '"That is only because you do not know me yet, of course. Come in. I expect you are here to see my exasperated young assistant."' Dario laughed. 'She means me.'

'I am, Scholar. Thank you.'

Prakesh signed again. 'You might have to dig him free of the work I've piled on him this morning. Try not to listen to his complaints.' She reached for the boxes, and the conversation between them was clearly over. She moved with impatient speed back to her desk, leaving him and Dario to sort things out. It gave Jess a moment to take in Scholar Prakesh's office. If Khalila's room had been piled with papers and books, this one had the feeling of order, but ancient layers of it, built one atop another. Chalkboards lined the room, filled with jottings and notes in tiny, precise writing, some of it written in a rounded, beautiful language he didn't recognise. It was an oddly restful place, and, best of all, it was steeped in the crisp, autumnal scent of books. *I just want to take this all in,* Jess thought. It seemed like . . . home.

Dario gestured impatiently for him to follow, and Jess left home behind. He trailed Dario to the door of the office on the left. Dario sat down behind a desk, leant back, and folded his arms. 'What are you doing here, Brightwell?' Unlike Khalila, Dario seemed to have changed quite a bit. He'd put on a little muscle, and cultivated a Spanish-style shadow of beard that made him seem older. Even a little wiser. His hair had grown longer, too.

The attitude, though, hadn't changed at all.

'I see you've missed me.'

Dario gave him an incredulous look. 'Were you gone? My goodness. The time seemed to fly by, not seeing you.'

Jess took a seat in the chair across from the desk. 'Still charming,' he said. 'Just for that, you don't get any pastries.' It seemed odd to switch from this comfortably contemptuous banter to news about Thomas, so he offered, 'I didn't know you knew sign language.'

'My baby sister was born deaf,' Dario said, which surprised Jess to the bone. First, that Dario had a baby sister and second, that he'd be considerate enough to go out of his way to communicate with her. 'That was one of the reasons I was assigned to Prakesh, besides being so handsome and charming.'

'So, this is working well for you?'

'As well as I could have dreamt. The Scholar's a wonder. I learn so much every day.' Dario's expression turned serious, and he leant forward in his chair to stare at Jess. 'Why do I have the feeling you've come here to ruin all that?'

He kept the story short, if not sweet. Dario's face took on a blank masklike expression while he spoke, and his eyes went narrow and very dark. No smiles. No sarcasm.

'So,' Dario said, once he'd told him everything he knew, 'we go and get Thomas. When?'

In that moment, Jess liked him very much.

'No idea yet. Stay in touch with Khalila – I'll send word through her. Help her with research.'

'If you need to question anyone, let me know. I'll come along.'

'You mean, you'll hold them while I beat them?'

'No,' Dario said. 'You'll hold them while I cut the truth out of them. This is for *Thomas*.'

'I didn't think you—'

'Liked him?' Dario waved that away impatiently. 'He's one of us.'

Simply said and plainly heartfelt. Jess nodded. 'Dario. Be careful. Keep your wits sharp.'

'And my dagger sharper? Yes, scrubber, I do have a brain. I know what we face here.' Dario pulled a piece of paper closer and picked up a pen. His fingers were shaking. He put the pen down again and flexed them, as if they troubled him. 'Anything else?'

'Enjoy the pastries.'

He was opening the door and preparing to leave when Dario said quietly, 'Jess.' It was rare that Dario called him by his first name. 'Do you think they're hurting him?'

'Yes,' Jess said. 'And I think they'll keep hurting him until we get him back. So let's get him back.'

He closed the door, said a polite farewell to Scholar Prakesh – that sign, at least, he knew – and headed back down the stairs. He was halfway down when his Codex chimed for attention, and he paused in the middle of the stairs to open it and check, as others moved around him with impatient looks.

It was from Glain, written in her sharp, impatient printing. *Get your bum back to the barracks before someone misses you. NOW.* That last was underlined with vicious black pen strokes. He could almost feel the anger and worry smoking off the page.

He reached for the stylus and replied, *On the way.*

EPHEMERA

Text of a treatise from Heron of Alexandria on the uses of automata in Library service, in the second century of the Library, in response to minor damage made to the Alexandrian Serapeum by vandals.

. . . insofar as the mechanical sentries are concerned, I see no reason that such devices cannot be used to frighten away evildoers bent on mischief inside the grounds of the Library precincts, and those of the museum, university, and zoo. It would be whimsical to fashion these automata on the shapes of creatures both familiar and fabulous to us. Lions have long been seen as noble beasts of tremendous power and cruelty; I should imagine a mechanical lion would turn away any casual vandal in search of easier targets, and it reflects well on the ideals of our Library.

There might also be made use of the sphinx, for this wise and legendary creature is everywhere a symbol of royal power and strength. To go a bit more fanciful, serpent automata might coil on columns, and perhaps even such devices in the shapes of horses could one day carry our soldiers to battle. Think of the possibilities!

I shall establish herewith a new field of study into this matter, with the express purpose of developing such methods of self-defence for the Library and those who understand and support our noble purpose. Of course, this will need to be done in secret. Such devices are of no possible use if their inner workings are made public.

May the gods bless our struggles, and our light ever push back the darkness.

CHAPTER FIVE

Getting out of the Lighthouse meant, in the end, waiting for a whole flock of Scholars to leave at once, and striding along with them as if he were meant to be one of them. Jess quickly offered to carry a heavy load of equipment for the small, overweight man leading the party, and that had earned him instant friendship – at least, until he handed it back at the end of the road and headed for the High Garda compound at a run. Running felt good on such a bright and perfect morning.

When he arrived back, he searched for Glain. Her quarters were empty, but he finally spotted her walking the halls in the company of Captain Feng. He couldn't read her expression, but he doubted she was with the man by her own choice. The conversation seemed one-sided.

Despite Glain's worries, no one seemed intent on ordering him today, so Jess indulged in some much-needed sleep, then rose with the intention of doing some reading. As he stepped into the hall, he realised that the door at an angle to his on the other side – Tariq's room – was standing open. He'd got halfway across the hall to say hello before the memory caught up with him of Tariq slumped against the wall. *Tariq was dead,* and someone was in his room. He stopped in his tracks.

Inside the room, Tariq's closest friends, Wu and Bransom, packed up his few belongings. Jess felt it like a hammer to the chest as he watched Recruit Bransom – as sturdy and muscular a young woman as Glain – wipe away tears as she picked up Tariq's personal journal, embossed with his name. The cover, even at the distance at which Jess observed, was smeared with dried blood, and she scrubbed restlessly at it with the sleeve of her own shirt. Her hands were shaking.

Someone will write the final lines in that journal, he thought, *detailing the dates and circumstances of Tariq's death.* Jess might even be mentioned by name. Then Tariq's family would read it, weep over it, hold a memorial to read aloud from it, and finally send it on to the Library's archives, where he would become a permanent part of the knowledge of humanity. Immortality, of a kind.

We're just paper on a shelf, in the end. Jess felt an unexpected surge of anger, because no matter how honest and forthright Tariq had been in his journal, it couldn't encompass *him* – the sharp humour, the way he'd cleverly cheated at dice, the shady jokes he'd loved and often told. The way he'd died. And for what? Tariq was gone, and Jess still felt the tension and release of pulling the trigger and sending Tariq sprawling against that wall where he'd died. Never mind that his shot hadn't been fatal in itself; it had left his friend helpless for the slaughter that came after.

Bransom looked up unexpectedly and saw Jess. She looked wounded and vulnerable, and tears glided down her cheeks . . . And then he saw the flare of real rage.

She slammed the door in his face.

In a subdued, soured mood, Jess spent the rest of the day in the barracks Serapeum – a small offshoot that contained a few dozen shelves of permanently loaded Blanks that held books most often requested, and a wall of ones waiting to be filled. He took one from that section and sat down to page through his Codex to find what he wanted. He remembered – thanks to Scholar Wolfe's ruthless grilling about the vast list of books in the public collection of the Great Library – that there were one or two extremely obscure histories of crimes against the Library. Maybe someone, somewhere, had included clues to secret prisons. The research might be useful.

Best of all, though he knew someone, somewhere was watching what he ordered to read, he had a long history of reading historical texts. Even if the Archivist had a watch on what he read, this wouldn't appear out of the ordinary.

Jess missed handling originals. He'd grown so addicted to the feel of those books, the individual differences in the bindings, the leather or fabric covers, the weight of papers, the smell. They were a very different experience than these Blanks, which all felt so . . . *sterile*, somehow. Words that could be readily dismissed and replaced didn't have the same moral weight to them, to him, but he recognised he was a rebel and an outcast, even here among those who loved the Library.

Another reason to never lower his guard.

He was immersed in text and making handwritten notes to himself on a separate sheet when he sensed someone standing close by. He looked up to see the faces of Garrett Wu and Violet Bransom, and instantly knew it wasn't a social visit.

Jess put the book aside and his pen down before he stood up to face them. 'I didn't do it,' he said. 'Tariq was shot from above. Ask Sergeant Botha.'

'You shot him first,' Bransom – they never called her Violet, and Tariq had coined her official nickname, Violent, the first day – said, and with one shove, she put him back down in the chair. He didn't resist. It gave him excellent leverage to kick knees and break bones. 'I saw it. He went down when *you* shot him.'

'He was aiming at a Scholar. You know, the one we're sworn to protect at all costs? Are you actually telling me you wouldn't have done the same?'

'You're lying,' Wu said. He wasn't a bad guy, and Jess normally got along with him, but seeing that stiff, angry expression, he knew getting along wasn't on the cards today. 'Tariq would never betray us. And he'd never shoot a Scholar. That's sick!'

They'd never accept the truth, and Jess didn't blame them. Tariq had been a friendly sort, likable. Jess had taken pains to *not* be part of the group. He'd wanted to stay apart, after the pain of losing his friends from his Postulant class.

And this distrust was what caution and distance had earned him.

'I'm telling the truth, and Botha backs me up about how Tariq died. Whether I shot him or not makes no real difference. *I didn't kill him.* A sniper from the rooftops did.'

'And you think you did your *duty,*' Wu said. The boy's fists were clenched hard at his sides, his stare very dark and fixed. Jess knew the look. He'd faced it before. He kept his attention split, because Bransom would be the one to make the first move, if one was coming. 'You'd do it again, wouldn't you? To any one of us.'

'Yes, I'd do it again, to save a Scholar's life. And so would you!' He was getting angry now, could feel it like a sunburn blooming under his skin. 'Tariq was working with them. Maybe he wasn't the only one.'

Wu's face went a dangerously dark shade. 'You saying we're *Burners?*'

There was, Jess knew, no insult he could have given that would be greater, but there was no taking it back, and it didn't matter. Neither of the two facing him was listening anyway; they had their minds well made up about what they thought. He was wasting his breath.

The area had quietly cleared of other soldiers. Disputes between people of equal rank weren't prohibited, unless officers were present. Bransom was about to kick it off, he thought, and he prepared to shatter her left kneecap, but just then a calm voice from the doorway said, 'Is this a private two-on-one fight, or can anyone join?'

Glain Wathen stood there, looking dangerously still, despite the mild tone. A superior officer.

It broke the tension like a hammer on glass, and Wu and Bransom stepped back. 'Squad Leader,' Wu said, but the look he gave Glain was chilly. 'Just working something out.'

'Then do it where I can't see you,' she said. 'If any of you start something here in the Serapeum, you're all on report, and I promise you, you do *not* want to see my temper just now. Are we understood?'

Her fingers tapped the seam of her trousers, and Jess knew that particular tic of hers; it meant she really was spoiling for a fight. The others must have known it, too, or at least they were aware of the dangerous light in her eyes. Bransom nodded and stepped away from Jess, and after a slight hesitation, Wu followed. 'No problem, Sergeant,' Bransom said. 'We'll . . . catch up later.' *When Wathen's not around* was strongly implied, but Jess didn't much care. At least they gave fair warning.

Jess watched the other two walk out, and when they were

out of earshot, he said, 'Do I really look so feeble I need help, *Squad Leader*?' As he said it – snarled it, really – he realised that he'd been ready to fight. Eager, even.

So was she, because in three long strides Glain was across the room, grabbing him by the collar and dragging him upright from the chair. He knocked the Blank off the table, and the thump of impact froze them both for a moment as they looked down.

Then she shook him. Hard. 'Go on, Brightwell, test me today. See how far you get!' He looked into her eyes, and his own restless anger and frustration faded because he saw its mirror in hers. He slowly held up his hands, and she let go and stalked a few steps away. Paced. After a moment, she bent and picked up his book to pass it back to him.

'Should I even ask what's put you in this mood?' he said. She cut him a look so sharp it had edges on it.

'Captain Feng. He made it abundantly clear that I have some choices to make,' Glain said. 'Hard ones.'

'Your career or your friends,' he said. 'You knew that was coming, didn't you?'

'I never wanted any of you as friends! I came here to succeed, and that requires focus. You know that. I know you do.'

He did. He was capable of the same ruthlessness when required. Achievement here at the Library was an altar on which one sacrificed many things . . . friendship being the least of it. To go on up the ranks, knowing what he did now – that would require sacrificing his morals. Ethics. His soul.

He also knew that Glain wanted – no, needed – to succeed. She tried not to show how much it meant to her, but it was as clear as the Lighthouse's beacon. 'Do what you have to do,' he told her quietly. 'No one will blame you. Least of all me. I'm a selfish bastard, anyway.'

She let out a strange, pressurised little laugh, and then caught her breath. Fought for control for a moment, and when she'd achieved it, deliberately relaxed. 'We can't talk here,' she said. 'Come on.'

She led him back to her quarters, and waited until he was inside and the door shut again before saying, 'You went to the Lighthouse, didn't you? Were you seen?'

'I don't think so,' he said. 'I talked to Khalila. She's willing to help.' Out of habit, they both kept their voices low. Best to assume unfriendly ears were everywhere, especially now.

Glain frowned. 'I don't like involving her,' she said. 'Of all of us, she's the one with the most to lose. And what about Dario? Do you trust him?'

'I don't always *like* him, but trusting him is another matter, and of course I do. Fair warning: he'll still give us grief just because it's his nature,' Jess said. 'He's angry about Thomas, though. I trust him to do whatever's required.'

She nodded and sat down on Jess's bed, leaving him to pull his desk chair close. 'What were you and the others clashing about back there?'

'Tariq.'

She hadn't been expecting that, and he saw the shift in her body language. Some might have seen it as defensive, but he knew it was more self-defence against her own pain. 'I should have realised that they'd blame you and said something first. Sorry.'

He shrugged a little and kept silent. Nothing much to say.

'I've sent the death notification to his family,' she said. 'It was my place, as his commanding officer. I suppose I had to learn how that felt sooner or later. Would have rather it had been later, and for a better cause.'

'What did you tell them?'

'Not the truth, of course. I said it was a training accident, very regrettable, and that he performed his duties with great integrity and concern for his fellow recruits.'

He let that sit for a moment before he said, 'Did you suspect him at all?'

'Not really. I knew he had questionable friends. I certainly didn't expect him to try to put a bullet in a Scholar!'

'And here I thought you automatically suspected everyone of the worst.'

'Let's just say I never assume the best. But Tariq's dead, and it seems likely he was killed by those who paid him, for failing in his mission. Agreed?'

'Agreed,' Jess said. 'Do you suspect anyone else in the squad?'

'I have to suspect everyone. Including you, I suppose.'

'Well, that's fair.' Jess cleared his throat. 'About Thomas . . . Feng said you had to make a choice—'

'He did,' Glain said, and met his eyes squarely. 'And I have. You know what it is?'

She and Dario have something in common after all, Jess thought. They didn't agonise about a decision. They just made it, and damn the consequences.

'Khalila and Dario are trying to find us more information about the secret prison,' he told her. 'What you said earlier, about the Black Archives . . . do you think there's a chance that information about Thomas might be there?'

'It's where the Library keeps anything secret, so of course.'

'I'll ask Dario to look into it. We need to move faster than this,' Jess said. 'I can't get Thomas out of my head. What if—?'

'If you're thinking about what he might be going through—'

She let in a breath and blew it out slowly. 'Don't. There is nothing you can do to stop it, and guilt is a useless exercise.'

He laughed, but there wasn't any humour in it. Or in him. 'What else should I think about? Our bright future here?'

'No need, because we don't have one. Wouldn't, even if it had nothing to do with Thomas. I lost one soldier for good and another to serious injury. I almost lost a Scholar. That was Feng's point to me today: how poorly I'd performed, and how much of a *favour* it would be for him to recommend me for advancement. If I accept that favour, he'll own me. Nothing's worth that.' It hurt her to say it – Jess knew that – but he saw no sign of it in her expression. Tough girl, Glain. And now she faced losing her dreams, and did it with the same courage as always.

He felt a tug of deep respect for her in that moment. Perhaps even a little love.

'At least we'll be able to meet with Khalila and Dario easily, if we're not constantly on duty.'

The eyebrows rose again. 'You want to put *me* face-to-face with Dario? I might have to punch him before I trust him.'

'You can trust him.' At her look, he shrugged. 'I know. Still surprises me, too.'

Glain sat back with a creak of wood and crossed her arms. She was out of uniform now, in a simple loose white shirt over form-fitting trousers, with the same boots she always seemed to favour. *If she's lost her place, she's lost her world*, Jess thought. 'You know, our odds are so bad as to be worthless. You and me, Khalila, Dario, Wolfe, Santi – *if* we can rely on Santi, who'll have to choose his own loyalties – against the Library? It's ridiculous.'

She was right. Even corrupted, the Library still commanded

the absolute loyalty of tens of thousands of good men and women, and had the reverence of billions. That was a testament to what it *should* be, though. Not what it was. That was the dream that Jess loved, really – the dream of the Library as a shining beacon of knowledge to the world.

But a light that cast so many shadows.

'It's getting late,' Glain said, which jerked him out of his musings and, as he blinked, back to the cool evening of the room. Dinner was fast approaching. 'You'll talk to Dario? About the Black Archives?'

'I will.' He groaned as he stood. His body was sore again, and all the older bruises and cuts clamoured for attention. 'Are you going to the dining hall?'

Glain smiled very briefly. It was a rare enough event, and it made her almost human. Almost pretty. 'Are you asking to escort me, like some girl you're romancing? Jess. Don't waste your time. I'm extremely unavailable.'

'Tragic,' he shot back. 'Be serious. You know I've got—'

'Morgan,' she finished for him, when he stopped. 'Yes. You do enjoy a challenge. Now she's a princess locked in a tower. That makes you want her even more, doesn't it? I think you've read too many tales of knighthood, Jess.'

That effectively silenced him while he processed the words; a flush of anger ran through him, followed by a chill of something like understanding. Was that why he loved Morgan? Because of the *challenge*? He couldn't deny that it might be a part of it. Damn Glain and her sharp eyes. Challenge and guilt.

'I'm not saying that because I'm jealous,' Glain continued, still with that maddening, calm smile. 'You and me? No. Agreed?'

'Yes.'

'Good. Now there's no confusion.'

How like Glain, to take action to dispel *any* uncertainty that might exist, however awkward that might be. The cold blast of it was shocking, but it did clear the air.

'Remind me never to be polite to you again,' he said, and she laughed this time, came around, and draped a comrade's arm around his shoulders.

'Of course I will.'

Days passed, and other squads finished their final tests. Recruits were dismissed or assigned to new duties, and their wing of the barracks emptied and filled with another quota of aspiring High Garda soldiers.

But there was no word on their future. That was worrying, and Jess enquired – carefully – among other soldiers. There were a few examples of squads whose fate had been held in suspense for a while, but only a few, and almost all of those had ended up dismissed. The delays, Jess thought, had to do with debates within the higher ranks.

Maybe Captain Santi was fighting for them. And losing.

Jess was just as glad, because he spent his days chasing down obscure information through the Codex, and nights with Red Ibrahim and Anit, looking through rare volumes for anything that might give small details about what happened to the enemies of the Archivist. What he *did* find wasn't heartening; almost everyone accused of heresy was recorded as executed, though those executions were done privately now, rather than the vast spectacle they'd once been. The Alexandrian prisons that had once existed in the early, brutal days of the Library were long torn down. There might be a few cells beneath the Serapeum, but Khalila's work had turned up guard rosters, and by matching up those assigned to duties, she'd been able to create a dizzying map of assignments that accounted for every one of the High Garda guards assigned to the Archivist. There would have to be *some* whose duties remained unaccounted for, if they actually guarded a secret prison.

Wherever Thomas was, he wasn't being kept in Alexandria.

'We should press Wolfe,' Khalila said, as she, Jess, Glain and Dario sat together in a small cafe near the water. Twilight dyed the sky a rich teal, though Jess couldn't much appreciate the beauty. All the information she and Dario had unearthed was proving to be useless. No nuggets of gold had turned up. The inaction drove him mad. 'Surely he *must* remember more than he's telling.'

'He might not,' Dario mumbled around a mouthful of curried chicken; Jess had already cleaned his own plate. 'There are Medica techniques and potions to block memories. If they treated him with those, it's not likely he *can* remember on his own.'

'What do you mean by that? Can he remember with help?' Glain asked. She'd long finished her meal, and now sat idly watching the white-sailed Egyptian fishing ships glide into the harbour towards home. 'More potions?'

'More likely it would require the help of a Mesmer,' Dario said.

'Mesmer,' Glain groaned. 'Don't tell me you believe that tripe.'

'Mesmerism is a scientific fact,' Dario said. 'Anyone can learn to do it. Doesn't take ability, like being an Obscurist. But their skills are closely guarded secrets. We had one at court.'

'Don't tell me you learnt how to Mesmerise,' Khalila said. 'I can never trust you again.'

'I tried, but, lucky for you, he refused to teach me. It is a real skill, though. It can recover memories in some subjects.'

'Mesmers are one step away from illegal,' Khalila said. 'Even if you found a Mesmer you could trust to undertake it, the outcome's doubtful. If the memories are there, they've been locked up tight. Breaking that lock could be dangerous.'

'We'll save that for a last resort,' Jess said. 'I've found references in some black-market books to a Library prison in Rome. Ancient references, though. Nothing recent.'

'Rome would be logical,' Khalila said. 'After all, next to Alexandria, it's the city most loyal to the Library. The Basilica Julia is almost as large as the Serapeum here.'

'You've been to Rome?'

'Once,' she admitted. 'My family toured the Forum and other famous sites. It was overwhelming. I've never seen anything like it. To be honest, I would think we'd have a better chance of rescuing him from Alexandria than Rome.'

'Well,' Jess said, 'it was just a reference, ages old. Might mean nothing. The Artifex could have him anywhere. Anywhere the Library has a foothold.'

It was a depressing thought, and silence fell heavy. A breeze blew cool off the water, ruffling Khalila's scarf and dress, and Dario said, 'We're not going to find him this way. The Archivist isn't a fool. He won't leave clues right out in the open. We have to dig deeper.'

'Where? It's a large world, Dario.'

The Spaniard looked away, out towards the harbour, and said, 'I applied for a position with the Artifex Magnus. We all know he's the Archivist's right-hand man.'

'You *what*?' Glain barked, and she'd got it out a bare instant before Jess would have said the same. 'Are you *mad*?'

'Someone has to get close to him. Gain his trust. I can do

that.' Dario shifted his stare back to each of them in turn. 'I'm the best suited – bright enough to be useful; not enough to be a threat. I'm ruthless. I have wealth and excellent family connections. And I have a certain charm.'

'I give you credit for leaving that to last,' Jess said. It was a surprisingly accurate and unflinching self-assessment. He hadn't thought Dario quite so insightful about his own gifts and flaws. 'What about your post with Scholar Prakesh? I thought you were happy there.'

'I am. But I thought we all agreed: this is for Thomas. I assume I'm not the only one willing to sacrifice.'

'You are not,' Khalila said, and looked down at her folded hands. 'I confess, I already applied to the Artifex as well.'

'You *what*?' Dario turned on her with a stare, which she met squarely.

'Don't look so shocked,' she said. 'I am capable of just as much folly as you, you know!'

'I don't want you to—'

'Dario. What you do or do not want applies to *you*, not me. I didn't ask your permission, and I don't seek your approval!' Khalila's voice had taken on a hard edge, and Dario was the first to look away.

'Congratulations,' Glain said. 'You're both wildly independent, and now the Archivist has to be wondering why *both* of you would want to get close to him at the same time. Clearly, neither of you are cut out to be spies.'

'Forgive us – we didn't grow up criminals and self-made adventurers!'

'Dario, you know nothing about me,' Glain said. She didn't sound angry, just a touch amused.

'I meant the *criminal* part for Jess.'

'Yes, I got that,' Jess said. 'It's not a bad idea, getting close to the Artifex, but I doubt he'll take either of you up on it. He's not a stupid man.'

'Just a cruel one,' Glain said. 'We need more. Much more than this.'

'What about . . . ?' Jess hesitated, then plunged in. 'What about the Black Archives?'

They were all silent. He expected at least one of them to scoff, to dismiss it as rumour, but Khalila finally said, 'I'll look into it.'

'Carefully,' Glain told her.

'I know. I should go,' she said. 'I have more work to do tonight. Dario?'

'Go on,' he told her. 'I'm drinking.'

'I'm not,' Glain said. 'Khalila, I'll walk you back.'

Jess started to get up, but Dario kicked him in the shins under the table, hard enough to make him wince. 'I'll have a cup,' Jess said, and gave the other young man a sharp-edged smile. 'See you later.' Glain and Khalila walked away into the early evening, and Jess stared at Dario. 'Well?'

'Something for the two of us. I didn't want them involved.'

'Why not?'

Dario shrugged. 'It's a job for two, not four, and I know Glain. She'll push her way in if we let her.'

'And you don't like her.'

'Well, I don't like either of you, to be fair. But you're the one with the skill I need.'

'Which is?'

'Smuggling,' Dario said, and gestured to the waiter. 'That's why we both need a drink.'

'You can't be serious,' Jess said, and looked up at the tomb of Alexander the Great.

Dario hadn't told him where they were going, or he'd have refused it outright back at the cafe. Maybe the wine had lulled him too much, because he'd agreed to at least take a look. And now, here he was. Looking.

Next to the Lighthouse and the Serapeum, the tomb of Alexander was the single most recognisable structure in Alexandria . . . a memorial that had survived in all its original gaudy glory. It crouched in the centre of the lush park square, looking exactly like what it was: an overdone tribute to an oversized legend. Marble clad, of course, with statues of gold at each corner on each of four levels. The other statues that lined each level were stone, or looked to be, at least – warriors, horses, gods. On top, Alexander's chariot was drawn by mighty warhorses frozen in midcharge, and the Boy King's statue showed him as handsome and glorious as the gods themselves.

A pretty dark-eyed girl strolled past the two of them, and gave Dario a bright smile as she trailed a hand over the flowers planted on the path. The Spaniard smiled back and bowed to her, which elicited a giggle. Jess sighed. 'Tell me we aren't here just so you can peacock to the ladies.'

'It's an added benefit,' Dario said. 'I'm supposed to meet someone here who may have a book for us.'

'Meet who, exactly?'

'Am I supposed to ask for formal introductions when buying illegal things? I was under the impression it was more of a casual acquaintance.'

'Where did you meet this person?'

'I *enquired*,' Dario said. 'I'm not without skills, you know. If you must know, he's a sailor out of Rome. He said he has a stolen log book from a prison there.'

'Every city has a prison!'

'This one is run by High Garda. Not local police.'

Jess didn't like it. 'Do you know him at all?'

'No. Which is why I want you here, with your long history of . . . questionable things. I'll pay for the book, you take it away from here, and we will all live to read whatever it is I'm spending a ruinous amount of my savings to get.'

'Dario, buying black market is *not* your strength. You should have told me. I could have—'

'There wasn't time,' Dario cut in. 'Are you going to help or not?'

This wasn't the spot Jess would have chosen for such an exchange, either: too many casual strollers in this park, some with families. Too many ears to bear witness, and he hadn't missed the fact there were two sphinxes roaming the park, too.

The sphinxes weren't the only threats. One of the golden corner statues – Hera, he thought, the queen of the Greek gods – turned her head and tilted it down to regard them as they passed, though if she were holding up a corner of the building, she probably couldn't step away. Jess didn't care for even that much attention. And then he saw out of the corner of his eye that one of the sphinxes had padded down the path and stretched out in a long, low crouch not far away. It wasn't directly watching them, but the nearness of the thing made his instincts scream with alarm. It wasn't so much that he was afraid they were following him – though he had to admit, he was more than a little haunted by the idea they were – but that he didn't care for their closeness during such a highly illegal activity.

Not that Dario would even think of that. He seemed to take automata as just part of the landscape.

'I don't like this,' Jess said. 'It's too open, too obvious. Sphinxes. Call it off. We can meet somewhere safer.'

'I can't call it off, and I didn't pick the spot,' Dario said. 'This is my one chance to get this book. Go if you're too afraid. But I'd think someone so well versed at criminality would have a little backbone.'

'There's a difference between courage and blind arrogance,' Jess said sourly. 'Where is this contact of yours?'

'He'll be here soon.' Dario seemed oblivious to the threats. Jess's throat tightened as they neared the sphinx, and it turned that pharaoh's head towards them. The eyes gleamed dull red, then brightened.

'Dario, we should go.'

'Ah, there he is.' The idiot *waved*, and Jess spotted a man in plain working clothes trudging down a path towards them.

Somewhere in the bushes, Jess heard a rustle. He turned his head towards the noise, and saw that another sphinx watched them through the hedge. The human-shaped face stared with eerie concentration, and the eyes burnt bloody red.

Jess forced Dario's arm down. 'Inside. Get inside.'

'No, he's right there—'

'*Follow me.* Now!'

Jess turned and launched into a run back towards the tomb's entrance. He heard the crack of breaking branches and didn't look back. Dario was just a step behind, and caught up as the sphinx let out a sound like the high shriek of a hawk. It was coming for them. Jess put on a burst of speed, digging into his strides and lengthening them, and within four long steps he was past the hedges, and in another ten, halfway around the tomb building, with Dario struggling to keep pace. Screams rose as the pursuing sphinx rounded the corner at a lion's lope, and people who'd been casually enjoying the park dove out of its path and ran for the exits. Jess tried not to think about the damage it could do to innocent bystanders. He'd seen the raw, red destruction left by automaton lions in London. He and Dario were risking not just their own lives, but those of everyone caught in this place.

Jess and Dario darted up the marble steps. 'Why are they chasing us?' Dario demanded, gasping for breath. Jess hadn't even felt the run. Dario needed to get out from behind his desk more. 'We're Library! We're wearing the bands! What in the name of God—?'

'They already knew! Your contact sold us out. Or someone sold him out,' Jess shot back. 'Did you think you could just stroll over and get handed something the Library *kills people for*? With no experience and no training, in a public place? Idiot!'

Dario was utterly out of his element, all his composure shaken. For all that he'd survived Oxford and the disasters that came after, he'd never, until this moment, truly seen the Library as his enemy. He'd never understood what it meant to come face-to-face with its dark side. Jess almost envied him that. And almost pitied him.

But there wasn't time for either.

He'd never been inside this tomb before, but Jess knew the first level was a kind of museum, showing artefacts from Alexander's time – his armour, his sword, and more. With any luck, the sphinx's instructions wouldn't allow it to enter these precincts, where it could damage and destroy priceless history. But in case that wasn't true, Jess led Dario up another, interior set of stairs, two at a time, to a shadowy landing. His heart was pumping, but not completely in fear; there was a kind of exhilaration to this that was addictive. A deadly game. But still a game.

Outside, the sphinx shrieked again. The other answered, and somewhere mingled with it was the bone-shattering scream of a human being in mortal pain and distress – a scream that cut off abruptly.

Dario's eyes were wild as he said, 'Did they—?'

'Kill your contact? Probably. Or some innocent who got in the way.' Jess wanted to punch him for his deadly ignorance. 'What did you think you were playing at, Dario? Were you trying to impress me?'

Dario swallowed hard, opened his mouth, then closed it. 'Maybe I was.' Some awareness crept back into his expression, and he looked around. 'I've never been in here. Have you?'

'No.' *Another idiocy*, Jess thought; Dario should have scouted this place thoroughly, on many occasions, at different times of day. He should have known how to get in, out, every possible route of escape. 'Come on. We're going up.'

The next level held the glass coffin of Alexander, and though he knew he shouldn't, Jess found his steps slowing. There was a sense of terrible reverence here. Alexander's withered, leathery body – embalmed and dressed in a set of gilded armour – lay under thick, ancient glass . . . or crystal, maybe. The body was smaller than Jess would have guessed. Alexander had conquered most of the known world as little more than a boy, and Jess wondered what he'd have thought of all this – of the tomb, the honours, the Library that had conquered the rest of the world in his name. Had he really wanted to be displayed like this, as his own museum piece?

Surrounding the coffin, set in alcoves in the walls, stood statues of weeping men and women, their hands covering their faces. Lifelike and frightening.

Dario's voice came hushed, but it still made Jess flinch. 'Are those . . . ?'

'Automata? Yes. Don't touch the coffin. They're probably guardians.'

Jess stayed well away from Alexander's corpse and took the next set of stairs up again, with Dario at his heels. They emerged into a large, empty veranda open to night breezes, furnished with stone benches and seats. It afforded a fine view of the sights of Alexandria, but no way up to the small roof or out. When Jess looked down on the gardens below, it didn't surprise him to see that all casual visitors had vanished into the night. It was just him, Dario, and two pacing sphinxes below, staring up with intense red eyes. Terrible odds.

'Where are we going to go?' Dario asked. He sounded justifiably worried.

'Go down,' Jess said.

'The sphinxes—'

Jess took in a deep breath. 'You go this way. I'll draw the sphinxes to the other side of the building. Stay here and watch. When it's clear, climb down.'

'Excuse me – *climb down?*'

'Swing over the edge, grab hold of a statue, shimmy down to the next level. Repeat. You can make it.' It never occurred to him that it might be terrifying; he'd grown up seeing that kind of activity as normal. From the look that Dario shot him, clearly he didn't share that idea. 'Do you want to try to outrun the sphinxes instead?'

Dario silently shook his head and moved to the edge. 'Are you sure none of these statues I'm supposed to grab onto are automata?'

'I can't guarantee it,' Jess admitted. 'Best of luck.'

Dario glared. Jess didn't really blame him. 'Go with God,' Dario said. 'And also to the devil, scrubber, for making me do this.'

'I'll take whichever of them will make me faster,' Jess said. 'Give me two minutes to lead them off. Good luck. I mean it.'

Dario nodded and offered his hand. They shook, and Jess backed up and ran down the steps they'd ascended. The sphinxes would be expecting him to emerge from the tomb's only door. He wouldn't want to disappoint them. But he did want a good head start, so he stopped a floor up, in the area lined with glass cases, and eased between them to reach the statues beyond. This was the layer with rearing horses and warriors, and, luckily, they all *were* stone, or he'd have been dead in seconds. The sphinxes hadn't seen him yet and were crouched at the tomb doorway.

It would be a long jump and hard fall, but he'd had worse. Jess took in four lung-expanding breaths, then launched himself forward into a flat dive. He had a terrifyingly good view of the sphinxes' twitching tails as he sailed over them, but he'd done it well enough; the dive carried him to a landing point several feet behind them, and he curled into a ball before impact, rolled up, and was digging feet into the gravel and running before the sphinxes even knew he'd arrived.

It didn't last more than a couple of fast heartbeats. He heard the twin shrieks of the automata, and didn't need to look back to know they'd risen to join the chase.

Go, Dario. Get out. Those were all the good wishes he could spare for his friend, because he had to concentrate on angling his body just right to take advantage of the footing, the breeze at his back, the way his feet rose and fell. He needed every possible fraction of a second to live through this . . . And then he saw the corpse lying ahead of him on the path. It was the body of the man they'd been set to meet – a sailor fresh from a boat, or so Dario had said. Didn't matter now; he was just a sad heap of meat and crushed bones, but lying next to him was a leather drawstring bag.

Don't risk it, Jess thought. *You don't have the time.*

But it was impossible to resist the impulse. He veered close to the body and reached down just enough to snag fingers in the bag's strings. He lost a half second and could feel the sphinxes gaining ground. *I won't make it*, he thought, and had a vision of himself crushed on the ground like that nameless sailor.

The bag he'd grabbed was unexpectedly heavy and it would slow him down. The knowledge – if there was any to be had from whatever was inside it – wouldn't help him if the sphinxes caught him, but it *might* give him an advantage if he used it right.

Jess turned and threw the bag as far as he could the way he'd come, into the park. The twist of his body gave him a heart-stopping view of the sphinxes loping behind him, just a body's length behind him, and then he was facing forward again and running with real desperation, breathing pumping faster and faster as he spotted the park exit ahead.

One of the sphinxes peeled off and chased the thrown bag; he saw the flash out of the corner of his eye.

But one stayed on him.

There was nothing to do but pray that once he'd passed the boundary of the tomb's precincts, the sphinx would let him go. They were made to be territorial, after all. Not even the Library wanted the monsters tearing through crowded streets in pursuit.

He could feel the sphinx gaining behind him and realised, with a sudden horror, that all his best speed, his finest running, wouldn't put him through the exit before it reached him.

He was going to be caught.

So Jess did the only thing he could. He threw himself flat

and hoped momentum would force the thing to miss him.

He was lucky rather than good . . . the sphinx had just leapt as he flung himself down, and as he curled into a protective ball, the back feet crashed down on gravel just a handbreadth away from his head. He could see cables flexing under the metallic flank of the thing and scrambled up, hoping to be away before it could adjust and turn.

He slipped. The loose gravel betrayed him, and before he could recover he was on his knees and the sphinx had turned to him. It padded towards him. Unhurried. Remorseless. The human face held no expression at all. The sinuous copper skin seemed to stretch and mould to the simulated muscles beneath as it moved, and Jess thought, *Do something*, but there was nothing he could do.

He held still, hardly daring to breathe. The human-faced head of it was on a level with his eyes, and utterly, unsettlingly alien; he was reminded of the cobra, swaying in the darkness as it considered biting.

The sphinx parted thin metal lips and revealed razor-sharp teeth behind – the teeth of a lion in a man's face. Deadly sharp.

Don't. Move.

He felt a whisper of air as it drew in a bellows of breath, and he realised he was doubly dead now. He was wearing the smuggling harness with not one, but two, illegal books inside. The harness's coatings should have masked the smell of bindings and papers, but if the Archivist wanted him dead, this creature needed no further excuse.

The switch, he remembered from the book. He also knew that those razor-sharp teeth, and the massive lion paws with equally pointed claws, ensured that one wrong guess would absolutely be his last. Anit's brothers had both faced this moment.

They'd both died.

Jess didn't allow himself the luxury of doubt, because he knew that he was seconds away from death if he did nothing; the automaton's mouth was already opening wider and the eyes burning hotter, and one chance was his *only* chance.

He reached under the chin of the human face and felt a small depression. As the sphinx's head whipped sideways to bite his arm, he pressed down hard.

The head slowed its turn, but the teeth still closed around his arm.

Pressed down.

He felt the slicing sting of metal and knew it was too late, he'd lose his arm at the very least, *God, no* . . .

But then the sphinx just . . . stopped, with a sound of gears grinding to a halt. The jaws still pressed down, but the bite was shallow, just a little blood and pain that he made worse by having to pull himself free. Jess was panting now, shaking, pouring sweat, and as he watched the sphinx's face, he saw the eyes flicker red, black, and then go a dead, leaden grey.

It stood still as the statue it resembled. Frozen on the spot.

Jess heard the shriek of the other sphinx returning, and launched himself around the frozen automaton. Hedges snapped and flailed at him until he achieved gravel again, and then was running, running, with the gardens falling behind him, and the lonely, angry shriek of a sphinx chasing to the borders of the tomb's park.

The scream followed him like a vengeful ghost as he lost himself in the streets of Alexandria.

Sweating and staggering with weariness, Jess made his way back to the port and the Lighthouse. He avoided the guardian automata by climbing the wall – another exertion he didn't savour – and dropping down into the meditation grotto for some god or goddess lost in the dark.

He found Scholar Prakesh's offices closed and locked. Dario hadn't come back there, and he didn't know where he bunked.

Khalila was in. He pounded on the door, and it opened to spill him in. He found a chair and fell into it, still breathing hard. 'Dario,' he gasped out. 'Is he back yet?'

'What happened?' Khalila sank down next to him to catch his eyes. 'Jess! You're bleeding!'

'It's fine.' He brushed off her attempt to roll up the sleeve of his jacket. 'Where is he?'

She frowned. 'I don't know. In his room, I suppose. You know where that is?' Jess shook his head. 'I'll take you. And you can tell me what put you in this state along the way.'

She wouldn't take no for an answer, so Jess did tell her, and didn't spare Dario's folly in the retelling, either. She stopped in the middle of a flight of steps to turn and stare at him. 'You're saying that you *outran a sphinx?*'

'No, I'm saying I couldn't outrun a sphinx,' he corrected. 'I'm lucky to be alive, and no thanks to our little Spanish prince.'

'Jess . . .' Her lips were parted, but she clearly didn't know what to say to him. 'Allah must love a fool.'

'Let's hope that extends to Dario, too.'

She took him down four flights of stairs to what proved to be a residential floor, thickly carpeted and boasting carved doors of cedar that gave the whole hallway a rich, woody smell. She rapped on one of the doors, and it almost immediately swung open.

Dario was still alive. Injured, Jess saw, but alive. Relief flashed in his eyes when he saw Jess, but he quickly buried it. 'Scrubber,' he said, and stood aside to let them come in. 'Happy to see you still standing.'

'What happened to your leg?' Khalila asked, and helped Dario limp to the bed.

'I twisted my ankle falling off the damned tomb of Alexander,' Dario said. 'I challenge you to find anyone else who can say that. What happened to your arm?' That last, Jess realised, was directed to him.

'Sphinx,' he said.

'You just always have to win, don't you?' The joke was almost a reflex, because Dario stared at the blood and rips on his jacket with real concern. 'Is that a *bite*?'

'Their teeth are like razors, in case you ever wondered,' Jess replied. 'But I learnt something important.'

'That I'm a fool?' Dario asked bitterly. 'I'd have thought you already knew. You've said it often enough.'

'You're not a fool, just a dilettante at what I've been doing all my life,' Jess said. 'Never mind. We're both alive. That's what counts.'

'Did you get the book?' Jess shook his head, and Dario's expression set into a grim mask. 'Then it was all for nothing. I got a man killed for *nothing*.'

'Not exactly,' Jess said. 'I know how to turn off an automaton.'

EPHEMERA

Text of a coded, self-deleting Codex exchange between Morgan Hault and Jess Brightwell.

How could you be so stupid?

Don't blame me. I said it was a bad idea. I'd give you two guesses whose idea it was, but you won't need them.

I know you could have said no. You can't take these kinds of risks! The High Garda commander nearly caught you. I saw the report. I knew it had to be you.

Not every foolish thing in Alexandria is my fault.

Please tell me you got something out of it.

Nothing I want to tell you this way, even if you're erasing these messages. Too dangerous.

Try not to let him talk you into any more of this.

Careful. I might begin to think you care.

I always have.

Morgan, tell me what I need to do to make it right between us. Please.

There's nothing you can do. I'll do what I can for you.

I want to help you!

...

Morgan?

-X-

CHAPTER SIX

It was the heavy middle of the next night when Jess's Codex chimed, bringing him groggily awake. He turned on a glow and paged open the book to see a new message writing itself out in round, professionally inked letters. *Recruit Jess Brightwell to report to the Office of the High Commander in fifteen minutes.*

Now? He felt a lurch of unease. People disappeared conveniently in these barren hours. He remembered finding the disarranged state of Thomas's room back at Ptolemy House at a similar time of night, a smear of blood on the floor. Easy to just be . . . gone. But avoiding the summons would be inadvisable at best, impossible at worst, and he couldn't let them see fear. *What if they know? What if we've been identified from the park?*

It felt like dressing for his own funeral, but Jess donned a clean uniform and stepped into the hall . . . to find Wu, Bransom, and Glain already there, as well as the remaining members of their squad. Helva was still in the infirmary, and Tariq – his absence echoed loudly between them just now.

'High Commander's office?' Wu asked. Jess nodded. His eyes met Glain's for a moment, and he knew she was just as unsettled as he was. She'd taken the news of his near death calmly, but had also known, just as he did, that it might have been a temporary escape.

'Form up,' Glain said. 'If this is our last time together, then we do it right.' She meant it both for them as a squad and as a personal message to him. Jess appreciated the sentiment.

The squad fell into stride through the long, clean hallways, past the turn that led to their quarters and off into wider, more lush spaces, and then into the courtyard where the Spartan turned his head sharply to focus on Jess as he passed. Jess refused to look at the thing. Instead he kept his concentration on keeping stride with Wu and Bransom and trying not to think why the squad – the *whole* squad – had been so summarily summoned.

The High Commander's office was in a tightly guarded central building, one that required presentation of their official Library bracelets to a seated sphinx automaton twice Jess's height – an eerie thing that stared at Jess from the lifeless simulation of a human face with utterly alien eyes as it examined his credentials. A growl of discontent rumbled somewhere deep inside the thing as it stared at him, a vague and terrifying dislike that might, at any moment, break into a full-throated shriek and baring of those needle teeth. *Did it know? Could it? Do the sphinxes communicate somehow?*

Evidently they did not, because the sphinx turned attention to Bransom, the next in line. It took a real effort of will for Jess to turn his back on the thing and walk. Glain, having her own bracelet examined last, caught up to him in several long strides and whispered, 'Near thing.'

'But still a miss. I'm beginning to believe that they just don't like me.'

'Automata don't like or dislike anyone. They're machines!'

'Not completely,' he said. 'Thomas once told me that they . . . think. It's not just gears and steam in there. It's something else.' He itched to open one up now that he'd read that coded volume, full of tantalising hints about how the thing worked inside. Thomas would have had exactly the same impulse; the German boy was an expert at mechanical things, constantly breaking down and building up their inner workings. He'd been fascinated with automata. *Still is fascinated*, Jess corrected himself. *He isn't dead.*

The group marched together at a brisk pace down clean stone hallways, inset with alcoves filled with warrior deities from around the world – African, Indian, Chinese, Greek, Celtic, Norse, Roman, Japanese, Russian. Finally, at the end of the hallway, in pride of place, stood outsized golden statues of Horus and Menhit, the local Egyptian war gods. The floor beneath their boots, shining and clean, was a mosaic design of sphinxes, and at the end, in the rounded vestibule of the High Commander's office, the Great Library's seal shone gold, inset in the marble. The place smelt of metal and oil, with a faint, acrid smell of chemicals and gunpowder floating above like fog. The smell of war. Jess still preferred the crisp, dry scent of paper and leather.

This is the end, he thought, and wondered if the others were thinking the same thing. *This is the end of my time at the Library. We've been held hanging, and now the sword is about to fall and cut us loose.*

My father will never take me back.

Glain stepped forward to knock on the huge ebony doors, but she didn't need to do so; they swung open without a sound, and after a bare instant of hesitation, she squared her shoulders and led the way in.

It was a long march through a very large room. Displays of arms and armour and vast shelves of Blanks lined the walls. At the far end of the space, in front of a wall inscribed with rows of hieroglyphs that looked millennia old, sat a desk with crouched lions for legs.

An old man sat behind it.

He watched as the four of them snapped to attention, and as he stared at them, Jess revised his judgement. The High Commander wasn't *that* old; his hair had gone a glossy grey, with black threading through, but it was like a layer of snow on concrete. His shoulders were still broad, his body straight, and he had large, scarred hands that had seen plenty of hard use. The High Commander was of African heritage, with skin so dark it held overtones of blue in the lamplight, and startling hazel eyes that looked as sharp and clever as Scholar Wolfe's.

'Recruits,' he said. There was nothing but a Codex and a single folded paper on his desk. 'Until your final test, your squad demonstrated an outstanding amount of potential.'

'Sir,' Glain said. 'Permission to speak?'

The High Commander's gaze fixed on her, and Jess was very glad it wasn't aimed at him. 'Denied,' he said. 'You are here to listen, Recruit Wathen, and not to provide me with excuses. To continue: this squad had a great amount of potential. The last test was, in fact, designed to simulate an ambush of your squad by hostile forces while you were in the performance of regular duties. In the course of that exercise, one of your squad was killed, and another injured. Is that accurate? You may now answer, Wathen. Briefly.'

'That description is accurate, sir,' Glain said. There was no emotion to it. She stared into the distance, somewhere over the High Commander's squared shoulders.

'The exercise was designed to test your innovation, your toughness, your responsiveness, your team's bonds. How do you feel that you performed in light of this, Recruit Wathen?'

'Sir, our progress towards our goal was steady and careful, and when presented with the unexpected challenge of Greek

Fire, we took cover and returned fire. We followed procedure. We defended our Scholar at all costs.'

'Ah,' the High Commander said, and leant back in his chair. 'The *Scholar*. There comes the interesting twist in this tale: you were not assigned a Scholar or anyone representing one. Scholar Wolfe's intrusion into this space was unauthorised and introduced random factors that call the entire exercise into doubt.'

'Permission to ask a question, sir,' Jess said, and pushed forward before he could be told no. 'If Scholar Wolfe wasn't authorised to be there, then how did he get in?'

It was a simple and revealing question, and the High Commander stared at him unblinkingly for a moment. Jess could almost feel the rest of his squad trying to shift away from him without moving a muscle.

'Scholar Wolfe forged credentials to allow himself access. We are still investigating the matter.' Clearly, he wasn't happy about Wolfe's refusal to cooperate further. The closed Codex on his desk hummed for attention, and he paused to consult it, then closed it again.

Glain took advantage of the distraction to say, 'The Greek Fire wasn't at exercise strength, sir. It was fully dangerous. And we are well aware that one of our own was meant to take out Scholar Wolfe, and died for failing. It's a testament to our squad's determination and training that this ambush did not succeed. Sir.'

'Your argument is that your squad *succeeded*, Sergeant? At the cost of one dead recruit and one seriously impaired, possibly unable to return to duty?'

'We are sworn to fight and die in service to the Library. Recruit Oduya tried to shoot our Scholar – a Scholar who, whether supposed to be there or not, was nevertheless our responsibility. So yes, sir. We did succeed.'

'Do you then accept responsibility for a traitor within your own squad?'

It was a trap, and in the hard silence that fell, Jess struggled with an impulse to blurt out a defence. Glain wouldn't thank him.

After letting the stillness weigh on the room for a moment, she said, 'I do, sir. If Recruit Oduya was compromised, I should have seen that and acted before he was able to commit such a crime. His death is on my hands, and I accept all responsibility.'

'I would expect nothing less of someone in command.' The man's voice had a low, rumbling timbre to it, and Jess could well imagine how it would echo across a messy battleground, rasping orders and shouting encouragement to his troops. Like Glain, a born leader. *Don't throw her away*, Jess thought desperately. *She deserves better.* 'At least you understand your duty, even if you failed to adequately perform it. Recruit Oduya did indeed receive additional payment from an unknown source, no doubt to act as Wolfe's assassin. He was backed up in his heinous crime by another, as yet unknown individual who was responsible for the shot that killed Oduya. The same individual no doubt substituted full-strength Greek Fire for the exercise formulation.'

Despite their training, Jess felt the squad shifting around him, exchanging glances. Glain stayed still and focused. Waiting for the axe to fall.

'After much consideration and debate, it has been determined that this squad was *not* at fault for the outcome of this exercise, and no punishment shall be assigned to the team as a whole. Recruit Brightwell, you first spotted the danger to the Scholar and protected his life. You also risked your own life to fetch assistance for fallen colleagues. Few of the regular ranks could have done better under the same circumstances. You are to be commended for your actions.'

Jess blinked. This had taken him entirely by surprise. He wasn't used to open praise.

'Squad Leader Wathen, you commanded your team well under difficult circumstances, but because of your failure to spot this traitor within your team, you are hereby lowered in rank. You will no longer enter the High Garda as the rank of sergeant as was originally contracted, but as a common soldier. Nevertheless, I do not feel your failure warrants dismissal from the High Garda.'

Glain let out a breath, a slow and trembling one. She didn't relax, but Jess could feel the wave of relief coming from her all the same. She'd have to give it all up if they went after Thomas, but that would be *her* choice. Failure would have been humiliating.

For the first time, the High Commander smiled. It only made him more daunting. 'Your squad kept a Scholar – whether he should have been present or not – alive. That matters. That is *everything*, except for the protection of original books, which would take precedence even over the life of a Scholar. And for that, I have decided to accept this exercise as your final test.'

Jess didn't dare speak this time, but after a long pause, he heard Wu say tentatively, 'So . . . we passed, sir?'

'You passed,' The High Commander replied. 'You will each receive your individual assignments soon via Codex. Squad dismissed.'

In a way, passing the test was more of a shock than failing; at least he'd been properly prepared to be sent on his way, without a future. Jess couldn't process the moment fast enough to really comprehend what had just happened. He'd got so used to assuming the worst that having the best actually arrive was somehow wrong, coming on the heels as it did of the escape from the tomb – and what had almost been his *own* tomb – in the park.

'Brightwell,' the High Commander said, and caught Jess mid turn. He spun back to face front. 'A moment.'

He heard Glain's footsteps hesitate, but only for an instant, and then she was gone. The door shut behind his friends, and he was alone with a man who could destroy his future in a breath.

At least he was used to that, after Scholar Wolfe and his harsh postulant training. And before that, life with his own father.

Jess stood perfectly still, perfectly at attention, while the man regarded him. Finally, the High Commander reached for a folded sheet of paper on his desk. It was sealed with gold, and stamped with the symbol of the Library. Jess opened it. His hands were steady, though his heartbeat jumped faster when he saw the name written at the bottom – a personal signature, not just a scribe's notation.

The Artifex Magnus, head of the Artifex division of the Great Library. One of the members of the Curia, who advised the Archivist. But, in reality, the Archivist's bully boy and henchman. A villain with elegant handwriting, it seemed.

The message read, *Our eyes are on you.* Nothing else. But on the heels of that unsettling mess at Alexander's tomb, it seemed even more ominous.

'Bad news?'

Jess's head snapped up, and he met the High Commander's eyes. He couldn't read the man at all and he couldn't trust him. So he folded up the note again, put it in his coat, and said, 'No, sir.'

He half-expected the man to ask harder questions, but it was late, and he was of too insignificant a rank. The High Commander brushed a hand towards him. 'Go.'

'Sir.'

He walked out on legs that felt less steady than those he'd

walked in on, and once he was out and the door boomed shut behind him, he still felt eyes on his back, as if gravity had increased its pull.

As he stood for a moment in the round vestibule, getting his mind together, for the first time Jess realised that there were *no guards*. The man in charge of the most feared army on earth had *no guards*. That was a stunning statement of his power.

That was when he looked up at the flanking statues of Horus and Menhit. The hawk-headed Horus and lion headed Menhit stared back, and, as he watched, Menhit shifted her weight from the traditional pose. She held a flail in one hand, and the flexible metal strips dangling from it whispered against each other as she moved.

He tore his gaze from Menhit back to Horus, who carried a spear.

Horus cocked his head, birdlike, to stare harder at Jess.

Our eyes are on you.

He jumped when a hand fell on his shoulder and pulled him back a step.

'*Cachu*,' Glain breathed. 'What is it about you they don't like – did you kill their pets? Come on!'

They walked fast, and Jess became horribly aware that all of the war-god statues they passed were turning their heads to stare. Behind them, Horus stepped down from his pedestal in the alcove on the wall and took a long stride down the hall. Then another. Behind him, Menhit descended after him, that hissing, sharp flail cutting the air before her.

It was all bluff. When Jess attained the end of the corridor, he looked back to see Horus stepping back up to his pedestal in an eerily smooth, flowing motion. *Threats*, he thought. *Intimidation*. The Artifex's stock in trade – and the Archivist's.

Extremes of emotion colliding inside him made him feel sick.

The rest of the squad stood clumped at the end of the hall, looking one step from running as Glain and Jess caught up.

'Why did they do that?' Violet Bransom sounded utterly shaken. 'Why would automata come for you?'

'They didn't,' Glain said. She sounded brisk and matter-of-fact, and if he hadn't known her well, he might have believed she hadn't been frightened at all. 'It was likely some malfunction. If they'd meant us harm, someone would be mopping our remains off the floor right about now.'

'Then why—?'

'I don't know,' Glain said, and cut Bransom off, with the definite subtext of *I don't care*. 'You heard the High Commander. The squad passed. We'll receive individual commissions by Codex. This may be my last opportunity to say it to all of you, but I'm proud of you. Very proud.' Her gaze touched each of them in turn, and last of all, Jess. He nodded.

'Thank you, sir,' Wu said, and Jess echoed it. 'Oh hell, Bransom, stop cringing like a child. You're a soldier now!'

'I wasn't cringing!' she said, and glared at Jess, as if it was somehow his fault. 'What about Helva?'

'Helva will be on Medica duty until she's well enough, but I imagine she'll pass too. They say she'll make a full recovery eventually.'

Jess drifted slowly away and let the group talk, as their good fortune slowly began to sink in. He continued to stare back down the hall, where the eight-foot goddess Menhit relentlessly swished her golden flail, her leonine jaws baring in a grin that showed sharp, cutting teeth.

Jess went back to his room and tried to go back to sleep, but his heart was pounding, his hands clammy, and he couldn't shake the feeling that the jaws of a trap were slowly, slowly closing around him. He couldn't lie still. Finally, he rose, dressed in common clothes, and paced his room restlessly as he tried to still the anxiety inside. He didn't want to wake up Glain, and Dario and Khalila didn't deserve to be rattled awake at this terrible hour, either, but he felt more alone than he ever had.

He sat down and picked up his Codex and turned to the page where Morgan's messages appeared. He knew it was useless, but he took up his pen and wrote, *I need to talk to you. Please. I need you.*

He watched the page, waiting for her familiar handwriting to appear, but it didn't come. Of course it wouldn't. She could reach out to him, but he couldn't do the same to her. He didn't even know if she was reading it. So he kept writing, almost against his will. *I feel very alone tonight. And I miss you. It's stupid, I know, but I miss the touch of your skin, the smell of your hair. The weight of you in my arms. Horus help me, I sound like a lovesick poet. I should thank the God of Scribes you'll never read this, because I don't deserve to write it. You still hate me. You might not ever want to see me again, and, even if you do, you might never feel the same as you did before. I know that. I just . . . I miss you, Morgan.*

Then he reversed the stylus and brushed it all out, erased as if it had never been, and felt more alone than before.

He needed the comfort of someone familiar. *I want to go home*, he thought, which was strange; he had few happy memories of London, really. And it had hardly ever been safe. Still, in this moment, he desperately wanted to walk in the door of his family's town house, to see the wan smile of his mother and see his father busy at his massive desk.

A bit of home.

After a moment of debate, and knowing it was bound to backfire on him, Jess gave in to temptation and went in search of his twin brother, Brendan.

The sentries posted at the gate asked where he was going, and he told the truth: visiting relatives. *I'm not a child running for comfort*, he told himself. *Father's been pestering me to find out what Brendan's up to, anyway.* Because Brendan should have left Alexandria long ago, headed back to London, but Jess had learnt his brother had taken up residence in the city instead.

Maybe his brother had broken with the family business. Maybe they were both outcasts now.

Leaving the compound this time felt like a giant load falling from his shoulders; he wasn't on a mission, wasn't under pressure to dodge, avoid, not be found out. He had been allowed off the grounds without argument, and now he walked into the cool, misty night of Alexandria with his hands in his pockets.

It felt, for the first time in a long time, like freedom, even with the weight of the copper bracelet of the Library still clasped around his wrist.

Alexandria at this hour was a relatively quiet place, except near the docks, where lights and noise and activity continued as ships loaded and unloaded and sailors found leisure. He avoided that; pubs here in Egypt were far different from the friendly, cosy places he'd grown up with at home. Add sailors in the mix, and they were almost always dangerous places, especially at this dark hour.

He knew the way to his brother's rented home; he'd walked past it a few times, studying it. But it occurred to him that along the way, he needed to make a stop at the shadow markets.

Growing up in the book-market trade, he'd been dragged along to these sorts of places since he was old enough to understand what went on there and the risks. He remembered, at ten years old, carrying a satchel of rare books for his father as they followed warren-like alleys into a particularly wretched little shop near Cricklewood. It had not, of course, sold books; it sold pens, journals, Codexes – all the products of the Library. The old man who ran it had opened up a trapdoor to a tunnel that ran below the shop, and well beneath the city, they'd found London's Graymarket, a moving, ever-changing feast of illegal books and those who craved them. There were always two or three clumps of nervous newcomers who'd found caches of books in dead relatives' homes and looked to sell them off for a quick profit; those, his father always targeted first, bought cheap, and allowed those otherwise upright citizens to scamper home with their guilty money.

Then he'd set up at a table on his own, and sell the *real* beauties to true collectors.

The Alexandrian market was nothing like that, of course; there were no tunnels here, or if there were, Jess had never found them, except for sewer drains. It meant that the Alexandrian smugglers had to be even cleverer and a good deal bolder.

He found Red Ibrahim's daughter, Anit, minding a table. There was absolutely nothing on it, not even a hint of what was for sale; everyone knew it was a matter of requests and fees, not options. She looked up at him as he approached and gave him a calm look. 'I have nothing else for you,' she said. 'I heard about your adventures at Alexander's tomb. Clever of you to escape.'

'Clever had help,' he said, and handed her a paper drawing of a sphinx, and the location of the switch he'd found. 'In memory of your brothers, Anit. Thank you.'

She said nothing for a moment, just stared at the page hard, then folded it up and slipped it into a pocket of her skirt. 'You're not negotiating for this?'

'No.'

She pulled the chain from beneath the neck of her dress and held the embossed ring that hung on it like a talisman. 'Then I'm in your debt.'

'If you mean that, there's something you could do for me. I'm trying to locate someone who can tell me about the fate of a boy who was arrested at Ptolemy House about six months ago, taken to the Serapeum, and questioned. I want to find out where he was sent after that.'

Anit sat back in her chair. 'This is not what we do, Jess Brightwell. We sell books. Not information.' Then she looked down, and said quietly, 'But I will ask.'

He nodded and almost walked away . . . but then came back, leant over the table, and said, 'Be careful how you go. I don't want to bring anything down on you.'

She actually laughed like a little girl. Genuinely amused. 'My father is the most wanted man in all of Alexandria; I am quite used to being careful. But thank you for your concern.'

She was right, of course – not that it made him feel any better about having involved her.

Then he went about his real business of the night, to a deserted street on the outskirts of the University district. It held spacious homes built in a modern style, but with bows to Egyptian design and sensibility. Expensive, this area. Well-known for being the home of several prestigious Scholars. There was even a statue to the great inventor Heron on one corner, though, to Jess's great relief, it was only made of stone and was not an automaton.

He still hesitated in the shadow of Heron's statue as he studied the house in front of him. It was large, comfortable, with Egyptian fluted columns and red- and gold-painted decoration.

A small fountain whispered in the courtyard, sending a little silver mist into the air. It was a private sort of place. He liked it.

Jess moved quietly up the shallow front steps and knocked. His brother opened the door.

For a moment, they stood there staring at each other – still eerily similar mirror images, even now, though Brendan's hair had grown long and messy around his face and he'd gained a few pounds. Egyptian life either did not agree with him or agreed with him too much. Hard to say which at the moment.

'You're supposed to have left town months ago,' Jess said. 'Idiot.'

Brendan was wearing a loose silk sleeping robe, and he stepped back, rubbed his face, and said, 'Get in before someone sees you.'

Jess stepped into a darkened entry hall. He had the impression of expensive tastes, beautiful decorations and furniture, but it was a strangely empty sort of display, as though an expert decorator had done everything. No real personality to it. And, of course, no books. Not even a Library shelf of Blanks. Brendan wasn't much of a reader.

'What are you doing here?' Brendan asked. He shrugged, and got a hard-eyed glare from his brother in response. 'For God's sake, do you know what time it is, Jess?'

'I've passed training,' he said, because he realised he had to say *something*, and Brendan gave him a disbelieving stare.

'What do you want? Congratulations? A nicely wrapped gift? Weren't you supposed to be a full Scholar by now?'

'Aren't *you* supposed to be back home?' Because Brendan wasn't supposed to still be in Alexandria. 'The last letter from Mother almost seemed worried about you.'

'Almost,' Brendan said. 'Well. That's something.'

A girl of about Jess's own age appeared in the doorway. She was dressed neatly in a loose white gown belted with gold, and her hair was swept back smoothly in a braided queue. Pretty features, sharp cheekbones, skin the colour of blushed copper. She met Brendan's eyes with remarkable ease to say, 'I see you have a visitor. May I bring you anything, sir?'

Brendan said, 'Coffee, please, Neksa. Jess?'

'Coffee,' he said. 'Thank you.' Jess watched the girl go her way and waited until she was out of earshot before he said, 'You know, you don't have to pretend with me.'

'What?'

'She's no servant.'

Brendan, to his credit, didn't give it away if Jess's observation surprised him. He sat down in a gilt-framed chair with lion-head arms and covered a healthy yawn. 'What if she isn't?'

'Well,' Jess said, and took a chair across from him, with a wide black table between them, 'that would explain why you haven't gone home. She's pretty.'

'My personal life's none of your business.'

Jess grinned. 'Scraps, it's always been my business. So, what's the difficulty? Father doesn't like her? Mother wants you married off to some bloodless girl with twelfth-removed royal connections?'

'Jess,' Brendan said, and rubbed at his forehead, '*why are you here?* Please God, tell me, so I can get back to bed again before dawn arrives.'

I needed you. And I worried, Jess thought, but he could never say that. He and his brother had never been close, not nearly as close as he felt to his friends, but they were brothers. And he did worry. 'Father sent a letter. You were supposed to be home long ago. I know you're not staying in Alexandria to look after me.'

'And this isn't a question you could ask me in the daytime?'

'We aren't daytime people,' Jess replied, to which truth his brother had to give a smile of acknowledgment. More of a grimace, but still. 'You can't be staying this long in Alexandria for entertainment. It's business.'

'Why would I tell you? You'd just run back to your real Library masters and tell all.'

'Scraps.'

Brendan's flash of temper surprised him, as his brother leant forward and all but shouted, '*Stop calling me that!*'

It never failed to get a rise out of him. 'You don't trust me – I know that. I even understand why. What happened? Why didn't you go home?'

He didn't really think his brother would answer, but Brendan finally looked away and said, 'I lost a shipment. A large one. Rare books.'

'Lost it—'

'To the Library. It was a mistake, and, yes, I should have known better, and Father's never going to let me forget it until I make up for it. So, yes, you're right: I'm after something big. Big enough to make him forget his disappointment.'

Jess shrugged. 'Cost of the business, isn't it? Father already wrote me off as a lost cause; he won't take the chance of losing the only son he's got left.'

'You're dreaming. Do you actually remember our father?'

Brendan might have been right about that. Eerie. In some ways, talking to his twin was a bit like having a conversation with himself. 'Maybe the books are better off with the Library. It's a long, dangerous trip for them all the way to London.'

'I knew it,' he said. 'You've gone over to the other side, haven't you? Trouble with being a spy: sometimes, you start believing your own lies.'

'Just the opposite,' Jess said. 'The Library's shown me very thoroughly that I can never be part of it at all. And I know I won't be welcome back home, either – not with a price on my head from the Archivist. Da would rather see me dead than on the run from that.'

'Well, then, he'd have to include me, too,' Brendan said, and pointed at his face. 'If your face is on a wanted poster, we're easily mistaken for each other, and I'd hate to end up on the bad end of a lion with poor eyesight.'

The girl, Neksa, brought a tray with small cups of coffee – three cups, not two. She put one each in front of Jess and Brendan, then put one at an empty spot beside Brendan and sat down. 'Oh, don't bother,' she said, when Brendan started to speak. 'He already knows I'm not a servant.' She offered her hand across the table to Jess, and he took it. She had a remarkably firm handshake. 'Neksa Darzi.' She was wearing a Library bracelet, Jess realised, and it was a silver one – which outranked him by a considerable, easy margin. Not a gold-banded Scholar with a lifetime appointment and all her needs supplied, but a silver contract guaranteed her a comfortable career ahead of her. 'I am a Librarian here in the city. This is actually my house; I inherited it from an uncle. I have no real use for it, so I've rented it to your brother.'

Jess couldn't get his bearings for a moment. Brendan, who was a born-in-blood book thief, was snuggling up to . . . a Librarian?

'So you're his . . . landlady?'

She laughed and took a sip of her coffee as she gave his brother a sidelong look, and there was no mistaking Brendan's smile or the sudden light in his eyes. 'Among other things.'

He wanted to ask if she knew what it was his brother did for a living, but he couldn't, not seeing that silver bracelet on her arm. Either she knew and was playing an extremely dangerous game for which she couldn't possibly be prepared, or else she didn't know at all, which . . . was worse. *Maybe this really is why he's stayed so long*, Jess thought. *Because of her*. And that was a tragedy waiting to happen.

'I see,' Jess said, and managed a good impersonation of a smile. 'Always happy to meet someone my brother likes so well. Better than he likes me, anyway. He can't stand being around me for more than a day or two.'

'Damn well true,' Brendan said, and drained his coffee in a gulp. 'Neksa, I'm sorry, but private family matters. You understand?'

She finished her coffee, sighed, and rose to put a slender hand on Brendan's shoulder. He reached up to cover it with his own, and didn't meet Jess's stare. 'I'll see you in bed,' she said, and bent to kiss him very lightly and sweetly. 'Don't stay up all night. Jess, you are welcome here anytime, of course.'

'Thank you, Neksa,' he said, and watched as she disappeared through the doorway. Jess stood quietly and moved to the hallway.

Empty. She was gone.

He closed the door with as much care as he could before rounding on his brother to say, 'Are you *mad*? She's wearing a silver band!'

Brendan grabbed his wrist and twisted it up to put Jess's copper bracelet at eye level between them. 'I don't think you've got much cause to throw stones at me!'

Jess pulled free. It wasn't hard. 'Does she know?'

'About what?' Brendan's bland denial was maddening. Jess outright glared at him this time, until his brother finally shook his head. 'She knows I'm a trader. Nothing more.'

'You understand that this –' Jess gestured at the fine house, at the girl who'd left the room '– *this* is why our parents keep writing to me! You're going to drag her down with you. There's no possibility she comes out of this unhurt, and if you really care about her—'

'Who says I do care about her?'

That stopped Jess cold. He stared at his brother with an unpleasant churn in his stomach. 'What in the *hell* are you doing?'

'My job,' Brendan said. 'Unlike you. Father pinned his hopes and a large part of his fortune on you coming here and excelling, and instead you're just a spear carrier. A nothing, dead in battle a year from now. What use are you to us?'

'What use is *she* to us?'

'We need someone inside, in a position of real authority and access. It obviously won't be you. So she's a present to Father to salve the vast fortune I lost here – a direct way in to the highest levels of the Library.'

'You're not planning to abduct the girl!'

'Of course not!' Brendan seemed to be honestly puzzled why Jess would think of it. 'She's in love with me. Through her I can gain access to information you never could.'

It was a cold plan, and it felt dishonest in ways that had nothing to do with mere theft. His brother had always been a schemer, but Jess didn't think he'd ever been *this* bitter cold before. 'Brendan,' he said. 'Where does Neksa work?'

His brother gave him a slow, cold smile. 'She works for the Archivist. Oh, not a trusted advisor, obviously; merely a clerk. But she sees things. Knows things that could be of huge benefit to the Brightwell business.'

'I don't—' Hard to believe he was saying this. 'I don't think you should do this.'

'Why not?'

'Because it's—' *Because it's a filthy betrayal of a woman you've pretended to love.* 'Because it's wrong.' Even to his own ears, that was weak.

His brother laughed. It sounded bitter. 'Everything we do is wrong. Haven't you noticed?' He regarded Jess for a moment and sat back, pushing his hair from his eyes. 'You've gone soft here in the heart of luxury. You've forgotten that everything has a cost.'

Jess shut his eyes for a moment. The hard pulse of caffeine in his bloodstream had started a dull headache, and he felt his blood pulsing in his neck. The sickly sweet taste of the coffee fuelled a roiling in his stomach that had less to do with the drink than his own disgust. 'She loves you. Even I can see that. Don't you feel anything for her?'

His brother's face, a mirror of his own, was as hard and unforgiving as the face of an automaton. 'She's a means to an end, Jess. The sooner you learn to shed your sentimentality, the better off you'll be. Now. You didn't come here to check on me – I know you better than that. Why did you? And don't tell me Father sent you.' He looked, just for a moment, less cynical. Almost concerned. 'Jess? You look . . . troubled.'

I'm taking on a battle I know I can't win. I felt trapped and desperate, and I thought my brother would tell me everything would be all right. I wanted to feel . . . safe. Just for a while.

But he should have known better. The Brightwells weren't a family. They were a business – first, last, always.

'It doesn't matter,' he told his brother, and made for the door. 'Never mind.'

EPHEMERA

From a personal journal by Brendan Brightwell, written in family code. Burnt in Alexandria on departure.

I know how this will sound, but Jess – my brother and I, we've never been right. It's as if we compete for the same breaths even out of the womb, and he's always been just a little bigger, a little stronger, a little older. I've always run just a half step behind in his shadow, and God knows there have been times where I hated him just for existing. Like he's stolen something from me.

So how can that excuse what I'm doing to Neksa? I don't know. Maybe because Jess has to be the hero, I have to be the villain. The dark to his light. Or maybe I'm just trying, for once, to prove that I'm better at something than he is, even if that something is cruelty. Leaves a bloody taste in my mouth and ashes in my stomach every time I think what could happen – no, will happen – to Neksa if all this comes off. She's just a key to a lock, is all. That's what I keep telling myself. Access to the Archivist himself – isn't that worth any cost, any price?

In one stroke, I'll eclipse my brother, earn my father's undying respect, become a legend in our black-market world. People will fear and respect me.

Surely it's everything I've ever wanted.

And yet I'm sitting awake tonight, writing this down, because I lied to Jess, and he believed me. I told him I didn't care about Neksa, and, God help me, that was the biggest lie of my life. She's not just a key, not just a tool, not just another woman I can push away. She's . . . I don't know. Everything.

I never meant to fall in love with any girl, much less a good, true Library girl who trusts me not to hurt her. I've spent months telling myself that I'm just biding my time, building her trust until it's time to use her as I see fit, but tonight, looking into my twin's eyes, I realised that the only person I've really been lying to is myself.

I can't do this. I can't hurt Neksa. I love her too much to do that, and now that I've faced it, seen the full extent of my failure here in Alexandria, I have to go home and beg my father for forgiveness. I have to leave Neksa and never look back, because I'll do her far greater harm if I stay with her.

I blame Jess for making me finally see it.

Well, I have to blame someone. Can't blame myself, can I?

CHAPTER SEVEN

Three more days passed. Their compatriots received commissions and were folded into High Garda companies, but no word of any future for Glain and Jess. It was worrying for a day, and quietly terrifying after that. Glain constantly asked what it could mean, and Jess had no answers, only fears he refused to speak aloud and tried to bury under other concerns. Surely, Glain would find a good home in one of the elite companies.

He was not so confident of his own prospects.

While they waited, the two of them were rarely out of each other's company. To fill the time, they researched the Library's secret prisons and met with Dario and Khalila to discuss their findings.

The problem was, proof was thin on the ground. Thomas *might* be in three different places where secret prisons were strongly rumoured to be hidden: Rome, Paris, Moscow. If Jess had to place a bet, he'd have put his money on Paris – the country of France was, after all, a Library territory, fully owned after the rebellion against the Library that failed in the late 1700s. The few remaining French people were allowed to live in Paris were required by law to perform in the historical re-enactments – the rebellion, the Library's conquest, the executions. It was a perfect place, in Jess's opinion, to hide prisoners. Who'd dare to even go look?

Trouble was, every new location led to impassioned speculation but no definitive answers to tip the scales towards one of the choices.

'Well,' Glain said over strong coffee in their usual cafe, 'we can't go looking for him blind. We need more information than we have. Much more. Somehow we have to find it.'

'I agree,' Jess said, and to his surprise, Dario was saying the same thing at the same time. They exchanged looks, and Jess let Dario continue.

'We need someone with more access than we can have. What about Morgan?'

'What about her?' Jess shot back, suddenly on his guard.

'She can access hidden information, can't she? It's the whole reason they're called Obscurists.'

'I can't contact Morgan. I have to wait for her to write to me.'

'And she hasn't? Maybe your charm's finally wearing off,' Dario observed. 'Maybe she's found some lucky man to fill her days inside the Iron Tower.'

Jess's hand tightened on his fork, and for a brief, bloody moment he imagined that – or worse, that she *hadn't* found someone else, that someone else had been found for her. He didn't want to talk about that. At all. 'Morgan can't help us,' he snapped. 'Move on, Dario.'

'I have, actually. I think we should involve someone else who can—'

'No,' Khalila said. Her tone sounded flat and a little angry. 'Dario. We discussed this. You *can't* involve anyone else inside the Library!'

'And anyone outside it is of no use – Jess has proved that. All his fancy criminal connections can't get us what we need, and every day, *every day we wait*, Thomas suffers.' Dario glared at Khalila, a thing Jess had never seen him do, and Khalila held the stare firmly. She might be a quiet girl, but shy? No. She didn't back away from a fight. 'It's three cities – we've narrowed it to that. We just need confirmation. If it's someone we can trust—'

Sickly, Jess thought of his brother and Neksa. He *could* ask Brendan to use Neksa to verify the information. If she really did work for the Archivist, she might not have to do anything but look in a book and say yes or no. Easy. But that meant he was complicit in ruining the girl, and that . . . that was a bridge he couldn't cross.

He didn't have to, because Dario said, 'I didn't wait to get your approval. I told Scholar Prakesh everything we knew about Thomas. I asked for her help.'

There was a breathless silence, and Khalila's eyes widened. She tried to speak, failed, and finally managed to say, 'You *what*?'

'Without asking us?' Glain jumped in.

'I'm tired of waiting for someone to drop an answer into our laps,' Dario said. His cheeks had an angry red tinge now, and he met Jess's eyes. 'Well? Aren't you going to join the outrage?'

'No,' Jess said. 'You know Scholar Prakesh; I don't. I know she's highly placed and very well respected. She'll be hard for the Archivist to dismiss and harder to make disappear. It might well be the best choice we have.'

Glain kicked him under the table for breaking ranks, but the fact was, Dario was right. Except for that one guilty thought about Neksa, which Jess knew he had to hold as a last resort, he'd pulled every lever available to him.

'I don't like this,' Khalila said. 'What if she's discovered? She's a Scholar, not a spy!'

'She's been close friends with the Archivist since he was a postulant, and she was once the Artifex's lover,' Dario said, and refilled his coffee cup from the small pot on the table. At Jess's gesture, he filled that cup, too. 'She knows the Library in and out. Even better, she knows the people we need to investigate. Who better to find out what we need to know?'

'She's an old woman, and you put her at risk,' Khalila insisted. 'What if something happens to her? Our duty is to—'

'Our duty is to our friend,' Jess said. 'If you don't believe that, Khalila—'

'I never said that! Of course I want to save him!'

'Doesn't sound like it. Are you having doubts?' Glain gave her a stony look and sat back in her chair. 'Thinking of your own future inside the Library, are you?'

Khalila stood up, colour high in her own cheeks now, and yanked her silken Scholar's robe on over her long dress. 'I'm thinking that you have put an innocent old woman at risk. I'll be late for prayers. And I'd better say a prayer for all of us.' She walked away quickly in the direction of the neighbourhood's mosque, and though Dario leant back in his chair and watched her, he didn't rise to escort her.

Jess started to rise, and Dario said, 'Let her go.' His face was set and unreadable. 'She'll feel better after she prays.'

'Well, wouldn't we all?' Glain said. 'So there's no point in protesting – you've already done this without us. Right?'

'Right,' Dario said. A muscle jumped in his jaw. He was still watching Khalila as she moved down the street, and Jess could sense the desire in him to follow. 'Scholar Prakesh is careful and she's good. She's willing to help. There's no reason not to accept that. We've done our best and got as far as we can on our own, haven't we? Sooner or later, we have to admit we need assistance. You idiots weren't going to do it. Someone had to.'

He isn't wrong, Jess thought, but he still had a terrible, sick feeling. This was moving beyond their control, quickly. Too many people, too many emotions. *But if it gets Thomas back ...*

'Next time you want to run off on your own, count to ten and come talk to me,' Glain said. 'You're a hothead, Dario. At least let someone else give you a chance to convince you it's not a good idea.'

'I did,' he said, still staring after Khalila. 'She didn't.' When Jess checked over his shoulder, he saw that the girl had disappeared around the corner.

Glain drank her coffee without another word, threw money on the table, and nodded to Jess. He stood up with her. 'We'd best get back,' he told Dario. 'You'll be all right?'

Dario gave them a bright, entirely shallow smile. 'Aren't I always?'

When Jess looked back at the end of the street, he saw Dario still sitting at the table, toying with his coffee cup, staring off towards the corner where Khalila had disappeared.

Just one day later, Jess read the terrible news in the *Alexandrian Times*. He always kept a copy of the thin sheet in his quarters and checked it twice a day for the updated news as the articles changed and were written in fresh. It was the evening edition that carried the bold headline: Prominent Scholar Dead in Carriage Accident. The hand-drawn illustration showed an old woman in Scholar's robes stepping off the curb in front of a steam carriage, utterly unaware of the death hurtling towards her.

Scholar Prakesh was *dead*. He read the news over twice,

letting the details sink in slowly; she had been walking to the Lighthouse late in the evening and evidently had not seen the carriage approaching before she stepped out into the path. She couldn't have heard it coming, Jess realised, being deaf. *But she's walked this city all her life*, he thought. *She'd know by instinct to constantly check around her.* He felt a horrible, sinking sense of guilt and anger. This hadn't been a random street accident; Scholar Prakesh had been out asking questions, trying to help them.

He carried the paper with him on the way to Glain's room, but she wasn't there. Not in the common rooms or the gymnasium or the Serapeum or the target range. He sent her a Codex message and got no reply.

So he set out for the Lighthouse.

Scholar Prakesh's office lights were on, and Jess pressed the button that would have alerted someone inside, but there was no answer. He knocked. Still nothing. When he tried the door handle, it opened, and he stepped inside. Prakesh's office was just as he remembered: a warm combination of clutter and organisation. Her handwritten notes were still on the chalkboards that lined the room.

He walked to the left, to Dario's office.

Dario sat behind the desk. He had a glass in front of him full of a dark red liquid, and a bottle beside it. He looked up when Jess appeared in the doorway, lifted the glass, and downed half of it in a gulp. 'Sit down,' he said. 'Join me.' He put out another glass from a desk drawer and unsteadily poured it full. Jess took it and sniffed. Not wine. It had an interesting herbal, fruity smell. 'It's Pacharán, from Spain. Gift from my father.'

'What is it?'

'Alcohol,' Dario said. 'Come on. We're drinking to my vast

stupidity. Where's Glain? Surely she wouldn't miss the chance to rub it in.'

Jess said nothing. He sipped the liquid. Strong, all right, with a deceptively fruity taste. Dario had been crying; that was clear from the red, swollen state of his eyes. He'd also had a fit of temper. Papers littered the floor, no doubt brushed off the desk to make room for the drink.

'I was wrong,' Dario said. 'Say it.'

'You took a chance,' Jess replied. 'We've all taken them. I'm sorry it came out this way. She was—'

'She was brilliant. *Brilliant.*' Dario's voice broke, and tears beaded in his eyes. He tried to blink them away, but they broke free and he had to angrily wipe them away. 'She liked me. She trusted me. I got her killed.'

'It might have been an accident,' Jess said, but it sounded hollow even to his own ears.

Dario tossed off the rest of his drink and refilled the glass. 'Shut up and drink.'

It took some time, but Jess finished what he'd been served, and before he was halfway through he was feeling the effects. Dario had two glasses to his one, and no doubt more before that. He tried to pour another out for Jess, but Jess quickly pulled the glass back. 'That's enough,' he said, and reached over to stopper the bottle. 'You've had enough, believe me.'

'It wasn't an accident,' Dario blurted, and drained the last of his drink. 'She never walked in front of a carriage in her life. It was murder, and it was because of what I did. Her blood is on my hands – don't try to tell me anything else.'

Jess didn't. He let silence set for a moment, then said, 'We all knew this would cost lives. Ours, our friends, maybe our families. Going against the Archivist is a blood sport.'

'*He killed a Scholar*,' Dario said. It was almost a whisper, and his voice shook and nearly broke again. '*Me cago en todos los santos*, he killed one of the best of us, and for what? To hide his dirty secrets? No. Khalila's right. This has to stop.'

'I never said to give up.' Khalila's voice came from behind Jess in the open doorway. 'I never will. Dario, I'm so sorry.' The gentle sadness in her voice made Jess take in a breath, and as he turned his head, she moved past him, around the desk to open her arms. Dario lunged up and into them, and put his head on her shoulder to cry in silent, wrenching sobs. It lasted only a moment, and he murmured a quiet apology as he pulled back.

She kissed him. It was a sweet, gentle kiss, and Jess found himself looking away to give them some privacy. She stepped away first and took in a slow breath as Dario sank down again in the chair. 'What have you been drinking? I think I might be intoxicated on the fumes.'

'It's not *haram* for me,' Dario said, and reached for the bottle. She moved it out of his reach. 'Khalila. Please.'

'You're beyond drunk enough,' she said. 'And this is the end of your mourning. If they've killed a Scholar, we are all in danger, and you need to be alert. I need you at your best. We all do.'

He sat back in his chair, staring at her, and then nodded. 'You're right. From now on, we stay together.'

Khalila turned to Jess. 'The same for you. Stay with Glain. Watch your backs.'

'Thomas—'

'There's nothing we can do for Thomas if we're dead,' she said. 'Stop asking about him, about secret prisons, about the Black Archives, about *all of it*. In a month, we may be able to start again, but they *are* watching. It will take only a stroke of the Archivist's pen to kill us all. You know that.'

He did. He hated it with a cold, aching fury, but Khalila's words were wise. Any sane person would pull in their head and proceed with caution.

Jess stood up. The Pacharán had worked all too well, and he felt his head spin a little. *The Archivist won't have to push me in front of a carriage*, he thought. *I'm liable to stumble in front of one all on my own.*

'Stay safe,' he told them, and embraced Khalila first, then Dario.

Then he left the Lighthouse.

He'd lied. He didn't intend to proceed with caution. It was far too late for that.

He intended to make sure Scholar Prakesh hadn't died in vain. If that meant selling his soul to his brother, then he'd pay the price. However high it was.

When he knocked on Brendan's door, it was late for most in the area, but hardly too late for a Brightwell. Still, he got no answer. Jess stepped back and studied the high windows. All dark. He didn't believe that his twin, of all people, would be so quickly to bed, whether Neksa was in it or not.

Calling out for him was a stupid idea. Jess moved down to the far end of the wall, which surrounded a garden, and effortlessly climbed over it and dropped down on the other side. Darker there, though a fountain whispered in the corner, and lotus flowers drifted on the surface of a pond.

He found the side door, quickly touched his fingers to the household god next to it, and got out his tools. Not a bad lock, but, then, thieves always bought the best. It took him more than a minute to open it, and then he stepped inside, into the soft shadows and the smell of sandalwood incense. Quiet.

Too quiet, he thought, for Neksa and Brendan to be here. And then he sensed movement and ducked instinctively into a crouch. Just in time for the club to crash into the wall behind where his head would have been. Jess lunged forward in the next second and found himself pushing a strong, lithe, curved body back against the wall.

He immediately moved his hands to more neutral territory and said, 'Neksa? Neksa, it's Jess! Jess! I'm not going to hurt you!'

She went still for a few seconds, and then he heard the sound of the club crashing to the tiled floor and a trembling intake of breath. *'Jess?'* Then he actually felt her steady herself and her voice grew firm. 'Let me go!'

'All right,' he said, and made sure to kick the club away into the dark before he did let her loose. That had been a very respectable attempt to kill him. 'I'm looking for my brother.'

'By sneaking in the side door?'

'You didn't answer the front.'

'He's not here,' she said, and turned a switch on the wall at her back. Lights hissed on, gradually brightening. She left them low, for which Jess was thankful, and he saw the swollen redness of her eyes and nose. For all her bravado, she looked devastated. 'He left this morning.'

'Left,' Jess repeated. 'Are you sure?'

'I found this when I got up this morning.' She silently reached into a pocket of her dress and handed him a sheet of folded paper. Jess took it and held it up to the light. He recognised his brother's hand, the jagged points and long loops. It was a terse message, saying he'd had enough, he was going home, and that he'd send for the rest of his things soon. No affection. Only the vaguest of goodbyes. Even for Brendan, it seemed abrupt and cold.

'It's from him, isn't it?' she asked, and he slowly nodded. 'Why? Why would he leave so suddenly? Why would he not talk to me first? I would have gone with him. I love him! He knows that!'

He doesn't love you, Jess wanted to tell her, but that seemed cruel. He wanted to be relieved, but the timing couldn't have been worse; he needed Brendan. *No, you don't,* the old cold part of him told him. *You need her. And you can still use her.* His father wouldn't have hesitated. He'd have threatened exposure, pushed past Neksa's shock and anger and tears, and made her into a tool to be used as needed. That was what Brendan had been intent on doing. That was the Brightwell way.

She can help you get to Thomas! Scholar Prakesh died for this. The least you can do is do what has to be done.

He stood there for a long moment, the note in his hand, and just looked at her. At the undeniable heartbreak in her, and the dignity and the vulnerability.

Then he pressed the note into Neksa's hand and said, 'Lesson learnt. You shouldn't trust either of us.'

He was gone before she spoke again.

Captain Niccolo Santi answered his door on the third volley of knocks with an expression Jess could only identify as irritated. Out of uniform, he still looked tall and imposing. 'Are you insane? Go home.'

'No. I need to talk to you.' Jess heard the hard, bitter edge in his voice and the determination, and the captain must have, too. He stepped back and swung the door wider as he turned away.

'Close it behind you,' Santi said over his shoulder. 'And lock it.' Which Jess would have done, anyway. 'What happened? You look like something hell spit out.'

Hard to choose what to give him for an answer. *My brother's fled town without a word to me.* Or, *We caused the death of a Scholar.* He couldn't quite bring himself to say any of it.

Inside, the small house was clean, orderly, and comfortable. The main feature of the room was a table with four chairs, bare of plates or glasses but loaded with a stack of Blank books, all open. Christopher Wolfe sat at that table in a dark red silk dressing gown with small reading glasses perched on the end of his nose as he compared one book to another. 'Good evening. It is evening, isn't it?'

'It's the black middle of the night,' Santi said. 'But close, I suppose.'

Wolfe folded the glasses, slotted them into the centrefold of an open book, and said, 'You were told to stay away from us, I believe, Brightwell. It was very good advice.'

Santi sat down at the table beside Wolfe and put his head in his hands. 'He's as bad as you. Tell him to stay away, and he'll do just the opposite. I don't know why you pretend to be surprised. You should know them all better by now.'

When Wolfe didn't answer, Jess did. 'Captain, you heard about Scholar Prakesh?'

'Yes,' Santi said, and looked aside at Wolfe. 'I meant to tell you, but you were busy, and—'

'What about Prakesh?'

'She's dead,' Jess said, before Santi could reply. 'It's our fault. We asked her for information that could have led us to Thomas.'

Paralysis lasted for a few heartbeats, and then Wolfe angrily shoved the books in front of him off the table, onto the floor. Santi winced, and Jess quickly bent and rescued the volumes.

He found Wolfe's glasses and put them on the top of the stack.

By the time he'd finished, Wolfe had got to his feet and turned away to pace the end of the room. 'I hope you realise what you've done. You've not just sacrificed Aadhya Prakesh, but yourselves, as well. Every one of you will be picked off before you know what's coming. What were you *thinking*?'

'We were thinking about Thomas!' Jess shouted back. 'The longer we hide from this, the more he'll be hurt! Broken! You, of all people, *you know that*!'

Santi looked at Wolfe with a stilled expression. His long fingers curled too tightly around the edge of the table, and then he nodded. 'I know, too,' he said. 'I was there when Wolfe crawled bloody to this door. I'm the one who saw what was done to him. And we are *not* taking this risk blindly.'

'That's the point, sir. That's why I'm here. We're all going to die if we don't take action *now*. We need to get Thomas and get out!'

'Not without more definitive information.'

Jess swallowed, and said, 'I think part of that answer is locked up in your memories, Scholar. You were taken, just like Thomas. You were even taken for the same *reasons*. Maybe they took you to the same place.' He spread his hands. 'We've tried everything else.'

'No,' Santi said.

Wolfe ignored that. 'There's no guarantee that anything I recall will help,' he said. 'Still less will it be real proof that's where they're holding Thomas.'

'It's more than what we've got right now, isn't it?'

Wolfe looked at him for a moment without any expression, and then shook his head. 'I can't recall any useful details. What they did to me was very effective.'

'Leave it, Jess,' Santi said. 'I'm sorry, but this has gone far enough. I have to look after Christopher's safety now.'

'There is no safety – you said so yourself.'

'I told you, *leave it alone*. This isn't some adventure; it's a bloody war. They pay me to be a tactician, and I can tell you this: *we can't win*. We don't have the numbers or the weapons or the knowledge. We're defeated before we start, and, yes, I *will* look after the one I love before all else, and devil take the rest of you if it comes to that!'

Wolfe didn't seem to hear any of that as he paced, but suddenly he said, 'Brightwell. Can you secure a Mesmer who knows his business and can be trusted?'

Mesmers weren't common in Alexandria, but there were a few, and some who plied a trade more in the shadows than the light. The entertainers – the ones who made volunteers dance like chickens or pretend to fly – those had been certified by the Library. There were others whose motives were more purely profit driven. 'I think so,' Jess said.

Santi said, 'No. Under no circumstances will I allow it.'

Wolfe said, in the same mild tone, 'Ignore that. He doesn't want me to remember more, of course. He thinks I'll shatter like a dropped vase if I do.'

'Will you?' Jess asked.

'Yes!' Santi said, and it was a shout compressed beneath an artificial calm. 'He'll destroy himself. And you've got a target on your back, Jess. Don't forget it.'

Jess shrugged. 'I grew up with the Garda chewing at my heels. Business as usual.'

'The Archivist's assassins aren't bound by the same laws as the London Garda or even my own soldiers. You *should* be afraid. He's killed far better than you.'

'Stop, Nic. Jess is right.' Wolfe stopped pacing and looked at Santi. The two men faced each other, and Wolfe seemed quiet, clear-eyed, and steady. He didn't look like the fragile, shaking man Jess had seen at the High Garda compound after the ambush. Nor did he look like the driven, angry man who'd taken on the role of teacher for Jess's class. The man had too many secrets, buried too deep, for Jess's comfort. *Ironic*, some sliver of Jess's mind whispered, *considering how much you keep from him. From everyone.*

They were alike, Jess realised: both mistrustful, prone to hide emotions from others. Both with scars they hated to show. The difference was that Wolfe had Niccolo Santi. They'd braided their lives tightly together, and it would take a sharp sword to cut that tie.

He envied them that love. He might have hoped for it once. But she was gone.

'Don't do this,' Santi said. 'I'm begging you, Chris, don't. You'll kill yourself.'

'Better I kill myself in a good cause than let the Library simply erase me. The Archivist has already destroyed my work. We both know he won't allow me to live on much longer. If dying is my fate, at least I can try to change Thomas Schreiber's before it comes.' He reached out for Santi's hand. 'I will happily remember every cut, every burn, every blow if it helps set that boy free. Please don't stand in my way.'

Santi bowed his head for a moment, stepped forward, and rested his forehead against Wolfe's. 'You fool,' he said, and kissed him, sweet and slow. 'Don't ask me to watch you tear yourself to pieces.'

He let go of Wolfe, went into the bedroom, and closed the door behind him.

Wolfe said, 'I can't blame him for that; he remembers how I was after. But I'm stronger now. I will manage.'

'Sir—' Jess's voice went cold in his throat, and he couldn't finish for a long, struggling moment. 'Thank you.'

'Don't thank me.' The look in his dark eyes was chilling now, lightless, the same as when he'd been the unwilling proctor for their class of innocent postulants, knowing so many would fail or die. 'I'm not your hero. It was my doing that made you all targets in the first place. If you'd never met me, your life would have been happier. It surely would be longer.' His smile was awful – full of bitterness and heartbreak. 'Now go find me a suitable Mesmer, and let's get this over with before Nic comes to his senses.'

Finding a Mesmer wasn't hard; finding one who didn't have ties to the Library was much more difficult. In the end, Jess had to settle for one, on the advice of smuggler friends, who was known for conducting under-the-table thefts from wealthy clients, some of whom he convinced to rob *themselves* and forget they'd done it. A gifted man, no doubt about it – just not a very nice one.

In person, Elsinore Quest was a rabbity little fellow who hunched his shoulders and ducked his head and almost never met Jess's eyes. But when he did, Jess realised why. There was a certain steeliness to his gaze that would certainly have put some of his victims off too soon. Better to seem inoffensive and incapable of violence, particularly if someone wanted to entrust mind and will to you.

Quest kept up a steady stream of chatter on the carriage ride back, which was unbearably annoying, since all he talked about was the weather. It was typical for the time of year – warm and humid – and Quest seemed to think that it would be the death of him.

If only it were true, at least it would stop his endless droning.

'You understand what I'm paying you to do?' Jess interrupted, when he recognised the streets they were crossing. They were close to Wolfe's house. 'And what I'm paying you to forget?'

Quest's flow of complaints shut off as if someone had closed a valve inside him, and he raised his gaze to meet Jess's. The man was in his forties, most likely, with weathered, ill-kept dry skin and greying, thinning hair, but his eyes – blue as the faded Alexandrian sky – were still vital and powerful. 'Don't worry about me, young master,' he said, and smiled. 'I've forgotten more deadly secrets than you can ever imagine existed. One more is no bother, especially at the price you're paying. Though I should point out – just for business purposes – that I sent a message off to a colleague about where I'd be and who you are. In case some . . . mishap occurs.'

In other words, he wasn't a fool and he knew the risks. Jess nodded. He didn't take offence. Everyone in the shadow trades had to look out for their own backs.

'Half now,' Jess said. 'Half when you're done.'

'Reasonable,' Quest said, and turned to look out the carriage window. The steam powering it puffed white and wispy behind them on the still, quiet night air; the streets were deserted, which Jess thought was a good thing. The fewer witnesses to Quest's visit, the better. 'Ah. We must be close.'

The carriage slowed, and Jess jumped out to offer the driver the standard fare of five *geneih*. Quest climbed down slowly, as if he was old and fragile, and shuffled after Jess to Santi's door.

Wolfe opened it and stood aside. He was fully dressed now in a loose black shirt and trousers and boots. There was no sign of Santi, and the bedroom door was still shut.

'Elsinore Quest, Mesmer,' Jess said. 'Scholar Wolfe, who'll be your subject.'

'Very pleased to meet you,' Quest said, and weakly offered a handshake. Wolfe ignored it until the hand dropped awkwardly back to Quest's side. 'We will need relative quiet. Ah, this corner chair will do. Please sit down, sir. Make yourself quite comfortable. It's very important that you be quite comfortable and let all your cares fall away, let them blow away like sand on the wind . . .'

There is a certain strange rhythm to the man's voice, Jess thought, and tried to pinpoint what it was that so unsettled him – and, at the same time, what soothed him. He'd already started his work, then. Odd; Jess recognised that the man had used the same tones in the carriage, during that endless flow of weather observations. Had Quest tried to use his talents on him? *Had it worked?* No, surely he'd have known if it had. *Wouldn't I?* The doubt made his mouth go dry.

Maybe this hadn't been such a good idea.

Wolfe sank down in the chair that Quest indicated, and as the Mesmer pulled another chair close, Jess saw the bedroom door silently open. Santi stepped out. The captain moved to stand beside Jess and said, in a low voice that couldn't have carried to Wolfe, 'If this goes badly, I will stop it.'

'I know,' Jess said. 'It might not even work – sometimes it doesn't . . .' His voice faded because Wolfe had already closed his eyes. Quest's voice dropped to a low, calm rhythm, and Jess couldn't catch what he was saying now as he bent close to Wolfe. The Scholar's head slowly tipped forward.

Wolfe raised one hand – or, at least, the hand rose. There was no corresponding shift of balance from Wolfe's body, no sign that the movement of that hand and arm had been directed from a conscious mind. The rest of him stayed completely still.

Quest reached out and pushed on the top of the floating hand. It hardly moved at all. He nodded in satisfaction and looked over to Jess. 'He's ready. What do you want me to ask?'

That fast? Jess blinked. 'Ask him about his time in the cells—'

'Wait,' Santi said. He sighed. 'I hate that you've forced him into this, but at least we can spare him some agony. Ask him about being taken to prison, then ask about any time he was taken *out* of a cell. Nothing about what happened to him; only locations and surroundings. Do you understand?'

'Of course,' Quest said blandly. 'You're looking only for where he was being held. I understand.'

'Good.' Santi's gaze bored into the man. 'You'd better.'

'Trust in me, friend. I know my business.' Quest leant forward and rested his hand briefly on Wolfe's shoulder. 'Now go back. Go back to the day that you were taken into custody. Do you remember?'

The reaction was immediate and terrible. Wolfe's whole body tensed, shifted, and seemed to pull inward. His head did not rise, but Jess heard the change in his breathing from across the room. His skin went cold listening to that harsh, painful panting. But they couldn't stop now. Wolfe had agreed to this.

'Tell me about the day you were taken to the prison,' Quest said. His voice was gentle, rising and falling in those faint, odd rhythms. 'There is nothing to fear. You are only seeing, watching a play of light and shadow. You are an outside observer of what occurs. There is no pain. You feel no pain at all.'

The harsh breathing eased, just a little, but when Wolfe's voice came, it sounded rough and uneven and utterly unlike him. 'I was . . . here,' he said. 'They came for me here.'

'Here, in this house?'

'Yes.'

'And where did they take you?'

'The Archivist's office at the Serapeum,' Wolfe said. 'He asked questions—'

'Let that go. Where were you taken after he finished with you?'

Wolfe didn't answer. Beside him, Jess felt Santi's muscles tensing, as if bracing for a blow.

'Scholar? Where were you taken?'

'Below.'

'Below where?'

'The Serapeum. To a cell.'

'Stop,' Santi quickly said. 'Skip over that. Ask him where he was taken after that.'

Quest gave Jess another questioning look, and he nodded. Santi was right. Asking Wolfe to recount whatever happened to him in the cells below the Serapeum in Alexandria wouldn't help them at all. Thomas wasn't there.

Paris, Jess thought. *They'll have taken him to Paris.*

But when Wolfe answered the question, he said, 'The Basilica Julia.'

Rome. Jess swallowed hard as he remembered how passionately he'd argued for Paris with his friends; he'd nearly persuaded them it was the only logical choice and to go tearing off in pursuit of Thomas there. *Thank you, Khalila. Thank you for holding out for more information.* They wouldn't have more than one chance at this.

And even this information, he cautioned himself, wasn't true proof. An indicator, certainly. But not proof.

'How were you taken there?' Quest asked.

'By Translation.'

Quest leant back, frowning, and looked at Captain Santi. 'There isn't a Translation Chamber inside the Basilica Julia proper, is there?'

'No,' Santi said. 'It's in another building altogether, about a mile away. He can't be recalling it right.'

'Scholar Wolfe, when you came out of the Translation Chamber, where were you? Can you describe it?'

'Hallway,' Wolfe murmured. 'Inside the Basilica Julia.'

'How do you know you were in the Basilica Julia?'

'I saw the Forum from the windows. I know Rome.' Of course he did. A travelling Scholar like Wolfe would recognise a great city like that from even the briefest glance. 'A long, straight hallway. A door at the end.'

'Tell me what you could see from these windows,' Quest said, and Jess grabbed a piece of paper and a pen that Wolfe had left on the table. He wrote as Wolfe described his view. Jess made a quick, rough sketch, marking exact things he'd seen. 'All right. This door at the end of the hallway: was it guarded?'

'Automaton,' Wolfe said dully. 'A Roman lion.'

'And was this door locked, as well?' Quest asked. That was an excellent question Jess wouldn't have thought to ask. The Mesmer obviously had some experience at this sort of thing.

'Yes.'

From there, Wolfe spoke of being led down steps, along a long, sloping corridor of ancient stone, with cells built along one side. Turn after turn. Jess wrote it all down, and Quest continued his steady, passionless questions: how many soldiers did he see? How many Library automata? It was important, even critical, but Wolfe's distress grew ever more visible the farther they delved into this particular piece of the past. He moved back and forth now, a constant rocking motion, and his arms had closed over his stomach. Protecting himself, Jess realised. He felt sick himself, watching. Next to him, Santi was as still as a statue.

'Did anyone ever come to take you out of your cell while you were inside it?'

'Yes.'

'And where did they take you?' Quest asked, which seemed an innocent enough question. He was only trying to map the rest of the prison, which was smart.

Wolfe let out a sound that raised the hair on the back of Jess's neck, and Santi almost lunged forward, but Quest's gaze flicked to him and the Mesmer shook his head. 'Breathe, Scholar Wolfe. Relax,' Quest said. 'You feel no pain, remember? There is no pain now; you are merely watching this from a distance. It isn't happening to you at all. Step back. Just step away and let it go.'

The terrible keening sound went on and grew sharper, and even the Mesmer seemed taken aback by it now. He reached out and put his hand on Wolfe's shoulder. 'Scholar,' he said. '*Scholar.* You are now outside of the cell, do you hear me? You are standing outside the cell. There is no pain at all. You feel peaceful. Calm.'

It was no good. Wolfe's buried scream was growing louder and he wasn't listening.

'That's enough,' Santi shouted, and lunged forward. 'Bring him out! Now!' He sounded as shaken as Jess felt.

'All right,' Quest said. 'Scholar Wolfe! Scholar!' He briskly tapped Wolfe's forehead, then his shoulder, then the back of his hand. '*Exeunt!*'

Wolfe's cry stopped cleanly, and he slumped back in his chair, utterly limp. Santi shoved Quest out of the way and sank down to a crouch beside Wolfe to take his hand. He was checking the other man's pulse, Jess realised, as much as holding it.

Wolfe slowly raised his head. His colour was terrible and his eyes looked dull and strange, but they were open, and after a blank moment that seemed to stretch forever, he looked directly at Santi and said, 'It must have been terrible if you look so worried.'

Jess saw the intense relief flash over the captain's face before his expression closed again. 'Not so bad,' Santi lied. 'And now you're back.'

Wolfe put his hand over Santi's, and there it was again: a little flash of gentleness, sorrow, love. Jess looked away, and when he turned back, Santi was rising to his feet and turning to Quest. 'You, Mesmer,' Santi said. 'Get out. If there's any whisper about any of this, I'll kill you.'

'Sir,' Quest said, 'I am a *professional*. There is no need to threaten.' He hesitated for a moment and then said, 'And as a professional, I would be wrong not to tell you that something terrible was done to your friend, and that will fester inside if that wound isn't lanced. I am willing to offer my continued services at a reasonable—'

'It's none of your business,' Santi said. 'Jess. Get rid of him. Now.'

Jess nodded and grabbed Quest's arm to tow him to the door. He handed over the second, heavier sack of *geneih* coins – the half Quest was due, plus a hefty bonus. 'Leave,' he said. 'Forget about this. He's quite serious about killing you if you don't.'

'Risk of the trade,' Quest sighed. 'But take my advice for your poor Scholar. Find someone who can guide him through that pain. He needs help. I've seen it kill stronger men.' He seemed earnest in that moment and not at all trying to make another fee. As if he were actually, legitimately worried.

'Thanks,' Jess said, and meant it. He hailed the little man a carriage. 'Don't make me find you again.'

Quest grinned suddenly. His teeth were surprisingly white. 'If I didn't want to be found, you'd never manage it. One street rat to another, you know that's truth.'

Then he was gone.

Jess went back inside. 'Is he all right?'

'Still here, Brightwell. Thanks for your concern,' Wolfe said. His voice sounded unnaturally low and hoarse as he cradled his head in both hands. 'Did you find out what you needed?'

'Yes,' Jess said. 'I think so.'

'Then get out.'

'I'm sorry you had to do this—'

'*For the love of all the gods, get out!*' Wolfe raised his head, and his eyes were wet and streaming with blinding tears of pain and fury. He grabbed for a book and hurled it at Jess with great force. It was only a Blank, but Jess understood just how out of control the man was to fling it.

'Jess,' Santi said. 'Go. You have what you wanted. Now I have to help him live through the consequences.'

Jess swallowed hard, nodded, and rolled up the notes he'd made. He closed the door at his back and leant against it for a long moment with his eyes shut. He tried to forget the awful, tortured sound of Wolfe's keening.

On the way back to the barracks, he sent coded messages using people he trusted to alert Khalila and Dario to what he'd found out. It was only fair to tell everyone at once. Everyone but Glain, who'd probably deck him hard for what he'd done to Wolfe. Her, he could leave for last.

He was halfway to the barracks when he turned a corner

and saw a person lurking ahead, wearing a coat too warm for the weather with the hood raised. His instincts pricked him hard as needles, and he slowed his steps. The shadowy figure melted into an alcove halfway down the block; there weren't many people out in these dark hours, and the moon was half-hidden behind high, thin clouds. Perfect conditions, he realised, for an assassination, if the Archivist meant to launch one.

Jess moved with deliberate, casual confidence, and eased his knife free of the sheath at his belt as he walked on. He had to use his left hand to keep the knife from view of his would-be killer, who lurked on the right. He wondered whether he should whistle. Might seem too much.

He kept his speed calm and steady as he drew near the alcove, then past it, and when he felt movement behind him, he turned, grabbed hold of the person rushing at him, and jabbed the point of his dagger up under a soft chin.

The hood fell away. The moon whispered out of the clouds overhead and threw a soft, pale light over both of them

Jess's lips parted and he let go, because the girl facing him, the girl he'd almost killed, was Morgan Hault.

EPHEMERA

From *On Further Nature of the Elements*, a late work of the great Archimedes, collected from that master Scholar in the first years of the Great Library. Available on the Codex.

I have many times been asked to explain the nature of the divine fluid of quintessence, the unseen barrier through which all things must pass to change form. I direct your study to the minerals of the earth. The baser metals are found below the surface, in the darkness and silence, and are lumpen and unformed. The finer metals and minerals – silver, gold, all precious ores and gems – are found in an organic structure of life. They grow, tree-like, slowly through many years, rising up through the invisible richness of quintessence, and are transmuted from the base to the precious as they rise towards heaven.

All things live. That which begins as inorganic becomes organic through the divine power of quintessence. And so we must learn to control this unknowable element, to discover how to make metals, minerals, the organic and inorganic alike transmute and transfigure, above and below the earth.

This knowledge is obscure, but it must be sought. It must be codified, taught, and revered, for only through this great work will the secrets of the world be revealed.

And those who seek it, I call Obscurists, who will cast the light of quintessence upon the darkness.

Let us now discuss how the principle of First Matter may be used to create new forms, with the help and guidance of the gods.

CHAPTER EIGHT

Morgan seemed too pale, he thought, and in the same breath she seemed ethereally beautiful. Her unpinned hair cascaded down over her shoulders in messy, springy curls, and she was dressed in a plain dark dress that reached down to the tops of leather boots. The only jewellery she wore glittered in the moonlight: the gaudy, engraved collar that circled her throat. The golden collar of an Obscurist.

He dropped his knife to his side and wanted badly to put his arms around her; everything in him said it was the right thing to do.

But he knew it was wrong from the tension in her body, the flash in her eyes. Still, for one dizzying instant he imagined holding her and kissing her, and the feeling of her lips under his seemed as real as breath. The smell of her, roses and spices, washed over him in a flood.

Jess took an indrawn breath that seemed to fill him with her presence, her reality.

'You're here,' he said. 'You're really . . . here.' It seemed impossible. No, it *was* impossible, by any imagining; she couldn't leave the Iron Tower. If she could have, surely she'd have run away, not come *here*.

But then her hand brushed his, and he knew it wasn't a dream or a trance or anything but real. She was here. Alive. Morgan smiled, and his heart shattered into pieces, because it was a guarded smile, not a happy one. 'I won't be here long,' she said. 'I've managed to stay out for almost a full day, trying to find you. You do hide yourself well.'

'Then you can stay out longer? Get far from here?'

She was already shaking her head. 'No, I'll never make it out of Alexandria. They'll find me soon. I haven't found a way to take this off yet, and until I do, they can track me.' She withdrew her hand and traced fingers over her collar, the symbol of her enslavement to the Library. Some sanity came back to him, and with it, doubt. Maybe they'd turned Morgan. Maybe she was a lure meant to distract him from another, more serious threat. He didn't see anyone or feel anything, but she was a stunning distraction. He couldn't take his gaze away from her for long enough to keep a good watch.

So many things he wanted to ask her, but he settled for, 'You must have had some great reason to come now. What's wrong?'

Something clouded her face for a moment, and it almost looked like . . . fear. 'There were other reasons, but mostly . . . mostly, it's about Thomas. Jess, I think he could be held in Rome! I found reference to an ancient, very secret prison—'

'Below the Basilica Julia. I know,' Jess finished. 'I'm sorry. I just found that out. But . . . do you have proof that Thomas is actually there?'

Morgan seemed shocked and then a little angry. He didn't blame her. 'Proof? No. But I thought – I thought you'd want to know, that it would give you something more to investigate. And instead I risked my neck to come here to give you information you already *had*?'

She really does seem pale, he thought. Even in the Iron Tower, there must be sun somewhere for them to enjoy, and she hadn't got enough. She seemed thinner, too. And even discounting the deceptive shadows of the night, he read the weariness on her face. The frustration.

'Did you find records about him? Is he all right?' Jess asked, when all he really wanted to ask about in that moment was her. What she was enduring in the Iron Tower. Whatever it was, he knew it was his fault she was there. They both knew it, and it stood between them like a dark, brooding shadow.

'I know he's still alive,' she said. 'The Artifex seems to believe he has a use for him. Something about the design of the Library automata. From the reports, Thomas had notes in his Codex that might help improve the automata against the Burner attacks. They'll want to get that from him, at least. If he proves useful, they'll keep him alive. And if they think they can trust him, they might even . . .'

'Let him go?'

'No. But move him somewhere not as terrible. It *must* be terrible, Jess. From what I've read . . .' Her voice faltered, and it took a heartbeat for it to return. 'Wolfe suffered horribly there. They were going to kill him before his mother finally intervened. I didn't know human beings could be so . . . cold. So cruel. And especially not . . . not in service to the Library.'

Jess did, unfortunately, though it seemed to him there were always more terrible surprises left in the world. 'How long before they find you?'

'I'm not sure. They'll have searched for me inside the Tower first, probably most of the day. If the Obscurist is involved, it won't be long now.'

'Then we don't have much time.' His body felt hot and cold

at once, and the feeling in his stomach was like standing in a very high spot, looking down at the drop. He took her hand and held it. 'Morgan, please. I need to know if you can ever forgive me.'

'For sending me to the Tower?' she asked, which was blunt and painful, but he nodded. 'Most days I don't blame you. Some days I do. I tell myself they would have caught me eventually, that you just spared me pain and injury and maybe even death fighting the inevitable. But it still hurts. As long as it does, I can't . . .'

'Can't feel the way you used to,' he finished for her, and she slowly nodded. And there it was, the drop he was falling off of, a long spiral down to an inevitable painful impact. 'All right. That's fair enough.' All the nerves in his fingers seemed painfully aware of the feel of her skin, the softness, the warmth. The way her hand curled around his and held on.

'No, it isn't fair at all,' she said. 'I'm sorry, Jess. It isn't that I don't care for you – I do. I just—'

'Let me make it up to you. Come with me,' he said. It was an impulse, a wild thing he couldn't quite control. 'I'll take you away somewhere.'

'Where?'

'Away. Anywhere.'

'Jess, they'll find me.'

'Then we'll run.'

'*They'll find me.* Until I can get this collar loose, it's no use even trying!'

'And if you do get it off?'

'Then maybe things will be different,' she said. There were tears glittering sharply in her eyes. 'This isn't easy. I'm sorry.'

Jess stepped closer, and she didn't back away. He eased

her hair back from her face and let his fingertips linger. After imagining her for so long, having her here seemed more like a dream, except for the velvet evidence of her skin. *Easy.* Nothing about how he felt for her was that. He knew he loved her, but it was shot through with dangerous thorns: guilt, jealousy, fear.

It occurred to him in that moment that for all his missing Morgan before, he'd missed nothing but a fantasy. As Glain had said: a challenge, distant and safe. But this girl, standing in front of him now, was far more real, honest, and complicated.

And he wanted her more than he ever had.

They were so close, too close, and Morgan's eyes widened. She stepped back and brought their conversation back to the practical. 'I almost forgot. There's a Translation Chamber in the Basilica Julia; it's private, only used for access to the prison, and only to and from the Alexandrian Serapeum.'

'Wolfe remembered a Translation Chamber,' Jess said. 'Nic didn't believe him.'

'It's very secret. But I think I might be able to change the destination and take us somewhere besides Alexandria. *If* I can get free of the Iron Tower again and join you.'

'You're free now.'

'You're not ready to rescue him yet. Are you?'

'No,' he admitted. 'We're not even completely sure he's there. We keep looking for proof.'

'I wish I had more to tell you,' she said. 'I'll keep looking. I'm sure I can crack some more of the codes that the Artifex uses—' She broke off with a gasp and touched the collar at her neck. Her gaze met his and held.

'They're coming,' he said. She nodded.

'I can't let them see you with me, or you'd be arrested. If I escaped and ran on my own, that's one thing, but the penalty for you . . .'

'Maybe they'd put me in the cell beside Thomas. That's one way to do research.'

'It's not funny! Jess—' He kissed her. After a second of surprise, she kissed him back, warmth and sweetness and a frantic kind of passion that said more than words. And then she pushed him away. Hard. 'Go *now*. They can't find you with me. Please, just go!'

He turned and ran. When he looked back, he saw Morgan walking calmly to the opposite end of the block, where a steam carriage glided to a halt and armed High Garda poured out to surround her. She didn't fight them.

Look back at me. Just look back, Morgan.

She didn't.

Jess waited all night for a Codex message from Morgan or Khalila or Dario.

No messages came.

By dawn, he was desperate enough to use his Codex to try to send a message himself, despite the fact that he knew it would be monitored. He tried Khalila first, then Dario, but neither replied. *Something's happened*, he thought, and the fear climbed his spine as if it were a ladder, to lodge cold in the back of his brain. *They've been taken away. Or . . . or worse.* Would the Archivist risk another tragic accident in a matter of days? Or would he simply have them vanish, and make up whatever story he needed to pacify their loved ones?

Jess imagined how that polite, pretty fiction would sound in his case. The Archivist's sorrowful letter would arrive in formal calligraphy, and it wouldn't tell the truth, like, *Your son was dismembered by an automaton – so sorry*, but talk of some quiet, mundane death. Illness, probably. He morbidly pictured the scene back at home, where his mother and father would receive news of his death with the same quiet stoicism they'd used to greet the death of his older brother, Liam. Maybe Brendan would actually be sorry to lose him.

Just as he was trying to decide whether or not his father would shed any tears, his Codex flashed a message. His High Garda orders had arrived. This morning, he was to report to Captain Niccolo Santi's company, which would become his permanent assignment for the next year. He stared at it for a long, strange moment, wondering what in God's name the Archivist intended by granting him what he'd wanted, and was startled out of his chair when someone knocked loudly on his door.

Glain stood outside, and when he opened up, she thrust her open Codex in his face. 'Santi,' she said. He silently held up his own orders. 'What does this mean?'

'I don't know,' he said. 'Nothing good.' He told her about Dario and Khalila, and Glain paled under the deep tan she'd acquired. 'We need to go to the Lighthouse.'

'We can't,' she said, and pointed to his orders again. He'd stopped reading after seeing Santi's name, but she was right: there was more. 'We're ordered to report for duty. Now.'

He and Glain made it to the parade ground just in time and were intercepted by someone Jess recognised: the centurion who'd helped them on the exercise ground, when Helva had been hurt and Tariq killed. Centurion Botha.

There was no recognition or even interest on Botha's face as he stepped into their path. 'Orders,' he snapped, and Glain briskly flipped her Codex open to show them. Jess followed a second after. Botha examined them and the imprint of seals embossed under, and shoved the books back into their hands.

'Century Two, Blue Squad. Report to your squad leader.'

Over Botha's shoulder, Jess saw Captain Santi, who was listening to a lieutenant intently. He looked very different now from the man who'd been defending Wolfe; all traces of that emotion had vanished, and he wore command like an invisible crown. No time for mere new recruits.

Glain had already saluted Botha and turned away, and Jess quickly followed suit and moved off at a lope after her. They both knew the standard configurations of a company, and, finding Century Two, then Blue Squad, was simple enough. The squad leader there watched the two of them step into formation with cool, judgemental eyes. 'Nice new uniforms, recruits,' he said. 'Don't worry. We'll beat the creases right out of them. Welcome to Blue Squad.'

Around them, the other members of the squad gave a deep-throated bark in unison. The squad leader smiled. 'Also known as the Blue Dogs. I've looked at your scores. Not bad. We'll expect better, of course.'

The young man – *two or three years ahead of us*, Jess thought, *but with the air of someone twice his age* – turned with that very brief greeting and walked to take his place in the rank, at the far right of their squad. Jess, standing on the end of the line, had a good view of the platform where Santi stood. He was gathered now with his centurions, and at his nod, the centurions jumped down to walk the ranks.

Botha had a voice loud enough to carry halfway to China, and he used it to full effect to shout, 'Century Two, report by squad to supply wagon and reform! Fast and orderly!'

Instantly, the first squad in the century peeled off and ran to a supply carrier that was parked not far away; Jess tried to watch them without turning his head, but got little but a headache for his trouble. It took just under five minutes for each squad to run over and return, and he realised that they were picking up weapons and travel packs.

Travel packs.

As they jogged to the supplies, he managed to whisper to Glain, 'We're on the move. Did you know—?'

'No,' she snapped. 'Shut up.'

'But what about Dario and Khalila—'

'Shut *up*!'

It was the work of seconds to grab weapons from the hands of the armourers, plus a travel pack; Jess wasn't used to putting one on quite so quickly, but he managed to get the buckles fastened and be back in the Blue Dog line with only a slight delay. It earned him a lean-out stare from the squad leader. He kept himself at perfect attention until the other young man looked away.

He was burning to ask where they were going, but he was now, officially, High Garda, and High Garda soldiers didn't ask. Glain had done him a favour by insisting he pack his personal journal and wear his smuggling harness with his stolen books inside. He'd never go back to his room in the recruit barracks. When he came back, the few belongings he had left would be moved to new quarters in the regular company barracks. He was, finally, in his place. Everything to this point, Jess realised, had still felt like preparation – like schoolwork, not life. But now, in full battle uniform, wearing the heavy weight of the pack and loaded down with weapons he knew he would have to use, it all felt . . . different. More ominously real. *This is my place. This is my life.* The weapons were live and lethal, and he would be expected to use them.

Dario and Khalila. We've lost them. He couldn't leave

Alexandria without knowing where they were, what had happened. He'd thought they would have time to find out, but now . . . now they were being sent out without warning. Maybe to battle.

Hard not to flash back to Oxford and the terrible war that had overtaken them there as they rescued books and librarians. Jess had spent months fighting back nightmares in which he saw the slaughter, the desperation, saw his fellow postulant Joachim Portero die. It had been a cruel and terribly real introduction to the chaos that the Great Library had been built to guard against. During that chaos, it had been hard to see the Library as a villain, though he knew very well that the Library was no stranger to death, oppression and cruelty. The Library had taken Thomas. Walled up Morgan. Separated him from everything he'd come to care about. Now they might have stolen away two of his remaining friends, too.

The idea that he was supposed to fight *for* it was obscene. He wondered how Santi stood it, knowing what he knew.

A line of carriers rolled up in a hiss of white steam, and one by one, Blue Dog squad received an inspection not from Santi himself, but from one of his top lieutenants, a round-faced woman with startling greenish eyes in a very dark face. Those eyes missed nothing, and when they lingered over Jess and his pack, he felt a chill. 'You,' the lieutenant said, and gestured to him. 'Come with me.'

Glain broke from her rigid attention to send Jess a startled glance as he followed the lieutenant out of ranks to a spot at the back of the carrier. A thick white wisp of steam left a damp streak across his face as it drifted past, and the lingering smell of bitter metal. 'Is there a problem, sir?'

The lieutenant fixed those intimidating eyes on him. 'You're Brightwell,' she said. 'Correct?'

'Yes, sir.' He felt sweat tickle down the side of his face. 'Problem, sir?'

She leant forward suddenly, and it was all he could do not to flinch. She didn't blink as she stared into his eyes from a distance close enough that their noses nearly brushed. 'You're acquainted with Captain Santi.'

'Yes, sir!'

'Then know this: if you presume on prior acquaintance, I will *end* you. Is that understood? You speak to Captain Santi when spoken to *by* him. You will not approach him. You will not send him messages. There is a chain of command, and you are the link at the ass end of it.' Every word was as bright and sharp as a razor, and she never blinked. 'If I catch a whisper of a rumour to the contrary, I will destroy you. Understood, Brightwell?'

He sucked in a breath and said, 'Understood, sir!'

'Good.' She held there another beat, then drew back and nodded. 'I've been instructed to tell you to stop looking for your friends. They're safe. That comes directly from the captain himself, and if I hear you've stepped over that line, I'll destroy you twice over. Now fall in.' She gestured sharply to the squad leader, and he counted off as each of the squad members lunged up into the carrier. Jess climbed in, as promised, last. The ass end of the chain, just as the lieutenant had said, but he couldn't shake the other part of her message.

They're safe. Santi had said so. What did that mean? Had Dario and Khalila gone into hiding? Had they come under some kind of threat? *Can't ask.* It was going to kill him to resist.

He tried to focus on the other soldiers in the carrier. Apart from Glain, he knew none of them, and not a single face seemed familiar or even friendly. The seats were arrayed facing each other in two rows, with space between for packs, and Jess struggled to unbuckle his and lay it in the assigned space between his boots.

The carrier lurched into motion, throwing him against the deep, padded seat. Circulating cool air only cut the heat but didn't defeat it, and didn't hide the smell embedded inside this vehicle: sweat, blood, a whiff of old fear. The smell of battle. It took him back to Oxford, and he felt cold despite the heat.

'What did the gold band want?' Glain asked, and Jess realised that she was right: the lieutenant had been wearing a gold band, a career appointment. He hadn't noticed until Glain brought it to mind.

'Nothing.' He couldn't tell her, not here. She seemed to accept that and nodded.

'Well, you do know a good deal about nothing, so that makes sense.'

'Where do you think we're going?' There had been enough carriers pulled up to move Santi's entire company – and that, he thought, wasn't normal. Usually squads were sent out, or, more rarely, centuries. Even heading to Oxford, Santi had taken only a half century as escort. Taking the whole company meant real trouble.

'The hot spots are in England,' the man across from Jess said. He was older, with a dust of grey in his dark blond hair and a neatly trimmed beard and moustache. The accent was familiar – *English*, Jess thought. *Manchester, maybe*. 'The Welsh are still pushing up towards London.'

'We're not going to England,' said a shorter man next to him. 'We're heading to Rome.'

Rome. Jess felt his heartbeat speed up and he couldn't stop a look at Glain, who maintained her usual mask of cool indifference. 'Why?' she asked. 'Is Rome about to fall to the Welsh, too?' She made sure, in saying it, that her native Welsh accent was on full display.

There was a ripple of laughter. The Englishman across from Jess didn't crack a smile, and there was a dark look in his eyes. *Easy*, Jess thought. *These aren't our friends. They're trained killers.*

'I heard the Artifex Magnus is inspecting the Serapeum there,' someone else offered. There were nods and more serious expressions; they all knew the Artifex was a prime target for the Burners, which was the principal enemy they had to fear these days.

The Artifex was also the red right hand of the Archivist. He might not be the second most powerful in the Library – that honour went to Wolfe's mother, the Obscurist Magnus – but the Artifex ran a close third. If the Archivist ordered someone dead, it was the Artifex who arranged for the murder.

And they would be guarding him from threats. Ironic.

Jess shut his eyes for a moment, ignoring the chatter around him, and then reached in his bag and pulled out his Codex. He opened it to a specific page, the page where Morgan's messages appeared, and took out a stylus. He wrote down, in flowing, tight letters, *They're sending us to Rome. Is it a trap? Please answer. I need you to answer. Please.*

The words stayed for a moment and then faded away. The page was blank.

The page stayed blank.

'Put that away,' the man across from him said. 'No messages on missions.'

Jess should have known that. He nodded and put the Codex away, and tried to hope that being sent to Rome was just some lucky, happy coincidence.

He was too cynical to believe it for long.

'On your feet!'

Jess hadn't realised he'd slept until the squad leader's shout roared over him, magnified by the very suddenness of it; he jerked awake and was up fast enough that he banged his head on the low ceiling of the carrier. It had stopped moving, though he could feel the faint vibration of the steam engine still working. The impact was hard enough to make his vision spark, and the pain radiated through the top of his head like an acid bath, but he grimly stumbled out after Glain, into what proved to be a heavily walled courtyard large enough to hold all the vehicles and soldiers disembarking from them, but only just. Overhead, the sky had turned a teal that told him twilight was approaching, the day well gone. He'd slept a long time. He supposed he'd needed it, but he'd missed meals and – most important now – a latrine.

Wherever they were, it wasn't Rome, but it also didn't feel like Alexandria. There were drifts of fine dirt on the smooth surface of the courtyard that crunched under his boots as he turned to see the soaring structure of a pyramid-shaped building. A Serapeum, a daughter branch of the Library. This one was made of searingly white stone, with the slice of gold at the top that he realised, on squinting, was a spire holding up the Library's seal. The shadows drowning half the courtyard seemed deeper than usual.

He formed up with the squad, and the Blue Dog squad leader – he still didn't know the young man's name – moved quickly down the line to inspect them. He was shorter than Jess but radiated a commanding presence that made Jess straighten just a bit more.

'Where are we, sir?' That was Glain, surprisingly.

Even more surprisingly, the squad leader seemed willing to answer. 'We're at the port city of Darnah. Ships are waiting to take most of the company, but we lucky few will be going on with the Captain directly.'

'Directly,' Glain said. 'You mean by Translation.'

The squad leader grinned, dispelling all his years and authority in one flash of teeth . . . and then getting it back in the next instant as he said, 'Exactly what I mean. Move. Consider this an honour. We're in the advance guard of the Artifex Magnus today.'

The arrogant old man was making *Niccolo Santi* guard him. It was a deliberate insult; there was no doubt of that. The Artifex had been the one to take Wolfe to prison and oversee his . . . conversion, just as he'd taken Thomas. It had to be a constant struggle for Santi not to shoot the bastard in the back.

If Santi can stand it, I can, Jess told himself. He tightened the straps on his pack and followed Glain down the wide tunnel that ran at a slant beneath the Serapeum.

No doubt parts of this vast pyramid were devoted to spacious, beautiful areas where the public could browse the Codex and load up Blanks with texts; librarians would be working, serene and helpful. A Scholar or two might be conducting his own research in a secret archive of local documents. There would be reading spaces, light, and beautiful views from the windows. That would be the public face of the Library, the one that even Jess had always known.

That was not the Library he saw here in the tunnels. As the majority of Santi's troops continued down the stone-walled hall beneath the pyramid and headed for the docks, Santi led them off to the right, down a narrower passage lit by flickering glows above. The glows were chemical, an older style, and sputtered unsteadily with a greenish cast to them. It made all the faces of Jess's companions seem eerily lifeless.

Not a thing to think about before Translation. The last time he'd been through this, he'd seen a classmate die and one broken by it. But he'd survived it once, and knew he could again. *I am a soldier now*, he told himself. *Soldiers take risks.*

The group accompanying Santi consisted of the green-eyed lieutenant whom he'd sent to intimidate Jess, their squad, and another, more seasoned group of veterans who seemed totally at ease with the situation. One of them, a man who seemed ancient to Jess but was in reality about his father's age, caught sight of Jess's face and laughed. 'Don't worry, boy, you'll come through in one piece,' the soldier said, and shoved him ahead through an open set of double doors. 'Might not enjoy the trip, but at least we travel in style here. Seen a lot worse!'

The old soldier was right. This *was* far different from the Translation Chambers Jess had seen in Alexandria and in their last arrival point in England. The one in Alexandria had seemed chaotically full of machinery, steam, pipes, gears, sparks. It had felt at once ancient, untidy, and unfinished. Maybe it had been under repair.

The one in England had seemed bare and grubby. He'd have expected Alexandria to have the best of everything, but as he stepped into this Translation room in Darnah, he was struck by how sleek it was. The floor was bare stone, cool beneath his boots. The ceiling stretched high, and what machinery was visible was only glimpsed behind barriers or rafters above. A single bronzed cable dropped down from the unseen machinery to hang down in a circle of light, in which lay a curved, reclining chair made of the same stone as the floor, with a metal helmet next to it.

'I wish I understood this better,' Jess said to Glain, who gave him a quelling look. 'What? It would make me feel better knowing if I'm to be torn to pieces and put together again.'

'Didn't you pay attention at all in alchemy classes in school?'

'My schooling was more . . . practical.'

'The principle's simple enough: the Obscurist uses the element of quintessence to pass you through a fluid that rectifies your form in one place and purifies it in another. The quintessence exists everywhere at once. All things pass through it in creation and destruction.'

'Are you quoting a textbook?' he asked her, and she smirked.

'Why not? You never read it.'

'I was wrong. This little lecture didn't help at all.' He paused and looked around. 'The Artifex. Is he here?'

'He arrives later. We go first to secure the arrival point,' she said. 'I'd think you would have already figured that out.'

Of course the evil old man would think of his own safety first; he'd wait until Santi's security was in place, then join him. Then be escorted directly to whatever it was he found so important to do in Rome. Was it to see Thomas? Was that why he was heading there? Jess had a flash of the Artifex Magnus's severe, bearded face, and felt his fists clench. He deliberately relaxed them. Ironic that he'd been chosen to protect someone he most wanted to see dead. He wouldn't find himself shedding a lot of tears if the Artifex suffered a heart attack during Translation, but he'd do his duty. He had to.

Didn't mean he had to like it.

Ahead, Captain Santi was speaking to his lieutenant, who listened with perfect focus, nodded, and turned towards the rest of them. 'Attention!' Her voice cut clean through the chatter, and they all stiffened into inspection stance. 'We'll be travelling by Translation, which means that when your name is called, you will sit in the chair, fit the helmet on your head, and follow instructions. To answer any questions you have: yes, it will damn well hurt. Yes, you are allowed to scream if you feel the need. Yes, we are allowed to mock you for it later.' She smiled, and there was a ripple of laughter from the veterans. 'We have two new recruits in the Blue Dogs.'

The squad made that chesty barking sound again, and this time, Jess and Glain both joined in. Without being ordered, they stepped forward in unison.

'Show these dogs how it's done, new dogs. You first.' The lieutenant pointed to Jess. *Of course.* He stared at her for a beat, then saluted silently and walked towards the chair. Glain said quietly, 'Do us proud.'

Jess didn't give any sign he'd heard. He sat on the cool, hard surface of the reclining chair and swung his legs up. The pack on his back was bulky and uncomfortable, but he ignored that and reached for the Translation helmet, which was surprisingly light. Unlike the one in Alexandria, this one seemed more finished, more integrated, though it still had protruding tubes that glowed with a strange light. It fit snug around his head, and as the padding pressed down, he felt cold metal points touch his scalp, not quite sharp enough to pierce. They felt like chips of ice against his sweating skin.

A man in gold Library robes stepped forward. He was younger than Jess expected, of Chinese heritage, and around his neck he wore the wide golden collar of an Obscurist. 'You've done this before,' he said to Jess in a conversational tone as he reached for the bronze cable descending from the roof and connected it to the top of the helmet. The snap of it clicking in place seemed to echo through Jess's bones. 'Good – you know what to expect. Deep breaths.'

'*In bocca al lupo*,' Captain Santi said.

'*In bocca al lupo*,' Jess replied, and nodded to the Obscurist. 'I'm ready.'

The phrase meant 'in the mouth of the wolf', and that was what it felt like when the Obscurist put his hands on Jess's helmet and the machines powered up around them. It felt like the wolf had him in its jaws as power surged down into the conductors in the helmet and ate him from within, like a wild storm, like a hungry animal, ripping him to pieces in a slow, torturous explosion of blood and bone, organ and flesh, and he heard himself give a short, agonised cry . . .

And then darkness, and the slow waves of sick pain, and he compulsively sucked in a breath as if he'd never breathed before. Everything felt wrong; every nerve burnt with fire and salt, and he rolled on his side with his stomach lurching violently. He was lying on a reclining chair similar to the one he'd been on before, but instead of a helmet beside him, there was a metal bucket.

He grabbed it and vomited up his breakfast. A Medica professional in Library robes was there to steady him, and she checked him over with brisk efficiency. 'You'll be fine,' she said. 'Water's over there. If you have headaches later, report them. Oh, and take the bucket. There's a sink over there. Empty and wash.'

She set down another bucket by the chair, stepped back, and waited, dismissing Jess from her concern. He staggered over to the sink and dumped the bucket, washed it, and by the time he was done with that task, he heard Glain behind him, gasping for air. He put down the bucket and turned. She looked sick and blank for a moment, then controlled her breathing and sat up. She didn't quite vomit, but he could see from the press of her lips that she was seriously considering the option. The Medica helped her up, and Glain almost immediately shook free. 'Brightwell?' She blinked, and he knew she was having trouble focusing her blurry eyes.

He stepped into the light. 'Here, Glain.'

'Good.' She tried for a smile, but it didn't look right. 'You only half screamed. You're getting better at this.'

'You, too,' he said. 'Fast recovery.'

It wasn't protocol, but no one else except the Medica was in the room, so when she held up her hand, he clapped it in salute. 'Dario and Khalila,' he told her in a whisper. 'Santi's lieutenant told me they're safe.'

'Safe how?'

He shrugged in answer. 'Don't know. But there's more: Wolfe remembered. The secret prison is in Rome. Morgan confirmed that. We just don't have final proof that Thomas is inside.'

Glain had a thousand questions, he could see it, but this wasn't the time. They took up an at-ease position against the wall and waited for the rest to arrive.

Watching arrivals was almost as sickening as going through it himself. Jess stood stoically as one after another, the other members of their squad formed in swirls of blood and bone from the air, solidifying into themselves in the support of the stone chair. Most of the other soldiers made it without giving in to the nausea.

Santi's lieutenant arrived and swung her legs off to push herself to her feet after just a bare few seconds, as if she'd only sat down for a rest. Santi came right behind her, and with even less time for adjustment. Neither of them seemed impaired in the least.

'Form up!' the lieutenant barked, as Santi walked on. She followed, and the rest of them fell in behind in perfect order.

Then they boarded carriers again. Jess remembered Santi's observation that the Translation Chamber in Rome was at least a mile from the basilica, and he'd been right, but at least it was a short ride. Jess hardly had time to get uncomfortable before they were ordered out again, formed up, and walked down a long stone-and-column hallway to an arched entrance that glowed with the light of sunset. Beyond were a long, steep fall of worn stone steps; on the steps lounged an entire pride of Library lion automata. They sat still, like the statues they resembled, and they were different from the English versions. These had larger manes that stood out stiffly and curled down in ringlets on broader chests. Magnificent and *huge*. Beyond a doubt, deadly.

Santi opened his Codex and scrawled something inside it, and Jess saw all ten of the lions turn their heads in a smooth, eerie motion to look back at them. Their eyes flickered from dark to red, and one by one, they rose to their feet and began to pace the perimeter. Five remained on the steps, while the others patrolled farther.

Beyond the steps stretched Rome, and though Jess had thought the wonders of Alexandria had numbed him to everything else, the sight of the city stopped him cold. The square – no, this corner of the *Forum* – was surprisingly small and crowded with marvels. Temples of white marble blushed now with pink and gold by the sunset, and giant golden statues of the Roman gods stood, with citizens passing beneath their feet without any thought for the splendour above. Pigeons lined the broad shoulders of Jupiter and the outstretched arm of Juno, both statues taller than any of the other monuments.

The famous hills of the city rolled on above, and the spreading palaces and homes of the rich beyond that, growing larger and more lavish the farther up they went.

It even smelt richer here than in Alexandria – fresh pines, lush soil, sweat, the sharp, pickled vinegar of the fish being sold across the way in a food stall. That last made Jess's stomach roil with hunger.

Everywhere he looked, there was the shimmer of marble and gold in the fading light, ancient wonders and modern marvels, and it was so beautiful it didn't seem possible it had been built by the hands of men.

'Done gawking?' one of the veterans asked him, and he jerked back to awareness of who, and what, he was. Not a visitor who could take his time admiring the sights, but a soldier on duty. The veteran gave him a wide, sudden grin. 'Nothing like Rome, boy. Gets us all the first time.'

'And every time after,' said Santi's lieutenant from behind them. She didn't sound impressed or amused. 'Green Squad, you are down below, on the square. Blue Dogs, up here. Anything gets past Green Squad and the automata, it's yours to deal with. Stay alert. Rome's Burners always are.'

The idea that Rome had Burners lurking in these majestic, ancient shadows made Jess feel an actual pain in his chest. He'd seen what Burners could do with their bottles of Greek Fire and the destruction they could cause. A small bottle was enough to burn a man into bones. Large glass bombs of it could reduce beauty to ruins, melt the gods, destroy one of the world's greatest sights.

He hated what the Library did to protect itself, but there were times when he understood *why*. So much could be lost, so easily, to such hate.

Jess was ordered to a post quite near the arched door where they'd come out. It had a thick metal door that Santi's lieutenant closed behind her as she went inside, and Jess heard the heavy *chunk* of locks engaging.

It occurred to him then to turn and look back and up at the large, square structure they were guarding. It took a moment to come into focus, and when it did, he felt his body go hot as adrenaline flooded in.

He was standing on the steps of the Basilica Julia, facing the Forum. Though they had no proof, Thomas's prison might, even now, be only a few feet below where Jess stood. The realisation of that made him take a step back and look down at the ancient stone under his boots.

'Focus,' Glain said. She knew what he was thinking. 'We do our jobs. Consider this reconnaissance for the mission.'

She was right, and he needed to get his bearings again and put Thomas, and any possibilities, out of mind. This could well be the place, but it was definitely *not* the time.

He took a breath to wrench his mind away from the possibilities and analyse the situation in front of him. They were out in the open, with no retreat behind, and ten automaton Roman lions stalking among them. Jess knew how the lions worked, how they thought, and he also knew that they weren't particular about innocent victims when something rang their alarms. The automata in Alexandria had been alerted to watch him; had these? So far, none had so much as glanced in his direction. The citizens passing through the square below, coming and going to temples, government, businesses, courts, shops, restaurants, they didn't seem to notice the increase in security, but Jess saw a pattern nevertheless. The area around the Basilica Julia cleared, and those who might have crossed in front instead took a longer route around. No one looked at the lions or at the soldiers or even at the basilica itself.

It was fear he was seeing. No one was quite allowing it to rule him, but all were conscious of the danger.

You're not guarding the Artifex or a prison, he told himself. *You're guarding your fellow soldiers. The Scholars inside the basilica. You're guarding original books that need protection.* That helped steady him.

Jess remembered his encounters with Burners – sadly, too many in his young life – and began to scan the crowds below. In his experience, the fanatics had a certain purposeful look to them; it wasn't easy to work yourself up to self-immolation, and every Burner had to accept that his or her mission would probably end in death. They had a common look.

His gaze swept back and forth, back and forth, and then snagged on something he couldn't quite identify. He wasn't even sure *why* he'd noticed that particular group of people clustered together, apparently consulting a map. When he focused, they seemed like typical tourists, attempting to find their way to a landmark.

Then he realised that one by one – and not all together – they were stealing glances at the basilica. After each look, the one who'd taken it would lean in and say something to the others. Then another would take a brief look.

There were five of them, three men and one woman, most older than Jess but not by much. Young, idealistic, and perfectly suited to be recruited to a cause.

Jess's skin shivered into warning goosebumps, and he heeded it and signalled to Glain, who drifted his way. She covered ground but didn't seem to move quickly. It was a gift she had that he never could quite master. 'What?' she asked him, and stood apparently at ease, though her eyes were never still.

'By the feet of Mercury,' he said. 'That group of five. I don't like it.'

She studied the men and said, 'Neither do I. Watch them.'

She moved off, heading for the squad leader. *She is good at this*, Jess thought; she made it seem like a natural stop, just a standard check-in, and neither of them gave away any alarm.

Glain took out her Codex and wrote something, then snapped it shut. *Alerting Santi's lieutenant*, Jess thought, *that there might be trouble*. He didn't know if the Artifex Magnus had arrived or if he was keeping Santi waiting; probably the latter. The Artifex had always seemed to be a man too full of his own importance.

The group of five was joined by more. Seven now. Eight. Each had some kind of carrying pack, and they were careful with them. How much Greek Fire could they have? Too much, if those backpacks were full of bottles and containers.

Below him, pacing in front of the stairs, one of the Roman lions paused and turned its head with smooth grace to stare at the group standing next to Mercury, and Jess saw the articulated body crouch lower.

Behind them, the door into the basilica opened. He didn't turn to look. All his attention was on the lion, which took an elegant, smooth step down, then another. Others of its pride took notice and began to descend towards the Forum.

'Run,' Jess heard Glain whisper. 'Run, you idiots.'

But the group of eight standing in the shadow of the statue of Mercury, very near the golden wings on his sandals, just stayed where they were. Watching the lions come closer.

They'd be slaughtered.

'Something's not right,' Jess said. 'Glain—'

'I know,' she said. 'They should have run.'

It was a *plan*.

And he sensed it was working.

Jess took it all in at a glance: the lions clustering together as they advanced to circle the eight in the square. The soldiers still on the steps, watching as the pride of automata stalked their prey.

No one was looking anywhere else.

It was only because he turned that he saw the first attack coming: an arcing bottle that came not from the group in the Forum, but coming from *above*, from the statue of Jupiter on the opposite side of the Forum, closest to the basilica. 'Greek Fire!' Jess shouted, and realised the bottle was tumbling end over end. The liquid bubbled inside the glass as it passed over his head, and he ducked instinctively, but it would miss them by a good margin.

The bottle slammed to the steps twenty feet away, landing where a grouping of others from Blue Squad had been standing just a second earlier. But Jess's call had done its work, and they'd scattered. Only one was hit by cast-off drops; he went down, and another of their new squad mates yanked an emergency kit from her pack and dumped powder on the flames before they could bore through the cover of his coat.

Remarkable, how cool Jess felt, how focused. He calmly brought up his weapon, thumbed the switch to turn it on, and waited an instant until he felt the shiver of power run through it. The weapon fired in regular mode for closer range, but the bottle-throwing Burner was high up on Jupiter's shoulder, well out of range of the normal settings of the weapon.

But not for this one. It took a steady hand and good eyes, but Jess had both, and as he sank down to one knee for stability, he aimed the gun sights directly on the man perched on the shoulder of a god, preparing another bottle to throw.

Below in the Forum, the lions were roaring and alarmed screams went up. More guns barked behind him, but Jess had one, singular focus: this man. He could see the Burner's sweating face – reddened from heat and exertion and excitement – and could see the large bottle he had in his hand, ready for a second throw.

Jess's shot took him in the shoulder. The bottle tumbled out of the Burner's hand, not towards the Library troops, but down, plummeting past the god's muscled back and toga-draped legs to smash on the ancient Forum stones. It created a huge green blaze and a wave of sickly black smoke, but no innocents were in the way. They now scrambled to avoid the toxic spread.

The Burner stood up on Jupiter's shoulder. His right arm was a bloody mess, but he held up his personal journal in his left hand – the same personal journal they all kept. The same as the worn little volume in Jess's pack. 'Tell your precious Artifex! A life is worth more than a book!' he shouted. '*Vita hominis plus libro valet!*'

Jess, sickened, watched him deliberately fall backwards and disappear into the hissing flames below. If he wasn't dead from the fall, the Greek Fire would eat him to the bones.

'Down!' Glain yelled, and her hand shoved him forward as she hit the marble steps next to him. A leaping shadow passed over them, and Jess looked up to see that one of the giant Roman automaton lions had taken a position in front of them, facing the Forum. It set its metallic bronze paws and roared with such volume, it nearly deafened Jess.

When he raised his head, the entire incident was over.

The Forum was deserted – a suddenly blank stretch of old

stone littered with belongings and packages that people had abandoned in their haste to be gone. The Greek Fire behind Jupiter burnt brilliantly, stretching half up his legs, and in the flickering, sickly light, it looked as if the god might be melting, but no, it was a trick of shadows. Jupiter was made of hardy stuff.

There were eight dead bodies near the feet of Mercury across the way, crushed and lifeless. Jess swept the area again with a long, straight look, but he didn't see anyone else who'd been hurt or killed.

'Nine dead,' he said to Glain. 'For what?'

'For what it always is,' she said. 'A statement.' She was already on her feet and offered him a hand up, which he was happy to take. Strange; he seemed weak and a little shaky now, where he'd been ice-cold and focused before. 'They knew the Artifex was coming. This message is meant for him.'

'Thrown right at us, though. Seems more personal than that,' their squad leader remarked, coming up to them. He looked them over. 'Good job, new dogs. Didn't have a chance to acquaint ourselves earlier. I'm Tom Rollison, but most call me Troll.'

'Glain Wathen, sir. Jess Brightwell.' Glain answered for both of them.

'I know who you are. Wolfe's puppies. Word was you'd be trouble.' He looked beyond them at the blaze of fire behind the statue. 'Word was wrong. That was well done.'

'Brightwell's a better shot than most,' Glain said.

'Not bad,' Troll agreed. He glanced over Jess's shoulder and frowned just a bit. 'Seems you've made a new friend.'

Jess turned.

The Roman lion, standing taller than his head while on all

four paws, was *right behind him*, staring at him with unholy red eyes. It lowered its bronze-maned head and seemed to *smell* him, and a low rumble of a growl rattled deep inside the thing.

'Jess?' Glain asked, and took a step backward. 'Step away. Slowly.'

When he tried, the lion took a step forward.

'What the hell did you do to them?' Troll asked from behind him. Their squad leader sounded unnerved. Jess didn't blame him. He didn't dare look away from the lion's set metallic face, from the sickening red eyes. 'Wathen! Get out of the way if it's malfunctioning!'

She didn't want to go, Jess realised; she was standing next to him even though every instinct told her to retreat. 'Get away,' he told her. 'This is my trouble. *Move!*'

She backed away and down five steps to join their squad leader. *If I follow them, I put them in danger*, he thought, though it took everything he had not to seek the comfort of a group. Every cell of his body remembered running from the London lions outside of St Paul's. Those had a stone look to them, more muscular and brutal; these Roman lions had a leaner, sleeker build, and a bronze gleam that made their manes shimmer in the sun. Beautiful . . . and deadly.

I could turn it off. If the switch is in the same place.

He desperately didn't want to have to try.

'More coming up!' called someone from below, and Jess risked a glance to see that the pride of lions that had been down in the square was returning to the steps, flowing up in leaps and bounds past the other soldiers.

Coming towards him. Surrounding him.

This is it, he thought. *This is how I die.* Somehow that felt like a fate he'd always known was coming.

The lion facing him deepened its low, rumbling growl, and he felt rather than saw the others of the pride moving in around him. He heard Glain shouting something, but she was somewhere outside the closing circle. Jess felt the hot burn of air from the lion's nostrils as it moved forward and nudged his chest.

It wanted him to run. *Of course.* If he reacted, if he ran, then there'd be an excuse for the slaughter. *They were on high alert during the Burner attack. Unfortunate miscalculation; if only the recruit hadn't lost his nerve . . .*

This was the Artifex's doing, just like the Egyptian gods outside the High Commander's office. Jess realised in a blinding flash, as if a bottle of Greek Fire had been dropped on his brain, that if he ran, it would all be over.

And the Artifex wanted him to panic.

He leant down and stared into the lion's savage eyes and said, 'Come on, then, if you're coming. Take a bite. But if you do, everybody will know it wasn't an accident.'

He heard Glain's shocked intake of breath and felt that hot, brassy stench of the lion's insides wash over him as the creature opened its wide jaws to display bloody teeth . . . in a yawn.

It closed its mouth, stared at Jess for another long, horrible second, and then turned and padded away to stroll restlessly up and down the steps.

Guarding the building as if nothing had happened.

Jess straightened. He didn't say anything because, in truth, he wasn't sure he could at the moment. Better to look strong and silent than have his voice go as unsteady as his legs.

Troll stared at him as if he couldn't quite believe what he was seeing. 'I don't know if you're mad or lucky,' he said, 'but you've got brass guts – I'll give you that.'

Jess nodded and took up his post. One by one the other lions broke off and went about their business. When the last left him, he finally felt a sweet, cold wave of relief.

The Artifex wanted him dead, that much was certain, but he wasn't quite ready to make it a public execution. Not yet. He needed Jess to give him some excuse, however minor, to explain away the behaviour of the automata. Today would have been a fine one, in the chaos of the Burners, and Jess knew if he'd made the wrong move, he'd be another stain to clean up on the steps tonight.

Rome is a trap. It was too neat, too convenient, that suddenly they'd been dispatched here just after finding the information about the secret prison. The Artifex must have known their plans, or at least strongly suspected them. Khalila and Dario had gone missing. Maybe already locked away.

Disposing of Glain, Jess, and Santi would just be a sensible precaution. Get rid of the fighters; keep the Scholars out of the group who – in the Artifex's counting, maybe – could be controlled and used. It made a sickening kind of sense.

Below, Medica attendants came to claim the bodies, and a squad of firefighters put out the Greek Fire blaze. People began to filter back into the Forum in ones and twos, and then suddenly it was full again, as if nothing had happened at all. Only the blackened chemical stains on the stones behind Jupiter and the bloodstains on those near Mercury showed anything at all had interrupted a normal day.

Troll stopped next to him and scanned the people below with distant, cold eyes. 'Seems useless, doesn't it?' he asked. 'They put us out here, and the Burners take their shot at us, and they die.'

'It's a waste on both sides,' Jess said. 'But we can't let them win. They want to destroy the Library.'

He knew that wasn't strictly true; he'd been among the Burners once, had spoken to a local leader. They wanted the Library to change, just as Jess did . . . but their tactics were unacceptably violent.

Troll shifted his weight just a little. 'Any idea why the lions hate you so much?'

'No.'

'Hmm.' Troll surely didn't believe it for a moment. 'You know I have to report it. Even if I didn't, there's another squad leader who will. They might pull you out and try to find out what alerts them to you.'

Troll seemed to be fishing for something, and Jess didn't like it. He turned and looked at the young man directly to say, 'I'm not a Burner, if you're thinking it.' *But I knew some.* That was a secret the Artifex held in reserve, too. Guillaume, his classmate, had come from a Burner family; his bereaved father had taken Jess prisoner in France. If the Artifex wanted to make it seem Jess had become an agent, it would be child's play to make that appear reasonable. 'No offence, sir, but why do you care? I'm a one-day-in recruit. You should shed me and get someone else, according to any kind of logic.'

'Not that simple,' Troll said. 'Believe me, I wish it was.'

He moved off, stopping to check each of his squad members like any good commander. Jess didn't know what to make of him. Or any of this.

He was still considering the ramifications of it when he realised sometime in the chaos of the Burner attack, his Codex had received a new message.

It was gibberish. He frowned at the text, and then a second later realised he knew this code. It was his own family's highly secure emergency code, used only for the most urgent information. He'd memorised the keys to it when he'd been just a boy.

It read, *Your friend lives in the city of seven hills.* There was no signature, but one hieroglyphic bird sketched at the end of the code string. Not part of his family's code at all, and it reminded him of the engraving on the ring that Anit, Red Ibrahim's daughter, wore on a chain around her neck – the ring of one of her brothers.

The message was from her. His free gift of the information about the automata had done some good after all, because this was confirmation, at long last, that Thomas was alive.

And here, beneath Jess's feet, in Rome.

EPHEMERA

From a speech by a masked Burner leader, given in the territory of America, 1789. Held strictly in the Black Archives.

You hesitate now to lift your hands and weapons against your oppressors? We have the eyes of nations upon us, all eager to see us break these chains and rise, stand firm, be free of this dire and smothering control that has, year by year, been laid upon us.

We have been told that paper in a binding, ink on a page, is worth more than the life of any man, woman, or child. We have been pressed into the service of this false idol we call Knowledge for far too long; we have forgotten how to be free of it, how to think for ourselves and believe we, in ourselves, are worth the breath we take, the land we walk.

I say it openly and plainly: the Library is a cruel and evil oppressor. For long have we pretended it is not so.

It is time, it is time, it is long past time to rise and take knowledge in our own hands, rather than have it dripped out in cautious doses by an institution long ago rendered moot and lame, cowering behind a wall of power.

We will prevail.

Rise! Though we die, though our stories are lost and never placed on the shelves of the Great Library, though we lose our lives and our very nation, we will never give up one great truth: a life is worth more than a book.

So be it, whatever may come.

CHAPTER NINE

Santi's lieutenant reappeared and called in Jess's squad just as darkness took hold, though the Forum continued a brisk trade under the light of lamps. He was a bit sorry. Rome was just as lovely at night, with the glow of illuminated marble and household lights glittering from windows.

Though leaving the lions behind was a relief.

For the first time, Jess entered the Basilica Julia. They came in on the private side of it, away from the public Serapeum, and as they were led to the area where they were to eat and rest, Jess tried to place the corridor that Wolfe had described during his Mesmer session. *Has to be here*, he thought. *Wolfe could see the Forum from windows as he passed.* But instead of windows, they were led along a hallway that held alcoves and Roman statues. The way had to be hidden, he realised. Somewhere, behind one of these statues, there would be an entrance to a concealed hallway. Go left, it would take you to the Translation Chamber. Right, and a sentry automaton and a prison door.

He was so preoccupied with imagining it that it came as a shock when they suddenly arrived in the Basilica Julia's common hall.

It was teeming with people – Scholars, assistants, librarians.

The addition of a Santi's advance guard packed the place to bursting, but as the lieutenant led them towards the back corner, he saw it had been cleared for them. Several long dining tables and a private alcove. He expected to see Santi and his officers inside, but it was occupied by an old, white-haired man with pale European skin, arrayed in the very finest of Scholar robes and a purple sash to show his importance.

The Artifex Magnus.

Jess went cold inside for an instant, seeing him; the last time he'd laid eyes on the man, he'd been hearing him talk about Thomas's death. *The red right hand of the Archivist.* The old man, seated in a comfortable chair, conversed with two Scholars he kept standing, and, as Jess watched, one of them – a young Indian woman – bowed respect and moved away. She seemed thrilled to have been in his presence, and as she joined a table of others, he saw how the others admired her.

As if she'd accomplished something noteworthy.

That made Jess want to vomit. It was all show. The Artifex was a cruel, power-hungry man who thought nothing of breaking and destroying anyone who threatened his power. But these poor innocents saw him as a mentor, a sponsor, a man of great scholarship.

Something to which they should aspire.

The Artifex looked up as the last Scholar left his presence, and his sharp gaze moved around the room, snagged on Jess, and stopped. He blinked slowly, then turned his attention to a cup an assistant delivered, as if Jess didn't matter at all. Which, Jess thought, he likely didn't. But the Artifex had recognised him. No doubt of that.

Jess found a seat with some of his Blue Squad mates, and they ate with typical High Garda speed. Even so, he'd got only a few bites before he felt a hand press down on his shoulder.

It was the squad leader, Troll. 'Brightwell,' he said. 'With me.'

'Sir?' Jess stood up.

'The Artifex wants a report. I want you with me.'

Troll turned and led the way across the room. Jess caught sight of Captain Santi in the room; he sat at a table near one of the exterior walls and gave Jess and Troll a look as they passed that Jess couldn't read at all.

The noisy room fell away. It seemed as if the Artifex sat in a bubble of silence, far from the others, though it wasn't far at all, and then Jess was standing just a few feet away from him, from the man who'd coldly engineered the ruin of Scholar Wolfe, killed who knew how many, sent his best friend to a prison. And for what?

Power.

The Artifex's bright blue eyes fixed on him.

Jess wanted to curl his hands into fists and beat the smile off of him, but he forced himself to stay still as Troll said, 'Artifex, sir, you asked for a report on the Burner encounter outside. I'm pleased to say that we had no Library casualties, and no apparent civilian involvement in our response. Nine Burners died. Their information is being retrieved and forwarded to your Codex.' He turned towards Jess. 'Brightwell is a new addition to our squad, and was the one to alert us to the Burner attack on our flank. He saved many lives today.'

It dawned on Jess that the Artifex hadn't requested his presence; his squad leader was trying to *do him a favour*. Troll had no idea how wrong that was.

The Artifex's cold gaze fixed on Jess, and that smile deepened. It looked real enough. 'Well done, Squad Leader. You continue to show great promise, by all reports. I'm sure you will rise high inside the ranks. Captain Santi has an eye for talent.' There was a slight change in his voice as he said Santi's name, as if he couldn't quite keep the distaste at bay. 'Brightwell, Brightwell . . . Ah yes. You studied under Scholar Wolfe, did you not?'

'Yes, sir.' Jess had to force that out. His teeth ground together hard enough to hurt. *As if you don't remember, you bastard.* 'I was in his most recent class. The one you sent to the battle of Oxford.'

No reaction from the old man. None. Even his smile stayed warm. 'Ah yes, of course. Exemplary work, though the challenges were far beyond what we thought you'd face when we dispatched you there. Your class has proven quite exceptional.'

'Yes, sir,' he said. 'Those of us who survived.' If the Artifex read that as a challenge, so be it. 'You may want to have a look at the automata outside, sir. They might be malfunctioning. Seems like they almost attacked me. By accident, of course.'

'How unusual,' the Artifex replied blandly. 'I'll have my staff look into it. We certainly wouldn't want any accidents.'

'Sir.' Jess nodded slightly, which was all the respect he could stomach showing the man. He didn't intend to push his luck any further. But then the Artifex leant forward in his chair, and there was a cold fire in his eyes that made Jess's stomach tighten.

'Have you said hello to my new assistants?' he asked. 'They asked to be added to my research staff some time ago, and, of course, I could not say no to such excellent candidates once I realised their worth.' There was a vicious humour in the Artifex's eyes that was meant only for Jess. 'Friends of yours, I think.'

For an instant, Jess couldn't think what he was talking about. Not Wolfe, surely, and Santi was here in his capacity as High Garda captain. *He's insane*, Jess thought, and then he realised, as the Artifex gestured somewhere behind him, what the old man meant.

Jess turned, and Khalila Seif and Dario Santiago stood up from the table where they'd been sitting nearby. He hadn't seen them there; he hadn't been *looking* for them. Khalila gave him a tentative smile, but there was fear in her eyes. Dario – more handsome and well-dressed than ever – stepped forward and offered Jess his hand. 'Brightwell,' he said. 'Still just a recruit, I see. Nice to see you continue to keep to your natural level.' It was just the kind of insult Dario had always given him, but there was a warning flash in Dario's eyes and his handshake felt painfully firm. 'Maybe I'll request you as a special guard detail when I go shopping.'

Even for Dario, that was laying it on thick, no doubt for the benefit of the Artifex. He watched them like a vulture from the comfort of his overstuffed chair.

'As you wish, Scholar Santiago. I'll try not to accidentally shoot you.'

'Only on purpose, eh? You haven't changed, scrubber. I suppose that will do for a fond reunion. I have work to do. Scholar Seif?' Dario gestured to the table where they'd been working and took his seat with a thump. He made a fine show of ignoring Jess altogether.

Khalila walked towards him. 'It's good to see you, Jess. You're well?'

'I am. You?'

'Very well. I . . . had no idea you'd be here.'

'I could say the same of you,' Jess said, and what he really wanted to ask was, *Was it your choice?* But he couldn't. And, besides, he knew.

'The work being done here in the Basilica is truly exciting,'

Khalila said. 'Dario is studying the very pillars of history, you know. It is a field that has always interested me as well.'

Everything interested Khalila, which was one of the lovely things about her. 'I'm glad you find it rewarding.'

'Oh, I do. The Basilica is amazing, isn't it? So much history. Rome's roots go deep.'

'The feet of its mouldy old gods may go deep, but I still prefer Alexandria,' Dario said, without looking up. 'Rome's too damp for me, and too chilly this time of year. Like living in a tunnel. Khalila, we have work to do. I'm sure Jess needs to . . . patrol. Clean his gun. Something equally important.'

Khalila turned on him to give him a sharp look. 'Dario. He's our friend.'

'He's High Garda. Not our level, dear lady, if he ever was,' Dario replied. 'Let the scrubber be about his business. You're under no obligation to be nice.'

Troll suddenly stepped up to Jess's side, then moved past him to lean over Dario's shoulder. 'Did you have something to say about your feelings towards the High Garda, Scholar?'

Dario looked up, and his natural arrogance came out in a smirk that Jess wanted to punch. 'The High Garda has its place,' he said, and looked pointedly at Troll's boots. 'That place is not here, blocking my light.'

'Perhaps you should allow my assistants to proceed with their tasks,' the Artifex said, and sat back. He picked up his coffee once more. 'You're dismissed, both of you. Thank you for your service.'

Troll snapped a salute that wasn't at all necessary – the Artifex wasn't generally entitled to salutes – and strode away. Jess followed, minus the honour; he wasn't about to give the man more credit than he was due, even if it was interpreted as an insult.

'Unbelievable,' Troll said. 'Did you hear that? "*Thank you for your service*" – as if he cared. He didn't even reprimand that arrogant puppy Scholar. You came through postulant class with Santiago? Impressive. I'd have thrown the smug bastard off a bridge halfway through the first day.'

'I'd have helped,' Jess said. 'He's smart, though. Worse, he's clever.'

'The other one seemed nice enough.'

'Khalila Seif is the smartest person in this room.'

'A good friend to have, then. Not to mention attractive,' Troll said. 'You wouldn't mind if I struck up a conversation?'

'I wouldn't. Dario might.'

'I was afraid of that. Too bad. Killing him would wipe out my good conduct today.'

'Don't hold back on my account,' Jess said, but his mind was elsewhere. That display from Santiago had been classic, but it had also been out of place; the young Spaniard hadn't given him that particularly sour reception since their first days with Wolfe. They weren't exactly the best of friends, but they weren't enemies. Or, at least, they hadn't been when last they'd spoken.

Either something had changed for Dario or he was trying to tell Jess something. Dario and Khalila, working together. *Had they planned to be here?* No, surely not, or Khalila would have found time to warn him. The Artifex made it sound as if they'd asked to be added to his staff, but somehow, Jess doubted that; they'd applied, certainly, but he'd heard nothing of either being accepted. They'd been given no choice, and no time to tell anyone.

Rome's roots go so deep, Khalila had said, and veiled it in a cloud of compliments. Dario had added his own clues: *The feet of its mouldy old gods.* And *tunnel.*

Maybe, just maybe, they were trying to tell him they'd found something. Another way into the prison.

Jess sat down at the squad's crowded table, but he hardly saw their faces or heard the chatter. His thoughts were far away, locked on possibilities. On an insane and desperate possibility.

We're all here now except for Wolfe and Morgan, he thought. Thomas's rescue was almost within their reach. If Khalila and Dario really had discovered another way in, that was all they needed – an advantage. Get Thomas, get out, disappear.

Glain was staring at him from across the table, clearly worried. She waited for a few moments, smiling and talking to others, and then moved to a seat next to him when one became vacant. She bent close and said, 'I saw. Khalila and Dario.'

'I think they may have information that can help with Thomas—'

'Jess. We're all here *because he wants us here*,' Glain whispered. 'The Artifex can't touch Wolfe directly because of his mother, but us? Getting rid of us will isolate Wolfe. Destroy him.'

She was right. He'd been looking down the wrong end of the telescope.

This wasn't a chance for them to rescue a friend.

It was a threat to kill them all.

The rest of Santi's company arrived by ship the next morning. As early arrivals, Blue Squad got their pick of spots in the barracks built on the secured side of the basilica – which was, Jess realised, far larger than he'd ever imagined. An enormous building on a truly monumental scale, though only two storeys in height. It took nearly an hour to walk from one end to the other, and that was at a brisk pace. A solid two hours, then, to travel both floors end to end.

Not even Egypt was built on such a scale.

Most of the Library's side of the basilica was a warren of offices and laboratories, with long, straight halls running the length of the structure. Jess began a map while he waited for the lights to dim and his fellow squad mates to fall asleep. He planned to slip away once it was quiet and the snoring started, but the comfort of the bunk and the stress of the long days before pulled him down fast.

He woke up hard at the touch of a hand on his arm and found himself reaching for a knife with the speed of the criminal he'd once been . . . But he stopped when the scent of the girl crouched next to his bunk hit him. A light cinnamon perfume with a hint of dark amber. He connected that to Khalila even before her whisper said, 'Quietly. Come.'

Jess slipped out of his bunk, pulled on a pair of uniform trousers and a loose black shirt, slipped his boots on without bothering to tie them, and followed the drifting sweep of her dress through the shadows to the hallway. She hardly made a sound, and for a strong moment he wondered if he was wrong; maybe this wasn't Khalila. Maybe it was a vengeful Roman ghost whispering down the hallway, leading him to some terrible death.

She looked back at him with an impatient raise of her eyebrows, and he had to grin. Not a ghost. *Though a terrible death is still on the table*, some dour part of him said. He tried to ignore it.

Khalila led him down the hall to a closed door, which she opened with a key. It led to a small, enclosed atrium, open to the night sky, crowded with clipped hedges and a spreading olive tree. In the centre of the tiny garden, a graceful statue of a winged woman balanced on one foot with her drapes flowing in an invisible wind, and a hand holding up a laurel wreath –

Victoria, the Roman goddess of victory. Not an automaton, thankfully.

In the shadow of Victoria sat Dario, Captain Santi, and Glain. *A pitifully small crew*, Jess thought, *to go to war with the Library.*

'I'm sorry about earlier,' Khalila said, and gave Jess a quick embrace. 'We had to be careful.'

'Of course you did.' He nodded to Dario. 'I'd say it was an impressive display of arrogance you put on, but—'

Dario laughed, stood, and gave him an embrace as well – a quick one, with a heavy slap on his back that stung hard enough to remove any sentimentality from it. 'But it comes naturally, of course.'

'Did the Archivist force you to come, or was it your own idea to ride along?'

Dario and Khalila exchanged a quick look, and she said softly, 'Something of both, I'm afraid. We did apply to be on his staff, you remember. But he rejected us as applicants.'

'Until yesterday,' Dario added. 'When suddenly our presence was not just desired, but required.'

'He means to kill us here,' Glain said. 'That's why he brought us all. Death, or we join Thomas in the cells under here. Why else would he do this?'

Santi, Jess noticed, hadn't spoken. His head was bowed, as if he were lost in thought. 'Captain?' Jess asked. 'Do you agree?'

'I think he means this as a show of strength,' he said. 'And as intimidation. I don't think he'd quite dare to make all of us vanish at once.'

'He couldn't make *you* disappear. You're too prominent.'

'You think too small, Jess. High Garda soldiers die in combat. A nicely staged Burner attack, some conveniently destroyed bodies, and no one but Christopher will ever doubt the story.'

His hands, which had been resting on the bench on either side of him, clenched the lip of the marble and tightened, until his knuckles were almost the same pale shade. 'We're hostages for Wolfe's good behaviour, at best. And through him, his mother's. I don't think this is so much about us or him as it is a power struggle between those two.'

Wolfe's mother, the Obscurist Magnus, was a formidable woman, but trapped by her own power. Her influence didn't extend to freeing herself or those locked away with her. At the same time, the Obscurists had a fragile hold over the Library; without them, the essential functions – the Codex, the Blanks, even the automata – ceased to operate properly.

The Artifex *would* use Wolfe to keep her in check – and the rest of them as leverage against Wolfe.

'I suppose you were assigned the honour of escorting the Artifex at the last minute, too,' Khalila said to Santi. He nodded. 'I'm sorry. I know it's difficult for you.'

'I've defended Scholars I loved and Scholars I hated. Just part of the job,' he said. 'I defend an idea, not an individual.'

'None of that matters now,' Dario said. 'The Artifex sees us as chess pieces he can move as he wishes, and, eventually, he'll knock us off the board one by one, if not all at once. Are we just waiting to be killed?'

Santi said nothing. Did nothing. Jess stayed quiet as he watched him; he could see the man thinking, weighing, calculating odds and tactics. This was Santi's specialty, the art of war. Surprise and defence.

'No,' he finally said. 'We can't wait. Dario's correct. We're in a position of great weakness – away from home, easily disposed of. I think bringing us here was a demonstration of his power. He can't know we've found out anything.'

'We haven't,' Khalila murmured. 'Not for certain.'

'We have,' Jess said. He took a deep breath and told them about the information he'd received from Anit. 'Thomas is here. He is definitely here. Now.'

'Do you trust her?' Khalila asked.

'She wouldn't have any reason to betray me,' Jess said. 'Our families are old trading partners. Throw me to the lions, and she has the Brightwell clan to deal with after. Her father wouldn't want that.'

Santi nodded slowly. He looked up at them, and the anger in his face was chilling. 'Then we can't wait. We must get Thomas and get out of here. I'll send word to Christopher to join us, and we'll have to go into hiding, immediately. Jess? Can you arrange that with your family?'

Leave the Library. He saw Khalila and Dario exchange looks. They'd known this had to be coming, but it was all happening – and Jess surely felt it, too – so fast. 'Not Khalila,' Dario said. 'Surely no one would suspect her of anything. She could go back afterwards . . .'

Khalila cut him off. 'Dario. You don't decide on my behalf. I love the Library. I grew up believing I would spend my life serving it. But that ideal, the one they made us believe, it *doesn't exist.* I would rather spend my life fighting to change it. I can't continue to pretend to be loyal to it, not if all of you are gone!'

'Maybe that Library, the one we all believed in, maybe that could exist after all,' Jess said. 'It's not the *idea* that's bad; it's thousands of years of bad decisions and desperation. We could change that, but we can't do it from Alexandria.' He swallowed hard and glanced at Santi before he took the last step. The last risk. 'The reason Thomas was taken was that he invented a machine to cheaply and easily reproduce books. If we can get him, if we can build it and start distributing private books, it will change everything.'

Glain, Khalila, and Dario all looked blank. 'I can call up any book I like from the Codex,' Dario said. 'What use is something to make them, except to benefit smugglers like, well, like you, who can sell them to hoarders?'

'Sounds like a Burner invention,' Glain added, frowning.

'It isn't. And you think the Codex is your doorway into the Library? It's a little box they hand you – a curated, careful selection. They tell you what you can read. The Library shows you a fraction of what they have – trust me, I've seen tens of thousands of books go through my family's hands that never appeared on the Codex and never will. If we believe in the existence of the Black Archives, then we must believe that the Library hides what they think is dangerous – and it's old and conservative, and it believes *anything* can be misused.'

Khalila stared at him, but her mind was flying; he could almost see the thoughts and connections colliding. 'That explains a lot,' she said. 'There are holes in the progress being made, the science, if you look hard enough. And I have been gently warned away from certain questions. It explains everything if that research disappears into the Black Archives.'

'That's why Thomas is so dangerous. His invention inks print on paper, using precut letters. No alchemy, no Obscurists. It prints an entire page at a time. *You can make your own books* and no one – especially not the Library censors – can stop you from making more, spreading ideas, changing minds.'

He watched them think through that, and was impressed, again, by how quick Khalila was to grasp the implications. Pallor settled over her face. 'It would destroy the Library's power,' she said. 'If everyone could print and keep their own . . .'

'Then the Library can't choose what we learn, can't decide which science can and can't be pursued, and can't place books above human lives, because books *wouldn't be irreplaceable*,' he said. 'Books could be reproduced in the hundreds of copies. Even in the *thousands*. Everyone could have them. It changes *everything* about what they do, from that one simple idea.'

She looked sick. 'But, Jess . . . I don't know what the world looks like once that's done. Do you?'

'No,' he admitted. 'But if the Library overcomes its fears and uses that invention *first*, it can still be a force for good. It's been fighting the Burners for centuries, but Burners could be silenced simply by giving them what they want – the chance to freely own books and removing criminal penalties. Thomas's press allows for that. It sets the Obscurists free from the Iron Tower, too; they would go back to being Scholars, not slaves, because the whole basis of the Library wouldn't rest on them. The world . . . The world might be better in so many ways. *If* the Library agrees to change. But it won't, if the Archivist has anything to say about it.'

'This is . . . Jess, this doesn't just challenge the Library. It changes the entire world. What gives *us* the right to make that choice?' Dario asked.

'Nothing,' Jess admitted. 'Except someone has to. The Library's leaders made the choice for us again and again and again. It's time someone else had a try.'

Santi had watched the discussion silently, with bleak, calm eyes. Finally, he said, 'I don't think less of any of you if you want to take your chances with the Artifex. He's a powerful man, and behind him stands the Archivist, who makes the Artifex look as friendly as a pet. If you decide to rescue Thomas, if you even *help* rescue him, you forfeit everything you've worked towards. I won't lie about that. They will do anything to keep this invention secret. They have already killed, and will kill again.'

'I'm in,' Glain said. 'I'm a fighter at heart. I'll fight for what the Library should be.'

'It's the only logical way the Library itself can survive,' Khalila nodded. 'I value the future. That means I must do it or live a lie. Dario?'

He looked sorely tempted to back away, but the young man sighed, shook his head, and said, 'All right. But if you get me killed, I'll never let any of you rest. My ghost will be very persistent.'

Jess looked at Santi. 'You know where I stand. And yes. My family can hide us.' He didn't know that, but he knew that he would make it happen somehow. No matter what it cost him. His father was cold, but he was not completely cruel. *Promise him anything, anything at all. Promise him Thomas's press. Just get him on our side.*

'This is all well and good, but we still don't know how to get to Thomas,' Glain said. Khalila, in answer, dug in a satchel that she wore over her shoulder and pulled out loose sheets of paper that she passed to Glain, Jess, and Santi.

'I may not be able to get you in, but I can help with the exit from the prison. You remember what we said to you before?'

'Something about the old gods having deep roots in Rome?'

She moved next to Jess and tapped a spot on the drawing. It was a carefully inked diagram of the Forum, and each of the buildings and statues within the precincts. 'Here,' she said, and pointed. 'Below Jupiter's throne—'

'These are ancient tunnels,' Santi said, and looked up. 'How did you find this?'

Khalila nodded at Dario with a little smile. He raised his eyebrows. 'I didn't,' he said. 'It wasn't me. It was Scholar Prakesh; she left the information for me before she was killed. Both the records and the tunnels are ancient and very obscure, dating from early Roman religious practices. Unused for a thousand years, at least, but one thing about the Romans—'

'They built things to last,' Santi finished. 'You know how to access them?'

'I found references. I think I could figure it out.' Dario grinned humourlessly at Jess. 'Or our resident criminal could. The tunnels are a warren below, but from all the best research I could find, they connect to a sewer that is just below the prison. Not a working sewer, mind you – I'm not *that* dedicated. Its position on the Forum gives us a chance to melt into a crowd.'

This was, Jess thought, a fair and interesting idea, but he put little faith in millennia-old records without a firsthand scouting expedition. That might be more difficult, since anyone tinkering with an ancient statue of a god in the middle of the Forum might be noticed.

They wouldn't notice at night, he thought. *And not if I'm wearing a High Garda uniform. If I'm seen, I could just say that I noticed suspicious activity and went to check it.*

'The prison itself has human guards, and three automata on patrol within,' Santi said. 'Sphinxes and a Spartan. I'm not worried about the Garda. The automata . . .'

The automata were another matter altogether, and they all knew it. Glain had seen the ones surrounding Jess on the steps. They were already alert to him, ready to pounce in an instant. One wrong move and they would all be dead.

'We won't solve that tonight. We've already been out too long,' Santi said. 'Go back before someone discovers you're missing. Especially you two.' He nodded at Dario and Khalila.

Dario laughed. 'They won't worry. I made sure they knew I wanted to show Scholar Seif the beauties of Rome in the moonlight.'

'Dario,' Khalila said, 'tells everyone he's trying to seduce me. It does make a very good cover story.'

'Not that it's working,' he said gloomily. 'The best I've managed is a kiss. Not even a long one.'

'It was long enough.'

'For what?'

'For me to tell if you knew what you were doing.'

'You see how she treats me?' Dario said to Jess. 'I don't know why I bother.'

'Then you're even more of an idiot than I imagined,' Jess said. 'Be careful. Both of you. This isn't a game.'

'Spoken like someone who always loses when it is,' Dario said. 'Cheer up, English. We're survivors.'

Jess wished he hadn't said it. It sounded like a bad omen.

Going back to bed was impossible now. He told Glain what he planned to do – she argued, of course – and exited silently down the hall and through a secured door that led out into the public space of the Basilica Julia: the daughter library, the Serapeum.

Like all similar institutions, it never closed, but just now it was utterly empty of visitors. It was flanked on all sides by steady rows of tall white columns and shelves upon shelves of Blanks. At regular intervals around the floor stood marble podiums, upon which large volumes of the Codex waited.

Nothing in the Codex will help me with automata, Jess thought. *There might be other books, restricted from public view, that would hold hints and pieces of a key.* He'd need a Scholar like Khalila to gain access. Being just a copper-banded High Garda had its disadvantages.

He ran his fingers over the smooth leather spine of a book. It was more of a talisman than a comfort; he just needed to remind himself of why the Library was so important. Books had become a symbol of trust and libraries places of peace and stability. In all the chaos of the world that counted people as different levels of worthy, the Library served all equally. All genders, races, levels of ability. It was the one place they could all be safe.

It was a fragile idea, and the safety was a fiction; the existence of the Burners proved that. Armies didn't always obey the accords. Kingdoms fell. But the *ideal* was worth preserving.

I don't want to bring an end to this, Jess thought, and was suddenly afraid that was exactly what he'd be doing if they succeeded.

But there wasn't much choice. Not if Thomas was to be free.

Jess moved out through the outer Serapeum doors to the moonlight-washed steps.

Dario was right: Rome was magical at night. The marble glittered soft as snow, and the stars above were hard and bright, set in a deeply black sky. A breeze moved down from the hills and brought with it a warm smell of dusty olive trees and sun-warmed stones. He descended quickly. The lions were clustered together near the other end of the building, the end where the Artifex would be sleeping in peace, no doubt. If the old man thought about Thomas at all, it was probably only with satisfaction that he'd stopped what he saw as the downfall of the Library.

That thought strengthened Jess as he moved through the deserted Forum, past empty temples and the shadowy forms of gods. There were no patrols out that he could see, not in this direction, but he went quickly, anyway, moving shadow to shadow, checking constantly in all directions.

Then he was at the statue of Jupiter. It towered far up, and from this foreshortened view it looked massive and monstrous. *What if it's an automaton?* The thought struck him with real unease. A colossus like this could crush buildings, destroy armies. He put a hand on the metal. It felt warm, but a natural kind of warmth, residue from the day's sun.

The foot *looked* ancient and solid, and Jess ran his hands over the pitted surface, worn by time, and realised that ancient as it was, Jupiter couldn't have been here for more than a thousand years. This Forum had been a meeting place far longer than that. *Roots run deep.* Jupiter sat *over* the entrance.

He found the opening between the statue's feet, shrouded beneath the falling golden drapes of the toga. Just enough room to squirm under into the hollow space, and send a large rat squeaking away in alarm. Set into the cobbles lay an old iron grate. Jess pried it up with his knife and carefully put it aside. The opening was hardly large enough to fit through, but he managed, and dropped into a damp, echoing darkness that smelt of mould and the faint, pungent whisper of rot.

Jess shook a chemical light to life, and the yellowish glow washed over rough stones built in a strong, arched structure only a little taller than his head. It had a shallow trough in the middle, through which ran a slow trickle of moisture. And though – as Dario had promised – these sewers were long disused, except to channel rainwater, the smell of old waste lingered. The tunnel seemed sound, though he went carefully, tossing the light ahead as he went to be sure nothing dangerous waited. The darkness was complete and claustrophobic. The weight felt like an almost physical thing against his shoulders, and he tried not to think about the old stones pressing down. *It'll collapse someday*, he thought. *But not today. Keep your nerve.* It reminded him of the old tunnels beneath Oxford, but these were far older. He found etched stones set in the walls depicting a group of toga-wearing men gathered around a bull. The tunnel angled down. He felt the strain of it in the back of his legs, and had to be careful not to slip on mould, but then it levelled again and twisted in two directions. The basilica would be to the right, but just in case, he dropped one of the portable glows at the tunnel entrance before going on.

There was no sound here except for the faint rustling of rats and insects running from the light and the trickle of water in the tunnel's centre. He passed another plaque in the left-hand wall, then another, and then, finally, the tunnel split again. One side veered right and up. The other went down.

He dropped another glow and followed the left-hand path into the dark. It seemed to be a long journey, and then, suddenly, he heard something that didn't belong here. Something up ahead, a scraping noise that sounded deliberate. A faint whirring.

He doused the glow and blinked, because an afterimage of it remained printed on his eyes. No, the glow he saw was a faint red.

Growing brighter now.

Spilling over ridges and curves that he didn't understand at first, and then suddenly, chillingly, did.

There was a lion in the tunnel.

Jess stopped. Running would be useless; even at his best speed he doubted he could outrun the stride of a Roman lion in these cramped confines. The growling rumble of the thing echoed off the bricks, and he realised that he'd stopped breathing, as if it might hide him. It wouldn't. *Stay ready. Stay calm.* Running would be death.

The lion padded towards him at a slow, inexorable pace. He backed away, moving one slow step at a time, and like a terrible dance, the lion paced him move for move, gliding forward as he retreated.

Jess stopped cold in his tracks, staring at the lion. He wasn't looking at the ferocious, crushing jaws now, or the huge paws ready to smash the life out of him. The sphinx's switch had been hidden just behind the thin beard, under the chin. The Roman lions, though a separate design, would follow the same logic. Pick a spot no one in their right mind would reach for. Either inside the mouth, or . . .

Or just underneath it, beneath the lion's bearded chin. The challenge was that it was *much* harder to reach.

He heard the low, rumbling growl grow louder and echo in a continuous, angry pulse from the tunnel walls. The lion paused, very still, only a short distance from Jess, and the red illumination of its eyes turned everything bloody. It must have been confused, Jess realised; his High Garda uniform, the band he wore on his wrist must have made it pause and wait to see what he'd do. Any casual intruder would have already been dead.

That didn't mean the lion wouldn't decide at any moment that High Garda or not, Library band or not, he needed to die. *Don't hesitate. Just keep moving.*

Jess slowly raised his right hand. His fingers were trembling and twitching with the need *not to go near this thing*, but he controlled that and his natural desire to run for his life. His fingertips touched warm, slightly rough metal: the underside of the lion's jaw. A jaw that could open at any instant and bite off his entire arm. A mouth that held razor-sharp teeth longer than his fingers and were so much more terrifying than the sphinx he'd faced in Alexandria. *This is a bad idea. So very bad.*

Jess's sweating, shaking fingers slid along the creature's

jawline. The lion's eyes sparked as red as blood, and a rumble built inside. The jaws parted, an instant away from clamping onto his arm and ripping it from his body in a spray of blood and torn bone.

His fingers brushed a slightly depressed area in the metal. It could have been a dent, since the beast was battle-scarred, cast-off, consigned here to lonely tunnel guard. But he pushed *hard,* knowing it was his last chance, and felt something click sharply inside.

The lion didn't stop all at once. First, the rumbling died off, and then the glow faltered and flickered in its eyes. There was a ticking inside, like something very hot cooling off slowly, and then it was just . . . still.

A statue.

Jess pulled his hand back, still careful. Still wary. As the red glow died in its eyes the dark closed in and landed on him with the weight of real panic. What if he'd got it wrong? What if it was still moving in the dark and those jaws were opening? He fumbled for the glow he'd put aside and shook it back to life with so much enthusiasm, he almost dropped it.

The lion stared straight ahead, eyes dull grey now. One paw was slightly lifted and the body tensed as if ready to lunge forward, but it stood utterly motionless.

There were still sounds from inside the body – ticks, pops, scratches. A spring slowly hissing as it uncoiled. Jess's mouth was dry, and he felt giddy with relief. He tried to slow his breathing and had to stop himself from laughing aloud. After a few seconds, the exhilaration faded.

Mainly because he asked himself, *Why did they put it here? Why in this spot?* Surely it would have been a simple matter to position one right below the grate under Jupiter's feet, the better to catch an intruder before they even had a chance to discover any secrets.

If the lion had been put here, set to guard *this* spot, it meant it was important.

Jess squeezed past the bulk of the lion, moving carefully in case it should suddenly come back to life, and just beyond it lay the end of the tunnel. It emptied into a huge, rounded room lined with ancient mosaics dulled by time. But it was empty. This had once been some kind of ritual chamber, and on one wall Jess found a display of masks cast out of greenish bronze in frightening shapes.

He heard something directly overhead and looked up. *Footsteps.* They rang on metal, and as he raised the glow, he realised that there was a rounded, metal plate in the ceiling above. It looked solid and very old, and it was exactly where he would imagine a drainage grate would have gone. And who would remove a drainage grate and cover it with solid metal instead?

Someone who didn't want anyone coming or going through it.

There it is. The prison.

Jess stood for a long moment, gaze fixed on that metal barrier, and then he turned and retraced his steps past the frozen lion, up the tunnel, out from under Jupiter's robes, and back to the Serapeum.

EPHEMERA

Text of a letter from the Archivist Magnus to the Artifex Magnus, interdicted to the Black Archives by order of the Archivist.

It was a true tragedy to lose Scholar Prakesh in such a useless fashion; she was an extraordinarily bright woman. Just more proof that Wolfe's toxic influence has spread on to his students as well. Without her exposure to Santiago, no doubt she would have served the Library faithfully for the rest of her life.

We are reaching an impasse with the Obscurist Magnus as well. It might be necessary to bring her to heel one last time, by whatever means necessary. Her son might be broken, but he can still turn and bite. If you see any reason to suspect such might happen, make it clear to him that we have gathered up all those he cares for.

That should keep him in check, and, through him, his mother.

If not . . . well. You know my thoughts.

CHAPTER TEN

He arrived back just as his fellow soldiers were starting to wake, and except for the fact that he was already wearing his uniform, no one gave him a second look. He sat on his bunk and ate a pressed fruit from his pack, and wondered how to tell the others what he'd found. Too many ears. They needed privacy.

Glain could see he had news. She was clever enough not to ask, but he saw the level stare and the tilt of her head. *What is she seeing?* He had no idea. He was usually better at hiding in plain sight than that. Maybe it was the flush of triumph he couldn't quite shake. He just hoped that turning off the sentry lion hadn't triggered some alarms that would make exiting that way harder.

'You look happy,' she said to him, and took half his ration bar.

'Help yourself,' he said mildly. 'It's going to be a long day.'

She gave him a narrow look, which he answered with a grin, and then it was too late to play question games, as their squad leader called them to order. Jess fell into line beside Glain. Squad Leader Rollison walked down the line and fixed them each with a direct yet impersonal stare.

'Good work yesterday,' he said. 'So said the Artifex himself.

We don't get to earn that praise again, because today, the Artifex leaves the Basilica and visits the Roman Senate, and we're staying here. The rest of our century arrived overnight and will be guarding the route and the Senate. Our job today is to keep the Basilica safe, and, to that end, we'll be conducting roving patrols. Those of you who don't like sunshine, Burners, or those damned Roman lions, here's some happy news for you: we'll be staying inside. Those who were hoping for more glory today – and I mean you, Brightwell – you'll have to live with disappointment.'

'Yes, sir,' Jess said. 'I'll try to contain myself, sir.'

Lucky. Too lucky. He sensed some hand behind yet another windfall of good fortune, but he didn't know where to look. Could be the Artifex, setting him – setting all of them – up for a disaster. Or, rather more unlikely, it could be a better angel looking out for them.

'Routes,' Troll said, and all of them got out their Codexes. He scribbled down a map and labelled their names on hallways, and it appeared in rapid, neat strokes on the page in Jess's Codex assigned for orders. Jess had been paired with Glain, which seemed natural enough; Troll would have recognised they worked well together.

The hall they'd been given to patrol ran the length of the first floor on the Forum side of the building. Jess remembered the maps he sketched out last night and the one that he'd drawn from Wolfe's Mesmer session, and stacked them one atop the other in his mind to see the differences.

Wolfe's secret hall, the one that led from a concealed inner portal to the door that led down to the prisons, was on the other side of the wall from where they'd been assigned. Convenient, that. Too damned convenient. His feeling that they'd *just so happened* to be assigned here today and that they'd *just so happened* to be given a patrol so near to the secret prison entrance . . . it raised an itch on the back of his neck.

Better angels, or conniving demons. Something nipped at his heels.

He silently kitted up with the armoured Library coat and his weapons, and found Glain – of course – ready before him. Rollison was checking off his squad as they left the room, and held out a hand to keep Glain and Jess back. They were the last out of the room.

Troll turned to Glain and Jess, closed his Codex, and said, 'Follow me.'

'Sir?' Glain asked, but complied. He didn't explain; just set off at a quick pace. They fell in behind him as he led the way through a maze of doors that finally ended in a blind storage area lined with shelves.

'What is this?' Glain asked, and added only as an afterthought, 'Sir.'

'It's where you wait,' he said. 'Captain Santi and the others are coming. Don't worry, I'm – I can't say I'm one of you, but I've known Captain Santi a long time. He and my father were friends back in training. After my father died, he and Wolfe made sure I had a place to live, enough to eat. I owe him this much.'

He turned to go. Glain grabbed his shoulder. 'Wait,' she said. 'Do you know what—?'

Troll brushed her hand away with a move so smooth it almost seemed effortless. 'No. I don't want to know. It's a favour for a friend, and that's where it ends. When you're done here, make your patrols.'

He left without a backward glance and shut the door.

Glain frowned after him and said, 'Do you trust him?'

'Do we have a choice?' Jess leant against the wall. 'I found the tunnel Dario talked about. It's clear all the way down. I could hear footsteps above, and they weren't from the Basilica. They had to be from inside the prison.'

'No guards?'

'There was an automaton lion,' he said. 'I took care of it.' He tried to sound offhand about it.

'You *what*?'

'Off switch,' he said. 'I told you, I did it to a sphinx the night everything went wrong with Dario.'

She thought about it and shuddered. 'That was a sphinx. I've seen the size of these lions. Not sure I'd have tried facing one down there in the dark. And you should have let me know what you were doing! If you hadn't come back . . .'

She was right, of course. He should have left word. It had been a stupid risk; that fact had finally registered with the rising of the sun, and he could have disappeared without a trace into the dark, crushed and rotting beneath the prison. Worse than that, he could have destroyed any chance they had of finding Thomas. 'Sorry.'

'Do it again and I'll kill what the automaton doesn't eat.' She meant it – or thought she did. Her Welsh lilt came out strong when she said it. He didn't have time to reply – if he'd thought of anything to say to that – because there was a noise beyond the door, and as they both turned towards that direction, it swung open.

Santi. Khalila. Dario. Santi wore his uniform and carried a full pack and weapons. Khalila had opted for a dark grey dress with her robe thrown over the top and a head scarf, and carried a pack of her own. Dario was in plain, sturdy clothes and his Scholar's robe. They all looked tense.

'Someone tried to kill Captain Santi,' Khalila blurted.

Glain, who'd been about to speak, was stunned into silence, so Jess jumped in.

'What? How?'

'Poison in the fruit in my room,' he said. 'No way of knowing who put it there, but I think we can guess.'

'The Artifex.'

'He's done toying with us, and I think he'll close his trap now . . . he deliberately left us all behind while he went off to the Senate. We're out of time.'

'But we didn't bring all our things,' Khalila said. 'Can we go back for them?'

'No. You can't. If you turn back, you stay behind. Are you staying?'

'Don't rush us,' Dario snapped. 'It's a big decision, you know, to turn our backs on our futures. Our families. Everything we've ever believed.'

'No, it isn't,' Khalila said, and took in a deep breath. 'We've been thinking about this for a long time, Dario. I thought we'd already decided where our loyalty had to lie. Mine is with them. Is yours?'

'Sweet flower . . .'

'Don't. If you want to go, just go. This isn't the time for your charm.'

Dario studied her and then slowly nodded. 'All right,' he said. 'All right. Yes. We go.'

Santi looked grim, and never more in command. 'We go. Now.'

The timing is terrible, Jess thought; he had everything he would carry for a duty patrol, but no extras. The rest of his kit was still back stowed beneath his bunk. *It will have to stay there*. He'd abandoned more things than he'd kept in his life, anyway.

'The hallway Wolfe talked about is on the other side of the far wall, the one with the statues,' Jess said. 'Probably some access. I'd guess behind the statues, through one of the alcoves.'

'According to Wolfe, there will be guards and an Obscurist on duty in the Translation Chamber on the other side of the wall; Glain and I will take care of that end. At the end of the hall, there's an automaton and a door. I have Greek Fire for the automaton . . .'

'No,' Jess said. 'I can get us past it.' Santi looked at him and frowned. Jess met his gaze and held it. 'I can, sir. We both know using Greek Fire in a confined space is risky at best.'

'All right.' Santi didn't sound convinced. 'Jess will get us past the automaton. After that, the locked door.' Jess nodded to that, too. 'And then we go down into the tunnel. There will be more automata. Three of them, according to Christopher. Two sphinxes and a Spartan. Can you disarm those as well?'

'I can get the sphinxes,' Jess said. 'I don't know about the Spartan, sir.'

'That'll have to do. There are four High Garda on duty in the prison. If I know any of them, I'm going to try to save them, but if not . . . If not, we may have to fight. If it comes to that, let me, Glain and Jess take the lead.' He turned to Jess. 'You scouted the tunnel exit that Khalila and Dario discovered,' Santi said. 'Is it clear?'

'How did you know I—?'

'I know you. Is it clear?'

'Yes.'

Santi took in a breath. 'Then we go.'

As simply as that, they were abandoning all they'd planned

for their lives, all they'd worked towards. For Santi, it meant throwing away an entire career spent gathering honour and trust within the Library. For Glain, the destruction of a dream she'd held since childhood. For Khalila, a future so bright, Jess couldn't bear to think of snuffing it out. Even Dario was giving up something priceless.

I'm the only one who has nothing much to lose, he thought. He'd already lost all the illusions that had brought him to this moment. What he had left now was just a hope that whatever came after this would prove to be better.

One by one, they nodded.

And they headed for the hallway that Jess and Glain had been assigned to patrol.

'What about Wolfe?' Jess asked. 'He's alone in Alexandria. Anything could happen to him there, especially once they know what we've done. He'll be executed.'

'No,' Santi said. 'It's taken care of. Now spread out and find the entrance.' He stepped up to the nearest statue – the one of Minerva – and felt around behind her in the alcove. Jess held back, letting his gaze move over the gods in succession . . . and settling on one in particular. Pluto. Roman god of the underworld.

He stepped up and felt behind, along the smooth plaster of the alcove. Nothing. But as he did, he braced himself on Pluto's marble arm, and it moved beneath the black toga the statue wore.

The alcove clicked open.

'Here,' Jess said. 'Come on.'

'Dario, bring up the rear. Keep watch,' Santi said. He had his weapon ready, and, Jess realised, so did Glain. Jess quickly followed their lead and waited at the opening. 'Jess, go right and see to the automaton. Glain and I go left. Dario, Khalila, stay here until we signal.'

Jess ducked through and immediately turned right. The hallway was just as Wolfe had described it in his Mesmer trance – a long, straight run with windows that overlooked the Forum. Not glass, certainly, because that would make them easy targets for vandals or Burners. These would be made of something harder and unbreakable. No use giving a desperate captive the chance to throw himself out and escape, either.

Jess heard the lion's rumbling growl before he'd taken three running steps in its direction and slowed to a fast walk. The lion wasn't waiting for him; it was pacing towards him, the cabled length of its tail twitching side to side and slamming into walls and windows. It left gouges where it hit. The creature was a big thing, the same size as the one he'd faced down in the tunnels. Seeing it coming at him in harsh daylight was chilling indeed.

You know this. You can do this. The problem was that this lion was in motion, and very probably about to break into a loping run; it didn't have the same confusion the one in the tunnel had shown, and it was *not* undecided about the situation. It had been built to respond to intruders, no matter what uniforms they wore.

Jess broke into a run again, closing the distance fast, and ten steps from it, he threw himself into a slide on the slick marble floor. The lion, confused, tried to slow, but momentum wouldn't allow it to check so quickly. Jess slid right underneath its open jaws, which hit the floor with a heavy *clang* just as his head cleared the space, and grabbed one of the thick metal legs to stop his slide. At the same time, he reached up for the depression beneath the lion's jaw, found it, and pressed as hard as he could.

He heard the roar that had been building inside the thing skew to a strange whining noise and die. The lion took another step forward and froze.

Jess pushed himself out from behind it and cut his arm on the tail when he grabbed hold to stand up; the barbed end of it, he realised, was razor sharp. Even standing still, the thing was capable of harm.

The door lay just beyond – locked, as Wolfe had said. Jess never left without his handy set of picklocks – the lessons of a devious childhood – and pulled them out of the pack and set to work as quickly as he could. He heard the sounds of fighting behind him. Santi and Glain must have met with resistance.

He'd just pushed the last tumbler in the door when Khalila dropped down beside him and said, 'How can I help?'

'You can get out of the light,' he said. 'Are they coming?'

'Yes. Dario went to help them.' She stood up and looked back over the lion's shoulder. 'How did you know how to do this?'

'What, lock picking? Comes naturally. I'm a criminal, remember?'

'I meant the lion, Jess.' She was waving now, giving urgent *hurry* signals. 'Get the door open – they're coming!'

They were. He heard the footsteps. Glain, ever the athlete, chose to throw herself under the lion, as Jess had, and slid neatly through, then rolled back to her feet and leant on the still metallic body to aim her weapon back down the hallway. She fired, and Jess recognised the sound: stunning rounds, not lethal. She didn't intend to kill her fellow High Garda soldiers, no matter what their orders might be.

Dario came next, and behind him . . . behind him came Santi, and . . . Scholar Wolfe. Wolfe, like Dario, wore Scholar's robes, and his shoulder-length hair had been tied back in a tight knot. 'Wolfe?' Jess spared a precious, astonished second to stare at him. Khalila jabbed him in the shoulder to remind him to keep working. 'How did he get here?'

'Translation,' she said. 'Santi wouldn't leave him alone in Alexandria. That would have been a death sentence. Jess, are you sure you can—?'

'Got it,' Jess said, as the last tumbler clicked and fell away. 'Is he all right to be here, do you think? Wolfe?' He couldn't shake the memory of Wolfe's swallowed screams as the Mesmer tried to calm him. Whatever was buried under that calm, Elsinore Quest had been right: it was poisonous and powerful. Must have been hard to keep it locked away.

'I don't know,' Khalila admitted, as Jess rose and pulled on the door's handle. 'I can't imagine how it would feel to . . . go down there. But it's *Wolfe*. We can't leave him behind for the Archivist, can we?'

She was right. They were all in it together and would rise or fall together. And Santi was staying close to Wolfe, only a step or two away, as if well aware of the risks.

Jess slammed the metal door back against the wall and took the lead, heading down a ramp into the dark. As his eyes adjusted, he realised there were lights, just low ones that blazed brighter as he approached – sensing his presence somehow. *There'll be three more automata*, he remembered. The Alexandrian sphinxes would be smaller than the lions, though no less dangerous. The Spartan . . .

He didn't know what to do about the Spartan.

The tunnel twisted to the left, and he looked back before he took the turn. Khalila and Glain were behind him, then Dario and Wolfe with Santi. As Jess turned the curving corner, he saw steps going down. The smooth plaster of the walls changed to old Roman stone. The lights continued to brighten around them, and Jess moved as fast as he could.

A High Garda soldier stepped out into his path, and Jess

prepared to shoot, but Santi put a hand on his shoulder. 'No,' he said. 'Sergeant Reynolds?'

The soldier lowered his weapon – not completely, just enough to ease Jess's mind a little. 'Captain Santi? Sir, you're not supposed to be here.'

'Let me pass.'

'I can't do that, sir.'

Glain shot him. It was a quick, economical movement, and the stun round dropped the man to his knees. A second put him completely down. Santi checked the man's pulse and nodded. He wasn't happy, but Glain had done the right thing. Talking would get them killed.

The second soldier who came rushing in fired. Glain shot back, but he was wearing armour, and the stunning shot had no effect.

Jess had his weapon set to full strength and fired. He put two rounds into the armour, which was enough to knock the man down and unconscious, but – he hoped – not enough to kill.

A chorus of high-pitched shrieks split the air. There was another blind corner ahead, and beyond it would be the cells . . . but the sphinxes were between them and Thomas. *Two of them. How do I stop two of them at once?* It seemed impossible now that he was here, listening to the screams coming closer.

'Khalila,' he said. 'When the sphinx comes, there's a depression underneath the jaw, behind the pharaoh's beard. You need to press it. They should hesitate, seeing you in a Scholar's robe and a gold band. I'll get the other one.'

She stared at him with wide, incredulous eyes for an instant, then nodded. No discussion, no questions. She stood beside him, ready, as the two sphinxes rounded the corner together, loping out of rhythm with each other but with the same deadly grace. The one making for Jess screamed again and bared needle teeth, but the one on Khalila's side of the hallway seemed confused. She held her hand up to show her gold band. It slowed, cocking its inhuman head.

Jess feinted to his left, and when the sphinx on his side lunged, he jammed his gun crosswise into the needle-sharp jaws. One of the paws swiped for him, and he heard Glain shout a warning even as he twisted to avoid it. He didn't dare risk a glance at Khalila. *This* sphinx wasn't going to hesitate to kill him, and he didn't dare take even a second of attention away. It moved like a snake, like something unnaturally fluid, and his sweaty fingers slipped as he tried for the switch beneath the jaw. He missed, ducked a swipe, and heard metal crunching as the sphinx bit down on the gun. He tried for the switch again and got knocked off balance by a metallic head butt hard enough to send him flying backward. A massive paw armed with razor claws raked a path through the floor where he'd been. He hit, rolled off the wall, and came back low and fast.

This time, he flung himself around with one arm over the lion's head and swung onto the beast's back. The heat coming from it at this angle felt intense even through the layers of his uniform, but he ignored that, ignored the blood dripping from fingers that had grazed sharp claws on the way up, and wrapped both arms around the thing's neck as it reared to try to throw him off. When it crashed down to four paws again, the mangled gun fell from the sharp-toothed mouth, and the sphinx's head whipped around at an impossible angle to bite.

He got to the switch, somehow, just before it sank those teeth into his neck.

As he slid down, leaving the sphinx frozen in that unnatural, twisted position, he realised that Khalila's sphinx was equally still . . . in a crouch, at her feet, like a particularly dangerous pet.

'Maybe I should let you do this from now on,' he said with a grin that felt half-mad, and she let out a laugh at least as uncontrolled. 'We've still got one soldier and a Spartan to deal with. Reinforcements will come.'

'Then we should hurry.'

That was a new voice coming from behind them, and as Jess turned, he saw Glain and Santi had beaten him to it with impressive speed. They levelled weapons at the newcomer making her way down the steps, and Santi lowered his weapon first.

Morgan.

Glain said, 'It can't be. How in Hades did you . . . ?'

Morgan smiled, but it wasn't for Glain at all. She was looking through the rest of them, straight to Jess, and the smile was for him.

'I brought what I could,' she said. 'But we have to go quickly. I disabled the Translation Chamber to keep reinforcements from coming through from Alexandria, but Captain Santi's troops will respond soon, and we don't want to have to kill anyone.'

'Morgan?' Khalila asked, and then repeated it with more force. 'Morgan!' She rushed to her and clasped her in an embrace – one that the English girl returned full force. 'I didn't think you could leave the Iron Tower!'

'That's a story for later,' Morgan said. Jess couldn't take his eyes from her. *How is she here?* The Translation Chamber, obviously, but . . . It hit him then that the collar around her neck was gone.

She was free. *Free.* Just as she'd said she'd be.

He couldn't quite believe his eyes, until she pushed past the others and wrapped her arms around him, and then he *had* to believe it – her familiar, remembered warmth, the scent of her hair, her skin. It felt right, having her in his embrace again.

Dario, of course, was the one to say, 'Not that I'm not delighted to see you, too, Morgan, but can the welcomes wait? We're on a schedule.'

He was right, of course, and Jess stepped away. Not without regrets.

Glain wasn't smiling. She was watching Morgan with cool, assessing eyes, and now she said, 'This is strangely opportune timing. I thought it was impossible to escape the Iron Tower.'

'That's what they want us to believe,' Morgan said. 'There are several ways, actually, but getting the collar off was half the battle. I've spent months searching for a way to get out and stay out. When I found it, I waited until Scholar Wolfe made his move to join you. So the timing is exact. *Not* opportune.'

'You can understand her doubts,' Dario said, which was weaselly of him, sympathising with Glain while still not agreeing. 'We haven't seen you since you were driven off by the Obscurist Magnus, apparently never to be seen again. One thing we know about the Library: it's fully capable of turning us against each other.'

'You think you can't trust me?' Morgan's face set hard and she returned Glain's stare, not Dario's. 'While you were being pampered and groomed, free to do as you liked, I was locked away. You have *no idea* where I've been.' She touched the skin at her throat: too pale, from long months of being circled by the collar. But the collar was gone. 'I left my chains back in the Tower. And I'm not going back. If you don't think you can trust me, fine – I'll go my own way. But I'm not leaving until I see all of you safely out of here.'

Jess silently moved to her side, because suddenly there *were* sides, and at the very worst time. It lasted only a second, a terrible second, because Santi snapped, 'No time for this. We trust her because we have to trust her. Now *go*.'

He moved past them, and Glain went with him. Dario and Khalila were next, with Wolfe, who was also – to Jess's slight surprise – armed. The gun blended in with his black robes.

He seemed to falter a little, as if the memories had overwhelmed him. Morgan held out her hand to him. Wolfe looked at it as if he'd never seen such a thing and walked on.

'Well,' she said, 'he's not changed at all.'

'Come on,' Jess said. 'Dario's right. There's still Thomas to find.'

'I was so worried you'd move faster than I could and I'd be too late,' she said, and her grip on his hand grew stronger. Almost painful. 'I knew you'd left Alexandria. I was afraid – afraid something terrible would happen to you.'

'To me?' He forced a smile he didn't quite feel. 'Nothing ever happens to me.'

'Oh, I remember you collapsing with a wound that almost killed you after Oxford. You don't fool me.'

'Shh.' He'd heard a scrape, and his instincts had spiked hard enough to hurt. There was a blind corner just ahead, and Wolfe was already passing the turn.

The noise had come from *behind* them.

Jess pushed Morgan ahead of him, towards Wolfe, and – though he'd sworn seconds ago he never would – let go of her hand. His shove sent her stumbling into the wall at the corner, and she turned back with a surprised expression that turned to horror, and Jess knew.

He did the only thing he could: he threw himself hard to the side, into the old stone wall, and a sharp-tipped bronze spear stabbed hard down into the floor where he'd been standing.

The Spartan automaton pulled the spear back with economical grace, turned its head, and the red eyes blazed at Jess from a distance of only an arm's length away. This was no sphinx, no lion; it was in the form of a man, muscled and lean. Upright.

It slammed its left forearm towards him, and Jess ducked. He didn't quite move fast enough, and the blow that grazed the top of his head made the world go soft and strange. Not pain, exactly, but he knew it was there somewhere, floating like a cloud that hadn't quite rained yet.

'Jess!' Morgan's scream pierced the fog like the Lighthouse's focused beam, and he scrambled out of the way as the Spartan thrust down again. The spear tore through the leg of his uniform trousers and grazed his flesh; he felt skin part, but again, no pain. The spear's tip was too sharp to hurt, like a Medica's scalpel. He was seconds from dying and he knew it. All he could do was scramble and try to estimate where an engineer, a *good* engineer like Thomas, would have placed the safety switch for this particular design. He didn't know. It looked like a man, taller and broader and faster than a man. The face under the Spartan helmet was as unmoving, uncaring as any beast. *It won't bite, at least*, he thought. The mouth was half-hidden under the helmet . . .

The helmet? No, too high up. He'd never reach it. If he tried any approach from the front, he'd be killed before he could even try a switch, if one even existed in a spot he could find.

He was going to die. Maybe he'd known that from the first moment he'd seen the Spartan automaton on the High Garda grounds. He remembered feeling a shiver of premonition about it.

His brain was racing like a river in full flood, uncontrollable in its search for some way to survive. It directed his body without conscious thought, rolling, diving, scrambling on all fours like a crab, and when the Spartan lifted one sandalled foot to crush him, he remembered something.

Something from a favourite book he'd read a dozen times as a child. *Talos, the bronze Titan who fought Jason and his men aboard the* Argo. *A metal man who could not be hurt, could not be defeated.*

Talos had been stopped by the removal of a plug at his heel, which had drained away the vital fluid that moved him. So the story went.

The engineers who'd designed the Spartan had read the same stories, dreamt the same dreams.

Jess hit the ground behind the Spartan and reached out blindly for the back of the statue's legs with both hands, sliding fingers down the unnaturally warm bronze. It twisted around, shifting position to spear him like a fish. He saw the head tilting down towards him. The spear lifting.

His hand found a slight depression in the metal of the automaton's heel on the left side, and he pressed in with his thumb and rolled aside, gasping for breath, hoping he'd not just killed himself.

It was just as well he moved, because the Spartan retained enough power to bring the spear down one last time, hard enough to pierce the stone where Jess had been lying. It would have pierced his skull just as easily. He heard the whine of the gears inside grinding to a stop, the springs unwinding, and felt a surge of weakness that nearly put him down flat again. Then he felt giddy. He'd just become the world's foremost criminal expert in stopping Library automata. That was worth something on the open market, surely.

'You're bleeding,' Morgan said, and reached down a hand. He checked the floor around him, and, yes, he was, but not badly. A rain, not a flood. He grabbed hold and let her haul him to his feet, and then hung on to her for steadiness as the hallway rocked and spun around them. 'Can you walk, Jess?'

'I can walk.' He wasn't sure, but it was something to aspire to. 'I'm all right.' He wasn't. Definitely wasn't. 'Let go.'

'No,' she said, and there was no arguing with the way she said it. 'Why is that you're always hurt when I find you? Is that my fault?'

He wanted to laugh, but the fog was clearing, and in its place pain had taken up a steady, red throb. Laughter would split his skull in two. 'We need to find Thomas.'

'I know,' Morgan said, and her strong arm around his waist helped him find his balance again. 'Come on.'

The third High Garda soldier they'd expected was down by the time Jess and Morgan arrived. Santi glanced at them, but then his gaze locked on Jess and the blood. 'Are you all right?' It was only half concern. The other half of the question had to do with the viability of their escape if he wasn't.

'I'm fine,' Jess said, though he knew he wasn't. 'I won't hold you back.'

'Stop chattering,' Wolfe said, his tone was as cold and bitter as winter. 'Jess. Locks.'

For a blank second, Jess didn't understand his order, and then he fumbled for his picklocks and moved past the men to the door of the cell.

'Jess,' said a quiet voice from beyond the bars. It sounded rough and strange, somehow familiar, and when he finally looked straight into the cell, he saw his best friend, Thomas Schreiber, sitting on the floor of the stone room. He was shackled to a metal ring in the wall. The big, young man had lost weight, which somehow made him seem larger without that comfortable layer of padding. He no longer looked as young and innocent as Jess remembered. He'd grown a beard, and his hair was a matted mess down to his shoulders. He was dressed in a plain oatmeal-coloured shirt and trousers that were much worse for wear.

Jess wrapped his hands around the bars, partly to keep himself from falling as dizziness hit him, and said, 'Got yourself in a mess, haven't you, Thomas?'

'Jess,' Thomas whispered. Even with the beard, the hair, the changes in him, his smile remained gentle and kind. His eyes had an odd shine to them, and it took Jess a moment to realise it was tears. 'They took our machine. They destroyed it.'

'Never mind. You can build another,' Jess said. His throat felt tight and his eyes burnt until he blinked his own tears away. No time for that nonsense now. 'Let's get you out of there.'

He bent to the lock, but his fingers felt clumsy and his reasoning felt suspiciously slow. *I have to do this*, he thought. *I have to get him out.*

And then Khalila tapped him on the shoulder and handed him a ring of keys. 'From the last guard,' she said.

Maybe I do have a cracked skull, he thought, and almost laughed. Three tries before he slid the key into the lock, and then the catch clicked open with a crisp sound that seemed to echo around the stones. Jess heard his friends letting out held breaths, and grinned despite the ache in his head and shoulder. He swung the door open and rushed in to kneel next to Thomas.

He had to pause, because Thomas was looking down at him, holding out his shackled hand. 'It's good to see you, Jess,' Thomas said, and his voice faltered. It sounded different now.

Tears blurred his eyes. '*Mein Gott*, I thought – I never thought you'd really come. I didn't think any of you knew. They told me . . .'

His voice faded away. Jess ignored the hand and grabbed him into a hard, fast hug. Best Thomas couldn't see his face. Then he went back to the work of freeing him from the chains.

Scholar Wolfe was still outside the bars, and Jess realised he probably couldn't bear the idea of stepping inside ever again. Wolfe said, 'They told you we were all dead, didn't they?'

Jess felt Thomas nod wearily, and blotted moisture from his eyes with the back of his sleeve as he worked the stubborn lock. Until this moment, he'd thought of Thomas in the abstract, just as he'd last seen him. Unchanged. Seeing what they'd made of him brought things home in ways imagination couldn't.

'They described it,' Thomas said. 'For every one of you. How you died. I tried not to believe it, but . . . but it's hard not to here. This becomes all you know.'

'They lie.' Wolfe's voice sounded low and silky, dark as midnight. 'It's their favourite tactic – I know it well – to break your mind and your spirit. I'm sorry it took so long to get to you.'

'If we'd tried to come earlier, the lies might well have become true,' Santi said, just as Jess clicked the last shackle open. He winced when he saw how raw Thomas's ankle was beneath.

'Can you walk?' Jess asked. Thomas, for answer, stood up. And even though Jess knew how tall his friend was, it surprised him again to see him towering over them.

'Of course,' Thomas said, and then tried to take a step and had to grab Jess for balance. 'Slowly.'

Santi's expression didn't change, but it was clear *slowly* wasn't an answer he wanted to hear in strategic terms. Their time was running out fast. 'Then let's go,' he said. 'As fast as we can.'

'Wait!' Thomas turned to look at the walls of his room, and for the first time, Jess realised they were densely covered with small, scratched drawings in Thomas's precise hand. Machines. Automata. He'd drawn what looked like one of the Roman lions, then drawn it as if it had exploded into pieces, each one shown in context with the skeletal frame. 'I need to remember these! I have to remember. I didn't have anything else to work with – they wouldn't give me any paper . . .'

'No, time, Thomas. We need to move,' Glain said. 'They're coming.' There was a note of tension in her voice that convinced Jess instantly, and he pulled Thomas towards the door. There would be no moving the young man if he really wanted to resist, but Thomas went, although reluctantly, turning to memorise his drawings. Once out of the cell, though, Thomas turned to the front, put his back against the bars, and sucked down a deep, trembling breath, as though for the first time it was dawning on him that they were here, it was not a dream, and he was *actually free.*

All of Jess's pulling wouldn't move him.

'Thomas?' He kept his voice quiet, firm, and calm. 'We can't stop here. The Garda are coming, and they will put us all in those cells. We have to go.'

'I know,' Thomas said. He closed his eyes and then opened them, and they'd taken on a blind, hard shine. 'It isn't an illusion, is it? You're here. This is real.'

'Yes. It's real.'

Thomas was silently weeping, and Jess wanted to hurt someone responsible for that. Badly.

'Keep going,' Jess called to Santi, who was taking the lead

with Glain. 'There's a round metal plate in the floor that used to be a drain. Find it and burn through. That puts us in the sewer underneath. I've marked the way once we're down there. Oh, and there's a lion. I hope it's still stopped. I took care of it last night.' Strange that it seemed the least of their worries at the moment.

'Another one?' Khalila turned, eyes wide. 'How long have you known how to do that?'

'Since the night Dario almost got me killed at Alexander's tomb,' he said. 'Ask him.'

She whipped around to do just that, but Dario held up his hand to stop her. 'Later, desert flower, for mercy's sake,' Dario said, before she could begin the interrogation. 'I know your curiosity is stronger than your sense of self-preservation, but I still don't know how he did it, by the way. I ran for my life like any sensible person.'

'*Jess* didn't run!'

'And thus proves my point.'

Wolfe turned on them in a storm of black robes and bitter, angry eyes. He was, Jess thought, all but shattering down here, in this place where he couldn't shut out the memories of his time behind these bars. 'Do you think this is a game?'

Even Dario fell silent at the vicious tone and, more than that, the way Wolfe's voice broke in the middle. He was trembling. Sweat shone hot on his face, though it was cave-cool down here. Santi – still on alert – reached back and put a hand on his arm, Wolfe dragged in a tortured breath and nodded.

'Are there others?' Jess asked Thomas. 'More prisoners here?'

'Yes,' Thomas said quietly. He was watching Wolfe as if he understood him perfectly. As if he was watching himself.

'A few. Most don't stay long. They – they're taken away.'

'Released?' Morgan asked.

Thomas shook his head. Jess didn't want to ask any more.

They were hurrying along now and keeping their voices low. Jess heard nothing behind them yet, but he was sure pursuers would be coming fast. The prison was larger than he'd thought and stretched in a long, straight hallway of cells, some occupied, and he couldn't look inside, *couldn't*, for fear he'd see the face of someone he knew staring out. Khalila had, just ahead of him. She'd stopped, grabbed the bars of a cell, and was looking inside. When she turned to Jess, her eyes were blind with tears. 'We have to let them out,' she said. 'Please. Help—'

He took out the keys, but his hands were trembling. Nearly useless. *Focus*, he told himself, but he wasn't sure he could. It was all too much, too fast. Dario silently took the keys and tried them, one after another. The desperate person behind the bars didn't seem to care; it was impossible for Jess to tell the gender or age. It was just a dark shape huddled in a corner against the wall, chained as Thomas had been.

The keys didn't work.

'Maybe they're on one of the other guards. I'll get them,' Dario said, and went back the way they'd come. He didn't get far before he reversed course and came back fast. 'No time,' he said. 'They're coming. Go. *Go!*'

'But—' Khalila looked absolutely tormented. Dario took her by the arms and pulled her away from the cell. 'No, we can't—'

'We must.' He held on when she tried to yank away. 'Khalila. *Querida*. Look at me. *We can't help them if we're all dead!*'

He was right. It hurt, and he was right, and Jess finally dared to look into the cell, into the face of the one they were leaving behind.

He didn't know the man. That was a terrible relief, and then a terrible guilt, too. 'I'm sorry,' he said, and helped Thomas as they followed Dario and Khalila down the hall.

He didn't look in any of the other cells. Wasn't sure he could stand it.

The left turn ahead dumped them into a large, circular room with age-scrubbed frescoes on the walls. It was lined with . . . What were these things? Mechanical devices. Jess tried not to think what they were intended to do, but the spikes, straps, wheels, gears made it all too evident once he focused on the evil things.

It was a torture chamber.

There were no exits.

Jess froze for a moment, thinking, *What did I just do?* But then he pushed past the others into the centre of the room. This was the right place; he *knew* it was. This chamber was a perfect round replica of the one below their feet, off the sewers. But there was no sign of any metal plate in the floor.

It has to be here, he thought, and pushed aside the thudding headache to concentrate. His eyes fixed on a device in the middle of the room.

'Here! Move this!' he said, and pushed at a particularly large construction that looked like a bed, but with gears and ropes and straps stained with old blood. The stench of it – of the whole room – made his throat close up, but he gritted his teeth and shoved, and Santi and Dario joined him. The machine moved with a long, agonising screech of metal on metal – because it had been partially blocking the round metal plate set in the centre of the floor. The plate was stamped with the screaming face of a monster with snakes for hair – a gorgon. Ancient work. It had been sealed for a very long time.

Santi removed the Codex from his belt and – to Jess's surprise – dropped it on the ground before he took a sealed, padded bottle from his pack and said, 'Leave your Codexes here. Stand back.'

Jess hadn't thought of it, but Santi was right, of course; the Codex that was so familiar a tool to him could be used against them. *It could be tracked, couldn't it?* The Archivist would have Obscurists on it in moments. Morgan had already dropped hers, and so had Wolfe. Jess put his down on the floor, obscurely careful about it, and watched as Glain did the same. It took Khalila and Dario far longer to decide to let go of this last tangible symbol of the Library; Khalila put hers down reverently, as if it might break, and whispered something that sounded to him like a prayer as she pressed her fingertips to the cover.

Then Santi opened the bottle and poured the thick greenish contents over the stack of books. They flared up into a brilliant pyre, and Jess pulled Thomas and Morgan back from the billowing toxic smoke. *We're Burners,* Jess thought, stricken. *Now we're Burners.*

Through the hanging pall of smoke, as he started to cough, he saw Santi taking out two more bottles that he poured over the gorgon face of the metal plate. This time it didn't burn; it bubbled as it distorted the gorgon's snarl into a slack-mouthed scream, and then hissed and melted it away altogether. The plate was thick, but the chemicals would do the job . . . if they had time.

Jess heard sounds from the hallway. He moved towards the opening, and what started as distant running footsteps rapidly came closer. They were still in the other corridor, fast approaching the sharp corner. He exchanged a look with Glain, and without a word spoken, they moved to take up positions. He was, by common consent, the better shot, and before anyone appeared at the intersection, let loose a short burst of lethal projectile fire that chewed head-high holes in the old stonework. A vivid warning to the troops around the corner. In the next second, before the echoes died, he switched the weapon back to a stun setting – enough to put someone down, he hoped, if he scored a good shot. From his angle, he'd get the first pick of targets, and Glain would clean up.

The first man to the corner was Blue Squad leader Rollison. Troll threw himself into the opening with fearless disregard for his own safety, maybe hoping that Jess would hesitate to fire, but Jess didn't: he planted his shot precisely on target, into the armour just above Troll's stomach. It would, he vividly remembered, knock the wind right out of a man.

Troll dropped like a suit of empty clothes, mouth open as he gagged for air. Glain got the next soldier to appear, Jess the third. The rest hesitated and dragged their injured comrades back to cover.

'We're through,' Santi said from behind them. 'Glain, get down to the next level. Go. *Now.*'

'I'd rather hold this position, sir.'

'I need you to be sure our escape route's secure. Take Wolfe with you and don't let him resist.'

Before either of them could protest, Santi walked right past them into the opening. Into the hallway. Glain hesitated then – as she would, being Glain – followed orders, grabbed Wolfe, and pushed him towards the open dark hole in the floor.

Jess took in a deep breath and focused on Santi, who was putting his own life on the line to buy time. He raised his weapon to provide what cover he could, though if anyone on the other end decided to rain fire, Santi wouldn't survive.

Captain Santi strode halfway down the hall and called out, 'Zara?'

There was a short silence, and then Santi's lieutenant – the green-eyed woman – stepped around to face him, with her gun pointed squarely on his chest. 'Sir,' she said. 'What do you think you're doing?'

'You know what I'm doing. You saw the cells. Don't tell me you agree with what they do here. What *we* do here. The Library is us. We allow this to happen, Zara.'

'Whether I agree with it or not, I can't let you take prisoners out of custody! There are ways we can make protests. Channels for—'

'Do you really think that the people who made this place care about protests or channels or laws? Come here and look, Zara. *Look at what they do.*'

The woman didn't answer. She stared at Santi for a long moment, and Jess couldn't tell what she was thinking. Not at all.

Then she said, 'Nic, please. Don't make me do this. We can make a story that you were forced into helping them. I don't know, but we'll make something work. You can't throw away your career. Your *life*! I know this is – it looks bad. But it can be fixed. It *will* be fixed!'

'It won't,' he told her. 'I'm sorry. They'd never believe I didn't know what I was doing. And I did know. I went into this knowing full well how this would go.' Santi's voice was gentle but firm. 'Zara, I'm not asking for you to join me. I'm asking you to just come with me and look. If you don't agree once you've seen what is in this room, then shoot.'

She blinked slowly, looking at him, then at the troops surely queued up behind her, just around the corner. 'I'm going with him,' she said. 'Give me one minute. If I don't return, shoot to kill. Is that understood? They may be wearing Scholar's robes, but they are traitors to the Library. No mercy.'

'Sir.' The echoing voices sounded dark and sure. Wolfe and Glain were already gone, as was Morgan. Dario and Khalila were helping Thomas through the opening and struggling with his weight. He dropped out of sight. Dario quickly gestured at Khalila to follow, and she let him take her hands and lower her down. With one last glance at Jess – *Almost apologetic*, Jess thought – Dario jumped through and disappeared.

Santi walked his lieutenant down the hall towards Jess. 'I don't want to fight my own people,' he said. 'No more than you want to fight me.'

'Why are you doing this? Just tell me that.'

'Just look.'

Santi walked her into the round room filled with machines – machines built to cut, to tear, to pull, to cause suffering and anguish. There was no other use for them. The stained walls and floor told the story without any words. The smell of pain and blood and despair was louder than screams.

Zara stopped in her tracks. She stared at the room, the gruesome equipment, the floor . . . and then back at Santi. She started to speak, then shook her head.

'Christopher was here,' Santi said. 'He was *here*. Do you understand now? *This* is what they don't tell us. *This* is who we serve. Who those people have made us.'

'No. It's not—' She took in a trembling breath. 'Someone has to keep order,' she said. 'Our hands aren't clean, either.'

'The High Garda fights wars; we don't torture the innocent *or* the guilty. This is what they made us into. I'm asking you to say you arrived too late to stop us, Zara. That's all I'm asking.'

The woman stood very still, looking at the room, hearing the silent screams trapped here, and Jess saw tears glitter in her eyes.

Then she lifted her gun and trained it directly on Captain Santi. From where Jess stood, he couldn't tell if she had set it for lethal force or stun, but the look in her eyes said she meant to kill. 'Surrender now, and maybe the Archivist will show you mercy.'

'Mercy?' Santi's voice was as dark as the dried blood on the walls. 'Look around. Does it appear to you the Library has an abundance of that? Shoot me. You'll have to, to stop me.'

She would, Jess realised. She wasn't like Santi. Like Jess.

She couldn't admit her world was a lie and everything she'd done had been in the service of something dark.

Jess fired, but he was too late. She fired at exactly the same moment his bullet hit her armour.

Zara and Santi fell at the same time.

EPHEMERA

Text of a letter from Pharaoh Ptolemy II to the Archivist Callimachus, in the time of his reign, long may his name be known.

From the scribe of Pharaoh Ptolemy II, to his most excellent servant Callimachus, Archivist of the Great Library, in the twelfth year of his glorious reign:

Great King Ptolemy, Light of Egypt, has wishes to endow you with his great wisdom on the subject of the loyalty of the Great Library, this sacred endeavor, to the throne of Egypt, as has been blessed by the gods from the first rays of dawn on the eternal Nile.

It is his wisdom that always must the Library exist to cast glory upon Egypt and the Pharaoh, and any thought that the Library shall be a power unto itself is a dangerous and heretical whisper that must be crushed out.

Knowledge is not a pure goal. All that you gather together shall lift the Pharaoh, sacred be his duty to the gods and the people of Egypt.

So speaks he, in his great and divine wisdom.

A notation to this document from Archivist Callimachus, sent to the Scholars of the Great Library.

A great decision is now upon us. Will we be nothing but a mirror for Pharaoh to gaze into, to see himself as beautiful and powerful? Or do we follow our truest calling, that of benefit for all who seek to learn, and gather up this knowledge in the name of the seekers, the scholars, the teachers, the students? Is what we do nothing but a prop for a king, or is it a lever by which we move the world?

It falls to us to decide this. It will be difficult. It will be dangerous. Pharaoh has power and strength, and if we declare ourselves independent from his power, we must defend that with our blood. More, we must seek that same hard course of independence from every kingdom, every philosophy, every religion that would take us as their own prop, their own polished mirror in which to gaze.

I say, let us throw the bones and see what fortune brings us. Knowledge is power, so they say.

If so, then we have more than any king.

CHAPTER ELEVEN

He's dead, Jess thought, and felt a wave of sick horror. *My fault.* She'd been aiming for a killing shot, and he should have been, too. He'd tried to save her, and she'd killed Captain Santi . . .

And then Santi pulled in a long, ragged breath. He gasped for air as the flexible armour in the centre of his chest smoked, damaged by the shot. But it was over the plate. It had protected him.

She must have chosen her target as carefully as Jess had.

Zara still breathed, but his own shot had knocked her completely unconscious. Wouldn't last long. They'd have to move fast; the clock was ticking down for her soldiers, as well.

Jess grabbed Santi's arm and dragged him to the hole, yelled 'Catch him,' and slid the captain through feet first. Then he gritted his teeth, got on the other side of the torture device that had been blocking the hole, and shoved with all his might. It grated a few inches – enough to disguise the opening, at least for a few moments. There was just enough of a gap left for him to skin through, if he didn't mind the scrapes.

Jess sucked in his breath and wriggled down just as he heard the other soldiers yelling for the lieutenant. He landed hard – no one caught him – and rolled right into the metal bulk of the lion still blocking the tunnel.

It was still stopped, thank all the old and new gods.

Dario yanked him to his feet. 'Move!' Dario said, and squeezed by the frozen automaton lion. Just beyond, Glain and Wolfe were holding Santi upright and Khalila was helping Thomas, nearly buckling under his weight. Jess hurried over to help. Glain had used one of the portable lights from her pack and they all glowed an unearthly yellow-green. In that light, Thomas looked like a corpse newly risen from the grave.

Santi looked almost as bad, but he was moving on his own, clumsily.

'You were supposed to watch out for him,' Wolfe said to Jess with a poisonously angry glare.

'I did,' he snapped back. 'Come on. This way. Thomas, can you make it?'

'I will have to,' Thomas said. 'Did you shoot someone?'

'Yes.'

'Was that in the plan?'

'No.'

'We're well off the plan now,' Glain said. 'And we've got no map to guide us.'

She didn't mean the path; that was distinct. Jess's markers were still clearly visible. She meant the soldiers on their trail, and the hue and cry that was sure to run faster than they could. Zara would wake up soon, and if they hadn't already discovered their way out, she'd tell them where to look.

'We need a distraction,' Jess said.

'We need an army,' Glain corrected. 'And as I see it, we're about a hundred short of even a small one.'

'Shut up and run,' Dario told her as he replaced Glain on

Santi's left side. 'You haven't changed at all. Still a gloomy girl with a bitter disposition. Cheer up – we're together again!'

If he hadn't been wearing Scholar's robes, she probably would have flattened him for that, but Glain settled for a scorching look and took the lead at an easy, long-legged lope. Jess broke out his light and took more and more of Thomas's weight, especially as the tunnel began to incline upward – strong he might be, but the German had been chained in place for too long. As they approached the upper exit of the tunnel and the grate, Jess boosted Glain up, then Thomas. Thomas helped pull up Khalila, Morgan, and Dario, and Wolfe and Santi came last. Jess grabbed Glain's hold to avoid Wolfe, who still looked at him with blank anger, and climbed quickly up.

They all crouched in the shadows beneath Jupiter's robes. The Forum beyond was busy, which was a gift; Jess sent a silent prayer up to his Christian God, who must have called in a favour or two for this small miracle in a land loyal to other deities. The Library hadn't sent the word out yet to clear the Forum.

'How far are they behind us, sir?' Glain asked Santi. He was still breathing raggedly and favouring his side, but he seemed better. Functional, at least.

He was checking over his weapon, and didn't look up as he replied, 'Fifteen minutes until they're in the tunnels, if we're lucky, and I wouldn't count on luck.'

'We have to get back to the Translation Chamber in the basilica,' Morgan said. 'It's our only way out. It's how we planned to leave!'

'The devil of battle is that plans change,' Santi said. 'And if we go that way, we'll have to go to ground somewhere and let the beehive settle before we try anything. Either that or risk the public exits.'

'They'll be waiting at every one,' Wolfe said. 'Rome isn't an easy city to enter or leave. They can make sure we don't slip away. Morgan's right: Translation is our only way out.'

'Then we use the High Garda chamber, where I arrived.'

'Nic. It'll be guarded and on high alert, and you know it. We must go back into the basilica.'

'I'd far rather deal with High Garda than a pack of automaton lions hunting just for us, with orders to rip us apart.'

'I'd rather not die,' Dario said flatly. 'So perhaps we should think on it.'

'If the problem is with the automata . . .' Thomas's voice came quietly, tentatively, and they all hushed to look at him. He almost seemed to flinch from the sudden attention and looked away. 'If that's what you need to fight, I might have a way. There's an inventor in Rome, Glaudino. I visited his store on Via Baccina a time or two when I was younger. We should go there.'

'Do you think you can trust him?' Wolfe asked, and Thomas shook his head.

'No, of course not,' he said. 'He's very loyal to the Library. He'd never help us.'

'Then I don't see how this helps—'

'Because he works with the lions,' Thomas said. 'I'll need Morgan with me. And Jess.'

'Why?' Santi demanded. He caught and held his gaze, and Jess saw a visible tremor run through his friend. Santi must have seen it, too, because he paused and softened his tone. 'I'm sorry, Schreiber. We're all on edge. What will you do there to help us?'

'I can make one work for us.'

'One what?'

It was Morgan who answered for Thomas. She'd got it

more quickly than Jess. 'An automaton lion,' she said. 'Oh, Thomas, brilliant. Brilliant. Do you think we can do it?'

'Glaudino's workshop repairs the Library's automata,' Thomas said. 'We should be able to fix one and make it work for us instead.'

Santi's mind gears were turning again – Jess could see that – and he waited while the captain reconfigured plans, calculated odds, came up with an answer. 'How long would you need?' Santi asked.

'I don't know. A few hours,' Thomas said. 'Not much more. The workshop won't be guarded, I think.'

You think. Jess didn't voice his doubts. It was still a good chance, and he knew Santi thought so, too. Glain looked more grim about it, but, then, she usually did.

'We're too noticeable as a group,' Dario said.

'I do need Morgan,' Thomas said. 'It takes an Obscurist to do some of this. And I'll need Jess.'

'Fine. Brightwell and Hault, go find the workshop; Glain, go with them. Wolfe and I will take Seif and Santiago with us. We'll meet you there on Via Baccina as soon as we can.'

It seemed equitable, and it separated the ones most hunted – Thomas and, conceivably, Morgan – from the rest, and Jess and Glain provided trained protection, even if Jess didn't exactly feel his best. Jess nodded and helped Thomas up. 'Morgan, you come with me. We have to scout and see where they've sent the lions out in the Forum.'

She nodded and gave Thomas a quick hug before going with Jess to peek under Jupiter's robes. They had to get on hands and knees to crawl under, and as Jess helped her up, he spotted a High Garda soldier walking towards them. On impulse, he turned to her and said, 'Run.'

It wasn't a good plan, but she had a much better one. She melted against him, kissed him, and he entirely forgot what he'd been about to say, because the feel of her, the taste, the rich and wonderful *reality* of Morgan pressed against him drove any thought of imminent danger away, just for a few critical seconds.

By the time he pushed her back, the soldier had passed them by, shaking his head. Why wouldn't he? Just another boy kissing a girl.

'Don't do that again,' he told her, but he was still pressed against her, mouth hovering too close. It felt like the world had tilted under his boots to keep him there. 'This is dangerous work, you know.'

'I know,' she said, and her eyes burnt into his with real intensity. 'Go buy me a scarf. Hurry.'

'A what?'

'A scarf. I need to cover my face.'

He realised that she was right, and hurried off to the nearest stall. It was floating with colourful silken ribbons fluttering on the breeze. He caught one that he thought would bring out her eyes, passed over *geneih*, and then spotted hats. He bought three of them.

'Thanks,' she said, as he handed her scarf and hat, and wound the silk high enough to conceal part of her face. 'Get Thomas.'

Jess bent down to motion for Thomas to come forward. He scrambled out, clumsy and breathless. Someone – Wolfe, Jess realised – had given him a black Scholar's robe. It was too short on him, but voluminous enough to hide his prison-eroded clothing. Jess clapped a hat on Thomas. It looked a little ridiculous, but that was the point: it hid his matted blond hair and cast so much shade, it was hard to make out his features. Many tourists here wore sun hats. He put his on as well.

Glain came last and fell into step with Jess. They looked for all the world like two guards escorting a visiting Scholar and his companion on a pleasant day out in Rome. They were halfway across the Forum when Jess said, 'Do any of us have an idea which way we're going?' He was eyeing the Library's lions, which were restlessly, aggressively patrolling the Basilica Julia. So far, they'd not been sent out hunting. They needed to be away from the Forum before that happened.

'This way,' Glain said. 'Lucky for you, I study maps of a city I'm being sent to defend instead of napping in the transport.'

She led them quickly and calmly out of the Forum and to the Via Baccina, while Morgan walked arm in arm with Thomas, subtly supporting him when he faltered. There were no lions following yet, but Jess imagined they'd be fanning out through the Forum now, searching for the fugitives. Every High Garda soldier in the city and every local Roman Garda would be alerted soon, if they hadn't been already.

Behind them, distant screams. The lions had been loosed, and when Jess looked back, he saw crowds of people moving fast away from the direction of the Forum. Panic would be spreading quickly.

'Do you think they got out?' Morgan asked.

Thomas patted her hand gently. 'With Santi and Wolfe leading? They got out. Don't worry.' He was panting, Jess saw. Not much energy left. He hoped this workshop Thomas had mentioned was close.

'What's waiting for us at the workshop?' Glain asked Thomas as they walked up the next hill, away from the chaos of the Forum. Thomas slowed with every step as they made the climb, and crowds were thinner here. They'd be more easily noticed by anyone trained to look. 'Don't tell me *wait and see*, or I'll forget I'm your friend, Thomas Schreiber.'

'I'm your friend, even if you forget that, too,' Thomas said. 'I won't lead you into too much danger, and I won't keep you in the dark. Signor Glaudino's workshop is the primary repair shop for the automata of Rome.'

'Wait,' she said, and turned to face him, still walking backward. 'Are you telling me you're dragging us into a shop *full of lions?*'

'I don't know if they're *all* lions,' he said. 'Most, probably. There are a few made in the shape of Roman gods, and, of course—'

'Are they working?'

'Oh, some of them will be, since Glaudino will have fixed them.'

'We can't fight automata, Thomas!'

'We won't have to,' Thomas said. 'They'll be switched off. How else would Signor Glaudino even begin work on them? Jess, you and Glain have to take the master and his apprentices and lock them away, and give Morgan and me time to repair and change one. Do you think you can do that?'

'We can do our jobs,' Glain said. Then she sent Jess a look, and he knew exactly what it meant.

Is he really capable of doing anything after spending all that time in a cell?

Jess lifted one shoulder in a very small, almost invisible shrug.

Because they had no real choice.

Glaudino's workshop turned out to be a large building, but not well secured. Jess assumed that nobody in their right mind would want to steal from the man who repaired Library lions, though, and so it was an easy matter for him and Glain to slip in the side gate. Stepping inside the building from an open sliding door, Jess came face-to-face with his own worst nightmare: an entire pride of Library lions.

But as Thomas had promised, they were all switched off, frozen in whatever pose they'd had when the button had been pressed. He heard Glain's sharp intake of breath when she moved in beside him, and felt her shudder as she fought, and conquered, the urge to retreat. 'Are they dead?' she asked him.

'They were never really alive,' he said. 'And they're shut off.'

Glain sent him a sharp look. 'How *did* you learn that trick, by the way? I've never heard of anyone managing it before.'

'Desperation. Luck. Free exercise of my illegal trade. Take your pick. Come on – I hear voices this way.' Jess followed a clear space between the lions towards the back of the room, to a separate workroom where voices conversed easily in Italian. Stepping through the door, he found three men sitting at worktables and on benches. There was a lion crouched in the middle of the floor, motionless, and it had a pathetic air to it; someone had removed part of its bronzed hide and pulled out bundles of cables that spilt over the floor like wiry intestines. The lion's face was frozen in a strange expression, as though it didn't much like what was being done to it.

The oldest of the three men – Signor Glaudino, at a guess – looked up at Jess's arrival, frowned, and switched from Italian to the more standard Greek that was the common Library language. 'She's not ready yet, this one. Tell your master we will deliver as agreed tomorrow. Yes?'

'No,' Jess said, and raised his gun. Glain stepped in beside him and mirrored the action. 'Apologies, *signores*, but I need you all to move into that closet, please.'

'Why? What is this?' Signor Glaudino was a peppery little man, and he puffed out his chest and stood up to face them squarely. 'You are ignorant people, to think you can do this to us! I have a commission from the Artifex himself for my work! The High Garda will hunt you down as soon as I tell them—'

'You won't,' Glain said. She stepped forward, grabbed Glaudino's shoulder, and marched him firmly to the open door of the closet. After checking it, she pushed him inside and gestured for his two employees to follow. Neither of them looked ready to put up a fight. 'Codexes, please. Now.'

Each of them handed over their Codex volumes, which she stacked neatly on the nearest table, and then she searched each of the men with quick, efficient slaps. Glaudino squawked like a plucked chicken, but he was no match for Glain, who shoved them in, one by one.

Glaudino began banging on the door almost immediately. She sighed and shook her head. 'I tried to be nice,' she said to Jess, and then hit the outside of the door hard enough to make it shiver on the hinges. 'Shut up, or I'll tie you up and feed you to your lions!'

That got blessed quiet. Jess fetched Morgan and Thomas, who'd been waiting in the shadows, and when he walked them into the workroom, Thomas's blue eyes burnt like someone had lit a lamp in him. 'Yes!' he said. 'Perfect! You, poor lovely thing. What have they done to you, now?' He sat down on the bench, leaning over the lion, and Jess crouched down with him. Morgan took a seat nearby and watched with fascination as Thomas put his hands on the metal skin, very much as if he petted a very live, friendly animal. 'We will make you well. No, better. Much better.'

But then, in the next few seconds, the muted joy drained out of Thomas's eyes and he began to shake. He sank down to sit next to the lion, put his head in his hands, and began quietly to cry.

'He needs to work,' Glain said, but at least she had the decency to mutter it to Jess, not to Thomas.

'He will,' Jess said, and sent her a warning look. 'Leave him alone.'

'Do something,' she whispered back. But Jess felt helpless. He put one hand on Thomas's shoulder and felt him shiver at the contact, then relax. Morgan took Thomas's hand. Neither of them said a word, and Jess listened as Thomas's ragged, laboured breathing slowly steadied. He lowered his hands from his face but didn't look up at them.

'Sorry,' he whispered. 'I – *Scheisse*. I didn't think I would do that. Why did I do that?'

Morgan started to speak but then couldn't seem to find the words. She looked up helplessly at Jess, and he finally nodded and crouched down until he and Thomas were on a level. 'I've never been through what you have, but I've been in the dark a few times. Sometimes the light's just too bright.'

'What if I can't—?'

'Can't adjust? You can. You will.' Jess nodded to the lion. 'Even in the dark, you dreamt about your automata. They're nothing to be afraid of.'

Thomas sucked in a slow breath and then quietly let it out. He nodded and opened his eyes, and put his hand back on the lion's metal skin. It seemed to steady him this time. 'All right,' he said. 'All right. I just wish I had more references.'

Jess unbuttoned his uniform shirt and pulled it off. Beneath was his smuggling harness, dark with sweat; it had practically moulded to his body. He unbuckled it and peeled it off with a relieved sigh. The cool air on his damp skin felt as good as a bath.

They were all staring at him with varying degrees of fascination. Thomas finally asked, 'What are you doing, Jess?' He had opened the skin of the lion through latches Jess would never have seen, and was now restlessly running a length of cable through his fingers, testing it for flaws. 'Put your clothes on.'

'I will,' he said, and opened the smuggling pouch and took out the book and the folded translation sheets that lay inside. The book felt cool and dry, and he handed it over to Thomas. 'Here. This might help you.'

Thomas dropped the cable and began to leaf through the book – slowly at first, then with increasing eagerness as he compared the translations to the contents. Jess strapped the harness back on and replaced his shirt.

'What is that?' Morgan leant forward to watch Thomas read, and glanced at Jess for the answer when Thomas didn't seem to heed her at all.

'It's research notes from someone – someone with inside knowledge,' Jess said. 'A mechanical study of the automata – parts, how they work, all the details the Library never wanted to get out. I expect this is all that remains of the poor sod who wrote it down. They wouldn't want him spreading this particular word, would they? Thomas? Can you use it?'

'Yes,' Thomas whispered, and then again, stronger, 'Yes! And you see here, the metal ball, the container? That, Morgan will need to open; it is an Obscurist's creation. You know how to write scripts, yes? They taught you that?'

'I—' Morgan blinked, and then nodded. 'Well, yes. But I'll need some starting point. There should be a script inside there. If I can retrieve it and alter it—'

'Exactly. It's simply a matter of—A matter of—' Thomas,

who'd been doing so well, stuttered like an automaton powering down and dropped the book from suddenly clumsy hands. He was trembling, Jess saw. No, not trembling. Shaking. Badly. His teeth chattered and he squeezed his eyes tightly shut.

'It's no use,' Glain said quietly. 'Part of him's still in that prison.'

We don't have time to let him recover was left unsaid. They all knew it. Thomas was doing his best, with all his good heart, but he'd been through a horrible ordeal.

'Then we help him,' Jess said, and looked at Morgan, who nodded. 'Thomas. I've read the book; I translated it. Let me do this, and you just rest and tell me what to do. Can you do that?'

Thomas said nothing, but after a long moment, he finally nodded in a movement so abrupt it must have hurt him. *More like a convulsion*, Jess thought, *than agreement*. He seemed pale as milk now, and the bruises stood out like fading tattoos on his cheeks.

Morgan yanked a thick blanket down from a shelf and wrapped it around Thomas's trembling body. He huddled into the warmth, and she rested her hands on his shoulders and looked at Jess.

'I'm sure they have scissors somewhere in this workshop; I'll find some and cut his hair. Then I'll find him something better to wear. Jess. Be his hands.'

When Thomas opened his eyes, he whispered, 'Thank you,' and Morgan bent to gently kiss his forehead.

'I still have the little automaton bird you gave me,' she told him. 'It still sings. It kept me singing, too, Thomas. You helped me. Let me help you.'

He managed a smile for her, and Jess avoided looking at him too closely as he knelt down next to the huge Roman lion.

There was some similarity, he suddenly realised, between this machine and his friend. Both had damage.

Both needed to be healed.

Maybe by helping to repair one, he could fix the other.

Jess had mechanical aptitude, but next to Thomas, he was a rank beginner; he had to work slowly, laying out parts according to the book's instructions, and just over an hour into the work, he caught a glimpse of a closed bronze sphere where the heart of a normal beast would have been. It was the size of Thomas's fist and looked seamless, held in place by a complex series of clamps and a net of something that looked like gold. By that time, when he looked back to ask Thomas how to proceed, Morgan had succeeded in clipping back the hedge of Thomas's unruly blond hair, and with it trimmed closer, his face looked leaner and older than Jess remembered. She trimmed his bushy beard, too, which helped make him look like less of a Viking from the old stories. From some closet she retrieved a pair of workman's oversized pants and a shirt that were too large even for him. He undressed beneath the blanket – shy with the girls, even now – and once he was out of his prison rags, he seemed . . . better. Not himself, exactly. It was possible he wouldn't be the Thomas Jess remembered, but any Thomas at all would be better than none.

'I think I've found the container for the script,' Jess said. He reached in, and Thomas's hand flashed out to grab his arm and hold it back.

'Don't. It would kill you,' he said. 'Glaudino would never touch it himself. Only Obscurists can open those containers. Work around it for now, and loosen the clamps. Be careful.'

Jess nodded. He didn't like the idea of working near something that might kill him with a touch, but he liked the idea of Thomas's unsteady hands in there even less. He worked the clamps loose until he heard the ball shift inside the flexible mesh net, and then sat back. 'Morgan? I think this is your job now.'

She squeezed in beside him, and he showed her how to unfasten the clamps before moving back. She loosened the fastenings and the ball dropped into her hands, wrapped in its mesh net, which she peeled away and put aside. It looked harmless in her hands, like a shiny toy, but there was a shimmer to it that made him move well back. Morgan turned it in her fingers curiously, but she wasn't looking for a seam – wasn't looking at it at all, he realised – and the heat-wave shimmer on the ball suddenly leapt off the surface and into a haze around it, with shadowy shapes forming. Not letters he recognised in any language he knew, or even numbers; these were alchemical symbols and figures that only Obscurists knew. She stared at the swirling orb of symbols and slowly reached out to pluck out a few.

Jess moved closer again, but not too close, and paused when he saw her warning glance. 'It looks like magic.'

'It isn't,' she said. 'Well, not exactly. Alchemy is science, but science that acknowledges certain principles of magic. This . . . this is a mathematical expression of quintessence, Archimedes' fifth element that binds all things together.'

'It's glowing letters hanging in midair!'

She laughed a little breathlessly. 'Think of it this way: alchemists of old relied on the energy provided by tides, the moon, sun, planets in alignment. Every experiment was delicate and had to be balanced just so, or there couldn't be a proper result. Obscurists have an inborn talent to provide that energy from within and not from the world around us: we are born with quintessence. And the letters are only glowing in front of you because I'm cheating. I like to see what I'm doing.'

'And what are you doing?'

'This ball has a seal on it. It is a code of structures that must be passed through quintessence and altered, in order. This is how I read the code.'

'But—'

'Jess. Let me work! This isn't like solving a child's puzzle.'

He sat back, watching as her slender hands touched, spun, and changed symbols on the air. Finally, she took in a breath and said, 'There. That feels right,' and pushed her hands together. The letters vanished, and she reached out to place her fingers on the ball.

The ball seemed to vibrate and then folded back with a sharp hiss. Jess expected to see a tangle of wires and cables and gears, but it was empty except for a small rolled scroll of paper.

'What is that?' Glain asked. She seemed as fascinated as Jess.

'The script,' Thomas answered. 'The instructions that set the boundaries for the lion and give it the rules it must follow.'

Morgan nodded. 'Exactly. What do you want the lion to do?' She reached for a pen that Glaudino had left on a stack of papers on the table.

'I want it to be our champion,' Thomas said.

It took another hour to puzzle out how to put the lion back together, but they managed. Jess was proud of his handiwork – or Thomas's, really; he'd just donated his hands to the job. He sat back on his heels and looked at Thomas, Morgan, and Glain, and said, 'Ready?'

'Ready,' Thomas said. 'Let's see if she works.'

Glain's head suddenly turned in the direction of the outer workshop, and she took a step towards the door, then back.

'Santi and the others,' she said. 'They're coming in.'

Jess nodded and reached the switch beneath the lion's jaw just as the others crowded into the small workshop.

'What in the *hell* are you doing?' Wolfe asked. He sounded exhausted and, of course, irritable. He would be. They'd been a long time getting here, and no doubt there was a story to it Jess wanted to hear . . . but not now.

Wolfe was probably shocked when Thomas turned to him and shushed him, but Jess didn't look up. He was sweating and feeling uncomfortably close to this creature now that it was no longer in pieces. 'Here it goes.'

He pressed the switch and quickly backed up to stand next to Thomas and Morgan. 'This will work, won't it?' he asked Thomas. 'A little reassurance would be nice. We don't have room to run in here.'

Reassurance didn't come from Thomas, but from the lion. The dull eyes took on a shimmer, then a baleful red shine. It turned its head to fix those unblinking eyes on Jess, and . . . made a sound low in that metallic throat that sounded almost like a purr.

Jess was used to hearing them growl, but he'd never heard *that* sound before. Before he could ask Thomas if that was a good sign, the lion's head pushed forward and pressed against his chest, and the mechanical purring grew so loud, it vibrated through Jess's body. He awkwardly patted the thing's head. His whole body still felt tight and nervous. 'Good girl,' he said. 'Is it a girl?'

'Jess,' Thomas said. 'It's a machine. But I think I will call her Frauke. Do you like that name, Frauke?'

'It's an automaton. It can't like—' But the lion was turning from him to nudge her nose against Thomas's chest now. *Purring.* It seemed beyond odd.

Morgan came next, and she smiled when the lion's massive nose pushed at her. 'Frauke,' she said. 'It means "little lady", doesn't it? It suits her.' She stroked the metal ears.

'If you're finished making a pet out of this monster—' Wolfe said, and stopped as Frauke's head snapped in the direction of his voice and the purring switched to a low, ominous rumble.

'No, no, Frauke. He's one of us.' Thomas gestured to Wolfe, who looked back as if he thought they'd all gone mad. 'Come, Scholar, she needs to learn who you are.'

Wolfe didn't like it – at all – and that didn't change even when Frauke's growls changed to purrs. He suffered the nuzzling with a bitter expression of distaste before he moved well back, and pushed Santi forward in his place.

'Brilliant,' Santi said, and patted Frauke on the head. No hesitation there; he clearly liked the creature. Santi stepped aside to let Khalila crowd forward, and then Dario. 'She'll not only confuse our enemies, but confront them, too. No one questions a party of Scholars and High Garda walking with an official lion as escort, do they?'

The only one Frauke hadn't nuzzled was Glain, who still watched the door. When they all turned towards her, she shook her head. 'I'm not coming near that thing.'

Morgan tried. 'Glain. It's safe. You saw—'

'It's wrong. It's wrong that you just . . . *changed* it. Is it just that easy for you? Just rewrite a killer into a pet?' She glared straight at Morgan finally. 'It's Obscurists who make all this possible, you know. Without them, things would be different, wouldn't it? Without the automata, the Translation Chamber, the Library wouldn't have nearly the advantage, and we'd be fighting fair.'

'I'm trying to help!' Morgan said. 'And you know I never wanted this! I never wanted to be—'

'Whatever you wanted, you're one of them. Doing this proves it more than anything else you've ever done,' Glain said. 'And that's why we shouldn't trust you. How hard would it be for you to give us away?'

'She won't,' Jess said, and got the full, scorching weight of Glain's scorn.

'Says someone who can't ever be rational on the subject of Morgan Hault. We shouldn't do this. What if some other Obscurist *rewrites* this creature into a killer again?'

'It can't be done without the same process I went through,' Morgan said. 'It doesn't work that way. You can order them to do a limited number of things by Codex commands, but not change their loyalty—'

'I don't trust you,' Glain said flatly, and looked Morgan right in the eyes. 'I have no idea what happened to you in that tower. What might have been done to you. All I know is, you've shown up here and we've all just accepted that you're *safe*, like this lion. You aren't. You're even more dangerous.'

Santi stepped in the way, facing Glain, and said, 'Glain. She's given you no reason to distrust her, has she?'

Glain didn't want to answer that, but she finally muttered, 'Not as yet.'

'Then the matter's settled. Keep your eyes open and not just on Morgan, all right? We have enough enemies without inventing more.' She nodded but didn't change her position from the door. 'Go introduce yourself to the lion. That's an order.'

She looked at him for so long, Jess was afraid she'd refuse, but then she pushed past him and stood in front of Frauke to be nudged and catalogued like the rest of them. She didn't touch the lion. Didn't stand it for one second longer than she was forced to before she stalked away.

Frauke tried to follow, then checked herself as Thomas said, 'Frauke. Stay.' She padded back to Thomas's side and sat down, as obedient as a dog on a leash. 'Frauke, you obey our commands now, yes?'

Hard to tell if she understood that, but Thomas had been right: there was an eerie simulation of *thought* in these creatures. Even intention. It was impossible, looking at Frauke now, to see the relentless killing machine she'd been before. Glain was also right: Morgan had, with a few simple, powerful strokes of the pen, made a killer into a pet. That kind of power shouldn't exist, and it made him cold to think what could be done with it in the service of the Archivist. *This is how they've kept power. Frighten us with monsters. Kill us when all else fails.*

Maybe that was the nature of power. Jess didn't know, but he didn't like to think of himself as being part of it.

He held to one thought: if they could change Frauke, maybe . . . maybe they could also, eventually, change the Library.

EPHEMERA

Text of a message from the Artifex Magnus to the Archivist Magister, marked URGENT.

They are together. Free. They have the young Obscurist.

If they get away as a group, if Wolfe and Schreiber together can make their machine and teach others how to make it, then we lose everything. *Knowledge becomes a common currency, as cheap as paper and ink, and all of the sanctity of the Library is lost.*

It is what I told you from the beginning: there is no compromise with rebellion. You coddled Wolfe for Keria's sake, and now it has led to this.

We have no choice. This is a threat we must deal with, quickly and decisively, whatever it costs.

Reply from the Archivist Magister, marked URGENT.

You were right from the beginning, and I regret I was too cautious.

Kill them all.

CHAPTER TWELVE

The delay in the arrival of Santi's party had simply been as a result of caution; they'd stayed well away from any areas where they might have been noticed, and ate a long lunch instead – a fact that made Jess realise he was starving. Glain silently passed out rations and water, and let Thomas have three times as much as anyone else; it wasn't as good as the cold meats and cheeses that the others had enjoyed, but it'd do for now.

Glaudino, clearly out of patience with his confinement – understandably; they'd been locked in a small space for more than three hours now, and even with the food and water Glain gave them, they were likely to be miserable – began banging on the door again and threatening them with dire punishment. Frauke, crouching in the corner, swung her head in that direction and growled. Despite knowing it was wrong, Jess felt a guilty spike of pleasure. Nice having something deadly on their side. 'So, what about them?' Glain asked Santi.

'Tie them, but leave them without gags. They can yell for help as much as they like once they wake up.'

'Wake up – Oh.' Glain nodded. He walked with her to the closet door, aimed, and nodded for her to open it. He dropped

Glaudino first with a well-placed stun shot, then the other two, and dragged them out to tie their limp arms and ankles together. He and Glain settled the prisoners against the wall, and while they were at it, Jess turned to Wolfe.

'We still don't have an exit plan,' he said. 'Do we?'

'You do,' Morgan said, and moved to stand beside him. She put her hand on Frauke's stiff metal mane. 'If you get me to Rome's Translation Chamber, I can send you where you want to go. Let me help you. This is why I came, to make sure you could get away safely.'

'And to run away from the Iron Tower,' Wolfe said. She gave him a look, and he shrugged. 'I am not blaming you. I, of all people, understand.'

'There's a problem with that plan: no doubt that the High Garda will be thick as fleas in the Translation Chamber by now, not to mention on every road leading to it. They'll know that's our best escape,' Dario said. 'We'd be playing right into their hands. Maybe Jess's illegal cousins would be a better idea, grubby criminals that they are. I'd rather have a long, tiring ride in the back of a wagon than a cell under the Basilica.'

'It's too late for that,' Jess said. 'My cousins generally aren't in the business of being heroes. Our code is: *Get caught, count yourself dead.*'

'Pleasant folk you come from,' Dario observed. 'All right. Maybe we can buy our way out of the city. There must be someone who wants a fat purse and no questions asked.'

'There's another option,' Santi said, rising from where he'd finished tying up their unconscious captives. 'We can go where they *don't* expect us. Rome doesn't just have one Translation Chamber. It has two. Morgan? You came in that way. So did Wolfe. Did you destroy it or only disable it?'

Santi was right: they had a decent chance, if all of the basilica guards were out looking, of walking right into the heart of the enemy's stronghold and using it for escape.

'And what then?' Khalila asked. 'Say we get away. Where do we go? Where's our safe haven? What chance do we have of staying free of the Library for any length of time at all?'

'None,' Dario said. 'Not unless we find allies, quickly. Jess isn't willing to put his neck on the block, so someone has to.' He looked across at Santi, and nodded towards the men unconscious on the floor. 'How long are they good for?'

'An hour, at most,' Santi said. 'What are you thinking?'

'I don't want to explain. Give me half that time,' Dario said. 'If I'm not back, then let Jess try to enlist his criminal brethren or run for the basilica. But I *might* be able to help with allies and a safe haven.'

'Dario!' Khalila grabbed for him, but he was quick, the arrogant Spaniard. He grabbed her hand instead, raised it to his lips, and then pressed the back of it to his forehead as he bowed. 'Don't go.'

'Why should Jess always be the one to run off on his adventures?' Dario sent Jess a wide, confident grin. 'Half an hour, scrubber. Start the clock.'

Then he was gone.

'We can't—' Khalila looked at Santi, then Wolfe. 'We can't just let him *go*!'

But they did.

Dario Santiago didn't come back.

The hour slipped away, and they waited as long as they could. Glain quietly suggested stunning Glaudino and his workers again, but Santi shook his head. Another shot risked real injury, possibly even death, and he didn't intend to leave bodies in his wake today unless they had no choice in the matter.

'He knows the plan,' Santi said. 'We head for the basilica. Twilight is our best time; people will be heading home or out to take the evening air. It'll be harder to recognise us.'

'No!' Khalila pulled away from him, from all of them, and backed towards the open door of the workshop. 'No, I'm not going to leave Dario behind. Jess—' She tried to get him to look at her, but he couldn't. Wouldn't. '*Jess!*'

'The captain's right,' Jess said, and hated himself for it. 'We can't wait. I'm sorry. He didn't say where he was going, and we don't even know where to start to look for him.'

'Then we *try*! We came back for Thomas! We can't just abandon Dario!'

She read their faces, and then, without warning, dashed for the door. Jess had seen that coming, though, and he was faster. He wrapped her in his arms, and she fought him surprisingly hard, with sharp, precise blows that almost made him let go. Almost. He protected himself as best he could. 'Stop. *Stop.* He'll be all right, Khalila!' He looked to Glain for help. She folded her arms. *Traitor.*

'No, he *won't*. You know he won't! He's not like you! He wants to show you that he can be just as clever, just as fast, just as . . .' She hit him again, this time a knee square to his family jewels, and he did let go. 'Just as *ruthless*! And if you ever lay hands on me again, I will kill you, Jess Brightwell!'

'I believe you,' he gasped, and struggled not to double over. Failed. He'd done his best, and when Khalila moved to the door again, this time it was Scholar Wolfe who got in her way.

She didn't attack Wolfe the way she had Jess. Maybe she didn't have the stomach for it when Wolfe put his hand on her shoulder and said, in that dark, strangely gentle voice, 'We'll find him, Khalila. But not now. Now we have to look after ourselves.'

'Scholar—' Khalila's voice was shaking. 'I can't abandon him.'

'You aren't. He knew the risks. He wouldn't want you to act impulsively, he'd want you to *think*. It's your defining feature. Your grace. Your strength.'

She took in a slow, shaking breath, and turned away. Her face was set and terrible, her eyes like dark pits, and she met no one else's gaze as she nodded. 'Then let us run,' she said, in a voice drained of anything but anger. 'Run and hide, like frightened rabbits. How does this change the world, cowering in the dark? They'll pick us off one by one. Dario is only the first.'

'We'll get him back,' Santi said. 'Dario's smart. He's tough. He will survive this.'

Maybe he'll survive because he never meant to come back. It was a sickening thought, but Jess was a practical young man. He didn't have Khalila's idealism, or her love-distorted view of Dario. *Maybe he's selling us out. In which case, we'd better move even faster.*

There was nothing else to say. Jess pushed pain to the background. He'd need to be ready to run or fight; this was still not guaranteed escape. *And if we get to the Translation Chamber, what then? Where do we go? London*, he thought. It was half instinct, going home, but it was also practical. His family resources could be commandeered from there, and his family had plenty of hiding places and bolt-holes; if he and Thomas showed Callum Brightwell the plans for the press, his father would be the first to recognise the potential. Reproducing books had the potential to increase his black-market business ten thousandfold.

No more black sheep of the family. Jess would be welcomed with open arms, and the Library would never lay a hand on any of them. Callum didn't hold with Burner theories, but he wasn't a man to despise a good alliance, either; the Burners would be equally interested in the press, and what it meant for them to break the Library's stranglehold. It could be done.

If they got away from Rome.

'Frauke,' Thomas said, and the lion immediately climbed to four paws, razor-barbed tail twitching. 'Follow.'

Jess took one last look back at Glaudino's workshop as they threaded their way through the outer room full of silent, still automata. It was an eerie sight, seeing Frauke ghosting silently along behind Thomas through her identical dead automaton twins. It was going to give him nightmares then next time he closed his eyes.

Then they were outside and pushing the door shut, and heading for the last place Jess wanted to face again. The logic of the plan was sound enough: the High Garda truly would be searching for them on the roads leading out of town, stopping carriages and transports, heavily guarding the central Roman Translation Chamber.

But not the heart of their own power. Besides, they'd already have realised that Morgan had disabled the secret Translation Chamber. It was likely they'd consider it totally useless.

Useless things weren't guarded at a time like this.

'We'll have to enter through the public side,' Scholar Wolfe said. 'There's a staff door at the back of the Serapeum that leads into the Basilica; it might be guarded, but not heavily. They won't expect us there.'

'What about the lions on the steps? They would have been alerted to us by now,' Morgan said.

Thomas sighed and looked back at Frauke, pacing steadily behind them with her eyes glowing bright, her head held high.

'I'm sorry, Frauke. But we will all have to play our part, I think.'
He looked scarecrow thin, all large bones and angles, and with
his hair and beard cut close he seemed so much older than Jess
remembered him. But still gentle.

How he managed that, Jess couldn't imagine. He'd lost his
optimism so long ago, he could hardly remember how it felt,
and he'd never been locked in that terrible, dark place. Never
been dragged into that torture room.

Thomas seemed all right, but Jess could tell it was a fragile
kind of strength, floating on a river of adrenaline and hope.
That tide would turn, and then the weight of the darkness
would press on him, as it did on Wolfe. Jess knew he'd need to
keep good watch on his friend when the shadows came for him.

Rome seemed utterly normal as evening fell, and the
sky faded from blue to a greenish teal. Stars emerged in shy
peeks, then gaudy sprays. Their little party passed brightly
lit restaurants, and Jess's stomach growled from the scent of
roasting meats and fish.

Having Frauke with them made a difference. People made
way for them, some with respectful bows, since Glain, Jess, and
Santi were all clearly armed High Garda, and the others, except
Morgan, wore Scholar's robes. Morgan walked next to Wolfe,
like a favoured student or a fond daughter.

And the lion, Frauke, paced behind them, a silent and
watchful guardian that warned off even Burner sympathisers
from any confrontation. Strange, how good it felt to have that
power at his back, at his command. Jess didn't entirely like it.
Too easy to become dependent on it.

But it did make their walk to the Forum efficient.

Standing in the shadow of Mercury's feet, in virtually
the same spot where Burners had died only two days before,

Wolfe and Santi assessed the situation of the basilica. As they'd predicted, it *did* seem quiet. People proceeded in and out of the public area of the Serapeum, and most of the pride of automata patrolled farther down. There was a lion crouched beside the open Serapeum door, scanning those who entered.

'Can you turn it off?' Santi asked Jess, and he nodded.

'I can if it's distracted.'

'That's my job,' Santi said.

'Nic—' Wolfe protested, but Santi cut him off.

'No. I'm the better option. They'll all have me first on the list; after all, I'm the one who betrayed my own company.' Even as he said it, Jess saw the pain that flashed through him, quickly banished to some dark corner inside. Captain Santi loved the High Garda; he loved the men and women under his command, and the responsibility he held for the lives of Scholars.

'Jess, your job is to turn it off. Let me handle the distraction.'

Jess nodded. Thomas said quietly, 'Frauke can help.' That meant Frauke could go in single combat against the other lion, but Jess was well aware that if that happened, things would get much worse, much faster. The rest of the pride would come, and Frauke wouldn't last long against numbers.

Neither would they.

'Stay together until we get close. I'll draw the lion off,' Santi said. 'Jess, you know what to do then. The rest of you, just head straight inside. Don't wait for us.'

Jess nodded and turned to Thomas. 'Keep Frauke with you. Of all of us, you may be the one they want most.'

Thomas knew that. His face was thin and pale under his new-cut hair and beard, and underneath his surface calm, he looked like he was fighting an urge to curl into a ball. He put a hand on Frauke's mane, and she purred that metallic, singing purr, and it seemed to help. 'I know,' he said. 'I won't go back, Jess. I can't do that.'

He'd rather die. *Wolfe would be the same*, Jess thought.

'We're going to make it. Trust me.' Jess tried to make himself sound positive of that and cheerful, and might have even succeeded, because Thomas pulled in a deep breath and nodded.

'I do. Of course.'

As Santi started to take the lead, Morgan suddenly grabbed his arm. 'No,' she said. 'Let me. It will know me as an Obscurist, but that means it will also be under strict instructions not to harm me.'

'You're sure of that?'

'Absolutely. It won't dare.'

Jess hoped she was right as they mounted the marble steps. She looked confident and bold, all right, with her head held high. The ends of the silk scarf Jess had bought her floated like dreams on the cooling breeze. She looked beautiful and fragile and brave, and Jess couldn't take his eyes off of her as they climbed.

The lion tilted its head down to regard their approaching group.

Morgan took in a breath and hurried up ahead of the rest of them, and the lion rose from a crouch to a standing position.

A mother with three young children ahead of them was startled by the movement and rushed her brood inside the Serapeum; Jess was grateful she did, because in the next second, the lion's eyes flickered red. It growled.

'Move!' Santi called, and Glain grabbed Wolfe and hustled him inside fast, acting – once again – on her built-in priority to protect a Scholar. Khalila stayed with Thomas, and Jess glanced back to see that Thomas wasn't following the plan; he was waiting, ignoring Khalila's pulls on his arm to try to rush him to the entrance. Frauke paced restlessly near them, growling now herself.

The Library lion paced down towards Morgan now, with his growl ratcheting up to an intimidating snarl. She backed slowly away from it, and Jess ghosted sideways, trying to work his way around it while it stayed focused on her. She circled and went backward up the stairs, and it paced to follow her. She let it back her up against the wall, and it pressed forward, snarling jaws inches from her face as it boxed her in.

Then it let out a curious roaring sound that he'd never heard before. That must have been a signal to summon help, and Jess realised that they were out of time and luck. He darted in to get his fingers on the switch under the lion's jaw, but it saw him coming and shifted weight sideways to block him. It was like running into a stone wall, and he was knocked into a sliding fall on the marble. As soon as he slowed, he rolled to his feet and tried again, slipping in under the swiping paw. The lion yanked its head aside as he tried to get to the switch, and this time, a batting blow connected squarely.

It sent him rolling down the steps in a breathless heap of pain.

As he blinked away bloody afterimages, he saw a shadow pass over him and heard the heavy crunch of a lion's body landing on the steps, then leaping away again. *No, no – it's going after Thomas.* But it wasn't the lion who'd sent him tumbling down the steps. It was *their* lion.

Frauke let out a wild, full-throated cry of rage and slammed into the Library lion with so much force, it sounded like two steam trains colliding. Jess tried to get to his feet and managed it, though everything seemed wavy and blurred. Someone was helping him – Khalila. Thomas rushed to take his other side.

No, don't, Jess tried to say but couldn't. He couldn't quite grasp what was happening now. Morgan was crouched in a heap near the doorway, covering her head as the two massive lions battled and tore at each other above her. He saw movement and realised more lions were coming, drawn to the fight.

Thomas and Khalila half carried him towards the door. The battling lions thrashed and roared next to them, bits of metal flying off as claws shredded bronzed skin, then a sharp snap as a cable was bitten through, the smell of spraying fluids, a metallic roar that was almost one of pain as one of the lions lurched unevenly, one leg useless.

'Frauke,' Jess said, and the wounded lion turned her head towards him. 'Kill.'

Her eyes blazed an intense, bright white, and she roared and threw herself into the fight, a fight she couldn't possibly win, and he knew he was killing her as well. He felt like a monster.

Thomas pulled him through the doorway, and he lost sight of Frauke just as her jaws closed around the paw of the other lion and yanked; metal ripped, cables shredded, gears scattered. Dark fluids spilt like blood. *She's winning*, he thought, but in the next instant, another Library lion, red eyes glowing hellishly bright, landed on Frauke's back and dug claws in.

The embattled first lion closed its jaws over Frauke's throat.

Jess looked away, though he couldn't help but hear the heavy *crunch* of the bite or the hissing spray of liquids, or the high-pitched metallic shriek that couldn't have been one of pain, but that was how it sounded to him, as Frauke died.

Then he was across the threshold and couldn't see any more. He heard screaming and panic, and realised that the Serapeum was full of innocent people and more lions were coming.

Wolfe rushed for a control lever by the door and pulled it.

The doors began to crank shut, and almost closed before a Lion got a paw between them. Metal shrieked and bent. The doors didn't quite close. They shuddered as a lion's body hit, and then another.

'Stay out of the way!' Santi shouted to them. 'Get against the walls! Don't get in the way when they come in. You're in no danger if you *stay out of the way*!'

The civilians were already following that wise advice, cowering in corners or near bookcases. The sound of the lions battering at the door, clawing and screaming echoed from the marble walls and floors as Wolfe took the lead, running across the broad, open central hall towards the far end of the Serapeum. The building passed in a blur for Jess, who finally was feeling his body again – not that it was a blessing – and got his feet working to move under his own power. Nothing broken, at least, though he'd be aching badly tomorrow. He had an impression of a vast, columned hall lined with row upon row of shelves – a whole section of precious originals sealed under glass, available only to authorised Scholars, but open shelves lined with prefilled blanks, or ones ready to be filled. Podiums held giant, permanently affixed Codex volumes. Roman statues graced alcoves, and for a bad moment he imagined those marble maidens and lads stepping down to grab them, but they were just statues, after all.

Wolfe made it to the door, but it was fixed with a heavy lock. Jess pushed forward and fumbled for his tools; his head wasn't clear, and it seemed to take forever for his fingertips to begin to sense the vibrations of the metal pins.

Somehow, despite the tension, the others managed not to yell at him, and he was grateful for the concentration. At last he felt the lock snap open under his fingers and sag open. He moved through and held it open for the others, and at the far end of the Serapeum, one of the double doors shrieked and fell as a Roman lion bounded through and skidded on the marble floor, roaring.

'Go!' Jess shouted, though they hardly needed encouragement. Santi came through first, ready to shoot any opposition, but the hall was empty for the moment. Glain stepped through last, still facing back towards the Serapeum's hallway as the lions crowded in. Jess slammed the door shut and locked it as the first of the pride fixed a red gaze in their direction.

Then they were running through the empty halls of the basilica. Jess managed to keep up without help, though he felt Morgan next to him, anxiously steadying him when he faltered. 'I'm fine,' he told her, and she sent him a breathless, disbelieving look. 'You were right about the lion. I'm sorry I couldn't—'

'It wasn't your fault,' she said, and her hand slipped into his. The warm touch of it pushed back the pain a little. 'Come on, Jess. Just a little farther.'

Santi led them through a maze of corridors, avoiding High Garda patrols responding to the summons from the Serapeum, and Jess recognised where they were now: the hallways close to where he and Glain, a lifetime ago, had begun their patrol. 'It'll be guarded,' he told Glain, and she nodded. 'Don't hesitate to shoot, no matter who it is.'

'I won't,' she said, and moved up to run with Santi. They rounded a last corner, and there, halfway down the long hall, stood the statue of Pluto with the hidden entrance behind him, and a group of five soldiers in front.

Blue Dogs – their own squad. Jess recognised the Englishman with the beard and a few of the others, and it hit him like a sick jolt.

Someone shouted, and the Blue Dog soldiers all turned to

face them. One of them fired, but it was a wild shot and dug gouges from the stone above and behind them. Santi and Glain fired back, and Jess managed to get his own weapon up, too. Two of the soldiers dropped immediately, and another one followed in the next second, but the two on the left abandoned the open hallway and took cover. 'Glain, Jess, with me!' Santi shouted, and they pelted forward. Another shot came their way, and this one wasn't wild at all; it was well-placed, accurate, and hit Glain in the meaty part of her thigh. She cried out and went down, and Jess blinked at the splash of bright red blood left on the wall where she'd been. He dragged her up and pressed her behind the statue of Juno, then ran after Santi, who'd activated the secret entrance behind Pluto. He skidded to a halt and aimed at the soldiers who had already lined up on Santi's back.

One shot, and missed, but Jess didn't. He placed his shots carefully, and both men dropped.

Santi looked angry and ill with it. 'Get them in,' he said. 'Look after Glain. We still have to take the Translation Chamber, and there may be more guarding it . . .' His voice trailed off, and his eyes fixed somewhere beyond Jess, towards the other end of the tunnel.

Jess heard a ringing, echoing roar.

He turned his head to see the Roman lion – the one he'd turned off on their way to rescue Thomas – racing towards them in a flat-out run, claws digging into the stone floor of the hallway as it ran and flung up chips behind it. His weapon wouldn't matter to it, not at all, and from the tenor of the roar and the red shine of its eyes, it didn't intend to take them prisoner. It would crush them, rip them, leave them bloody rags on the stones.

He heard Santi's quiet sigh behind him and recognised the resignation in it. Santi was giving up.

Jess damn well wasn't.

He dropped his gun and, as Morgan and Khalila ducked through the opening, with Glain held up between them, he went straight at the lion at a run. *Not this time*, he thought. *This time I won't miss.* He couldn't. They were in the path now, and the lion would crush them all, Scholars and Obscurists and High Garda alike. They were now enemies, and enemies had no safety.

Now.

He flung himself forward into a tight ball and rolled, slammed his legs down flat to stop himself as the lion passed over him, and then he was up, *behind* it, as it passed him.

'Jess!' Morgan screamed. She thought it had trampled him, and, near enough, he'd felt one paw graze his shoulder and leave a massive bruise, but he was alive. And now he grabbed hold of the automaton's whipping tail, careful of the barb at the end, and swung himself up on the broad, muscular back.

It was like riding a storm. The lion reacted instantly to the pressure, twisting and writhing, slamming against the wall; he dodged the barbed tail that tried to spear him from behind, and locked his arms around the massive neck before he swung his legs off and let momentum throw him forward. For a second he was dangling from the lion, and his head wedged in under the lion's jaw, preventing it from biting.

Now.

He let go, and as he fell, he stabbed his fingertips up onto the switch. It gave with a sharp click, and then he hit the floor and scrambled backward as the lion lunged at him, snapping its jaws.

It came to a frozen halt a handbreadth from his face.

'*Dio mio!*' Santi said, lapsing just for a moment into his native Italian, and then recovered a second later to lunge forward, grab Jess, and drag him backward to his feet. For just a moment, the captain looked at him with silent approval, and then he turned and said, 'We have to get to the Translation Chamber. Move.' As the others began to go, he said to Jess, 'I thought we were dead.'

'So did I,' Jess admitted. 'I just thought I'd rather go out fighting.'

Santi slapped him on the same shoulder the lion had bruised. 'I've decided I like you, boy.'

Jess somehow found himself grinning. 'Everybody likes me. I'm charming.'

'Shut up and move.'

Morgan embraced him with wild strength when he reached her, but it was only a moment's pause before they began running down the corridor after Wolfe and Khalila. 'Where's Glain?' he asked, and looked back. Thomas was helping Glain limp along; he'd ripped a strip from the black Scholar's robe to bind the hole in her leg, but she was still leaving a bloody trail of footprints behind.

'We need to get her help,' Morgan said. 'She's losing too much blood.'

'Glain's too damned tough to die,' he said, but Morgan didn't smile. She looked grim and scared, and he thought she ought to be. Their chances of surviving this day were looking smaller and smaller. They'd lost Dario; Glain was badly hurt. It had been a matter of seconds between his neck and a lion's jaws.

The odds were good that someone was going to die before they got out.

The Translation Chamber lay at the end of the hallway, a simple open alcove and a round room like the others Jess had seen; he realised only now that it had much in common with the round room below them, in the prison, where torture equipment had been set up. The difference was simply in usage. This room, too, was lined with tiled mosaics of gods and monsters, kings and warriors. In the centre of it lay a marble couch in the old Roman style, and a helmet that reminded him of the ancient legions. It was connected by a thick, flexible metal cable that descended from a hole in the ceiling. Like the Translation Chamber at Darnah, it was otherwise empty – no, even more barren. Not even a bucket and sink for those who might get sick.

And, more meaningfully, no guards. No Obscurist.

'Can you do this?' he asked Morgan, and pointed to the couch, the helmet. 'Turn it back on?'

'Yes,' she said. 'Where are we going?'

'London,' Jess said, and looked at Santi and Wolfe for confirmation. Wolfe shook his head sharply.

'Word is that the Welsh are already there,' Santi said. 'They're making quick work of English defences. We could be trapped in the fighting, and how do you know your family hasn't already pulled out?'

Jess turned to Morgan. 'Can you send a message to my father on the Codex, and make sure no one else sees it? I can give it to you in code.'

'I think so. What do you want to say?'

'Tell him I'll meet him at the warehouse. He'll understand. If he's not still in town, he'll warn us off.'

'I'll need a Codex,' Morgan said. Khalila ran back down the hall and retrieved one from a fallen soldier. Jess wrote out the words in code on a scrap of Glaudino's note pages, and Morgan quickly copied it into the message page. Her words, Jess realised, didn't even show on the page at all, as if the ink erased itself as soon as she put it to paper.

They waited tensely for a moment, and then the reply wrote out in Callum Brightwell's spiky, urgent hand: *Go careful*.

'He's still there,' Jess said. 'In London.'

'We still have a problem. The Serapeum is guarded,' Wolfe said.

'Not as much of a problem as you would think,' Santi replied. 'The High Garda will be out defending the perimeter; London Garda will be engaged with the Welsh. There are three of us in uniform – that's enough to cause confusion until we can win our way free. I know where the Translation Chamber is. We can make it outside, if your father can send us to safety after.' Santi studied Jess with cold intensity. 'Will he? No half-truths this time.'

'He will,' Jess said, and then swallowed hard. 'For a price. He'll need something in trade.'

'Something,' Santi repeated. 'Such as?'

'I don't know,' Jess said. 'I'll think of something.' But he already knew. His father would highly value the information about how to switch off the automata, but if it wasn't enough, Jess could offer the precious volume he'd translated for Thomas about the creatures. That was enough to buy all their lives ten times over. 'We don't have much choice, do we?'

Santi didn't look happy about it, but he nodded. They were well committed now, and any delays might mean capture, imprisonment, death.

Jess stretched out on the marble couch. 'I'll go first,' he said. 'I'll distract them with a story about fleeing a sneak attack on the High Garda in Rome. Send Glain after me.'

'I'm not sure that's wise,' Khalila said. 'She's injured.'

'That's why she has to go next,' he said. 'If I'm alone telling the story and she arrives . . .'

'It's confirmation,' Santi nodded. 'All right. Morgan, if you can do this, you'd better do it now.'

There wasn't much choice. Morgan fitted the helmet over Jess's head. He muttered the standard good-luck phrase under his breath and waited for the mouth of the wolf to close over him . . . But those jaws never shut. He felt the pressure of Morgan's hands on the helmet, but there was no surge of energy. No power ripping him apart.

He tilted his head to look back at her. 'What's happening?'

Her eyes were round and shocked, and she said, 'I don't know! It's as if—As if I'm blocked from that path. It won't *let* me send you to London!'

'Is it malfunctioning?' Wolfe demanded. 'Because we can't stay here, Morgan.'

'I know! It's not . . . The power's there, but it's only letting me go . . .' Morgan closed her eyes a moment, and Jess felt something this time – a slight tingle, like a surge of static electricity. She caught her breath and whispered, 'No. Oh God, *no*!'

'What is it? What's wrong?' Jess sat up and stripped the helmet off. Morgan's eyes were filled with tears, her hands trembling as she raised them to cover her mouth. When she met his eyes, the tears spilt over. 'Morgan!'

She gulped back what looked like sheer panic, and looked from him to Wolfe as she dragged her hands back down and balled them into fists.

'I'm so sorry. They must have—They must have known we'd try this. I can take you only one place from here,' she said. 'Just one.'

'Where?'

'Alexandria,' she whispered. 'Back into the Iron Tower.'

Wolfe stared for a moment, black eyes gone blank, and then shifted to send Santi a look. 'This is my mother's doing.'

Jess dumped the helmet on the floor with a crash. 'We can't go back to Alexandria. We have to fight.'

'Then we'll die,' Santi said flatly. 'And Glain won't survive that injury unless she gets help quickly. We can give up, or we can take a chance. The Obscurist isn't pledged to be loyal to the Archivist. She's loyal to the Library. There's a difference.'

'Hair-splitting,' Wolfe said, but then shook his head. 'It doesn't matter. Nic is right. We must chance it. It's that, die fighting, or—' He didn't need to state the alternative. They'd all seen it below in the cells. The torture chamber.

'Not the tower,' Morgan whispered, and it was just for Jess. 'I can't go back there. Jess—'

He grabbed her hand and held fast. 'Yes, you can,' he said. 'I'll be with you. I promise, I'm not leaving you.'

'Jess!' The wordless plea in her face hurt him, because he knew he had no way to answer it. He shook his head and saw the light go out in her eyes. He'd just betrayed her. Again.

'We're agreed?' Santi asked, and one by one they nodded. Even Morgan, though the pallor on her face spoke louder than words. 'Go.'

Jess settled the helmet over his head and felt Morgan's trembling, powerful hands come down on it. And this time, *in bocca al lupo*, the lightning came, and struck him apart into pieces and sent him shrieking into the dark.

EPHEMERA

An excerpt from the personal journal of Obscurist Magnus Keria Morning (interdicted to Black Archives).

I have always tried to believe. Always.

When I learnt that, as late as three hundred years ago, Obscurists were allowed the same freedom as other Scholars, that the Iron Tower was only a place of work and study, and not our gilded prison, I accepted that these changes were made purely for our own protection.

Then I read in the Black Archives that two hundred years ago, the Library ruthlessly crushed a revolt by the families of those kept here with us – our children, our lovers, our husbands and wives. Those we loved were killed or exiled. The Archivist set new rules. Crueller rules. We could no longer keep our families or even our children, unless the children were gifted as Obscurists.

My great-great-grandmother remembered a time when her husband lived here, and her children. She lost the ungifted in the revolt. It is not so very long ago, this change. This terrible, cruel desperation of our Archivists, striving to cling to power that is slipping away from them.

Maybe if I had not read so much, did not know so much, I wouldn't see how we live now as a horror. But I think it is just that. The Library, in its terror of losing a grip on us, has crushed us instead. Maybe the dwindling number of children born with quintessence is a sign that the Library's stranglehold is destroying us, and that the Library's days are numbered.

For myself, I should have never let them take my son away from me, or allowed them to take all those sons and daughters we still mourn. I hate every moment of my life as the jailer of this prison. I hate even more the necessity to follow these rules or be replaced by someone much, much crueller.

I am resigned to my fate. No matter what it costs, I will try to make it right in the end.

Keria Morning

Obscurist Magnus

In what I pray will be the last days of the Iron Tower.

CHAPTER THIRTEEN

Arriving in the Iron Tower was not what Jess expected, though he hadn't known *what* to expect, really. Guards seizing him? A sphinx pinning him down with a crushing paw? He did *not* expect to find himself coming awake in a garden of fresh, flowering plants: English roses, tulips from Holland, a blooming cherry tree from Japan gently shading the low, padded couch on which he lay. The rich, gentle scent of flowers and herbs filled the air, and he breathed it in over and over. It settled his stomach and filled him with a kind of calm he hadn't ever known before.

Jess rolled off the couch and to his feet, and felt only a little unsteady – mostly from the beating he'd taken back in Rome – and saw an Obscurist sitting on a nearby folding chair. He was an older man, with handsome, sharp features that spoke of Eastern Europe, possibly Russia, and he nodded calmly at Jess. 'Put the weapon down, please,' he said. 'You may, of course, keep it if it makes you comfortable. Just don't point it at me.'

Jess was still clutching his weapon in a nervous grip, but the man's quiet assurance made him feel a little ashamed of that. He angled the gun down. The Obscurist nodded in satisfaction. 'Good. Now sit down. There's tea.'

The garden room stretched high in an arch, but it wasn't open to the sun; light poured in from windows that circled the round walls, and from them Jess saw the familiar layout of the city of Alexandria – this time from a very great height. The only building that rose higher was the Serapeum, and he could see the tip of the pyramid stretching up another giant's reach above this place.

The garden around him spread out huge and bursting with colours, and it gave him a sense of the incredible scale of this tower. He'd always known it was huge, but never quite *this* large.

A city in its own right, surely.

Jess sat down on a bench and poured himself a cup of hot tea from the waiting pot; his hands were steady enough to hold it now, at least. As he drank, Glain came through. She arrived unconscious, and blood leaked in thick drips from the sodden cloth of her uniform's trouser leg onto the couch. The Obscurist stood up, suddenly very tall and active, and went to her side. He pressed a silver symbol on his collar and said, 'I need Medica here in the Translation Chamber. Now.' He picked Glain up – and she was not a light burden, Jess knew – and moved her to a clear spot on the floor, then clamped a strong hand over the wound in her leg to slow the loss of blood. 'You'll need to assist your other friends,' he told Jess. 'I'm Gregory, by the way.'

'Jess Brightwell, sir,' Jess said. 'Thank you.' This all seemed so strange. He'd expected to arrive in a dark, forbidding world filled with angry soldiers ready to take them down, or, at least, into a place no better than the torture chamber beneath the basilica. But there was a kindly man and tea, flowers, and a Medica team hurrying now into the garden to tend to Glain. Maybe they had no idea they were welcoming fugitives, sworn enemies of the Archivist. Maybe word hadn't come here at all, and once it did, the bars would finally close in on them.

He drank all the tea quickly, just in case. It was the first liquid he'd had in what seemed like hours, and he was severely thirsty. His uniform hung heavy with sweat and bloody from cuts. The one on his palm had split open again, and he took out his field kit and wrapped it in a fresh bandage. He was tying it off as Khalila came through. She seemed as dazed as he still felt by their new surroundings, and he got up to help her to the bench and pour her a cup of tea.

'What is this?' she asked, as if she truly couldn't comprehend it. Her head scarf had come askew, and strands of her glossy, dark hair showed around her face. She dragged it off and repinned it without the slightest self-consciousness, as if he were family. He appreciated that. 'Where are we? Is this the Iron Tower? I thought—'

'You thought it would be grimmer,' said Gregory, the Obscurist, as he got to his feet and came to them. 'Well, you wouldn't be alone in that, I'm sure. But it *is* our home, and we make it as pleasant as we can. How many of you will there be?'

'If we all make it through? Four more.' Dario's loss seemed greater now, their decision to leave without him even worse. He knew that was what Khalila was thinking, too. He could see it in the miserable hunch of her shoulders. 'Dario will be all right, Khalila. He's clever.'

'I know,' she said. 'And he does know Rome. He spent time there when he was younger. His father was an ambassador for Spain.' Jess had always known Dario came from wealth and influence, but not quite *that* much influence. 'I think, if he were in real trouble, he would go to the embassy. They would hide him, at the very least, and get him back to Spain, where his family could find him a safe place. But I think he'll want to find us again.'

'You mean, find *you* again,' Jess said. 'I doubt he gives a rusty *geneih* about my future.'

'You wrong him. You always do.' He put an arm around her, and she sighed and relaxed against him, just a little. 'I missed this. Being together. You've always been like a brother to me, from the moment I met you.'

'Ouch,' he said, but eased it with a smile. 'I never had designs on you, Khalila. I like being someone you can rely on, as much as I rely on you.'

'Jess. You don't rely on anyone.'

'I do,' he said. 'It comes as a surprise to me, too.'

Thomas came through, and was promptly and violently sick – no surprise, since he'd been struggling with so much, for so long. Gregory calmly went for a mop and bucket to clean up after him, and Jess and Khalila moved the boy to the bench, poured him tea, and helped him lie flat when it seemed he needed that more than the restorative. By the time they'd got Thomas settled, Wolfe arrived, then Santi immediately after.

Jess stared hard at the couch, so hard he could feel a vein pulsing in his temple. *Come on*, he begged her. *Come on, don't dally around. Don't let them take you!*

When Morgan's form coalesced in a red cloud of blood, bone and muscle, he was instantly on his feet and moving towards her. By the time she was gasping her first breath, he was at her side. Holding her hand.

She jack-knifed up into his embrace with a horrible, choking cry and locked her arms around him like she expected to be dragged away. 'No,' she whispered into the fabric of his shirt. 'No.'

He smoothed her hair and pressed his lips to the salty skin of her temple. 'Morgan. I'm here. You're not alone.'

'You don't understand,' she said, and her whole body shook with the force of her gasp for breath. 'I can't do it again. There's no other way out. They'll lock me here for good, and I can't, I can't . . .'

'Nobody's locking you in,' he told her, and he meant it. 'But we need to find out what the Obscurist wants from us. Trust me? I won't let you down, Morgan. Not this time.'

She shuddered and relaxed, just a little – enough that he was able to loosen her panicked grip on him. Jess helped her to the bench, the tea, and then turned to Santi and Wolfe, who were standing and talking to Gregory. Glain's leg had been efficiently bandaged, and she was being carried off to a surgery for repair of the torn muscle and blood vessels; on the way out, Jess reached out to brush her fingers, and she gave him a brisk, almost normal nod.

'You're in charge until I get back,' she told him. It was half a joke, and half not.

He nodded back. 'Not sure what I'm in charge of,' he said, 'but I'll do what I can. Glain. Don't die on me.'

'Well,' she said, and managed a weak, strange smile. 'As long as it's an order, sir.'

As they carried Glain away, the Obscurist Magnus appeared from a staircase, trailing an entourage of more than a dozen others who all wore the golden collars of service to the Iron Tower.

Wolfe's mother. She wore her age well and was beautiful in her own striking way. She also wore power like a crackling cloak, and Jess could feel the snap of it halfway across the room. Every head bowed as she passed, and even Niccolo Santi took a step back and nodded in tribute as she approached.

Not her son, though. Wolfe stared at her as if she were a stranger, and said, 'What is this? Are you planning to bargain with the Archivist? Use us as your chips?'

It was a sharp observation. After all, the Iron Tower now had something the Archivist wanted very badly, and all neatly tied with a gift ribbon: Wolfe, Santi, the rebel young Scholars, and an escaped Library prisoner. Quite a lever, if she chose to use it to move the man who ruled the Library. And the Obscurist surely hadn't gained, or held, her position by being politically inept all these years.

The Obscurist put a hand against his cheek. It was a contact that lasted less than a second, because he quickly stepped back. 'Do you really think I would do that, Christopher? Do you think so little of me?'

'No,' he said. 'I think so much of your sense of responsibility to the people in this tower. I'm a secondary concern at best. As ever.'

He couldn't have hurt her worse if he'd stabbed her, but it was visible for only a moment. Her expression stayed the same, except for a slight chill in her eyes. 'Everyone in this tower is my family,' she said. 'You, of all people, know that. They're *your* family. You were born here. Raised here. And, yes, it hurt to send you away, but you know why it had to be done. I've never stopped watching over you. I never will.'

Jess tried to imagine those words coming from his own parents and failed. He knew other families loved on that level; he'd seen it, like glimpses into a warm room from a cold street. But it was an alien thing to him, caring so much. He'd never experienced it until he'd – all unwillingly – begun to care about these people here in Alexandria.

His . . . family.

'You won't hide us from the Archivist,' Wolfe told his mother, and then, after a brief pause, asked, 'Will you?'

'That would be impossible. I can delay him for a bit,' she said. 'Enough time to plan for what you will do next. I'm not the Archivist's creature. I know that everything you've done has been for the good of the Library's mission. For its soul. No matter how you feel about me as a mother, I love you as my son.'

Wolfe walked over to inspect something in the garden – mostly, Jess thought, to hide a sudden vulnerability. The Obscurist watched him with a gentle, sad expression, then turned from him to Santi and gave him a wan smile. 'Nic,' she said. 'I'm sorry. Seeing you here means you've given up so much today. You've worked so hard to secure your place in the High Garda.'

Santi shrugged. 'I always said, if it comes to a choice between him and the Library, I'd choose him,' he said. 'I love him. That means I protect him, doesn't it?'

'It means everything. I'm glad you're all right. You're nearly as dear to me as he is.' Her words must have offended Wolfe, because he gave her a black look and moved farther away. His mother's gaze followed him. Worried. 'You took him into the basilica? What were you thinking?'

'I had to bring him with us,' Santi said quietly. 'If I'd left him behind, he'd have been arrested and ended up dead, or worse. At least it kept him alive.'

'Perhaps, but it's certainly taken a toll,' she said. 'I can see it, though he's hiding it well. I hope time here can help heal that.'

Santi considered that for a moment, then said, in the same level voice as before, 'Lady Keria, I respect you, but if you try to betray him in any way, I'll kill you. You understand? He's had enough pain from this place, too. And from you.'

He'd finally pierced her calm, at least a little, and her eyes –
so like her son's – flashed. 'Do you think it's easy, watching your
son suffer while you stand by doing nothing? Don't you think I
want him to understand—' The Obscurist stopped herself, let a
beat of silence go by, and then said, 'Very well. If I ever betray
him again, or you, then by all means, kill me.'

Santi blinked, but said nothing. *She managed to surprise
him*, Jess thought. And then the Obscurist's gaze turned to
their little group: Khalila, Jess, Morgan, Thomas occupying the
whole of a second bench. Morgan kept her gaze fixed down on
her feet as the Obscurist approached, until the woman's fingers
under her chin forced her head up again. Morgan didn't flinch,
and she didn't look away once their eyes had locked, even while
the Obscurist reached for the silk scarf around her neck and
tugged it loose to reveal the fish-pale skin of her throat.

'Incredible,' the Obscurist said. 'I've never met anyone with
your power or your blind foolishness. If you think it gives you
some kind of invulnerability, you don't understand the stakes.'

Morgan slapped the Obscurist's hand away from her scarf. The
collared guards nearby tensed, hands closing tight around knives,
but the Obscurist gave them a shake of her head. 'I won't be caged
up here! I won't be made into some slave – no, worse than that.
Some mindless part in a machine, replaced when it breaks.'

'You're far more than an automaton,' the Obscurist told her.
'You're worth more than most people who will ever be born
on this earth, Morgan. Archimedes taught that of all the five
elements, quintessence is the most rare, the most valuable, the
one that transmutes the ordinary into extraordinary. *We* are
quintessence. It's a divine gift, and like all gifts, we must use it
for the Library's greater glory.'

Jess wanted to push her away, but it was – oddly – Khalila who spoke in that moment, as clear and calm as glass. 'Archimedes said mathematics reveals its secrets only to those who approach it with pure love for its own beauty. But the Archivist has no love for knowledge. He wants only power. You are the club he swings to get it.'

'Archivists come and go,' the Obscurist said. 'The next will be better. You're no more than children. You can't possibly understand.'

Jess glared at her. 'We aren't children, and you don't need Morgan. You have a tower full of your *quintessence* already.'

'Not like her.' The Obscurist touched Morgan's cheek, and Morgan jerked away, eyes burning with anger.

Khalila stood up. It was a swift, controlled motion, and although it wasn't threatening, there was a cold look in her eyes that made the Obscurist's focus shift.

'You are Scholar Seif, if I am correct.'

'Yes, Obscurist Magnus.'

'I have heard great things of you. And I have a name. Please call me Keria.'

'I would not presume to be so informal. But if you touch Morgan again, if you try to take her away and lock her up, then you'll have to kill me. I won't make it easy.'

'Yes,' The Obscurist said. 'I can see that. You, Jess? Are you also determined to be foolish?'

'It's my finest quality,' he said blandly. Her smile had the power of a lightning strike.

'So I see. We'll settle Morgan's status later. For now, permit me to offer our help to the young inventor,' she said, moving to Thomas. 'Don't fear, Thomas. We'll see you are well cared for here.'

'Hypocrite,' Jess said. 'You knew where he was the whole time. As Scholar Wolfe said, we're all just pieces on your game board. You'll sacrifice any of us to get what you want.'

She had the same severe look as Wolfe, when she wanted to use it. 'Do, please, tell me what my plans are, young man. I'm sure it will be very informative.' He could just *hear* Wolfe saying that, in exactly the same tone, and though Jess didn't mean to, it made him laugh. Bitterly.

'Oh, leave them alone,' Wolfe said without turning. 'I know exactly what your plans are. *Mother.* And I can promise you, we won't cooperate in the least.'

There was a breathless silence for a moment, and then the Obscurist walked away, towards the stairs where she'd entered. 'Gregory will see to your accommodations,' she said without looking back. 'Morgan. Your collar will be replaced. It has to be done, so please don't injure yourself resisting.'

Morgan stared at the woman's back as if she wanted to plant a knife in it. Her hand gripped Jess's again tightly. He was lucky it was the one without a bandage.

Gregory walked over to stand in front of the two of them and said with a calm smile, 'Now, let's be reasonable about this. You can either submit gracefully or submit when you lose the fight, and your friends end up suffering for it. All right?'

He held up his hand, and another Obscurist moved forward to put a wooden box in his palm. When he opened it, Jess saw it held one of the golden collars. He felt Morgan's bone-deep shiver of revulsion and took in a slow breath. 'You don't have to,' he told her. 'Just tell me the word.'

'No,' she whispered. 'It won't do any good, Jess. I don't want any of you hurt.'

Morgan stood up, closed her eyes, and stayed very still as

Gregory clasped the collar around her neck and the symbols on the golden surface shimmered and shifted, and the latch just . . . disappeared.

Morgan sank down again beside him as if all the strength had drained out of her, and he put his arm around her waist. 'Easy,' he whispered to her. 'I'm right here.'

He turned his head and was suddenly, intensely aware that she was here, next to him, *real*. Being separated for months hadn't dulled the impact of her presence to him, or – he thought – of his on her. A burning wave of hot and cold swept over him, and he thought, *I can't let them have her. I can't.* It had been different before, but here, seeing the mute, horrible misery in her eyes and the defeat . . . He understood how much she hated this place, rich and splendid as it seemed to be. He didn't altogether understand *why*, but there was no denying it.

Gregory casually poured himself another cup of tea from the pot, sipped, and made a face. 'Gone cold,' he said. 'Too bad. You know, Morgan, you'd do well to be cautious. Keria Morning is the most powerful woman in the world.'

'I don't care who she is,' Jess said. 'Morgan is coming with us when we leave this place. And we *will* be leaving.'

Gregory laughed so hard, he slopped tea from the side of his cup. 'You, boy, are one to watch. I might watch you end very badly, but at least it will be a good show.' He put the cup aside. 'Come on. I'll show you to your quarters. The good news is that there is plenty of space here, so you each get your own rooms.'

'What's the bad news?'

'I wish I could even begin to guess the extent of it.' Gregory sounded dry and uninterested, but Jess couldn't imagine that the man wasn't *some* kind of important personage within the Iron Tower. He did notice that as they stood up, Morgan kept tight

hold of Jess's hand, and moved quickly away from Gregory as soon as the chance presented itself. *She doesn't like him. That's telling.*

'I hope Glain will be all right,' Khalila said, as she helped Thomas up.

'She's in good hands,' Wolfe said, turning in a storm of black robes to stride back to them. 'The Tower gets the best of everything the Library has to offer.'

'Except freedom,' Morgan said. He turned to look at her, and she dropped her gaze.

'Except that,' he agreed.

Gregory said, 'Come on, then,' and led the way out.

Jess supposed he shouldn't have been astonished by the interior of the Iron Tower, but he was, and felt as much of a bumpkin gone to market as he had on his first day in Alexandria.

The tower's central core held rooms. The garden room and Translation Chamber – which sat atop everything else – stretched across the entire expanse from side to side. Beneath that, stairs wound in a flat spiral around the outer walls of the tower, and Jess could feel the warmth of the Alexandrian sun radiating through the metal skin – muted, but not completely gone. Nevertheless, it was cool inside, an artificial sort of coolness that puzzled him, until he felt a breeze from a grate blowing unnaturally cool air. He mentioned it to Thomas, who nodded. 'It's like the heated air we use in the winter,' he said. 'Here, heat is as much the enemy as our cold.'

'I can understand heat, but how do you cool air down? Ice?'

'Chemicals,' Thomas said. 'There are some that freeze things. I suppose blowing air over a mixture of them might do the trick. I never thought of it before.' He seemed thoughtful, distracted by the question. That was good. He even seemed strong enough

to take the stairs alone, though with Santi's watchful support at the ready.

The cool air wasn't the only marvel Jess glimpsed. The lights were made of clear glass globes with glowing centres that seemed like trapped starlight. And they were *everywhere* . . . hanging from chains overhead, powering lamps sitting on tables. When he reached out to touch the nearest lit glass, it scorched his fingers as if he'd put them in an open flame. He felt like an idiot.

'It's powered by electricity,' Morgan said. 'The heat's a by-product.'

'I didn't think electricity could be used for illumination! I thought it was just a party trick, of no real useful application.'

'One of a great many things we've been taught that isn't true,' she said. 'Don't be fooled by all the wonders. It's a pretty prison. Still a prison.'

Gregory was already proceeding down another round of stairs ahead of them, and they had to hurry to catch up. Khalila seemed as fascinated as Jess with what they were seeing, though far less willing to risk skin in experimentation. She dropped back to chat with Thomas, and they had an animated conversation about the wonders of the square lifting device, quite like a small room on tracks, that rose and fell, carrying people from one floor of the tower to another. Electrical as well, Jess gathered from the densely technical discussion. Jess was used to the ever-present sound of steam pumps; it had been the constant heartbeat of London, and even in Alexandria the hiss of them was never far away. But here . . . here the power they used gave it an eerie, calm silence.

They arrived at a floor near the middle of the tower, and Gregory led them through a closed door. A central hallway ran straight through, bisecting the circle, and on each side of it lay more closed doors. 'There,' he said. 'One for everyone. Choose your own; they're all equally well appointed, with full baths and fine beds. You've even got a window in each, though I would recommend against trying to open them. Or break them.'

'Are we to be locked in?' Santi asked.

'Certainly not. You're free to come and go as you like. Explore the Tower. Just don't try to leave.' His gaze swept over them and fixed on Jess. 'We have sphinx guards downstairs. Ours *do not* turn off. Nor are they susceptible to rewritten scripts. Their behaviour is etched into their metal bones.' He checked an elaborately gilded clock that graced an alcove in the centre of the hall, between two of the rooms. 'Dinner will be downstairs in an hour. Morgan can show you the way. There are bells in your room. Pull them if you require anything. Someone will be on duty no matter the hour.' Gregory smiled, and for the first time he looked less than friendly. It was not a pleasant change. 'Morgan. After dinner, I will expect you back in your own room.'

She nodded, but said nothing. They watched as the Obscurist left and made his way down the stairs, and waited until he was gone before Jess walked to the door they'd entered and shut it. There was no lock to keep Gregory out. He wasn't overly surprised.

'Morgan?' Wolfe was looking at the girl now, turning her to face him. 'I know Gregory. I know what he does. Do you want to talk to me?'

'No,' she said. 'You can't help me, can you?'

He seemed to consider that for a moment. 'We'll see about that. Nic? Do you have a preference for a room?'

'One that isn't inside this damned tower?' Santi choose a door at random and swung it open. He stopped and seemed to reconsider. 'Or . . . I suppose I might grow accustomed.' The room, Jess realised as he craned to look, was enormous and luxurious, and the bed looked more lushly comfortable than anything he'd ever seen. Surely even kings didn't sleep that well.

Jess opened the door across the hall. It was a mirror image, just as rich. The fabrics were muted golds and crimsons, and the floor was covered with a carpet so soft it felt like stepping on pillows.

Morgan said, 'The rooms are all fine. He wasn't lying about that.'

He turned and found that she was already inside and closing the door behind her.

Alone. *Alone*. It suddenly hit him like a fist to the gut that he had Morgan to himself and their friends would, perhaps, understand enough to leave them their privacy.

But probably not.

There were no locks on the doors. That was going to bother him a great deal, he realised. He searched for some way to jam it shut, but found nothing.

When he turned back, Morgan silently came into his arms. She didn't speak, so he didn't, either, afraid to break this fragile truce between them. And then she began to cry.

He held her closer, wrapped in a protective hug. Her grief was a storm, and it sounded agonising and hopeless to him, and went on until he worried she might be lost in it. 'Hey. *Hey*. You're safe, understand? Morgan!'

'No,' she said, and grabbed the inner edge of the gold collar around her neck. She pulled at it with sudden viciousness, and he winced as he saw it bite into her skin. 'I'm trapped here, don't you see it? Of course you don't. All you can see are the pretty flowers and the beautiful rooms, but that's just paint over something rotten. I'd rather die than lose my will and be one of them, Jess. I'm not afraid of dying!'

She meant it, and it stunned him. He kept holding her, not sure how thin the ice was he was standing on. 'Do you want to tell me what scares you so badly?'

'They—' She seemed to want to answer, but he could feel the frustration, too. As if she couldn't find the words. 'I don't think you'd understand.'

'Try.'

'They give us examinations,' she said then, and he felt her shudder from the memory. 'Chart our monthly cycles. And when they think we are ready to conceive, they . . .'

His throat felt dry now and hot with anger. She was right: this was unfamiliar territory to him. He'd not grown up with sisters, and his mother had always been a distant visitor in his life. He had no real reference for these things. 'They match you?'

'Yes.' She looked up at him. 'When I ran away to see you, I avoided the day they'd marked out for me to be matched. But, Jess, I won't be able to avoid that again now.'

'Then you can fight!' he told her. 'You've never been afraid to fight!'

'I've seen what happens when you fight. My friend . . .' She took in a deep breath, held it, and let it out. 'I'm sorry, Jess. I didn't mean to . . . I'm just so angry. And frightened.'

'I won't let anything happen to you,' he said, which was a foolish thing to say, and from the look she gave him – half-grateful and half-pitying – she knew it.

'Don't,' she said, and put her hand on his cheek. 'Don't. Just say you'll be here for me now.'

'I will. I am.'

'Then kiss me.'

He did, and tasted tears and sweetness on her lips. It was a long, gentle kiss, and not entirely innocent of passion.

Morgan suddenly broke the kiss and put her forehead against his. The moment snapped him back to reality and it physically hurt inside, like something stabbing deep. She leant back and her eyes met his and held, and it hurt worse. He didn't move. They had a history of this, of finding each other and being torn apart by words or deeds, and he didn't want it to happen. Not now. *Not tonight.*

He rested his fingertips on her Obscurist's collar, this awful, beautiful thing, and it felt warm as blood to the touch; heat from her body or some kind of process within the gold, he didn't know. 'Morgan,' he said. 'You don't have to make this choice. It's not me or the Iron Tower. You don't have to – to pretend to love me to make me help you get out of here.'

'Is that what you think about me? That I'm *paying you off?*' She was angry. Hot spots of colour darkened her cheeks, and now she pulled away from him completely and stood up with her hands clenched at her sides. 'That I'm *selling myself to you?* I thought you understood me, Jess. I thought you understood how I felt!'

He held up both hands in a plea for peace. 'I meant only that it doesn't have to end with you settling for something you don't really want. Even if *I* want it.'

'You're an idiot!' She grabbed a pillow from the bed and flung it at him.

He caught it. 'Apparently!'

'I'm not going to sleep with you just to get out of being matched in the Tower, if that's what you're thinking!'

There was a ringing moment of silence after that, and he stared into her suddenly wide eyes.

'Would that work?' he asked her. 'If you did, would it—?'

'Get out!' she yelled at him, and picked up another pillow.

'Morgan, it's my room—'

'Out!'

He was too angry, too hurt, too full of stupid pride, to argue with her.

And he slammed the door behind him on the way out and went to Thomas's room.

Thomas was standing in his doorway, and with one look at Jess, stepped back and let him inside.

'I propose chess,' he said. 'There's a board in the room.'

That was nearly as perfect an answer to his problems as Jess could imagine.

EPHEMERA

From the personal journal of Morgan Hault.

I've done everything wrong. Everything. It's all coming apart. It's all my fault. I thought I could make everyone safe, and I thought that Jess . . . that we could patch up our differences and find each other again. Even if most of that separation was from me, because I was afraid to be hurt again.

But he doesn't understand me at all. And I hurt Sybilla. I left her behind when I'd promised to help her, too. I ran without even thinking about what that would mean for her. I ran to Jess, and then I didn't dare get close to him, and now . . . now everything is in ruins.

I'll be trapped here. Maybe I should accept what fate writes down for me. Maybe Dominic will be a kind partner to me. Maybe one day I'll be as contented and bland as Rosa, and believe every lie shovelled into my face.

I hope they kill me before I become just another

broodmare for the Library's futile attempt to cling to its past.

Damn you, Jess, for making me hope it could be any different.

And thank you, too.

I still love you. As unwise as that is.

CHAPTER FOURTEEN

'Mate,' Thomas said, and moved his knight into position. Jess groaned and tipped his king. It was his third straight game lost, but he at least felt somewhat steadier and a good deal more level-headed.

'Let's not use that term any more,' Jess said. 'Just say, *I win*.'

Thomas raised his eyebrows and smiled a little – the best that Jess had seen from his friend since finding him in that cell. 'All right. You know, as much as I enjoy this strange new feeling of winning against you, you should go back and talk to Morgan.'

'Not yet,' Jess said. 'She'd only throw another pillow at me. Or something more damaging.'

'I understand why she's angry. What are *you* angry about?'

What was it, exactly? He didn't know, except that he was angry at everything suddenly. Angry for Morgan, but angry *at* her too. Stupidly. It didn't even make sense. 'She thinks I'm taking advantage.'

Thomas's eyebrows rose to a ridiculous level, wrinkling his forehead like an old man's. 'Are you, Jess?'

'How can you even ask me?'

'Your motives are completely pure, then?'

Jess glared at him. 'Set the board, Thomas.'

'You sound like Dario just now, you know.'

'Are you trying to insult me?'

'Only a little.' He grinned outright this time, and Jess smiled back. With months of grime washed down the drain and his hair drying to puffball brightness, Thomas looked almost like his old self. He had some spark back in his eyes. But the grin faded too quickly. 'She's trapped here. I know how that feels. Now you begin to see it, too, how being helpless twists us around.'

'It didn't twist you,' Jess said. 'You've done very well.'

Thomas's expression didn't alter. 'I seem so, maybe. But I'm not the same. She's not. Her confinement isn't like mine, but don't let the soft bars fool you. Taking someone's will, someone's freedom . . . it kills the heart and then the soul.'

'It didn't kill yours.'

Thomas said nothing this time. He set up the board, white and black, and waited for Jess to make a move.

Jess didn't have a chance, because a knock came on the door. He was hoping for Morgan, but when Thomas swung it open, Khalila stood on the other side. She glanced quickly at them both and said, 'We have to attend dinner now. I don't think they gave us a choice.'

'See?' Thomas said to Jess. 'So it begins. The little deaths of freedom.'

They stepped out into the hall. Khalila stood quite alone, and Jess wasn't sure if her arms were simply crossed or if she was hugging herself for comfort. He knew what she was thinking and feeling, because he'd felt it himself when Morgan had been taken away. At least he'd known where she was and who'd taken her.

Dario was just . . . gone. Vanished. And there was no way to know if he was alive, free, imprisoned, dead. All Khalila could do was hope . . . and hope was difficult, knowing what they all knew about the Library now. *He's a smart one*, Jess told himself again. *Connections, money, friends . . . he'll be all right.* He wanted to say that to Khalila but knew how useless it would sound.

When she looked up and saw him, she forced a smile and said, 'I was just thinking about my family.'

That stopped him. Why had he just assumed she'd be pining uselessly after Dario? Was it because he was so caught up in his own thoughts of Morgan? 'Your family?' He knew he sounded surprised. 'Why? Are they all right?'

'I don't know,' she said. 'I've betrayed everything they believe in. Worse than that, I've so many Scholars in the family. Will they be all right, Jess? Do you think the Library will punish them for what I've done?'

'No,' he said. 'Of course not.'

'I hope not.' The desolation in her voice hurt. He remembered her proud uncle, escorting her on the train to Alexandria, and the constant messages she'd received from her father and mother and siblings and cousins. Khalila's life was full of love, and the decisions she'd made may have cut her off from that love. Would she have done that if he hadn't come to her with his mad speculations and schemes?

Another knife cut of guilt slicing a piece of his heart away. He had no answers for her, nothing but a whispered, 'I'm sorry,' which was no comfort. He wished she *had* been thinking of Dario. It would have been a simpler subject, an easier answer. This cut to the core of who Khalila was.

She made the choice, some part of him said, but he hated that he thought of it. Of course she had. That didn't make it all right. In some ways, it only made it worse.

While Jess stood helpless, Thomas walked directly to Khalila and wrapped her in a hug that lifted her nearly off her feet. After a second of surprise, she put her arms around him – as far as they would stretch – and put her head on his broad shoulder.

'I would be dead if not for you,' he told her. 'I would be dead to everything and everyone I knew if you hadn't come for me. All of you. Don't think I will ever forget what you've done for me.'

'I had to,' she said. 'I was glad to.'

'Even so,' he said. 'If you lose your family, I will be your family. Always.'

She took a deep breath and said, 'Thank you. Now put me down, you lumbering bear.'

He laughed a little and put her back on her feet. 'Sorry. It's like picking up a tiny bird. You should eat more.'

'So should you,' she said. Her smile was back. So was the light in her eyes. *It's remarkable*, Jess thought, *that Thomas can do that.* He had so much light inside him that it warmed those around him. 'Will you be my escort to dinner?'

'I will,' Thomas said gravely, and offered her his arm, like an ancient country gentleman. She put her hand lightly on it.

Jess was laughing at them, but it stopped quickly as Morgan opened the door of his room and their eyes met. He nodded to her warily. She nodded back. Her eyes looked red and swollen, but there were no tears now. And no forgiveness, either.

He was still considering what to say to her when the door to Wolfe and Santi's room opened and the two men stepped out. Wolfe gave them all a dour glance and said, 'What are you waiting for?' as he pushed past and opened the door at the end of the hallway. Santi followed, and then Khalila and Thomas.

Jess cleared his throat and gestured, and Morgan preceded him out.

It didn't really feel like peace.

Somehow Jess had expected a small, private room that would have been set aside for them, but instead the dining room of the Iron Tower was a large, open space filled with many, many tables and groups gathered at nearly every one. Most of those in the room fell silent and turned towards them as they entered, and Jess had an instinctive defensive reaction until Morgan murmured, 'They never see new faces here. You're novelties.'

Novelties. He felt Thomas flinch, saw Morgan avert her eyes, and it made him even angrier. *We're not your entertainment,* Jess wanted to shout. He began to have a small inkling of what Morgan's life might be like here, being the rebellious outcast in what seemed to be a group of true believers.

Morgan, gaze down, wasn't looking at any of the other tables, but they were all staring . . . and whispering and pointing. A young girl rose from a nearby table and walked towards them. She couldn't have been more than sixteen and had an unpleasantly smug look on her face, but what drew Jess's attention was the rounded swell of her stomach beneath her dress. It took him a long moment to comprehend what that meant, and then he shot a fast, unguarded look at Morgan. Her face – what he could see from this angle – had set into a bland mask.

'Sister Morgan!' the girl almost purred, and extended both hands as if she expected Morgan to grasp them in welcome. 'We're so glad you decided to rejoin us. We missed you!'

She managed to make it look like her own idea to clasp her hands in excitement and pull them back when Morgan didn't take the hint. Her smile turned brittle and a little vile. The silence stretched . . . and then Morgan said, 'Rosa, we're tired and hungry. Please excuse us.'

It was bare courtesy, and Rosa couldn't have missed it, but she somehow managed to hang on to that smile and put both hands now on the curve of her stomach. 'The baby's started to kick. Do you want to feel it?'

'I'm afraid we are all far too tired this evening,' Khalila said, which sounded brusque, but in the way that only Khalila could manage, also sounded warm and kind. 'Rosa, is it?'

'Yes,' Rosa said, and turned to her. She took in Khalila in one sweeping glance, head to toe. 'You're not one of us.'

'I am a Scholar,' Khalila said. 'How does that make me alien to you?'

Rosa dismissed her and went back to Morgan. 'Don't worry,' she said, and pitched her voice a little louder to carry. 'I know you missed your time, but Dominic is a patient young man. I'm sure you look forward to it.'

Dominic. Jess felt something dark settle into the pit of his stomach, because now he had a name for the Obscurist Morgan was expected to bed. *Dominic*. He scanned the room, wondering which of them it was. The puffy, pale one at the back with his attention fixed on his plate? The lean one watching them with silvery eyes? It would drive him mad, not knowing which one of them to hate.

Rosa started back towards her table but then turned back, as if she'd just thought of something. Pure, petty theatre. 'Oh,' she said to Morgan. 'I don't suppose you've heard about poor Sybilla?'

That, for the first time, broke through Morgan's mask, and she quickly looked up. 'What about her?'

'She had a . . . misadventure,' Rosa said. 'Perhaps you should visit her on the hospital floor.'

This time, Gregory stood up from one of the tables not far away, and though he said nothing, Rosa quickly ducked her head and went back to her seat without another word. Gregory sank down, too, but Jess could feel his gaze on them.

On Morgan.

'Well,' Khalila said as they took chairs at one of the few empty tables. 'I can see why the charm of this place might wear very thin. Morgan? All right?'

'Yes,' Morgan said, but in a toneless way that made Jess think the opposite. 'Fine.' She swallowed and forced a little cheer. 'The food's very good. The servers will bring what you want.'

Thomas, settling uneasily into a chair too small for him, said, 'Is there a list of choices?'

'No. You just tell them what you'd like. Wolfe was right; Obscurists are pampered. The best food, prepared just the way we want it; that's just one of many ways they try to make us forget we're—'

'Prisoners,' Jess finished.

'No,' Morgan said, and didn't look at him. 'Prisoners eventually get out.'

A servant wearing a gold band – didn't that go against the entire structure of the Library? – came to ask politely what they wanted for food and drink. With no slate of choices, Jess was too tired to think creatively; longing for a bit for home, though he didn't know why, he just ordered roast beef and mash. Thomas must have felt the same, since he ordered schnitzel. Morgan asked for chicken; Khalila for roasted mutton. It was all very normal. As soon as the servant walked away, Thomas said, 'The servants are pledged here for life as well?'

Morgan nodded. 'The difference is that they do get to leave the tower from time to time. Obscurists can only leave under the strictest rules and controls.'

'What about the ones who operate the Translation Chamber?'

'Our lowest caste,' she said. 'They have the least talent for writing scripts; they can only interpret what's already been written and infuse it with the quintessence to make it work.'

Jess thought it must be a strange blessing here to be a disappointment; it held the chance to take the outside air, see the world, at least a bit. 'Lucky devils,' he said, and got a look of agreement from her. Just a brief one, but it made him feel less cold. He'd lost his anger, he realised, and partly because it was becoming clearer and clearer to him that none of this had to do with a choice Morgan had made. She'd not chosen to be born with this talent; in fact, she'd done everything in her power to avoid coming here in the first place. She'd never sought out being an Obscurist.

Or children, he thought before he could stop himself. Rosa, with her self-satisfied glow and pointed jibes, made it clear just how Morgan was being taunted.

'Morgan,' he said quietly. 'Who's Sybilla?'

She froze for an instant in the act of reaching for her water glass, then completed the motion, drank, and set it down before she said, 'A friend.'

'And she's ill?'

Morgan said nothing, but Wolfe did. He looked angry. 'Not ill. Leave it, Brightwell.'

Another awkward silence, one Thomas moved to fill with a patently false cheer.

'Do you know the tower already?' Thomas asked Wolfe. 'You lived here. Such wondrous inventions they have here, I'd love to hear about all—'

'My mother determined I was without significant talent as an Obscurist when I was five years old,' Wolfe broke in. 'At ten, I was removed to the Library orphanage, where I received my training. I've never been back. So I know little about the inventions, Thomas.'

'A lot of time between visits from your mother,' Santi said. He was watching Wolfe closely, a cup of poured wine forgotten in his hand.

'Not long enough. I saw her the day they released me from the Basilica Julia prison,' Wolfe said. 'She brought me home. To you. She left before you found me.'

Silence at the table. Santi opened his mouth and closed it again, as if he couldn't decide what to ask or what to say; he finally just drank his wine. Wolfe followed suit.

The mood had fallen a little dark, and grew darker with the sudden approach of Gregory, who smiled at them as if they were old friends. 'Obscurist Hault,' he said. 'Your presence is requested. Dominic has missed you during your absences. Please come with me.'

Dominic, Jess realised, must be the red-haired young man who stood a few paces back. He was small, compact, and covered in a spray of freckles . . . and miserable. Jess had been prepared to hate him, but seeing how he avoided even so much as looking in Morgan's direction, he understood with blinding speed it wasn't the boy's choice, either.

Just a duty to be done.

Jess was rising to his feet to do something violent – to Gregory, if not to Dominic – when Wolfe quickly stood, faced Gregory, and said, 'I'd have thought you'd have learnt some manners at your age, but you're as bad as you were when I was a child. You'll have her the rest of her life. Isn't that enough?'

Gregory straightened to face Scholar Wolfe, and Jess realised there was real dislike between these two. It bordered on hate. For all Gregory's droll observations, he wasn't remotely friendly. There was something dark underneath his smile – more like a smirk now. Unpleasant and superior. 'Keria's always favoured you,' he said. 'Her precious little boy, born a disappointment. She fought to keep you long past the age when you should have been sent away, and when you finally were, she still never forgot you. All her love was reserved for you, and you can't even give her a kind word in return.'

'She doesn't look to me for kind words. She has you for that. You were ever the politician. And the predator.'

Gregory's smile froze in place, and shattered into a compressed, hard line. 'What are you implying?'

'Nothing,' Wolfe said. 'Except that you take a special, unseemly delight in your job.'

'And what do you think I do?'

'Play God with the lives of children.'

'Obscurist Hault is not a child. She is a young woman of tremendous potential who might one day prove as important, if not more important, than your own mother. It's in the best interests of the Iron Tower to—'

'To match her with an appropriate sire for her children? Oh yes. I know the game. I grew up with a mother who loathed the very sight of my father, and he hated her in turn. Odd, isn't it, that your forced inbreeding has created generations of progressively *less* powerful Obscurists? It's as if it doesn't actually work to force people into loveless unions!'

'You know nothing—'

'As one of your more notable failures, I'd say I know *everything*,' Wolfe said flatly. 'Go away, Gregory. Morgan stays with us.'

Jess stood up. Didn't say or do anything; just stood up. Khalila stood, too. Thomas. Santi. Last of all, Wolfe, with deliberate calm.

Dominic at last raised his head, and the relief on his face was very plain.

'This is a foolish waste of our charity,' Gregory said. 'We've offered you safety. Refuge. Care for your wounded. And you're throwing it back in our faces, and for what? You can't keep her. She belongs to us. To the Tower and the Library.'

'She belongs to no one. Let me be clear: the girl makes her own choices, for as long as she's with us. If my mother disagrees with that, tell her to come herself. I don't listen to self-important lackeys.'

Gregory's face turned an alarming shade of red. 'As you wish,' he said. '*Scholar* Wolfe.'

He walked back to his table, anger in every stiff motion, and pointedly turned his back to them. Jess didn't want to do the same. He didn't trust Gregory not to stick a knife in it.

Dominic was still there. The young man looked scared as a rabbit, but he stayed long enough to say, to Morgan, 'I'm sorry,' before he went back to his own table.

Not everyone in the Iron Tower was as content and smug as Rosa.

'Morgan?' Khalila settled back down in her chair and reached for Morgan's hand. 'They haven't forced you—'

'Not yet,' Morgan said. 'Thank you, Scholar Wolfe.'

He shook his napkin out and dropped it in his lap. 'Don't thank me,' he said. 'I did it to annoy Gregory.'

'Watch him,' Morgan said. 'He's a snake.'

'I'm immune to his particular poison. We knew each other as children, and he was five years older. You can imagine how that appealed to his cruel nature.'

She shuddered. 'I'd rather not. And thank you, whatever you meant by it.'

He shrugged as if it didn't matter and then the food arrived. Jess was pleasantly surprised to find his roast beef and mash was as good as a Sunday feast at home – one of the few consistently pleasant things he could recall about his childhood. They'd even mushed his peas. For a while, the five of them concentrated on their food. Someone had wisely allotted Thomas a double portion, and he ate it at an alarming speed that worried Jess for a moment; maybe the young German's stomach couldn't handle such a sudden rush of rich food. But Thomas seemed happy, and at the moment that was all that mattered.

'Glain!' Thomas suddenly put down his fork – he was more than halfway done with his second large schnitzel – and looked around at the rest of them. 'What is Glain eating? Is she allowed visitors yet?'

'You're free to ask,' Wolfe said. 'The Medica floor is below this one.'

'Soup,' Thomas said. 'I'll take her soup.' Without waiting for anyone else, he stood up and stopped a server, ordered a bowl to go, and quickly left with it. Santi, done with his meal, leant back to watch him go.

'He's making a quick recovery,' he said.

'Yes,' Wolfe agreed. He didn't look happy. 'Seems so.'

They exchanged looks – significant ones, Jess thought. 'He's strong,' he said, out of some impulse to defend his friend. Santi sighed.

'He wouldn't have survived without that,' he said. 'But strength won't keep the darkness away, and being on his own in a hostile place isn't good for him. Go. Find him.'

Jess didn't hesitate to take up that suggestion. And it led him to the Medica floor.

The floor, instead of having individual chambers, had been built open plan, with only suspended curtains sectioning off one patient from another. Most of the curtains had been tidily drawn back and secured, the beds empty. The Medica attendant on duty rose from her station to study him as he entered, then nodded towards one of the curtained areas. 'Your companions are there,' she said. 'You can stay a few minutes. No longer. The patient needs rest.'

Jess nodded and continued on, and found Thomas sitting beside Glain's bedside. He seemed fine, and so did Glain; she'd been propped up with cushions, and was trying to spoon up soup, but without much appetite that Jess could see. He pulled a chair closer and straddled it. 'I've been told that the Iron Tower gets the best of everything,' he said.

Glain swallowed her mouthful and reached for the water glass. 'Soup is soup. But they've treated me well enough.' She shot Jess a guarded look. 'How is everyone else?'

'All right so far,' he said. He knew she was asking mostly about Morgan, and he didn't want to answer that question. 'So, you're not going to die on us, then.'

'Don't you just wish? No. You're not so lucky, Brightwell.'

'Good.' He extended a hand and she clasped it, but quickly, and then dug back into her soup. Personal emotion always made her uncomfortable. 'Thomas thought of the food.'

'It was kind,' Glain said, and gave the German boy a brief, full smile. 'Did you eat?'

'Schnitzel,' Thomas said. 'But I almost regret it. I – My stomach can't take so much rich food so quickly, I think.' He'd paled again and his fingers drummed in agitation. Trying, Jess figured, to distract himself from thoughts of what he'd eaten in the cells, or the times he'd had to endure hunger. *Even the good things are tainted for him*, Jess thought, and it enraged him all over again. But it would get better, wouldn't it? Given time? *It hasn't for Wolfe.* Against his will, he recalled Elsinore Quest's advice: damage like this couldn't be buried safely.

'We should leave you,' Jess said, 'unless you need something?'

'I'll harass the staff if I do. That's what they're here for,' Glain replied. 'You concentrate on finding a way out of this. I'll join you tomorrow.'

'If the physicians say you can.'

'Tomorrow,' she said, and ate another mouthful of soup with grim determination.

Thomas seemed reluctant to leave despite his restlessness, and Jess had to convince him that they weren't abandoning Glain; he seemed eager for her not to feel alone, but to Jess it appeared to be more about Thomas's experiences shadowing the situation. Eventually, Glain persuaded him by rolling her eyes and said, 'Oh, for the sake of Heron, just leave me to get some rest, Thomas! I'm fine!' And as blunt as it was, it did the job of convincing him to follow Jess out.

As they left, though, Jess caught sight of a familiar figure slipping into another private curtained-off area across the way, and put his hand on Thomas's arm to hold him back. 'Wait here for me,' he said. 'I'll just be a moment.'

'Jess?'

'One moment.'

He didn't go into the private space, but he pulled the curtain aside, just enough to see Morgan sitting down at the bedside of another young woman. It took him a moment to recall it, but hadn't the snide girl Rosa mentioned something about Morgan's friend? *Sybil . . . no. Sybilla.*

Sybilla couldn't have been much older than Rosa – fifteen or sixteen, best guess. She was a slip of a thing, swallowed up by blankets and pillows, wan, pale, and unconscious.

As he watched, Morgan put her hand on the girl's shoulder,

bowed her head, and began to cry. Silent, wrenching tears.

'Sir,' the Medica attendant said sharply from behind him. 'Come away. Now.'

Jess jumped and turned and followed her away. 'Wait,' he said. 'What happened to her? The girl in the bed?'

'I can't discuss that.'

'Wait.' Jess drew her to a stop and met her eyes. 'What happened?'

She looked away all too quickly. 'I told you, I can't discuss it.' But she hadn't pulled away, either, and after a pause whispered, 'She took poison. She's not the first.'

He kept his voice as low as hers. 'Why?'

'Not everyone is happy with their fate,' she said, and then did pull away. 'Or suited to it. You should go. Now.'

Jess looked back over his shoulder at the closed curtains. Morgan must not have heard; he could see her shadow against the cloth, still bent forward. Still lost in her grief and fear.

I won't let it happen to you, he told her. *Whatever you feel about me now, that doesn't matter. I don't want to ever see you like Sybilla.*

He walked Thomas back to the safety of the others and waited on the stairs until Morgan walked out onto the landing in front of the Medica doors. She didn't look up to where he stood; she seemed tired and lonely, then she turned and took the stairs *down*. Away from him. Away from the rest of them.

Jess followed quietly and at a distance.

She descended two floors and went down a hallway, and as he stepped through and into sudden, thick darkness, he felt a knife prick the skin of his throat, and he immediately froze.

Then she sighed. 'Oh, Jess. Please go away.' Her voice sounded thick and unsteady, and he knew she was still crying or on the verge of it. The knife moved away, and he heard her start to turn.

'I'm sorry,' he said quietly. That earned another sigh, even more quiet.

'For what?'

'For not understanding. Staying away from this place should always have been your choice. Not mine.' He hesitated for a second. 'Your friend. Will she live?'

'Yes,' Morgan said. 'And that's almost worse. You see, they now consider her a danger to herself, so what little freedom she did have left will be taken away. She can't bear that. Yet she'll have to somehow.'

'Is he so bad? Her match?'

'No. Iskander is perfectly fine. But Sybilla . . . she was in love with someone else.'

'Who?'

Morgan turned and put her hand on his cheek. The contact was sweet and warm and unexpected, and he resisted the urge to put his arms around her.

And then she said, 'Me.'

He couldn't comprehend that for a moment, and then his stomach lurched and dropped two floors. 'You—You and Sybilla?'

'No, Jess, that's not what I mean at all.' Morgan's hand dropped away and he felt terribly, icily cold now. He felt her move away. The hallway was starting to reveal itself to him in shadows and highlights of dark grey, and he could see her now, just a shape. A cipher. 'She was *kind* to me. She was the only one, at first, and we spent time together. She liked me. I didn't realise – I didn't realise at first that she felt more for me than that.' The pain of that was still there in her voice, and he almost winced. 'And when I did, I didn't know what to say, except that I – I couldn't be with her. I felt awful about it; I think she saw me as . . . as a refuge from Iskander. But it was never . . . I never . . .' This time there was no doubt she was crying; he could hear the agonised hitch of her breath. 'Oh God, Jess. I didn't tell her I was running. I left her here alone. You betrayed me, and I betrayed *her*. I should have at least tried to help her get out of here, too. I knew she was just as desperate!'

He still felt light-headed; his heart was pounding so hard it hurt. 'It wasn't your fault. You felt you had to help us with Thomas. You know that.'

'It was more than that. I was running away from Dominic, too, that night,' she said. 'We both try to do the right thing, don't we? But no matter what we do, it keeps coming out *wrong*.'

He put his arms around her, and after a second of stiffness, she collapsed against him. He kissed her cheek, and she put her arms around his neck and held him tightly. 'I love you,' she whispered to him. 'I never stopped, Jess – I want you to know that. I just – I just felt so alone here, and the only person I could blame was you.'

She loves me. She still loves me. That brought him a stunned kind of peace. 'Forgive me?'

She kissed him gently on the lips. Sweet and a little sad. 'I did already,' she said. 'Now go to bed. I'll see you in the morning.'

He was unexpectedly tired, he realised as he headed back to his room, but there was no chance to rest yet. Wolfe's door was open, and Khalila, Thomas, and Santi were in with him. They all looked up when he passed, and Wolfe said, 'Brightwell. In.'

Jess took up a leaning spot on the wall. Wolfe paced, of course, as was his usual habit. Khalila and Thomas sat, quietly watching him. Santi poured Jess a cup of wine, and Jess took a sip before he asked, 'So, what's this?'

'This is us planning what to do,' Santi said. 'It's not going very well. Considering that no matter what we do, there's very little chance we can break free of this tower, and none at all we will get out of Alexandria alive if we do.'

'Nic.'

'There's no point in planning when we're too tired to think,' he said quite reasonably. 'Your mother's not likely to hand us over immediately is she? Or have us knifed in our beds?'

'No,' Wolfe said. He kept pacing, hands restlessly tugging at his robe. 'Hardly her style.'

'In that case, I have some news,' Santi said. 'Zara might not be a friend to me any longer, but I do have some in the High Garda I can rely on. I asked them to let me know if anyone matching Dario's description was captured either in Rome or elsewhere. There have been no arrests. He made it out of Rome safely, I believe.'

Khalila let out a trembling breath and whispered a prayer of thanks.

'Glain's doing well,' Jess said. 'She should be strong enough to join us tomorrow.'

'Or will join us, anyway?' Wolfe asked. 'Yes, I know the girl. She won't stay in that bed long.'

'And Morgan?' Thomas looked at Jess and raised his eyebrows. 'She's all right?'

'Yes. She's all right. I saw her to her room.'

'Morgan's in no danger at all here, at least not the kind we're in,' Wolfe said. 'Her problem is more desperate, but less violent. We have a day, two at most, before the Archivist himself arrives at the tower, and once he does, my mother won't have a choice but to hand us over. She can turn the Artifex away. Not the head of the Great Library.'

'Then we need to leave,' Thomas said. 'Perhaps the Obscurist will send us away to safety?'

'She says she will,' Wolfe said. 'I don't know if I believe her. My mother's ever been in pursuit of her own agenda. Sentiment doesn't often enter the equation.'

Like mother, like son, Jess thought, but had the sense not to say it. 'Any way other out of here?' he asked, but he already knew that answer. If there had been, Morgan wouldn't have been here as long as she had.

'It's possible,' Khalila said slowly. 'I've been researching the Iron Tower for months. I was doing it for Morgan, in case I could find any way to get her out safely. Just before we left, I found something strange in the records. Very strange. I took notes, but I didn't have a chance to verify the research.'

'And?' Wolfe asked, and she blushed a little.

'Just a moment.' She turned, and Jess thought she was retrieving something from a hidden pocket in her dress. Or under it. She handed over a single sheaf of paper to Wolfe. 'It's coded. Dario created the cipher for me. Do you need the key?'

Jess gestured for the page, and Wolfe passed it along. Jess blinked. 'When did he make the code for you?'

'When? Just a few days ago. He said we'd be better off that way. Why?'

Jess felt himself smiling tightly; how like Dario to both do something smart and at the same time demonstrate his arrogance. 'Because I recognise it. It's my family's code.'

'Don't tell me Dario's a long-lost cousin!'

'Just an ass,' Jess said. 'He asked me about the code once. I told him it was unbreakable. So of course he broke it. And now he's using it. Idiot.'

'The contents?' Wolfe prompted impatiently. Santi, who'd said nothing, pushed himself off the wall he'd been holding up to stand next to them.

'There's a hidden section in the Iron Tower. Several floors unaccounted for in all of the records that exist. What's above the garden level, where the Translation comes in?'

Wolfe frowned. 'Nothing. That's the top of the tower.'

'No, that isn't true,' Thomas said. His eyes turned blank, the way they did as he performed calculations Jess couldn't even fathom inside his head. 'There must be at least four more floors above it. Possibly five.'

'Morgan would have found that by now. She's had nothing but time to look!'

Jess sent Wolfe a warning look. 'If Thomas says it's there, it's there. Perhaps we could hide in these hidden floors. Perhaps there's even an escape of some kind there.'

'Don't you think if there was a way upstairs, someone else would have found it by now?'

Wolfe hadn't said anything, but he looked over their heads at Santi, who raised his eyebrows.

'We can try,' he said. 'But I have the feeling that anything that's secret inside the Iron Tower may be a great deal deadlier than it looks.'

Jess slept poorly, even as tired as he was. All the day's events kept jumping through his mind, and the knowledge that Morgan was here, within reach, left him feeling restless. When he rose at the first light of dawn the next day, his first thought as he looked out of the narrow, unbreakable window was, *This is the last time I'll see Alexandria*. One way or another, they'd either leave this place for good or die here.

Not surprising to him that Wolfe and Santi were already up

and dressed. Wolfe still wore a Scholar's robe over his plain shirt and trousers. Santi had put on his uniform. Khalila emerged just a few minutes after, fresh and lovely in a dark blue dress and head scarf.

She smiled at Jess. 'I couldn't sleep,' she said. 'You?'

He shook his head. 'I haven't seen Thomas yet. Maybe he's the late riser among us.'

But he wasn't. Glain was true to her word and appeared just a moment later, with Thomas walking at her side as she climbed the stairs. They were talking with an ease and animation that seemed vaguely surprising to Jess, given their circumstances.

And then Morgan. She'd changed into a practical costume: trousers and a grey jacket. Against the plain fabric, her gold collar seemed far too bright. She'd pulled her brown hair back in a twist. All business.

'The Artifex came to the gates just before dawn,' she said. 'I saw him arrive with soldiers. The Obscurist ordered him to leave. Very tense. I'm surprised there wasn't a fight.'

'There will be,' Santi said. 'Soon. He's not going to take no for an answer.'

'He won't have to,' Wolfe said. 'He'll send for the Archivist, and that's an end to it. And us.' He nodded to Khalila. 'We'll need to explore Khalila's information. Quickly.'

'About that,' Santi said. 'Wathen. How do you judge your ability to run today?'

Quick on the uptake, Glain. Her dark eyes flashed around at each of them, and she raised her chin and said, 'Whatever the day requires, sir.'

Santi nodded. 'Packs and weapons. Our time's running out. Either we find a way out this morning or we fight.'

And our odds aren't good, either way, Jess thought. He

reached out for Morgan's hand and her fingertips felt chilled in his. She knew, too. She had to know. This idea of Khalila's might be a useless effort, but it was all they had left.

'Where are you going?' Morgan asked, and Jess explained it as quickly as he could. She caught on immediately. 'Of course. There was something that always bothered me. The Obscurist would lock the garden entrance every few days. I thought she was conducting secret work via Translation. I didn't think it could be anything else.'

'You've never heard of any hidden floors above it?'

'No,' she said. 'Never. Not even a rumour.'

'Maybe they don't actually exist,' Thomas said.

'Then we'll have a nice garden stroll before we're taken out to be killed,' Santi said. 'I don't see any drawbacks.'

They took the strange moving room – it was, Jess learnt, called a lift, which made quite a bit of sense, given its function – up to the garden floor, a floor that, he realised, could only be accessed by Morgan's hand resting on the panel, while other choices were clearly visible with switches. 'Not everyone is allowed use of the garden,' she told them. 'Only the most senior in the Tower.'

'And you're one of them?' Wolfe gave her a look that said he clearly doubted that, and, of course, he was right.

'No,' she said. 'I changed the script inside the lift months ago. It thinks I'm Gregory. So far, none of them have figured that out, though they've found other changes I made. I suppose this is the last time I'll be able to use this one, too.'

'With any luck, it's the last time you'll need to,' Jess said. 'Can you use the Translation Chamber?'

But Morgan shook her head this time. 'Not after I used it to escape last time. They'll have made sure to lock it off from me this time. But I'll check, just to be sure.'

When the lift slid to a stop and the doors opened, they stepped out into the lush, warm garden. It was deserted except for the flutters of butterflies among the flowers and a subtle hum of bees that drowsily roamed the room near a hive at the far end. The Translation couch and helmet occupied the central gazebo of the room, but outside morning stretched towards noon beneath a bleached-pale sky, and the dizzy patchwork of Alexandria heaved with motion in the streets.

Eerily quiet here.

'They might already know we've come here,' Wolfe said. 'Morgan, see if you can use the Translation equipment.'

It was immediately obvious she couldn't; as she came close to the helmet and couch, a low humming sound rose and spiked, and a harsh blue spark stabbed out towards her. She yelped and jumped back, rubbing at the spot on her arm where it had struck. It left a burn.

'And that's our answer,' Santi said. 'Work quickly. Spread out. Find anything that might be a concealed staircase, a switch.'

They'd all been well trained in how to suss out hidden alcoves, floor tiles, concealed safes and shelves. Common practice among those who possessed book contraband to hide it from view. Scholars and soldiers learnt how to pry those secrets out early in their training.

But Jess had experience at *hiding* things, not just finding them. The Brightwell family expertise lent itself to a search like this, and instead of doing what the others were, he stood very still, looking around the large round room. *Those who built this place weren't trying to hide something completely. They'd want it accessible. No Obscurist is going to want to grub around in flower beds, looking for a switch or a panel.*

He let his eyes unfocus and wander, and suddenly, he was

looking at a statue. The largest statue, in fact, in the room: an image of hawk-headed Horus, from whose bowl flowed a continuous stream of water that snaked among the flowers and plants.

Horus, god of scribes. Patron of the Great Library.

Jess grabbed Thomas as he passed and pulled him over to the statue. 'Look for any kind of switch,' he said. They both began running hands over the cool marble, and then Jess felt a scarab ornament on the arm of the statue give to his touch. 'Here! It's here!'

He pressed it, and above them something hissed. What had seemed like just another part of the ceiling proved to be a plate – the bottom of a black iron staircase that screwed down from the ceiling, turning so smoothly that it must have been powered by steam or hydraulics. The whole thing was silent enough that it seemed as eerie as a dream.

'Incredible,' Thomas murmured, and ran his hand over the smooth black railing. 'We go up?'

'We go up,' Santi said. 'But I go first.'

Jess hung back to take rear guard. The staircase turned in a tight spiral around a central iron core, and above him Thomas said, reverently, 'Look at this. It's the same as the Iron Tower! No one remembers how this metal was created; it has the same properties as the Iron Pillar of Delhi, but—'

'You must be feeling better,' Glain said from just below him. 'Since you're lecturing again.'

'Sorry.'

'Oh, don't be. I'm happy to hear it.'

At the top of the steps, Santi paused and said, 'There's a door. No lock and no handle, so I assume it takes an Obscurist. Morgan?'

She squeezed her way past the others to the top. Jess craned his neck, wishing he'd put himself farther ahead, so he could see what was going on. *Someone has to bring up the rear, scrubber.* He could almost hear Dario's mocking voice. When had he started missing Dario, of all people?

It seemed to take forever, and Jess faced outward, towards the garden room. How long before someone – Gregory, perhaps – came looking for them? How long before he realised they'd gone missing and began to search? Not long, surely. He wasn't the trusting sort. *I should be up there*, he thought. *I'm the one who's good with closed doors.*

But Santi did know best, after all. Above there was a hollow *clunk*, and Santi said, 'We're moving!' Khalila, just ahead of Jess, glanced over her shoulder at him and gave him an encouraging smile.

'Come on,' she said. 'At least we can brag to Dario later that we saw something he didn't.'

Jess backed his way up the winding stairs, training his weapon on the room below until the last twist hid it all from view. Then he turned and hurried up after Khalila, across a shallow landing, and towards a black iron door that stood open.

Behind him he heard another hiss, and looked back to see the staircase moving again, this time spiralling back into the ceiling. *Counterweights.* It had been only their weight on the staircase that had kept it down after the initial descent. The design reminded him of Heron of Alexandria and all the marvellous bellows and gears that had driven the wonders of the temples in the early days of the Library.

Khalila had stopped in the doorway, and Jess stepped up beside her and stopped as well. He couldn't help it.

A vast, circular Serapeum spread out in front of them, but not like any he'd ever seen before. The Library's daughter facilities were always, always *orderly*, clean, well maintained.

This was like the ghostly wreck of one.

The Black Archives rose in a hollowed-out tower within the tower, ring after ring of shelves and cabinets crowding every available level, with an ancient, dusty flat lift on a track that must have been designed to spiral up from one level to another. The number of books, scrolls, tablets . . . it was *staggering* and chaotic. The smell of the place overwhelmed him – old paper, mould, neglect. A thick, choking patina of dust.

It made his father's warehouse of contraband in London, the largest that Jess had ever heard of, look like a modest rural shelf. There had to be tens of thousands of volumes here – no, *hundreds* of thousands, if not millions. The books had long ago overflowed from the shelves, and towering stacks of them leant against corners and tottered atop the bookcases themselves. The shelves, Jess realised, were thickly stacked with multiple layers of volumes, too.

Without even meaning to, Jess took a step inside the hidden tower, then another, as he tilted his head to look up. The levels of shelves reached up and up, spiralling to what seemed like infinity. *This isn't the Archives*, he thought. *This is something else.*

Wolfe's voice was hushed as he said, 'The Black Archives. I don't know what's worse: the number of things they've kept from us or the incredible hubris of the idea.'

The Black Archives. A story, a rumour, a fable. The place the Library kept everything too dangerous to circulate, too damaging to allow out to the public.

How could so many books be *dangerous*? And by whose standards?

Khalila walked to a shelf and reached for a book. Morgan

got there fast and grabbed her wrist before she could touch the leather spine. 'Wait,' she said. 'There could be traps or alarms. Before you touch *anything*, let me look first. That goes for everyone.' In truth, she looked shaken. So did Wolfe, for that matter. Even Santi kept turning on the spot, staring in shock with a mixture of wonder and horror.

Traps. The word finally penetrated Jess, and he swallowed. There could be traps on books. Jess tried to comprehend that and failed. The scale of the place continued to overwhelm him. *So many books abandoned here.* Criminal works walled up to die.

They waited while Morgan made the rounds of the shelves, looking, occasionally brushing her fingers across a shelf or a case. Finally, she said, 'It's safe. You can touch them now.'

Khalila took the book from the shelf. Her voice trembled as she read the title, '*Generation of a Magnetic Field by Use of Electric Currents*,' she said. 'Hans Christian Ørsted. 1820.' She put it back and pulled another. '*The Law of Reciprocity of the Magneto-Electric and Electromagnetic Phenomena and Applications for the Reversibility of Electric Generators.* Heinrich Friedrich Emil Lenz, 1833.'

Wolfe moved around the shelves, not touching, just looking. He said, 'This whole level has to do with applications of electrical fields. Heat, light, machines – all powered by electrical fields. These are things that I've only seen here within this tower. I thought it was an Obscurist's trick, powered by alchemy. It isn't. It's something engineers discovered centuries back. And they kept it from us.'

'But why?' Thomas's eyes had gone very wide. He went to Khalila's side and pulled more books, searching the titles. 'Why would they keep these amazing things from us? Can you even imagine how bright the world would be if we had these lights? What about using this electromagnetic phenomena to power trains or carriages? Could it be better than steam? Why would they—?'

'Because someone, when this work was first submitted to the Library, decided the very idea of it was dangerous. Uncontainable.' Wolfe's voice sounded weary, and angry. 'They looked into that future and decided it couldn't be controlled, and, above all, the Library wants *control*. Look around you. Look at what the Library *kept from us*. We all knew it was true. Thomas and I, we both have experience of what they won't allow to be known.'

'The press,' Thomas whispered.

'The what?' Khalila asked it absently, still fascinated by the titles of the books on the shelves, all the knowledge that they had never seen. Never imagined.

Wolfe was the one to answer. 'He means a letter press, ink blocks arranged in letters and pages. It allows books to be easily reproduced. The Library can't allow that, because then all this – all this *banned knowledge* – could be distributed without having an arbiter of what is good or bad, dangerous or helpful.' He clutched the book he was holding in both hands, and the line of his jaw was so tight, Jess could see the bone beneath it.

'And the authors?' Khalila asked. 'What would have happened to these authors?'

'Dead,' Wolfe said. 'Silenced. Either when their work was placed here, or soon after. The Library would have seen to that. A candle can make a bonfire. So it's snuffed out quickly.' The silence hung heavy as the smell of old paper and leather, damp and neglect. 'This is the graveyard where they buried our future.'

Khalila pulled in a breath and carefully, reverently, replaced the book she'd removed. These were, Jess realised, not just forbidden works; they were the only remaining memories of brilliant people – Scholars, librarians, maybe even just amateur inventors – who'd discovered something the Library wanted to keep hidden. There would be no personal journals in the Archives celebrating their lives. No scholarly papers. No record of their births or deaths. They had been erased.

These books were all that remained of a vast collection of lost souls, and instead of being cared for, being loved, they were jumbled and rotting like a child's abandoned toys. Jess felt it like a hot spear through his chest.

Then he got *angry*.

Thomas cleared his throat. 'All this is only for the development of electricity,' he said. 'What *else* is there?'

'There must be a Codex,' Wolfe said. 'Even the forbidden needs to be catalogued.'

'Here,' Santi said. He moved to a vast book, thick as a builder's block, with pages large enough to hold a thousand entries each. The book was chained to a podium with the same black iron links as the staircase and the tower itself. It sat open to the centre. Morgan moved her hand over it and nodded. Santi flipped pages to where, in a normal Codex, there would have been a summary of categories and coding. He stared, then slowly looked up at the stacked levels upon levels of books. 'It's—It's as long as the Codex for the Archive. Inventions. Research. Art. Fiction. Printing—'

'Printing,' Wolfe repeated, and he and Thomas exchanged a sharp look. 'Where?'

'The seventh circle,' Santi said. He seemed shaken. 'It's an entire *section*. I thought—'

None of them wanted to finish that sentence.

They all crowded on the flat lifting device, and a blank panel rose out of the iron plate. Morgan hesitated, then pressed her palm down to it. She gasped a little, and Jess moved towards her, but she flung out a hand to stop him. 'No. No, it has to be me. This place, it only obeys Obscurists.' She closed her eyes and focused, and the lift lurched into movement on the track. It rose as it circled, level upon level, and Jess tried not to look down. *So easy to fall from this thing*, he thought. The thin railings bordering it were no kind of reassurance at all.

The lift slowed and stopped, and Morgan stepped off. She touched the old wood of the bookcase that circled around, and in a moment said, 'It's safe enough. But be careful.'

Thomas moved next to her, facing a bookcase seven shelves high and at least twenty paces wide. 'All of this? Surely it can't be all about what Thomas dreamt up, and Wolfe before him?' Morgan plucked the first book from the bottom corner. 'Chinese. I don't read it—'

'I do,' Wolfe said, and took it to open to the flyleaf. '*The Printing of Ink to Paper Using Characters Carved in Wood*. By Ling Chao.'

'What year?' Thomas asked. Wolfe didn't answer. 'Sir? What year?'

'Translated from the Chinese calendar? Year eight hundred sixty eight,' he whispered at last. 'They've robbed us of this for *more than a thousand years*.' His voice shook, and he thrust the book back at Thomas to turn away and stare at the shelves that marched around the level. 'How many? How many times was this created and cut down? They've been destroying it over and over, all this time. *All this time.*'

Santi had walked away, all the way towards the end of the shelves, and suddenly he stopped, backed up, and reached out to pluck a volume out of the rest. 'Ah, *Dio mio*,' Santi murmured, and put his hand on the cover, as if trying to hide the title. The name. He turned and looked back at them, and they went to him, as if he'd asked for help. Maybe he had, silently.

Thomas took the book gently and opened it. '*On the Uses of Pressed Metal Type and Ink on Paper . . .*'

'*For the Safeguarding, Archiving, and Reproduction of Written Works,*' Wolfe said. 'It's mine. I was told it was destroyed. *All* destroyed. Everything I ever wrote. But it wasn't. They kept it.' Santi put his hand on Wolfe's shoulder and held on, head bowed, but Wolfe didn't seem to feel the offered comfort. 'They kept our work and let it rot.'

'So you see,' a voice rose from far below them. 'Every one of these is a life snuffed out. You see the burden I've carried, every day since taking my post. I'm the caretaker of a graveyard of ghosts.'

Jess, Glain, and Santi all reacted at the same time, and all with military precision – spreading out, bringing their slung weapons into line to point down. There was nothing obvious to shoot, just the Obscurist Magnus, fragile and alone, standing in the rounded area below beside the open Codex.

She stared up at them, and from here, so far above, Jess couldn't read her expression at all. 'Don't worry,' she said. 'I'm alone. Careless of you to leave the door open, though. I would have thought you'd have closed it, at the very least.'

Jess's fault. He'd been so distracted by what was in front of him that for that one moment, he'd forgotten what lay behind.

'Come here to gloat?' Wolfe's voice was bleak and empty now, as if something inside him had burnt down to the very ashes. 'Well played, Mother.'

'Not gloat,' she said, and without anyone's command, the

iron lift glided back down to her level and she stepped on. It carried her all the way up to where they stood, and as she walked towards them, Jess saw the pallor of her face, the strain. 'All my life I thought I knew the Library and what we were. What we stood for in the world . . . until I was passed the key to this room. For the past three hundred years, every Obscurist Magnus has been shown this place, and it breaks them. It broke me. The weight of all this waste . . . it's too much.'

'And yet you did nothing,' her son said. '*Nothing*. Even when—'

'Yes, I did nothing! What can any one person do to stop this?' The Obscurist pulled in a breath and looked away. 'When *your* book came here . . . I knew. I knew I couldn't continue this way. I tried to save you, you know. I tried to protect you.'

'*Protect him?* Do you have any idea what was done to him?' Santi crossed the distance to her in three long strides, and Jess didn't know what he would have done – hit her, flung her over the railing – but he didn't have the chance, because Wolfe caught up and got between them. Santi checked his rush forward and stared into Wolfe's eyes, and whatever he saw there, he turned away.

'I don't blame you for your anger, any of you. This is a horror. It's the worst sin of all the Library's many evils. I did my best to minimise it.'

'You mean, your least,' Wolfe shot back. 'Your best would have been to say no to all this. To stop it!'

'I couldn't stop it. Not without risking the punishment of everyone I hold dear. But you can, my son. You all can.'

Jess couldn't keep quiet any longer; his anger boiled over and he heard himself saying, 'You're the most powerful woman in the world, by all accounts. We're just outcasts. Criminals.

Traitors. They're likely to kill us today. What makes you think we can change *anything?*'

'Because you've already started.' The Obscurist had always looked mysteriously young to Jess's eyes, though clearly she was old enough to have a son Wolfe's age. But just now she looked every year of her true age, if not older. 'I spent most of my life *believing* that I could change things eventually; I would never have been able to continue as I did if I hadn't. I gathered up the power I could, and I forced the Archivist to take some of what was stored here and let it out in the Archives, bit by bit. But I sacrificed' – her gaze fell on Wolfe and held – 'too much. I told myself that things would change eventually, that I could make it happen. But I know the truth. The Library can't be changed from within. We're all too . . . too afraid. Or too cynical.'

'All you have to do is dump all of *this* into the Archive Codex!' Khalila said. 'You have the power to do it!'

'No. I don't.' The Obscurist touched her collar, the thick gold traced with alchemical symbols. 'There are things even I can't change, or I would have done it when I was young. When I was still brave.'

'So you want us to do it,' Glain said. It was the first thing she'd said, and she was absolutely white with rage. 'You coward. You ask us to bring down a giant with . . . a pebble!'

'The Jewish king David did,' Khalila said. 'Or so the stories tell us. Goliath fell to a slingshot and a stone. And the Library is a lumbering giant, dying of its own arrogance; it has to change or fall. We have the tools. The will. The knowledge.' She nodded to the book Wolfe still held in his hands. 'We'll have your printing press.'

Of all people, Jess had never expected *Khalila Seif* to propose such a thing. It was such a radical betrayal of the Library that

Jess's head spun from the whole idea. 'Well, we couldn't do it here, in Alexandria,' he said. 'Certainly not here in the Iron Tower. And we're out of time. The Archivist is coming, isn't he?'

'He is,' the Obscurist agreed. 'My delays in handing you over have already been noted; that will lead to my demotion, most likely today. Gregory has been wriggling to make himself the new Obscurist, and he'll get his wish, for all the joy it will bring him. No, it's inevitable. It's already done,' she said, as Wolfe started to speak. 'But I *can* get you out of here. Sending you on your way is the last gift I can ever give you, Christopher.' Her voice dropped lower, to a pitch Jess hardly even heard. 'Except my love.'

Wolfe said nothing. He stared at her as if she were a stranger, and maybe she was. *Families so often are*, Jess thought. The silence stretched, and then he said, 'What you're suggesting we do – it's like cutting loose a wild tiger. All this unchained knowledge will cause chaos and destruction, and what will happen can't be managed. I can't guess what will come of it. Can you?'

'No,' his mother said, and looked around the room. 'But it will be better than this sad place.'

'We'll need a safe haven, somewhere to build these machines,' Morgan said. 'Allies to hide us and help us distribute the books we print. Most of all, we'll need *these*.' She gestured at the Black Archives, the forbidden knowledge. 'With the right books, we can change everything.'

'Then take them,' the Obscurist said. 'Take as much as you can carry. I'll erase them from the records, and no one will ever know they disappeared. You'll have to carry them with you, and you can never come back here. Not as long as the Library controls the Iron Tower.'

'Go where?' Jess asked, but then he answered his own question. 'London.'

'Yes. Your family – blood and bonded by trade – is powerful and wealthy enough to hide you,' the Obscurist agreed. 'You'll need more than that, but it's a start.'

'Did you *plan* this?'

'I'm not gifted with so much foresight. But when I saw you together the day I came to get Morgan, and saw how much you all cared for one other, I hoped you would be the ones to finally, *finally* have the skills and the courage to do this. I knew you wouldn't let Thomas just vanish into the dark. You'd poke and dig, until you found him, and . . . this.'

Thomas's eyes were bright now, and very strange as he stared at the older woman. Was it anger? Jess couldn't tell, but it unnerved him. Badly. 'You didn't want them to have a choice, did you? Betray the Library or die. So you let them take me away. To motivate my friends.'

'I did what I needed to do,' Keria said. 'I always have.'

Wolfe was still between Santi and his mother, but in that moment, he looked like he might go for her throat himself. 'I thought I understood how cold you were,' he said. 'But there's no calculation for that. *Mother.*'

'Perhaps not,' Keria Morning said, and turned away. 'Choose the books you want to take. You won't get another chance.'

EPHEMERA

Text of a letter from the Artifex Magnus to the Archivist Magister, secured and coded at the highest level of security. Destroyed upon reading.

Are you sure you want to take this step? I don't normally question your directives, but this is a thing we can't undo. It crosses a boundary that we have never before broken. If anyone learns what we've done . . . You understand that it will destroy not just us, but everything we have given our lives to build and protect.

I must ask you to verify that this is exactly *what you want. That there will be no last-minute changes of heart. No reprieves. Because once the thing is begun, it can't be stopped, and it can't ever be repaired or replaced.*

What we're doing . . . I have a strong stomach.

This, I will tell you frankly, sickens me.

I need your order here on this paper. I need proof.

Reply from the Archivist. Destroyed upon reading.

I don't order this lightly. I have agonised over this decision. The weight of generations of my predecessors, who avoided it, rests solely on me, but we live in a far more dangerous world than any of them ever did. A world of increasing risk. Increasing dissent.

You have your orders, and I want them carried out to the letter.

Destroy it all.

CHAPTER FIFTEEN

This is like old times, Jess thought, stuffing illegal volumes into packs, and once the packs were full, into thick canvas bags that the Obscurist brought from somewhere in a storage room. He'd been born running rare, valuable books. The only difference was that this smuggling was done much more clumsily and more openly than he would've preferred and – was vastly more important.

Jess left the others to the frantic work of choosing what to take – arguments, he saw, were fierce and passionate between Wolfe, Khalila, and Thomas – and went instead with Morgan to a small table in a corner. She'd borrowed a Codex from the Obscurist Magnus, and now she placed it on the table between them.

'What do we need that for?' he asked her.

'You'll need to let your father know what happened and that we're coming through soon,' she said. 'The Obscurist can send us all to the London Serapeum, just like we originally planned. He'll have to help us get free of the guards there.'

'My father's not going to fight the High Garda! My father doesn't fight anyone. He's a smuggler, not some mercenary captain.'

She dismissed that with a wave of her hand. 'You're his son. He'll fight for you, Jess.'

'No,' he said grimly. 'He won't.'

That froze Morgan for a moment, but she shook her head. 'Then we have to offer him good reason. Surely what we're carrying will be enough of an incentive.' She used a thin-bladed knife that Wolfe had given her to carefully slit the endpaper of the Codex and peel it back; beneath that lay inked symbols that shimmered like metal in the dim late-afternoon light. She touched them and lifted her fingertips, and a three-dimensional column of symbols appeared, floating on the air as if they were made of burning fragments of paper. She studied them for a moment, then reached in and pinched one of them between her thumb and forefinger. As she pulled it out of the column, it dissolved into ash and smoke. She put her hand over the top of the shivering column and pushed it back down until her palm lay flat against the backing.

When she took her hand away, it looked exactly the same. 'That takes care of anyone trying to read anything written in this particular Codex,' she said. 'Now I'll link it directly to your father's. Give me your hand.'

'What?'

'I don't have a link to your father, but you do. It's necessary for it to be a personal connection.'

Jess shrugged and held out his hand, and before he could blink, she'd drawn that sharp little knife across his finger. The cut was shallow and he hardly felt it at all, but a line of blood welled up. Morgan grabbed a quill and dipped the end into the red, and he frowned at her as he sucked the wound closed. 'Shouldn't do that,' she said as she wrote a line in a blank page of the Codex – more symbols, then his father's name: *Callum Brightwell.* 'I might need more blood.'

'Make do with that,' he said. 'Have you ever heard of vampires?'

She gave him a wild sort of smile, put down the quill, and reached for a bottle of silvery ink she'd brought with her. She shook it, then uncapped it and dipped the quill into it. 'What I write here, only your father will see. By using your blood, I've mirrored this Codex to his. The ink will disappear in about a minute after I write, and it'll leave no trace on either book. So tell me what to say.'

Jess sank down beside her on the small bench. 'Say it's me. Tell him no one else can read it. It's safe.'

She did, writing quickly. There was a short delay. What if his father didn't answer? Would the message wait or disappear? Disappear, apparently, because as he watched, the letters began to fade away.

Then, suddenly, his father's pen moved in response, writing out words. *This isn't my son's handwriting. How do I know he's even there?*

'Does it matter who writes?' Jess asked her.

'Yes. I have to hold the pen or it doesn't work. Sorry.'

'That's inefficient. All right. Tell him . . . Tell him I still have nightmares about the ink-licker. He'll remember.'

He must have, because as soon as she wrote it, his father's response came fast. *Is Jess all right?*

Yes, Morgan wrote. *Jess is here. None but the three of us can see this exchange. My name is Morgan. I'm his –* Her quill stuttered a little, and then she wrote, *friend.*

This must be important, Callum Brightwell wrote. *Got yourself in trouble, Jess?*

'He assumes the worst,' Morgan observed.

'He's usually right,' Jess said. 'Tell him what we need.'

She wrote quickly, in pieces, explaining first that they were wanted by the Library, and next – at Jess's suggestion – that they were bringing incredibly valuable rare books with them. Last, what they needed as far as safe passage and hiding places. It was quite a bit for his father to take in, Jess thought; maybe too much for even naive greed to overcome. The page went blank. Nothing appeared. After a moment went by, Morgan looked over at him and tucked the loose strands of hair behind her ears. 'Should I try again?'

'No,' he said. 'Let him think.'

It took a torturously long time for Callum's words to appear again. When they did, it wasn't about Jess's needs at all. *Your brother is here*, the words read. *Word's been put about in Alexandria that you and your friends died in Rome. You understand my concern.*

'Concern?' Morgan frowned at the page and raised her voice, as if his father could hear her. '*Concern?* He thought you were dead, and he takes it so calmly?'

'I told you,' Jess said. 'He's not sentimental.'

She gave him a disbelieving look. He pointed at the page where more words were written. *Your brother's nickname. Now. Or we disappear and you won't reach us again.*

'He means it,' Jess said. 'Write *Scraps*.'

'What?'

'Scraps. Leftovers. You know. Just write it.'

She looked mystified but obeyed. Another blank space, and then Callum wrote, *He still hates that name. He says to tell you that. I'm glad you're all right, son.*

'That,' Jess said, 'is probably all the sentimentality you'll ever see from my family. Cherish it.'

Morgan refreshed her quill and frowned at the level of

ink left. She wrote, *Message back when you have everything arranged. We won't have much time.*

Done, his father wrote, and Jess could almost hear the clap of the book closing. His father would be on his feet now, tugging down his expensive silk waistcoat, pacing the thick Turkish carpet of his office. Brendan would be slouched in a chair nearby, listening to every word. He felt curiously reassured by that vision, and by knowing that though he wouldn't trust his family to save his life, he could trust them to see the profit in what he was bringing them. His life was just part of the deal.

Morgan capped the ink. 'I'll need more before we go,' she said. 'It's the one thing I can't make any other place.' She wiped the quill clean on a scrap of cloth and tucked it in the holder on the side of the Codex.

'You're taking the Codex? Won't they miss it?'

'Hardly anyone here bothers to request new books. We get almost everything mirrored to our Serapeum downstairs as it is.' She hesitated, stroking the cover of the Codex, and asked, 'Are you sure we trust him? Your father?'

He wished he could say yes. More than anything, he wanted to believe he could. But what he said was, 'You can trust he'll see the profit in rescuing us *and* the books. Once he realises the opportunities of building the press, I doubt he'll have a second of hesitation in throwing the full weight of the black markets behind this.'

'I'm sorry,' she said. 'That sounds like a harsh kind of love.'

It was a perfect description for his childhood. He'd not known anything else until he'd come here to Alexandria, and now he could look back on it and see how dry and arid it was.

But useful nevertheless. *I might be just as bad*, he thought. *I can't see my brother and father as anything but tools to be used.*

I should be better than that. He'd not even spared a moment to think about his mother – not that he wasn't fond of her in the abstract, but she'd never been present for him. Would she have cried over his death? Probably. But he had the awful feeling that it would have just been for herself and not for him.

'Don't,' Morgan said. She turned towards him and put her hand on his chin to turn his face towards her. 'Don't go into your head and leave me. I'm just as frightened as you are, you know.'

'You? The girl who defies the Iron Tower and wins? I doubt you understand what fear means to the rest of us.' He removed her hand from his chin, but only to raise it to his lips. He kissed the soft skin while looking into her eyes and saw her shiver. Felt her skin rise in chill bumps under his touch. 'Thank you.'

'For what?'

He pointed to the Codex. 'For reminding me there's more to life than what I grew up knowing.'

Wolfe, Khalila, and Thomas were still arguing. Morgan sighed and tilted her head that direction. 'I suppose—'

'That we should help? Yes. We'll be out of time soon.'

Morgan proved to be a calming influence, and Jess interrupted arguments when it became clear both sides had points, and within another hour, they'd scraped together a good deal more than a hundred volumes. Too many to carry. Jess and Santi took charge of weighing the bags and removing what couldn't be taken, though every one they abandoned put a cut on Jess's heart. *It's all right*, he thought. *Maybe we can come back later for more. She'll help us.* She'd said she couldn't, but Jess was seeing quite a bit of Wolfe in his mother's character, including the steel-hard stubbornness.

Keria Morning hadn't survived all these years as an enemy of the Archivist by giving up, giving in.

The Codex that Morgan carried must have changed, because she quickly drew it out and opened it. Then she frowned.

'Is it from my father?' Jess asked.

'No,' she said, and went to the Obscurist. She showed her the entry. 'It's from Gregory, to you.'

The Obscurist read the message, closed the book, and nodded. 'We're out of time,' she told him. 'The Archivist's guards have entered the tower. Gregory let them in, and I'm being ordered to surrender you all immediately. You must Translate to London. Now.'

'My father's not sent back a reply yet,' Jess said. 'Until we know it's safe—'

'It won't be safe here,' she interrupted him. 'They're coming. Now.'

Silence settled in with grim weight, and Santi said, 'Then we go.' It sounded like a death sentence. Jess swallowed hard.

Thomas silently took Glain's pack and added it to his own. She didn't say she was grateful, but Jess could see she was. Her leg was still painful and no doubt would slow her down in a running battle, but she bore the pain stoically. He expected nothing less. Glain would always do her best, until her best wasn't good enough.

Jess found himself missing Dario; the Spaniard's sharp humour would have been a nice addition just now. Khalila was steady and calm and as cheerful as she could be, but there was no doubt she understood this was a one-way step into total darkness. What they'd find on the other side . . . none of them truly knew. Jess certainly didn't.

The Obscurist stopped at the iron door and said, 'Morgan. I can do one last service for you, at least.'

Morgan flinched as Keria reached out and brushed her

fingertips in a line across the gold collar circling her throat.

It unlocked with a sudden, dry snap.

Morgan gasped and reached up to pull it off. Once she had, she stared at it as if she had no conception of what it was, until suddenly she let it fall to the floor with a heavy *thud*. The skin beneath was pale and moist. She didn't seem to know what to say, but finally she whispered, 'Thank you.'

Wolfe's mother nodded. She seemed very calm. Very . . . resigned. 'They would be able to track you through it if you'd kept it on. Morgan, I'll leave it to you to remove any tracking scripts that they try to link to the Library bracelets the others wear. It might help to leave them on for now. People hesitate to kill librarians.' She hesitated and closed her eyes. 'I've failed you in many things, Christopher. I won't fail you in this. You must trust me now.'

It was a leap Jess thought might be impossible for Wolfe, but he stared at her for a long moment and then crossed to her. He took her hand in his. 'I do,' he said.

'I don't deserve that, do I?' Her smile was broken and beautiful and very real. 'A mother should always protect her child. And I haven't.'

He stood for a moment holding her hand, and then suddenly pulled her forward into an embrace. It was fierce and fast, and then he turned away, head down. The Obscurist blinked away tears, took a breath, and said, 'It's time to go.'

She summoned the spiral stairs, and they descended quickly. The garden seemed deserted as they arrived, but Jess heard the sound of shouting echoing up from below. The Archivist's troops must have already arrived. They were searching.

'There's no time left,' the Obscurist said. 'I'll have to take the risk.'

'What risk?' Wolfe pushed forward, Santi just a step behind.

'I'll have to send you all at once. If I send you one at a time, half of you won't make it.'

'You can't do that! Even you—' Morgan stopped, looking at the others. 'It's too much for anyone. It will—'

'Kill me?' The Obscurist looked around at the beautiful, peaceful garden and sighed. 'So be it. I'll need you all to put your hands on the helmet—'

Jess felt the warning hiss of instincts coming alive, and his head jerked up and around, looking for the threat.

It was all around them.

The Artifex Magnus himself stepped out of the shadow of a spreading plum tree, pale blossoms brushing his long white hair. Behind him, around him, *all around the room*, more soldiers rose from concealment. Aiming their weapons.

Santi trembled on the edge of raising his own gun, then raised one hand, bent, and carefully placed the weapon on the floor by his feet. 'Disarm,' he said. His voice sounded flat and dead already. 'There's no point.'

Glain raised her weapon and sighted on the Artifex. 'There's every damn point.'

But she didn't fire, because the Artifex pushed someone unexpected out into the path of any of her bullets.

Dario.

He wasn't bound or restrained. He hadn't been wounded or beaten. He looked rested, well nourished. Well dressed.

And he couldn't look any of them in the eyes.

'Dario?' Khalila's whisper was full of stunned relief, and she took a step forward . . . and then he looked up and met her gaze. 'Dario.' All the life drained out of her voice. 'What is this?'

'Traitor.' Glain's hands were white around her gun, but she'd lowered it now to stare at the face of their friend. '*Y mochyn diawl.*'

He opened his mouth, hesitated, and then said, 'I didn't have a choice.'

Arrogant, clever Dario Santiago had sold them out. Of course he had. Maybe he'd been doing it all along; he hadn't had a chance to report their plans to rescue Thomas at the last moment because that had moved too quickly. But he'd tried to sell them out.

It came to Jess in a cold wave that if they'd actually escaped to London, it would have probably been a trap. Dario would have seen to it. He'd survived Rome alone because he'd never been in any real danger.

He'd gone to report to his spymaster.

Glain threw down her weapon with an angry snarl.

Jess thought coldly and seriously about putting a bullet in Dario. It would have been murder, absolutely and clearly murder. He very nearly did it, anyway.

Then he bent and put his gun on the floor, and as he straightened, the soldiers rushed in and grabbed each of them. No, not all of them. Not Morgan. Not the Obscurist Magnus. He supposed they'd been told to leave them alone.

Thomas had said nothing at all. Neither had Wolfe. They had identical expressions, Jess realised, as if something had drained out of them. As if their souls had already left their bodies behind.

It can't end this way. It can't. But it had, he realised, for so many others. The Black Archives were full of failures who believed they'd survive.

He'd end up on the shelves, too. All of them would.

'Don't!' Dario said sharply to a soldier who put his hands on Khalila. 'Don't touch her.'

'I don't want your protection!' she shouted at him. 'Traitor!'

'Maybe not,' he said. 'But you've got it, anyway.' He held out his hand. 'Come with me. Come away from here. You don't need to see this.'

'You're not going anywhere,' the Artifex said. 'Bring them. All of them.'

'But—' Dario looked confused and angry. A flush deepened the colour of his cheeks, and he rounded on the old man with clenched fists. 'You can't—'

'On orders of the Archivist himself, I can,' he said. 'You're all fools. None of you understand the consequences of what you've done.' The Artifex, Jess realised, was angry, and it wasn't just because of their rebellion. It was something else.

He walked straight to the statue of Horus, pressed the hidden switch, and watched the staircase descend. Then he led the way upstairs to the Black Archives.

'Bring them,' he said. 'They should see the price of their meddling.'

Back in the hidden rooms, they were pushed against the back wall and held there by the armed High Garda soldiers, who must have been the Artifex's hand-picked personal guard. Santi didn't appeal to them for help, and Jess didn't, either. They stood silently against the rough wall of the Iron Tower and watched as the Artifex stepped out to crane his head up, up, to look at the seemingly infinite spiral of shelves.

'So much,' he murmured. 'So much wasted.' He turned to them, and his old, seamed face was grim with anger. 'You've forced this. All of you, with your pushing and questioning and disbelief. You don't know how much we've saved you from: war, famine, pestilence, a thousand kinds of death. We've raised humanity from the mud, and you *still* chase after phantoms instead of appreciating the peace all around you.'

'Save us the speeches,' Wolfe said. 'Kill us, if you intend to do it.'

'I will,' he said. 'But first I have to do what I've been ordered. May all the gods damn you for it.'

He took a small leather case from a pocket of his robe and opened it.

A glass globe filled with green fluid rolled into his outstretched palm.

Jess pulled in a breath, but Wolfe was the first to understand, fully, the impossible. 'No,' he said. 'You can't. *You can't.*'

'I don't want to,' the Artifex said. He was crying. Tears streamed from his reddened eyes and lost themselves in the canyons of wrinkles beneath. 'But *you did this, Wolfe. You.*'

He threw the Greek Fire into the shelves of delicate, flammable books.

Jess screamed and threw himself forward, but it was too late, too late. The glass broke, the thick greenish liquid splashed over vulnerable spines and fragile paper, over faded ink and lost dreams.

And then, with the sound of a sickening, indrawn breath, it ignited.

Jess lunged at the soldier in front of him and slammed his forehead into the man's nose with a muscular *crunch* and a corresponding blackness that radiated through his skull like a ringing bell. He didn't pause, just put his shoulder into the staggering man's stomach and heaved up to toss the soldier off his feet.

The restraints tightened around his wrists like snakes constricting, and he felt a hideous whine inside his head. The first shelf of books was fully on fire with licks of greenish-white flame. The second above it smoked, and Jess could see paper blackening and curling at the edges.

Santi had put down a soldier, too. Glain hadn't; she was hobbled by her bad leg and had fallen herself. Together, he and Santi rushed at the Artifex. Jess didn't have a clue what the good of it was, but he had to do *something*.

They never made it, of course. Jess felt something hit him in the back and pitch him forward, off balance, to hit the floor hard. Santi hit just a breath behind him, and before Jess could scramble back to his feet, someone was pinning him down.

Jess raised his head and watched the shelves of the first level smoke, warp, spark, and burn. Book after book.

Level after level.

When the smoke became thick and choking and Jess could no longer see for the tears streaming out of his eyes, he felt himself being pulled backward by his legs, out into the sweeter air.

The Black Archives were gone.

And now all that remained was for the Artifex to finish them off.

He was being rolled towards the steps; Santi had already been pushed down them, rolling in an awkward ball. Jess would be next. The others had already been sent down, and he saw Khalila's stark, blank face staring up, Morgan beside her. Thomas was crouched on the floor in the open space of the garden, beside the Translation equipment they wouldn't have a chance to use. It would take too long, even if Morgan could operate it. What remained would be a quick, ugly death for most of them, and prison inside this tower for Morgan and Wolfe's mother. For ever.

Then Jess was tumbling down the steps, he tucked himself into as tight a ball as he could. He landed badly and cried out when his face hit the tiled floor; fresh red blood dripped from cuts on his face like liquid tears, brilliant even in the dim light. He coughed and coughed, trying to get the taste of bitter ashes out of his lungs, and between the retching spasms he realised he was still weeping for all the books he'd just seen die.

He felt fingertips brush the restraints holding him, just a quick touch, and the numbing pain of them loosed. Someone was kneeling over him. He heard the Obscurist Magnus say, in a strange and distant tone, 'You've given me no choice, Artifex. You know that. And I am a very bad enemy.'

'Not for long.' The Artifex was a blur on the edges of Jess's vision. He turned his head and blinked to clear his eyes. Wolfe's mother was kneeling beside him, and under the smudge of smoke and ashes, the look in her eyes was something so terrible, he didn't want to stare at it for long.

'You've killed so much of the past today,' she told him. 'Generations and generations of brilliance. But you know what you'll never kill?'

The soldiers of the Artifex were just as affected by the smoke as Jess; they were coughing, their eyes streaming and red.

So they missed seeing Thomas flex his wrists and break the restraints holding him. They missed seeing Dario, who'd been flung to his hands and knees on the tiles next to Khalila – still unbound, both of them – pick up the weapon that Glain had thrown down at the edge of the open space, near the bench.

Missed seeing Morgan draw her fingers over Wolfe's restraints and then over Santi's. Hers were already loose.

'You will never kill our future,' Wolfe's mother said, and as if it was a signal, as if they'd planned this, Thomas came up with a roar and lunged forward, taking down three guards at once, and Dario aimed and fired one perfect shot at the Artifex Magnus.

The Artifex fell. Dead or only wounded, Jess couldn't tell. He ripped his wrists free and grabbed for another fallen weapon, and in seconds he was firing, too, targeting one High Garda uniform after another. It was bloody chaos, and he couldn't see where his friends were, couldn't see anything except Wolfe's mother laying hands on both Wolfe and Santi and somehow, *without the Translation equipment*, unmaking them into a spiralling whirlwind of flesh and bone and blood. She reached Dario and Khalila, and they, too, vanished into a bloody mist. Gone.

Morgan and Glain, gone. It was just Jess and Thomas left, and Thomas had rushed back towards them. The Obscurist touched the piled mess of packs that the guards had left nearby, and that, too, vanished. Jess felt something hit him, but there wasn't any pain. A near miss.

Keria Morning grabbed hold of Jess and Thomas. The last two.

The one thing Jess was sure he saw was a High Garda soldier taking aim at her, and the ringing sound of a shot, and a vivid red hole in the woman's chest. A fatal wound.

But not quickly enough to stop what she'd already set in motion.

Jess pitched into a red, shrieking darkness that ate him whole.

EPHEMERA

Text of a letter between Callum Brightwell and Kate Hannigan, sent in code. Burnt on receipt.

We both know we're on opposite sides of this thing, but one thing's certain: this oncoming war, and the chaos it will bring, will only help us both. Let the Welsh have the city and claim their victory; the King and his court and all the ministers will be well away before they come. They'll leave the city to us: the rebels, the criminals, the ones they think aren't worth saving.

It's a fat target, and we can both enrich ourselves. Your movement needs money, and I've already sent your leader in France a tidy sum in trust – you can check with him if you like. Whatever riches you gather, you keep.

Allies are more important than politics these days, wouldn't you agree?

CHAPTER SIXTEEN

Jess opened his eyes on a dark, windowless room that stank of mould and the river.

River. Not the ocean. He knew this smell. It was even stronger than the vile stench of burnt books that still clung to his skin and clothes.

It smelt like . . . home.

The next second brought memory and a sharp stab of fear. *Was* he alone? Had the others been lost somewhere in that terrible, screaming silence? But no, he heard a scrape of movement and a moan and rattled, phlegmy coughing, all from different spots around him in the dark.

He heard Morgan whisper, 'Jess?' and flung his hand out towards her. He missed and slapped wet stone, then tried again. His fingers brushed cloth with hard edges beneath. A pack. A pack full of books. He rolled over, every muscle seizing in pain, and managed to crawl another foot closer. This time, he touched Morgan's skin. Her arm. 'Jess?'

'I'm here,' he croaked. His mouth tasted like sewage, and he desperately needed water to wash it clean. 'All right?'

She burst into frantic tears and threw herself into his arms, and he held on. He didn't know which of them trembled harder. It didn't matter. They'd seen something so terrible, neither of them would ever forget.

All that knowledge, lost. Wolfe's mother. So much gone.

Someone was upright, stumbling in the dark, and fell over something in the way.

'*Scheisse!*' Thomas! Thomas was alive. 'Jess? Jess!' He sounded desperate. Of course he would be. Alone in the dark again.

'Here,' Jess gasped. He let go of Morgan, though he kept tight hold of her hand. 'Thomas?'

'Here,' the other boy said faintly. 'I fell on something.'

Jess reached into the pouch at his belt and pulled out a glow; he shook it and held it out, and there was Thomas, sitting spread-legged on a damp concrete floor. What he'd tripped over was the mound of bags – packs, canvas duffel sacks.

The books. The Black Archive books.

The last ones. The survivors.

'Easy,' Morgan said, and knelt beside Thomas with her hand on his back. 'We're here. We're all right.' She looked up at Jess with a panicked question in her wide eyes. 'Aren't we?'

He didn't answer. 'Khalila? Glain?'

'Here,' Glain groaned, and Khalila responded a few seconds later.

'I'm here, too,' Dario said, very quietly. Jess swung the light around and saw the Spaniard against the wall, shivering. The light reflected weirdly in his eyes.

Tears.

'Jess. *Jess, stop,*' Morgan said, and Jess realised he'd been moving towards Dario with a deadly serious intent. 'Leave him! He helped us!'

'Leave a traitor to put a knife in our backs again?' Jess

still had the gun he'd been firing in the Iron Tower, and the deadly weight of it felt good in his hands as he stared at Dario. 'Khalila?'

'Leave him for now,' she said. 'We'll watch him closely. Where are we?'

'Smells like London,' Jess said.

'London smells very bad.' Thomas's voice was choked but a little steadier now. 'This isn't a Serapeum.'

'No. It's—' Jess raised the glow and looked around. 'Where are Wolfe and Santi?'

'Here,' Wolfe said. 'Nic?'

'It's not a Translation Chamber.' Santi, Jess realised, was already on his feet and shaking another glow to life. The sickly yellowish light revealed an empty hall with a high, arching ceiling like a church, but no windows to let in the light. *Underground*, Jess thought. *Somewhere near the river.*

A symbol up high in chalk caught his eye, and Jess held his glow closer. 'Smuggling route,' he said. 'Belongs to the Riverrun Boys.'

'Yours?'

'Competitors,' Jess said. 'My father's not the only smuggler in town. The Riverrun Boys specialise in things other than books. Drugs, mostly. Nasty bunch.'

'Charming,' Wolfe said. His voice was as low and raspy as Jess's. He'd breathed in a lot of smoke. 'Why would she send us here?'

'There wouldn't have been any chance for us at the Serapeum,' Jess said. 'Dario's betrayal would have seen to that. She must have known about this place. Maybe she's even been here.'

'Unlikely,' Wolfe said. 'My mother—Did you see—?'

'Yes,' Jess said. 'I did. I'm sorry.'

Wolfe said nothing. His eyes looked flat, lightless, utterly unreadable. The silence stretched a moment, and then he said, 'We should find a way out.'

Jess broke out a glow of his own, Glain had one too, and they separated into teams to explore the room. It was wide and bare, and the exit that the Riverrun Boys must have once used had been blocked up with stones. Solid ones. London Garda had found this place. *If she brought us all this way only to die in a trap . . .*

'Over here,' Glain called. She was leaning half her weight on Thomas, but she had a look of elation on her face. 'I think these are steam tunnels.'

Jess felt a wave of disquiet. 'Did you find a way out?'

'There's a staircase leading up. It's barred with a grate,' Thomas said. 'Welded shut, with the symbol of the English lion on it. London Garda?'

'Find something to force it,' Jess said, and began looking himself. 'We may not have much time.'

'Why not? What is it?' That was Dario, who'd finally got up from his spot against the wall. Jess picked up a piece of rotten wood and tossed it aside without answering. 'Jess, wait. I can explain—'

'I'm not listening,' Jess interrupted. 'Look for something to break those welds. Hurry.'

'Why?' Santi asked.

'Because if Glain's right, these tunnels vent scalding steam off the city boilers. We need to break out of here. Quickly.'

'How often does it vent?' Wolfe asked.

'I don't bloody well know! Every day? Every hour? The point is, we need to move. Now!'

That ended the questioning.

It was Khalila who came up with the solution, when a search failed to turn up anything else. She made an impatient sound, grabbed Jess's weapon, and said, 'Make it safe. Quickly.'

He did, sliding the safety switches and removing the cartridge, and she jammed it into the grate. 'Now, Thomas. You've got the best leverage, I think.'

'I'll try.' He sounded doubtful. His best effort popped half the weld loose, but then he stepped away, panting, flexing his arms. 'I'm sorry. I'm still too weak.'

Santi stepped up and took a try and almost got it. One last try with both of them shattered the last of the welding, and the grate swung open with a rusty, stubborn shriek of hinges.

'Stairs,' Glain said gloomily. 'Better let me go last. I'll just hold you up.'

Khalila shook her head. 'You come with me,' she said, and put her shoulder under Glain's. 'We're not leaving you behind, so don't start.'

They climbed up. When Dario moved towards the stairs, Jess shoved him back. Hard. 'Not yet,' he said. 'Why did you do it?'

Dario coughed, spat out black ashes, and wiped his mouth. 'Do what? I went to the embassy. I thought I'd get help for us from my father. Instead the embassy called the Artifex.'

'And you sold us out. Just that easy. Coward.'

'No.' Dario wiped angrily at his eyes. 'I would have given my life. But he had Khalila's *family*, Jess. I couldn't let him . . . I told him where you would have gone, to London, but you didn't show up there. He asked me where else you would go. I said you would try to find the Black Archives. Jess, I didn't know they were *in the Iron Tower.*'

Jess was silent. He'd effortlessly believed that Dario had turned on them. Why was that? What had Dario done to deserve that, really? Would he have done any differently with Khalila's family at stake?

Dario gulped in an uneven breath. 'I led him to you, is that what you want to hear? It's true! I didn't mean to do it or want to, but I did.' He was weeping, sobs hitting him like blows. 'Go ahead. Hit me. *Hit me!*'

Jess might have, if only to stop the other young man's self-pity, but he saw movement out of the corner of his eye and lifted the glow to check.

The opening in the ceiling had a thin curl of white mist coming out of it, like a lazy whisper. Something hissed far in the distance.

Something rattled. The hiss grew louder.

'I'll hit you later!' Jess said, and shoved Dario up the steps ahead of him. He felt a wave of sudden heat wash over him, damp as clammy skin. He scrambled up and nearly slipped on the foggy stairs; the steam boiling up from beneath came faster now, a hot white cloud that seared at his lungs when he gasped.

Dario grabbed him and towed him up the last few steps into the open air, and as Jess fell to his knees, a geyser of solid white steam shot up into the air behind him and climbed into the sky in a towering explosion.

Then it blew away in a hiss of hot droplets on the wind, and all that was left was a spray of water on the street where it had fallen.

Jess looked up at Dario, and for just a moment, he wasn't angry any more. Maybe that would come again later. Didn't matter.

He nodded. Dario returned it and walked away.

Santi crouched next to Jess. 'Can you breathe?'

'Yes,' Jess said. It hurt a little, but he didn't think it was as bad as he'd feared. His skin was tender from the steam, but no worse than an Alexandrian sunburn. 'I'm all right, sir.'

'Good.' Santi leant back on his heels and looked around. 'Where are we?' The day was cloudy, a typical enough London day, and the grey pall made everything look dim and ancient. Jess had no trouble placing the outlines of buildings and the expanse of the bridge, but it seemed darker than it should. Smoky.

'London. Close to the bank of the Thames River,' Jess said. 'Near Blackfriars Bridge.'

'How far to the Serapeum?'

'Walking? Not close enough.' He looked around. The bridge was some distance, but he saw it was full of people streaming across. Odd, that. There normally wasn't such congestion in the middle of the day to cross the river. He heard the distant honking of steam-carriage horns.

Morgan took out the Codex she'd put in the pocket of her dress. The quill had survived, and she unwrapped the padded bottle of ink and quickly dipped the pen into it to scribble on the open page. 'I'm telling your father where we are,' she said. 'And to call off his men at the Serapeum. There's no sense in risking them there if we aren't coming.'

Somewhere in the distance, Jess heard the sonorous noon strikes of Big Ben. 'What does he say?'

'Nothing.' Morgan chewed anxiously on her lip, and he saw the moment writing began to appear in the sudden relaxation of her posture. 'Ah, there – he says go to the warehouse. You know where that is?'

'Yes.' That didn't ease Jess's sense of unease, not in the

least. His father kept the warehouse utterly secure, and the eight of them were walking targets. Why would he send the Library's most wanted fugitives to his most sacred hiding spot?

He wouldn't. Not with any good intent.

'Ask him where Liam is,' he said.

'What? Who's Liam?'

'Just ask.'

After a pause, she read off the reply. 'He says he's at the warehouse,' she said. 'Why?'

'Liam's my older brother,' Jess said. 'He's dead. That means you're not talking to my father any more. And we're not going to the warehouse.'

Jess sat in the shadows outside his family's town house, eating a hot pie and watching the doorway. He'd been there for two hours, slouched in stinking rags with a nearly empty bottle of gin between his feet. It was cold and misty, and he now understood what the crush of traffic on Blackfriars Bridge had been about; it was all over the street corners, with urchins crying the news. The flexible sheet they sold him had constantly updating stories, war stories, quickly written out by scribes somewhere in a London office. There was a cleverly drawn illustration of soldiers in what looked to be Camden Town, by the street signs and shop windows. They were carrying the Welsh dragon flag and setting fire to buildings as Londoners ran in fear. A few uniformed London Garda were being overrun near the edges of the picture. It was stylised but effective. Chaos, it seemed, had moved on from Oxford and was spreading fast. London was a vast city, but in some ways it was also curiously small, and Jess felt the prickles of unease on seeing those familiar street names and shops burning.

If the Welsh had come this far, they weren't likely to be stopped now. Street by street, they kept up a relentless push towards Buckingham Palace, though it was likely the King and the rest of the royals had already sped off to safer strongholds farther north. Parliament would be just as deserted. It would be an empty victory, but an important symbolic one, for Wales.

The Library would be following standard procedure and evacuating all but essential personnel from St Paul's. But in the Serapeum there was a major holding place for confiscated original manuscripts, and there were many volumes on loan there, too. Those would need evacuation. The Library would have to divert troops away from chasing them.

In some very important ways, the chaos of war was a boon to them.

So Jess slouched on the cold pavement, looking like an anonymous soul lost to drink, and watched for any sign of his father. He saw none, nor any trace of his mother or brother or even the servants. The Brightwell household was quiet and cold, though the lights were on inside, and from time to time shadows seemed to pass the windows.

After another hour, just as it slipped towards night, the front door opened and Brendan stepped out. He looked as Jess remembered him from Alexandria, but back in English clothing as finely made as that which their father liked to boast, even down to the fancy silk waistcoat. He looked over to survey the skyline, maybe tracking signs of fire, then turned back and stretched. He looked very tired.

Jess took off his cap and stepped forward into the light. Brendan looked around, up and down the street, then made a sharp movement for Jess to cross the street. Once he had, Brendan grabbed him and shoved him inside with such force, it almost seemed desperate. He closed and locked the town house door behind them.

Inside, the place was just the way Jess remembered it, down
to the wear on the curled banister and the flower arrangement
his mother replaced daily on the hall table. It seemed oddly
smaller, though, for all the luxurious little touches spread
around. He turned on Brendan, intending to let loose a flood of
questions, but before he could, his brother embraced him hard.

'Idiot,' Brendan said. 'You bloody *idiot*!' He shoved him
back almost as quickly. 'What corpse did you pick those rags
off? They smell foul.'

'They're supposed to,' Jess said. He looked over Brendan's
shoulder. 'Where's Father?'

'I don't know. He vanished and we haven't heard anything
from him. Whoever has his Codex—'

'Is impersonating him, I know. Garda?'

'The Garda have bigger problems that the Brightwells. Must
be some Library spy. Welsh troops are burning through the city
from one end to the other, you know, and half the city's either
running in panic or planning to join the Garda to fight. He'd
been working on clearing the best pieces out for days.'

'We'll have to find him.'

'I was working on it,' Brendan said. 'I didn't even know
you'd survived, Jess.'

'I see you're in full mourning.'

'Well, I didn't fully believe it,' Brendan said. 'You're a bad
penny, Jess. Can't get rid of you. What happened?'

Jess explained it as briefly as he could. He didn't want to tell
Brendan about the disaster at the Black Archives quite yet. He
couldn't stomach talking about it. When he blinked, he could
still see those books dying.

See himself watching them die.

'Your friends? Where are they?' Brendan asked. 'I'm

assuming you didn't do the sensible thing and leave them.'

'They're close,' Jess said. Funny. He trusted his twin just so far and not a step more. 'Where should I take them?'

'The warehouse for now,' his brother said. 'Mother's carried off the family treasures with her to cousin Frederick. The warehouse is just a gathering spot for the men. The plan was that we'll join them there once we have cargo on wagons and safely away. But now that Father's gone, we probably should be gone from here soon, in case the High Garda come looking.'

'Brendan. About Neksa—'

'She's all right?' His brother looked at him, and it was an unguarded kind of dread. Jess had hit rather harder than he expected.

'She's fine. Broken-hearted, but last I saw, she was fine. You did a good thing, Scraps. Maybe you're not so bad at heart after all.'

'Shut up before I punch you,' Brendan said. 'Let's go.' He hesitated, then swept Jess with a disgusted look from head to toe. 'After you change and get rid of the lice.'

'This city,' Khalila said, 'looks like something a madman dreamt up. Didn't your architects ever hear of straight lines?'

Jess, looking at London with the eyes of experience, had to admit the girl had a point. The narrow, twisting streets, the blind alleys, the buildings jammed together on whatever plot of land had become available . . . it had no plan to it. Big Ben wasn't as tall as he remembered; some of the newer buildings reached much higher, though they somehow still had a look of weariness to them. The golden gleam of St Paul's in the distance was the only thing Jess could think would have been easily transplanted to Alexandria. Everything else was uniquely . . . English.

'At least it means slow going for the Welsh,' he pointed out.

'London's probably the hardest city to conquer in the world.'

'Yet they are managing,' Dario observed. It wasn't smug, just practical. He was watching the southwest, where the muddy glow of buildings on fire made the night shimmer. Jess could hear the sound of fighting, very dim and distant. Khalila gave him a glare. She still wasn't speaking to him, not at all. 'I hope this hiding place isn't far.'

'Just up there,' Jess said. Their group kept to the shadows; other London citizens hurried by in the opposite direction, many carrying suitcases or bags full of belongings, dressed in thick layers of clothing to lighten their loads. 'Stay out of sight of the Garda if you see any.'

They'd picked up the others a few blocks back, but now Morgan eased by Dario to take a place at Jess's side. She took his hand and looked him up and down, then over at his brother. 'Remarkable,' she said. 'It's hard to tell you apart.'

'Really?' Jess asked.

'Well. Not for me, of course.'

'That's better. I wouldn't like you mistaking the two of us at a critical moment.'

Jess adjusted his heavy burden of books. It felt larger with every step, or maybe it was just that he was growing tired.

'The fighting looks to be moving closer,' Santi said from behind them. 'We should go as quickly as we can. I'd rather not renew our acquaintance with our friends from Wales. They let us go once; I doubt they'd feel any obligation to do it again.'

'And we're not even Library any more,' Khalila said. 'We've got the same protection as anyone else on these streets.'

'Welcome to the rest of the world,' Brendan said. 'We rely on ourselves out here. Always have done, since the Library told us a book was worth more than we are.'

'But it is,' Khalila said quietly. 'A book outlives us all.'

'That's a legacy,' Brendan said. 'I'd rather have a life, if you don't mind.'

'Philosophy later,' Wolfe said. 'Run now.'

It was more of a walk, and though Jess worried their stuffed packs might attract attention, the growing chaos of the Welsh invasion worked to their advantage. Almost every person on the street carried something – a bag, a pack – and some even trundled carts. The wealthy, of course, steamed by in carriages loaded with all manner of valuables. He considered the merits of waylaying one of them and forcing the owners out at gunpoint, but that might set off a tinderbox of rioting. In the distance, looters broke windows and carried off abandoned goods. That was tragic, but would they fare better if left to burn? Probably not.

The only bad moment came when they rounded a corner four blocks from the warehouse and faced a troop of perhaps a hundred London Garda. The redcoats looked exhausted and filthy, and huddled in groups as they shared food and water. Fresh from the fight, it looked like there were plenty of wounded stretched in a row on the pavement, with Medica attending to them. Jess kept his gaze down as they moved around the soldiers, and hoped that nobody had thought to circulate their descriptions; together in a group, they were hard to miss.

Brendan, on the other hand, walked right up to an officer crouching against a brick wall, eating dried meat. 'Brightwell,' the soldier said, and glanced at Jess. 'I stand corrected. Brightwells. And I thought this day couldn't get worse.'

'Captain Harte,' Brendan said. He reached in his pocket and slipped out a silver flask that assuredly didn't hold water and passed it over. 'How goes the war?'

'We're trying to hold them at the bridges, but, to be honest, I don't think we have a hope. Bloody citizens are running like scared rabbits, and the army got themselves cut off in another battle. I'm surprised to find you lot still here.' He uncapped the flask and took a long pull, sighed with satisfaction, and handed it back. 'Look to your people. Get them out of here. I doubt we have more than an hour or two before this district's overrun.'

'Anything about my father?'

'Aye. Your da was almost taken, but he got clean away. Not surprised, really; old Callum's always been able to slither right out of a trap. I expect you'll meet up with him again sometime.'

'All right. Luck to you.'

'You as well.'

Brendan led them a step or two on. Harte called after him. 'Brendan. Library Garda's looking for your friends. Offering rewards.'

'Are you tempted?'

Harte shrugged. 'I know you'll make it worth my while to forget.'

'That I will.' Brendan touched his forehead in a mock salute and led them on.

The warehouse was an entirely unassuming structure at the end of a blind alley, hard to see and harder to find. It was usually guarded with lurkers out on the main streets and deadly bruisers at the doors. Not today, though. Today the doors stood open, and Brendan led them straight on inside.

It was empty.

Jess had never seen his father's warehouse empty before; there were always bolts and bundles of imported silk, pieces of fine furniture, boxes of expensive trinkets. His father had expensive tastes, but his real treasures had been concealed behind false walls and up high in the rafters – boxes and stacks of rare, original books. Beauties that ranged into antiquity, from the hands of the original authors or the most accurate copies. His father always sold quality, whether the items were legal or criminal.

There was nothing there now except a squad of hard men. Most were armed with knives and some with stolen guns liberated either from Garda or the army. Finding weapons wasn't a challenge for someone well-known in the shadow markets.

'Come out, Da,' Brendan said. 'I know you're here. They would have already run to the hills if you weren't.'

There was a laugh from the shadows, and then Callum Brightwell stepped out – grimy, thinner, with a cut on one cheek that had barely begun to heal. 'My boys. Come here to me.'

Brendan walked over and received a bear hug. Jess didn't move.

'I think I'll stay where I am,' Jess said. 'I can see you're overcome with joy that I'm alive.'

'I am,' Callum said, though there was no real sign of it.

'How did you get away from the Garda?'

'Hard fighting, boy. They got my Codex and twelve of my men. But they lost me. And you, apparently. Clever lad.' His father had lost his smile. 'Stop dithering. Your place is with us. I didn't send you to the damned Library to become a rebel. There's no profit in it.'

'There might be,' Jess said. 'If you'll listen to what we have to say.'

'Sure,' Callum said. 'But first I have a job for you. Tell your High Garda friends to lower their weapons or I'll have my men shoot and use the ones who survive it.'

That was a cold, clear threat, and Jess turned to look at Santi. Santi shifted his aim to rest on Callum Brightwell's forehead. 'I don't think so,' he said. 'Shoot me, I'll still pull the trigger. You know that.'

'I have two fine sons to carry on for me. Do you think I'm worried, Captain Santi? Yes, I know who you are; I like to know who has influence over my son. Including you, Scholar Wolfe.'

'Stop this,' Jess said, and took another step towards his father – but not far enough to interfere with Santi's aim. 'I'm not some Brightwell asset. I make my own decisions.'

'Yet you come running to me for help.'

'I'm bringing you an opportunity you'll never see again. It's business.'

'And we thought you didn't have the Brightwell heart,' Brendan said. He was smiling and his eyes were bright, and in that moment Jess knew his instincts had been right. He *couldn't* trust his family. Ever. 'We've got business for you to do first. Show us you're trustworthy, and then we'll look at this *opportunity* of yours. Or don't, and we'll kill some of your friends, if not all of them. Your choice.'

'Jess?' Santi asked. 'I'd like very much to shoot this man, but he's your blood. You decide.'

'Don't.' His heart was pounding and he felt sick to his stomach. The air still smelt of that faint trace of spices and old books that were so much a part of his childhood, but overlaying them now was the muffling scent of smoke. London was burning. So was his past. 'What do you want from us, Callum?'

'*Callum,* now, is it?' Two years ago, his father's glare would have cowed him. Not today. He met it with one of his own.

'It is,' Jess said. 'I'm not going to call you Father any more. Be grateful I don't call you worse.' He turned to Santi and Wolfe. 'You could kill them, maybe a few of the men, but they'll get some of us, too. It's not worth it.'

It took a long, tense moment, but their guns went down. So, unwillingly, did Glain's.

'Good,' Callum Brightwell said. 'Glad we sorted out our particulars. Come with us. We need the help of a Scholar.'

It was a long ride in an uncomfortable freight wagon to St Paul's, and while they rattled around inside the hard, empty space, Brightwell explained what he wanted. It was ominous and daring, and Jess could unwillingly agree that it might well be the chance of any self-respecting smuggler's lifetime.

St Paul's Serapeum had long been an unattainable target, though it contained some of the rarest, choicest volumes on display. But in the growing chaos, with the High Garda fanning out across the city searching for Jess and his friends, it was as vulnerable as it would ever be.

'It'll take a Scholar's robes to get us past the Garda barricades,' Brightwell explained. 'And a bright, shiny bracelet. Once you're in the building, they're busy boxing up things to send them to the Archives. A few liberated volumes might find their way clear with an enterprising thief in a black robe.'

'You expect us to help you *rob the Library*?' Santi asked. He looked at Jess's father as if he were a particularly unpleasant sort of bug he'd found in his stew. 'Are you completely mad?'

'You're no longer part of the Library, is what I'm hearing. You're on the run from it, like the rest of us poor criminals, so don't play the proper High Garda captain with me. I could turn you in as easy as dropping a handkerchief. You're lucky I'm generous, and you can be of some real use.'

'Nic,' Wolfe said. He was staring at Brightwell with flat, dark eyes, like he wanted to take a bite out of him, but his voice was calm enough. 'I'll do it.'

'No, you won't!' Santi shot back. 'You're too recognisable.

One look at you, and you're in the hands of the Artifex.'

'Of course it's got to be me. You don't have another gold-banded Scholar to—' Wolfe realised his mistake, but it was too late. Khalila held up her wrist, and her sleeve slipped down to reveal the gold bracelet. 'No.'

'I'm not as recognisable as you, and there are plenty of female librarians wearing a hijab. I will be fine.' She managed a smile. 'Of all of us, which one looks least like a thief?'

'No!' It wasn't just Wolfe this time objecting; it was all of them, talking over each other. Khalila looked at Jess, who *wasn't* objecting. He just nodded at her. She nodded back.

'Quiet, all of you,' she said, and opened her pack to dig out her black Scholar's robe. It was a little wrinkled and worse for wear, but in the current conditions of London, Jess doubted anyone would notice. 'Tell me what you want me to find.'

'Oh, use your best judgement,' Brightwell said with a deceptively kind smile. 'Something lucrative and rare. Two at least. Three if you can manage it.'

'You're not going alone,' Dario said, and grabbed his own robe from his bag. 'Jess, weapon?'

Jess ignored him. Glain glared but silently offered a knife, and Dario nodded and slipped it into the back of his trousers, under the cover of the robe. 'Once it's done, we'll meet you back here in the freight hauler.'

'Oh no,' Jess's father said. 'We're *all* going in. While you steal the books, we will be opening a way out.'

'Way out?' Jess echoed, and then he understood, just before Callum pointed a thick finger at Morgan.

'She,' he said, 'is the magic key to our escape. She'll send us to Lancaster, or as close as can be managed. Then we'll talk about opportunities, if you like, once we're safe in family territory.'

'I can't,' Morgan said. 'I'm just a student. I'm not—'

'You're an Obscurist, and by all the accounts that I've heard, you're far more powerful than the ones trying to teach you anything useful. Imagine what we could do with you, Morgan. You're going to open *many* doors for us, all over the world.'

The bad taste in Jess's mouth went sour. *Morgan, too.* She'd only just escaped from the Iron Tower, and already his own family wanted to put another chain on her, make her their pet Obscurist. Maybe she'd been right to run and hide before. Even from him.

'All right,' Morgan said, with a calm that surprised him. 'I'll send you to safety, *if* you let me send the others first.'

'I'm not as naive as I look, sweeting. You'd get them through and refuse to send the rest of us.' He took on a calculating look, glancing from Morgan to Jess and back. 'But I'll compromise. Never let it be said I'm not a fair man. You can send all of them ahead except Jess. Then you send me, Brendan, and my men. You and Jess leave last.'

It was a clever way to exploit the two of them again, and Jess knew it would work. It couldn't fail. She knew it, too, and nodded.

'You two Scholars, your job is to get inside and get the books without being noticed. Never mind what the rest of us do. Make your way to the Serapeum's chamber – what do you call it?'

'Translation Chamber,' Morgan said quietly. 'It's hidden behind a statue of Queen Elizabeth towards the back of the Scholar's Library.' She caught Jess's eye. 'I studied ahead, in case we needed escape.'

He loved her for that. For many things, just now. 'And how do you plan to get past the lions?' he asked his father, whose grin never slipped.

'With help,' he said. 'You don't need to know.'

Jess exchanged a quick glance at Thomas. His father had a frightening amount of inside knowledge, but he clearly didn't know that Jess could turn off the lions or that they could potentially convert them to their own cause.

Something to keep in reserve.

There was a rap on the front of the freight wagon, and Callum nodded. 'Get up,' he said, and rose, grabbing for a handhold as the lorry lurched. 'Don't cross us. Trust me, this is the best deal you're going to get.'

'I'm sure it is,' Wolfe replied. 'You strike me as such an honest man.' *The sarcasm is heavy enough to drown in,* Jess thought, and looking between the two men, he knew in his heart he'd choose Wolfe over his own father any time. As difficult and prickly as the man could be, at least he was honest.

The wagon wheezed to a lurching halt, throwing them against each other, and Jess all but lost his footing when Thomas bumped him. But then the back of the wagon clanked down and his father's men were rushing out with a purpose, shouting.

They were nosed against the Garda barrier, and the Brightwell bullies made quick work of the two London Garda soldiers on duty. There was almost no one at the barricades, but those who were there ran. By the time the second Garda soldier hit the ground unconscious, the area was all but deserted.

Jess heard screaming from somewhere frighteningly close, and as he turned that way, he saw a distant pinpoint of greenish light arcing through the dark, growing larger. It was a ballista pot of Greek Fire, and it hit no more than five blocks away, exploding and splashing the rooftops with luminescent liquid that began to burn instantly.

'The Welsh army is coming close,' Wolfe said. Brightwell nodded. 'Well?'

'We're waiting,' he said.

'For what?'

'For them.' A group of men and women ran towards them from a side street – ten of them, by Jess's quick count. They looked grimly serious as they exchanged nods with Callum. 'You're late,' he said. 'Go on, then. You've been paid well enough for it.'

The leader – a woman with black hair twisted in a thick braid to one side of her head, with features and skin that reminded Jess a bit of Joachim Portero – flashed him a smile, but without humour. 'We don't do this for *money*, criminal. We do it for principles.'

'I don't care why you do it,' Brightwell said blandly. 'So long as you succeed.'

She led her small force up the street towards the Scholar Steps, where Jess had once run for his life from lions – and those lions, he realised, were still there, crouched, waiting. They were the massively muscled English sort – shorter manes than the Italian version, without barbed tails. Designed to crush and tear. One rose to all four paws, turned red eyes towards the intruders, and let out a chilling roar.

The woman let out a bloody cry of challenge that was almost as chilling, reached into a bag at her waist, and drew out a glass globe.

Burners. My father's working with Burners.

He felt Morgan's hand closing hard around his arm and reached out to hold her closer. 'Nothing we can do,' he said.

The leader's throw landed accurately right on the lion's head and spread caustic chemicals down the metal face and into red eyes. Glass popped and sizzled, blinding it as the chemicals ignited and began to burn with a fierce intensity. The lion shook its head, trying to throw it off, but the thick stuff clung and melted, turning the automaton's face into a hideous, twisted mask of skeletal cables and clockworks.

The other Burners were throwing now, too, targeting the other lions. One automaton managed to dodge the rain of bottles and landed hard on a screaming victim – man, woman, Jess couldn't tell, and in the next instant it didn't much matter, because the scream cut off quickly. Some of the Burners weren't much older than him. Jess shut his eyes as the lions thrashed and roared, the bottles of Greek Fire flew and broke, and another Burner yelled in fear and pain.

Then Morgan said, in an unsteady, hushed voice, 'It's over.'

He opened his eyes again to see the last of the lions had collapsed on its side. It was melting into a tangled mess, cables twisting and snapping, gears and springs deforming. The metallic roaring faded to a strange, distorted whimper, and then . . . nothing.

Four lions lay dead – did automata die? – in a shimmering pool of Greek Fire, with two Burners bloody and crushed nearby. It was a terrible sight; the street and steps were scorched black from the rippling heat.

'Well,' Callum said from behind him. 'That was well worth the price.'

Jess didn't even think. He rounded on his father, fist pulled back, and as Morgan shouted his name, his brother grabbed his arm and held it while Jess shouted and struggled. 'Let go! *Let me go!*'

'Be smarter,' Brendan said quietly. 'He'll kill you.'

'I could have—' *Stopped this without people dying*, he

almost blurted out, but he could see Thomas's warning stare over Brendan's shoulder. 'I could have done this differently. *Burners*, Brendan. Since when do we work with *Burners?*'

'When it's smart to do it,' he said. 'Profit, not philosophy, remember? Relax, brother. We have it under control.'

Khalila and Dario, with Thomas and Glain, moved up the Scholar Steps; they were meant to go straight to the Scholar's Reading Room and grab as many books as they could. Each of them had their packs already loaded with originals, but Jess couldn't tell his family that now. He didn't trust them with that rare, precious knowledge. Or with the idea of the press. *Then where will we turn?* He didn't know. He felt sick, having led his friends here, to a safety that vanished like fog under the sun.

Once inside the columned entrance, Callum Brightwell led his sons to the left, where a statue of Queen Elizabeth in battle armour stood guard. There was no obvious entrance, and Brightwell gestured impatiently for Morgan to catch up. Just beyond them, Khalila and Dario had gone into the Reading Room, and Dario had already picked up an original volume to add to a small crate. Khalila passed him another. Her hands, Jess saw, were shaking badly.

Glain and Thomas hovered at the corner, watching over them in case of trouble, but so far, the room was far too busy for them to be noticed. Black-robed Scholars hurried from one table to another, stacking books with haste that spoke of real fear, while a second set in sand-coloured librarian robes brought over more crates and helped with packing. It looked like barely controlled chaos.

He froze as he saw a face he knew, one eerily familiar to him. It was a librarian named Naomi Ebele, who had not so very long ago been head of the Oxford Serapeum. She'd barely escaped with her life, along with the rest of them that day. He liked her. She was a strong, good woman, with a devout belief in what she was doing.

She'd recognise Dario and Khalila.

Just as he realised it, she *did* look up, and her eyes locked on Khalila and Dario and widened. She put down the crate she was packing and immediately walked in their direction.

Jess couldn't guess what they would have done or could have, but it didn't matter in the next moment, because Naomi never quite made it. There was a strange sound outside, like an impact on the roof overhead, and everyone looked up. Movement stopped.

Jess heard hissing and smelt the unmistakable reek, and as the first Scholar screamed it out, he realised what had happened.

Greek Fire.

The Serapeum was burning.

There was no greater sin in war than to destroy a Serapeum. The Welsh would later point fingers at the Burners or claim it was a mistake; Jess knew that. The Burners would be happy to claim a victory for their side whether they actually did the job or not. But St Paul's was burning. He saw the first licks of fire clawing at the ceiling above the Scholars' heads.

'Save the books!' Naomi Ebele shouted, and began slapping Translation tags on the boxes. She touched one and activated it, and the script buried inside it – like the scripts inside the lion, Jess realised now – drained a little energy from her to activate itself and dissolve the crate of the books, to reform in the Archives in Alexandria. Safe.

Khalila looked at Dario, face gone far too pale, and reached for one of the tags that Naomi held out. Around the room,

Scholars were dumping books into crates, attaching Translation tags, and hurrying them to safety.

Dario took a handful of tags from the table and began attaching them to boxes. Khalila put one on the box that they'd already filled.

'The devil is she doing?' Brightwell asked, and started to move for a better angle. Wolfe's hand held him back.

'She's doing her work,' he said. 'Not yours. Leave her alone.'

Dario attached tags and sent five before he staggered with the familiar weakness Jess remembered so well. Khalila managed four before she had to stop. It was enough. There were only a few boxes left now, and other Scholars were sending the last.

Dario palmed two extra discs and slipped them into a pocket, a move so practiced and sleek that Jess only noticed it because of his angle. Then he grabbed Khalila's arm and pulled her towards the door.

Naomi got in the way. The Librarian was a tall, strong woman, beautiful, and she didn't seem cowed by the fire now undulating across the ceiling above them. The other Scholars were using leftover Translation tags to send themselves home to the Archives. It was a last-resort escape, and some looked desperately reluctant, but, one by one, they dissolved in swirls and screams and blood.

No tags left.

Naomi didn't move. She stared at Khalila and Dario, and they stared back.

'Kill her,' Brightwell said to one of his men, and, quick as lightning, Santi had his forearm across the man's throat and the muzzle of his weapon pressed to the side of his head.

'No,' he said. 'You don't.' The man muttered an agreement, and Santi let him go, then turned the gun on Brightwell when

Jess's father tried to approach. 'You brought us here to get through the Translation Chamber. That can still happen, but we need to go. Now.'

Wolfe stepped into the doorway, and said, 'Naomi.' Ebele turned and saw him, and for a moment Jess saw her smile in relief . . . And then the smile faded when she realised he wasn't alone. It wasn't just Brightwell's people now; the Burners had crowded in behind them, stinking of chemicals and smoke. The hard-eyed woman who led them had a triumphant grin on her face.

'Naomi, please come with us,' Khalila said. 'You can't stay here, and all the tags are gone. *Please.*' She held out her hand to Naomi, who looked at her with real distaste and took a step away.

'In all my days,' she said, 'I never thought I would see Scholars standing with Burners. *Ever.* I would rather burn myself here than go with you.'

Dario sighed and reached in his pocket. He handed her a Translation tag. 'Don't do that,' he said, and coughed; the smoke was flooding in now, black and greasy. 'Save yourself, Naomi.'

'Come with me!'

'We can't,' Khalila said. 'Go.' She looked around at the reading room, the empty tables, the blanks still sitting on shelves and burning like torches. 'I'm sorry.'

This time when Dario grabbed her and moved her on, she went willingly. Naomi met Wolfe's eyes as she pressed the Translation tag, and said, 'May God forgive you, Scholar.' Then she was gone, in a spray of blood and bone.

Safe, somewhere else.

Morgan had pushed past Jess, and now she put a hand on

the centre of Queen Elizabeth's statue; it triggered a hiss, and the statue moved aside to reveal a short corridor. It was smoky, but the flames hadn't reached it yet. Brightwell plunged in first, followed by Brendan, and Morgan followed, reaching back for Jess's hand. The hall opened into a rounded room with a couch and helmet. The same as in all the other chambers he'd seen.

Smoke was already beginning to filter in and fog the air with a thick, chemical reek, and Jess coughed and began to realise that there wasn't time to send all of them, even if his father intended to keep his word.

He's going to kill them, Jess realised with a jolt of real horror. *Everybody but me and Morgan. He needs Morgan.* It was plain to him, the way that his father's men were positioned, isolating Thomas, Glain, Wolfe, Santi, and now Khalila and Dario.

'There's not time to send all of you!' Morgan shouted. The Burners had crowded in behind them and were pushing forward now.

'Oh, don't worry about that,' said the woman who led the Burners, and nodded to her men and women. 'There won't be as many as you think.'

At her signal, her people quickly, efficiently, and brutally swung into motion . . . and caught the Brightwell bullies by surprise. Ten men quickly taken down with blows from behind. Fast deaths, so fast Jess hardly even comprehended them. Now it was just the eight Burners who'd survived, plus Brightwell, Brendan, Jess, and his friends.

'Kate, you backstabbing piece of—'

'Manners, Master Brightwell. We're all friends here,' the woman said. *Kate.* It sounded too nice a name for her. Jess heard a crash from overhead; something had collapsed. The fire would get to them soon, and the smoke was already thickening. Harder to breathe. 'I'm sparing your lives. Get out. *Now*. Run. You're resourceful. And I'm giving you your son as a bonus.'

'I have two,' Brightwell said. 'I'll be taking both.'

She put a knife to his throat. 'The Library rebels belong to us,' she said. '*Go* or die – I don't care which you choose.'

Jess's father hesitated for a long moment, then turned his head and said, 'Good luck, Jess.'

'Da! No!' Brendan shouted, and tried to break free. Callum Brightwell held him tight. 'Jess—'

'Kill them,' Kate said, 'if they don't leave now.' One of her Burners pulled a weapon and pointed it, and Brendan finally stopped fighting. He and Jess's father ran.

Jess tried to acknowledge that it was the smart thing to do, the Brightwell thing, but all he could think was, *You left us. You left me.*

And it hurt.

Kate sat on the couch, put the helmet on her head, and looked at Morgan. 'Take us to the Philadelphia Serapeum,' she said. 'We are going to the City of Freedom.'

Philadelphia. The stronghold of the Burners.

Jess looked at Wolfe, at Santi. 'We can't do this,' he said. 'We can't.'

Wolfe said, 'I don't think they've left us any choice.'

They were going to America.

SOUNDTRACK

As always, I like to have some motivational music for the book. You might also enjoy checking out the songs! Remember: musicians need love *and* money. So please buy the music, attend the concerts, buy the T-shirts.

'Ticking Bomb'	Aloe Blacc
'Dark Horse'	Katy Perry
'Seven Nation Army'	The White Stripes
'Where's The Girl'	Terrence Mann
'Mugs Away'	Seven Nations
'Sundirtwater'	The Waifs
'The Engine Room'	Runrig
'Beggin for Thread'	Banks
'Crazy in Love (Chilled Edit)'	L'Orchestra Cinematique
'Bandida'	Audra Mae

'Flicker (Kanye West Rework)'	Lorde
'The River'	The Waifs
'Scarlet Town'	Gillian Welch
'Ain't Gonna Do It'	Kane Welch Kaplin
'Falcon in the Dive'	Terrence Mann
'Lighthouse'	The Waifs
'Sheila Put the Knife Down'	Junior Prom
'Ship to Wreck'	Florence + The Machine
'Graveyard Whistling'	Nothing but Thieves
'You and Steve McQueen'	The Audreys
'Can't Feel My Face'	The Weeknd
'Bad Blood (feat. Kendrick Lamar)'	Taylor Swift
'Juliet'	Emilie Autumn
'Across the Sky'	Emilie Autumn
'Clockwork Heart'	Abney Park
'Give 'em What For'	Abney Park
'Pity the Free Man'	Abney Park
'On the Fringe'	Abney Park
'Born at the Wrong Time'	Abney Park
'Sleep Isabella'	Abney Park

'I Am Stretched on Your Grave'	Abney Park
'Virus'	Abney Park
'Herr Drosselmeyer's Doll'	Abney Park
'This Dark and Twisty Road'	Abney Park
'The Secret Life of Dr Caligari'	Abney Park
'The Emperor's Wives'	Abney Park
'Airship Pirate'	Abney Park

ACKNOWLEDGEMENTS

I have many people to thank for the very existence of this book, including my husband, R. Cat Conrad (who has been *extremely* patient during a difficult writing process); my amazing assistant, Sarah Weiss (ditto); my agent, Lucienne Diver (double double ditto); and my editor, Anne Sowards, She of the Greatest Patience of All, Ever.

Special thanks to my sanity readers Tez, Sarah, Becky Tyree and Sarah Tyree.